MIDNIGHT
WORLD
VOLUME FIVE

DOWN WITH DARKNESS

DALIVIA PLAUT

DARK PLOT
PUBLISHING

• • •

First Edition, May 2020
Story by Dalivia Plaut
Written by Dalivia Plaut
Edited by Ireland Lelisio

ISBN: 978-1-7344831-1-6
Plaut, Dalivia, 1983—
Down With Darkness
I. Title. Fiction. Dark Fantasy/Horror

ISBN: 978-1-7344831-1-6 pbk.

Cover Design by Low Key
Book Design by Dalivia Plaut
Cover Photograph by joegolby/
IvancoVlad (istockphoto.com)

This is a work of fiction.
Names, characters, places, and incidents
are the products of the author's imagination.
Any resemblance to actual persons, living
or dead, is entirely coincidental.

Printed in the United States of America

• • •

Author's Note

The world presented beyond this page is a fictitious one, as are its characters. Any resemblance to actual persons, living or dead, is entirely coincidental.

MIDNIGHT WORLD VOLUME FIVE:
DOWN WITH DARKNESS

THE town of Nagamaki quietly resides in the shadows of the Okugawa Mountains in the western portion of Tokyo Metropolis, a rundown yet discernibly throbbing place that is often known to draw both tourists and those who live in surrounding prefectures due to its rich history, as well as its abundance of outdoor activities in its vicinity, including biking, hiking, and fishing. Over the past several decades, however, the town of roughly seven thousand residents—and shrinking—has become the home of a "legend," and for those living in Nagamaki, it's one that either goes shunned, unspoken, or, whenever the subject should arise with uncertainty, is rarely talked about and often done so with a faint murmur and a worried gaze.

Some forty miles west of the capital city, the lush foothills with all of its narrow, winding streets walled by tight living quarters and dilapidated buildings appear as if it's the undertaking of both man and the overgrowth of nature meshed in harmony. Heavy vegetation even stretches as far as the railroad tracks, which run alongside the town where the Umi Line frequently vibrates the town like the softest purr. Most of the residents use the Nagamaki Station, which provides a non-stop service for surrounding villages to the Tokyo Station. The homes are mostly what locals refer to as "modern," even though there are still traditional Japanese *sukiya-zukuri* style homes. A town hall, which blends in with an apartment building, is located in the center of Nagamaki next to a strip of shops, including a grocery store and the iconic noodle shop, "Eito's," which was featured in the cult film, *Shinto's Revenge Part 2*, directed by Nori Hirano. Admirers of Hirano are often spotted posing for photographs inside and around the popular noodle shop, which is filled with *Shinto* memorabilia and picture frames of the cast and crew hanging on walls. Occasional construction sites of cleared-out land are marred by shoddy fences, undeveloped projects, and building foundations left unfinished as a result of a rise in property taxes due to the sudden tourist boom, contentious land disputes, and on-going lawsuits. Nowadays, even though the differences between the two dialects rarely exist outside Nagamaki, most of the dialect in the area leans toward Yamanote, which is used by the old upper class, opposed to modern working class dialect Shitamachi, the pitch in accent between each kotoba varying with usage of certain words such as the word *tamago* carrying an accent on *ma* in ta-"ma"-go, whereas, in Shitamachi, there is no accent. With periodic clearing of clouds, the skies are often blanketed with a wash of newspaper gray, especially during misty mornings. The land is rather rugged and hilly with the Hichi River flowing through the most western part of town; and from the viewpoint of a foreigner, it appears sheltered from the looming mountains, which loll over the town of Nagamaki like ancient gods keeping guard on those who enter—and leave.

Funneling down toward the Kumodake Valley resides Lake Okugawa, which is not only essential in supplying water to the town of Nagamaki, but also remains one of Tokyo's, as well as the surrounding prefectures, most important sources of water.

On average, Nagamaki receives around sixty-five inches of rain per year during Japan's rainy season, or tsuyu, meaning "plum rain," which occurs at the same time of year when plums begin to ripen; and most of that rain comes in middle to late summer.

Very few people—Asians included—had ever heard of Nagamaki and the legend, both far and wide, behind the town until one clear day on September 21, 1987, when the clouds opened to a hard blue sky.

Like the murky run of Hichi River slithering its way around Nagamaki, like the motorists and like the railway with its clockwork-like rumblings, and like the automobiles, including cars, trucks, and mopeds, that zip along hairline streets, the continuity of nature, both man's *established* nature and the environment at his own disposal, requires the most fundamental quality of attention and without this quality, nature has a peculiar way of defending itself at whatever cost. On that late crisp autumn morning, a day in a year that had been forecasted as one of the wettest, the horrific cries of a local man named Kaito Takahashi fled from the dense forests in Kodama where rays of sunlight pierce beech tree tops and cut across the misty air like katanas, penetrating a once humbly subdued town not too far away, reminding the town, as well as its stoic people, of the horrors that lay bare only six years prior. Only a handful of townspeople had heard the screams, and those who had been bedeviled by the horrific sounds were left in a dubious state where fantasy naturally filled in the blank gaps of time. But, as time does what it does best, the details surrounding Takahashi's death would later manifest well after the case went cold and fester in the ready-minds of those who lay foot on Nagamaki's cursed soil. Exaggerations would grow. So, too, would that legend. However, of all the interpretations, one detail remained the most perennial and that, of course, was the manner in which Kaito Takahashi's body was discovered.

The reaction alone from the listener, which immediately followed the teller's description, was, in a way, a legend in itself. And rightfully so.

KAITO
SEPTEMBER 8, 1987 5:59 AM

AT exactly six o'clock, Kaito wakes up to the *hissing* sound of radio noise.

Shortly after, the hook from Whitney Houston's song, "I Wanna Dance With Somebody (Who Loves Me)" from her second studio album, *Whitney*, starts playing over a brand new General Electric red LED AM/FM digital clock radio model 7-4624.

Before Whitney could finish singing the word *heat*, Kaito strikes the snooze button along the wood grain cabinet of the alarm clock in a stabbing motion.

The radio quiets.

Kaito removes the blanket from his body, rolls out of the futon along the soft *tatami*, and unplugs the clock's cord from the electrical outlet in the wall.

Once more, the clock radio blasts Whitney's latest single.

Startled from the sudden spike in volume, Kaito stumbles to the clock radio and rips out the 9V battery from inside.

Kaito groans, his throat clogged with phlegm.

Some gift, Hiroshi.

After rising a few inches in a well-earned stretch accompanied by a yawn and a clearing of the throat, Kaito leaves the tatami room and makes his way into the kitchen, picking and scratching at his ass.

While Kaito puts a pot of water on a heated burner on the stove, he grabs all of the leftovers from last night's supper from the fridge and places each container of Tupperware along the counter for the preparation of breakfast.

Kaito removes the pot of water before the water comes to a boil and pours the hot, steamy water into a strainer of dry gyokuro tea leaves on top of the teapot.

While the tea is mellowing, Kaito begins to prepare breakfast for two, first by heating up the leftovers starting with the rice in a rice cooker, then next, warming miso soup in a pot on the stove. After the rice and soup are set to the right temperature, Kaito reheats the grilled large-mouth bass, which had come straight from Lake Okugawa.

Once everything is heated to perfection, Kaito dishes out the rest of the leftovers, including other side dishes such as *tsukemono, nori, natto,* a green salad, and a generous helping of *kobachi,* into several bowls as well as plates on a tray. He sets aside a bowl of rice, as well as a cup of green tea. Then pours himself a cup of green tea and places it next to the food on the tray. Lastly, he grabs himself a pair of chopsticks. He brings the tray into the *washitsu* and enters by sliding open the *fusuma,* which acts as a door. He enters the washitsu, carefully places the tray of food on a *chabudai* dining table made of rosewood and sits cross-legged on a *zabuton.*

A few minutes after Kaito finishes his breakfast in peace, he brings the leftover dishes back into the kitchen where, in the corner of his eye, he notices a bowl of rice, as well as a cup of tea on the counter. The steam from the rice is gone, he points out, same goes for the tea. For a moment, Kaito contemplates tossing both the rice and tea into the sink and pulverizing his weekly meal down the garbage disposal. Like any good cop, the thought passes.

As Kaito grabs the bowl of rice, his hand slips, causing the rice to spill over the floor. He clenches his jaw, his face reddens.

Accidental or not, Kaito reaches down and scoops the rice back into the bowl. Even hawks up a thick loogie from the back of his throat and spits it into the rice. With his used chopstick, Kaito mixes that phlegmy loogie into the rice. For good measure, Kaito flicks a couple of dry, flaky boogers into the rice as if it's his own personal seasoning and as he does with the loogie, stirs the boogers into the rice. Tainted food and all, the rice is placed on a smaller tray along with the cup of tea; however, before Kaito steps outside, he grabs an old, scummy pair of flip-flops, which he stores in the wooden *getabako,* a cabinet that derives its name from the word *geta*, along the side of the *genkan* and brings them to the back of the house.

Once outside, Kaito slips his feet into the flip-flops and walks along a natural pathway, passing a small garden of leafy herbs, vegetables, and plants, including *esharotto*, *soramame*, *naganegi*, *piiman*, *okura*, *tamanegi*, and *kyuuri*. At the end of the path, he stops in front of a *kura*, which is made of stone and tile roofing, kneels down, and sets the tray carrying the cold, tainted rice and tea on the ground. He digs out a key from his pocket and unlocks a steel padlock on the rusty chain wrapped and knotted around two steel door handles. He then pockets the key once the chain is unwrapped, unknotted, then removed, picks up the tray, and steps into the nearly pitch-black storehouse. In the corner of the room, the only source of light comes from a tiny window next to a square cell with cast iron prison-like bars; however, the window, given its eastward position, barely gives off any morning light along the edge of the cell.

Cautiously, Kaito creeps into the kura and places the tray in front of the cell.

From the inside of the unlit cell, a knobby tree branch extends from between the bars. With the end of the branch, the prisoner inside slides the tray underneath the narrow space underneath the cell.

Sniff.

Kaito can't see his face or his eyes.

But somehow, he can visualize that wicked-looking grin, the demon's grin.

Smells like you spit in my rice again, *Kaito*. You did, didn't you?

Remaining cautious, Kaito steps away from the cell and keeps his distance. Not once has he made a move toward Kaito. Which is extremely odd, considering his circumstances. However, Kaito makes sure not to take any risks.

Shut up and eat.

As his eyes adjust to the darkness, Kaito peers closer into the cell; and there, he witnesses the dark, twisted silhouette of a slender man reaching a spindly hand into the bowl of rice, scooping out five fingers worth, and placing his fingers into his mouth. The prisoner doesn't say a word to Kaito even after he swallows. Yet, he continues to savor his breakfast, as if he hadn't eaten in weeks.

ZARA
FEBRUARY 14, 2020 12:21 PM

I recently finished interpreting a PowerPoint presentation for two young Japanese businessmen from Okinagwa, The Watanabe Brothers, who were pitching a new "magnifying glass" feature which allowed its users to identify phishing scams and malicious software by dragging the mouse cursor over a suspicious link to the top dogs at Gumshoe, one of the hottest search engines north of Silicon Valley, when my left butt cheek vibrated.

Since I hadn't eaten any lunch yet and I was dying to check out an Italian bistro that I had recently opened to the public a couple of weeks ago in Sow Hollow, I actually thought about *not* reading the text, as if, by doing so, it would disappear in the data. But, as I ran through all the possible scenarios in my head, *what if* it was an emergency? *What if* it was a text from Po wishing me a "Happy Valentine's Day?" It was disheartening enough to hear it coming from random strangers throughout the morning, like that one barista at The Cup who was unabashedly spewing it to every Tom, Dick, or Harry, opposed to not even receiving so much as a simple acknowledgement from someone whom I once shared vows with. Oh, the unbridled power of "what if."

The text was, of course, from Lucy at Home Base.

No *"what are you doing?"* or *"are you busy?"* but, more or less, a demand.

Good grief.

TSUIHŌ

Footloose: Needed at The Burn Center at San Felisa Memorial Hospital ASAP. Will text you more details about the assignment as soon as they come in.

Assignment?

That was the first time I had ever heard Lucy use such a word.

Instead of asking me politely, Lucy was acting like Lieutenant Gordon sending out the *Batman* signal. Right, you could thank my thirteen-year old nephew, Titan, for that analogy.

Why couldn't she give it to Daniel or Hina?

Immediately, I started to think about the inception of where the most innocent exchanges between us went from friendly, even playful and, at times, diverting, to strictly professional. After all, I branded her with the fabulous nickname, *Footloose*, which was a play on words—her birth name, Luce—as well as a keen, actor-like observation of her ability to dance after a couple of shots of Fireball. She could've easily given the afternoon job to Hina considering Hina lived off Stone and Pleasant Street in Knob Hill. No doubt in my mind, the text was sent out of spite for me turning down her invitation to a small get-together at her apartment after a work dinner. Halfway through our entrées at Hibachi Lane and one or two sake bombs away from feeling a buzz, Lucy, who carpooled with two other colleagues from work, had given me what I could only perceive as a signal from the other end of the table—and I'm not talking about that kind of signal that came in the form of the glowing silhouette of a giant bat high above the skyline.

Any other smile would've been passed off as, suffice to say, innocent or even better, playful.

It was quite a flirty smile yet serious in nature, the turn of her lip lifting upward into her cheek, as though delicately being pulled by a fishing line. Her eyes trapped in mine. The last time I witnessed—or, at least, paid attention—to such a look was the night I met Porfirio. He was fifteen years younger than me, which, opposed to society's standards, as well as each *younger* generation's overcorrecting moral compass (sarcastically speaking), wasn't at all out of the ordinary for me growing up as a young girl raised by two loving parents who couldn't have been more farther apart in personality, as well as age difference, my father being two-presidents older than my mother. Sorry. I got you beat, Dad. The direction of my life was altered on that night I met Po, whom I would hesitantly call my husband seventeen years later and subtracting.

I looked over the text once.

Yellow frowning upside down emoji face, *sorry, still at Gumshoe*, was what my stomach was telling me to text.

> **ZaraSpears:** Be there.
> **Footloose:** Ty.
> **ZaraSpears:** You're welcome.
> **Footloose:** Detective Houser will fill you in on the details.

Detective, huh?

I received a rumbling in my gut, but it wasn't from hunger.

> **ZaraSpears:** Sounds good.

I haven't worked with the San Francisco Police Department since last summer when they needed me to interpret a thirty-six-year-old woman who was originally from Kyushu. She came to the country when she was only six years old. Both of her parents died when she hit the stage of rebellion. Her story was similar to my mother's. Only a teenager when she gave birth to two children. Japanese. Beautiful yet had the temperament of a tiger. The main difference between my mother and Ms. Ito: even though she had her moments when I was around the same age she gave birth to me, my mother wasn't disturbed enough to murder her two children. Ms. Ito buckled her two children in the backseat of her car; and instead of driving them to school, she deliberately pushed her car directly into San Francisco Bay because "the parasites" in her head told her to do it. The investigators needed me to interpret her confession, and she did. It was one of the hardest days on the job and, dare to say, the wildest. Despite all of the excitement, it was fair to say I sort of missed those kinds of jobs.

Since I didn't have enough time to grab a quick lunch, I nibbled from a two-day old protein bar that was partially melted in my purse and washed it down with cold coffee that I still had leftover from the early morning.

While receiving another text regarding information about the job, I arrived at San Felisa Memorial. According to Lucy's text, Detective Houser was scheduled to meet me outside the Rothman Burn Center.

Soon after reading the text, naturally, my mind began to race and fill in all of those holes of uncertainty.

Since I was a few minutes early, I waited in the waiting room until Detective Houser arrived. The front nursing station was littered with a bowl of hard candies and chocolates, a vase of red roses, and Valentine's Day cards, as well as a string of red hearts hanging above the station where a nurse sat with looked like a permanent smile drawn on her face. The sight alone of the decorations and cards—after all, the nurse appeared to be rubbing it in my face a little—weren't at all relieving the stress of the day and all the heartache it carried with it; in fact, it was only making it worse.

As I was about to silence the "vibrate" feature on my phone, I received a text from Hina.

Hina: Good luck, Sis. You're going to need it. Trust me!

I didn't really know how to respond to the text. The only thing that came to mind was that Hina arrived at the office not too long ago and like the social butterfly she was, made her rounds by chatting with each employee who paid her an iota of attention until she stopped at a desk in the very back of the office where sat a short, quirky, hipster-ish, bleach-blonde haired, four-eyed gal named Looselips, the, dare I say, cool, easygoing chick formerly known as Footloose, who informed Hina about the job at San Felisa Memorial.

ZaraSpears: Thanks?

Hina: Lucy told me you were at San Felisa Memorial.

Clearly, I chose the wrong occupation.

ZaraSpears: Should I be concerned?

Only a few seconds after I sent the text, my phone rang.

Hina was on the other end. I knew the job was serious as soon as I heard the joyless tone in her voice. Hina was *always* upbeat, even when recently informing me of her English setter's passing.

"What's up, Hina?" I asked Hina.

"I was actually supposed to take the job—did Lucy tell you?"

Hina's voice was unsteady.

Again, the floor started to crack and shift apart below my feet while my mind was quick to fill in those holes. Considering I was waiting outside a Burn Center, I totally forgot about her squeamishness. The woman would pass out from a paper cut.

"No," I said and pressed Hina. "She didn't. Why?"

"The other day I was called to San Felisa Memorial to help interpret a patient who was involved in a murder. Investigators wanted me to ask the patient for his consent to take his DNA. He could barely muster a few words, but eventually, he agreed."

"Murder, huh?" The plot thickened. Taming my excitement, I asked, "How old is he?"

"Early thirties, they presume, but you can't tell by looking at him. He was so badly burned that I could hardly get through a sentence. I know you have a much stronger stomach than me. So, maybe you'll have better luck than I did."

I could only imagine what the rest of the day might've looked like for Hina after she left the hospital. I was certain it involved a box of tissues, as well as frequent calls to Sean for reassurance—that is, if his condition was as worse off than Hina explained it to be. She was a delicate flower. From time to time, Hina was known to exaggerate.

"That sounds awful, Hina. Are you okay?"

"Yeah." Her voice jumped. A telltale sign of a lie. "I just feel so bad for the man. I mean, what kind of a person would do such a thing to somebody?"

I spotted two dark figures in the corners of my eye.

Turning the phone away from my face, I glanced at a man and a woman who were dressed like TV detectives.

"I'll find out soon enough. Listen," I said shortly to Hina, "I have to run. I'll talk to you soon, okay?"

"Yeah. Tell me how it goes."

"Will do. Bye."

"Bye."

I hang up with Hina and just as I imagined, the two standing by the front desk were detectives, who appeared to be on the lookout for someone.

This was my cue.

I walked up to the gentleman dressed in the black overcoat.

"Detective Houser?"

Detective Houser immediately reached out his hand.

"You must be Ms. Spears."

"Zara," I said, shaking his surprisingly smooth hand.

"Pleasure to meet you, Zara. I'm Detective Houser." He pointed at the stern woman standing next to him. "This is my partner, Detective Ruiz."

Her handshake was firm, military-like.

"I take it your friend, Ms. Araki, won't be joining us, is that right?"

"No," I said confidently with a closed, uninviting smile. "Just me today."

"That's a relief," Detective Houser said through the corner of his mouth.

I raised my hand. Again, I wasn't here for small talk, even though the detective clearly had other matters on his mind. I had a job to do.

"You don't have to explain."

Hina already filled me in, Buddy.

Detective held out his hand. He was wearing a golden Rolex. I swore that he could've been a hand model.

"Shall we?"

I followed the two detectives into the Burn Center where we met up with the patient's doctor, Doctor King. First name, Joe. I *wasn't* joking.

The doctor filled us in on the patient's condition, stating that he was going to be needing skin grafts since the third degree burns had covered over sixty percent of his entire body, most of the burns consistent around his face, as well as his upper body, including both arms. Dead skin and tissue were removed from all of the burned areas. The patient was also on a heavy round of antibiotics to prevent infections, as well as intravenous fluids to replace any fluids that were lost when the skin was burned.

We arrived outside the patient's room where a police officer was sitting in a chair next to the doorway.

Immediately, the sight of the police officer sipping from a cup of coffee sent me into a heightened state of both excitement and terror.

Detective Houser put his keen eye to good work and acknowledged my current unsettled state. He pointed out to me that the only reason the patient was under watch was due to the nature of the crime.

Simply put: it was for the hospital staff's safety, as well as the patient's.

"He's lucky to be alive," Doctor King said, more compassionately.

"After all of this," Detective Ruiz chimed in, "he's going to wish he wasn't."

"Forgive my partner's bluntness, Ms. Spears."

"Zara."

"Right," Detective Houser said smoothly, as if for a moment he was trying to hit on me. He spoke my name over a pause that warranted a second glance.

After shooting my eyes toward his hands, primarily his left, as if I was glancing at the sun, I immediately pointed out that the detective wasn't wearing a ring, only the pale outline of where a ring once rested. Of all the days for a man to find himself at the sharp end of Cupid's arrow, today was the day.

"So," I said sharply, warding off any awkwardness, "before we enter, is there anything else I need to know? For instance, does the patient have a name?"

"All we know so far," Detective Houser said, as he scaled back his smoothness, "is three dead bodies were discovered on a pier in East Park and our mystery man inside here knows exactly what happened. But," the detective flashed a grin, "that's exactly why you're here, Zara."

The doctor opened the door and entered.

"After you," Detective Houser said, showing me into the room.

Remaining professional, I mistakenly paused from the sight of the mysterious patient and without the detectives watching, took a moment to collect myself.

Poor Hina.

KAITO
SEPTEMBER 8, 1987 11:21 AM

AFTER a heavy morning of contemplation, which, over these past few months, has somehow been incorporated into his morning routine, Kaito finds himself back in the washitsu pulling out a large, rolled-up, burgundy towel from Manami's *tansu*, a cabinetry made from sugi tree, or Japanese cedar. His eyes cross the gory black and white photograph of a mutilated body lying in the bottom of the drawer. He immediately removes his eyes from the image and focuses elsewhere.

While still weighing his options, Kaito carefully kneels down on the zabuton and places the bulky towel on top of the chabudai. There, Kaito unrolls the towel, revealing a *katana*, a *wakizashi*, a revolver, and six rounds of ammunition, two of the rounds end up rolling off the edge of the chabudai. Kaito leans over and picks up the two rounds, placing one of them on the towel while holding the other one in his hand. He moves his eyes back to the katana.

Then, once more, back to that perfect round between his fingers.

Quick and easy, he thinks to himself.

Kaito can't help but draw his eyes to the katana.

Or, *slow and painful.*

As Kaito weighs his options—even though, in the end, the thought of his initial plan *always* came out on top—his attention is drawn to a news anchor talking on the small analog TV in the background. He turns to the other room where he partially catches the news anchor speaking about a recent murder.

Piquing his interest, Kaito leaves behind the katana and walks toward the TV where he learns more about the victim whose body was discovered in the Aokigatama Forest yesterday afternoon by two hikers. The body has been identified as a forty-three year old man named Eiichi Satō. Based on his suspicious wounds all over his body, the investigators believe it was a "homicide."

Kaito rushes toward the TV and switches it off.

He checks the time.

He's late for work. He doesn't waste any time. He leaves the house, gets in his car, and drives to the grocery store located a mile away from his house.

About an hour of uneventful work, mostly spent checking out the customers, some local, some tourists, and slipping into a daydream about a robber—perhaps a tourist or even a rude American—storming into the store to rob the place in order to release the built-up aggression he has inside him, Kaito can't take it any longer. During his downtime, he grabs the last newspaper from the shelf.

The murder of Eiichi Satō is plastered on the front page of Kai Shimbun.

Inside his 1985 brown Isuzu Gemini, Kaito reads further details on the local man's death, in particularly, the condition of his body when it was discovered; and his mind goes straight to darker places.

It's happening again. But how?

When Kaito returns home, he doesn't even bother removing the muddy shoes from his feet. Instead, he grabs a loaded revolver from the washitsu and wanders outside where he stops in his tracks along the pathway leading toward the kura.

A *flash* of his glory days comes back to him.

And for a moment, he finds himself wearing the badge yet again.

ZARA
FEBRUARY 14, 2020 1:12 PM

NOW, I know why she didn't take the job.

Which made me wonder why Lucy even gave her the job to begin with.

I pushed aside the patient's current condition and mainly focused on the job at hand. Following the two detectives' lead, I walked toward the side of the burn recovery bed, which was much larger than any ordinary hospital bed with a special inflatable mattress intended to evenly distribute the patient's weight, allowing for a more conformal shape while lying flat. Except for the two cutout holes for his eyes to see, the two smaller holes for his nose to breathe, and a narrow masked superhero-like slit to speak through, the patient's entire face, as well as his upper torso was mummy-wrapped in fresh white gauze. Both of the patient's arms were extended outward like a crucifix along plush padding and appeared as if they had recently been wrapped in gauze as well.

With a couple of nurses entering the room behind us, Doctor King stood over the patient and searched for his eyes with a tiny flashlight.

"Detective Houser and Detective Ruiz, who visited you the other day, have a couple of questions to ask you. Your interpreter," the doctor pointed at me and in return, I stepped forward into the patient's range of vision as if I was being summoned, "Ms. Spears is here to help translate."

Interpret, actually; however, it was the wrong place and definitely the wrong time to bring such a common mistake to the doctor's attention.

Somewhere, a good punch line was forming in my thoughts. Po entered my thoughts. He was perhaps the only person who loved my jokes and my dark sense of humor. I filed the joke away upstairs, hoping to tell it to him later.

Joking aside, Detective Houser took a step closer to the bed and spoke clearly for the patient, as if he was talking to a third-grader.

"I first want to start out by asking your name."

The detective turned to me and nodded as if he was giving me my cue.

In Japanese, I asked the patient what his name was.

"Ryuu Ishii," he said, his voice weak and gravelly.

I turned to the detective and even though the name was clear enough to interpret, I repeated anyway.

"He says his name is *Ryuu Ishii*," I said.

Bewildered, Detective Houser pulled out a notepad from his pocket and read from it, "What is your relation with 'Ichiro Higashi?'"

Strangely, I had heard that name before but didn't know where.

I interpreted the detective's question for the patient.

In return, the patient gave a response that left the detective skimming through his notepad.

"He says he doesn't know any man by that name."

"Is he sure?" asked the detective.

Once more, I interpreted for the patient.

"Yes," I said to the detective. "He is sure."

"Okay," Detective Houser said shortly, "let's start over, shall we? Why don't you start from the very beginning—"

"—What were you doing in East Park on the night of your attack?" the other detective, Ruiz was her name, asked over Detective Houser. Her demeanor was way more aggressive, as if she was tired of dancing around all of the formalities.

I was starting to see that cliché good cop-bad cop dynamic unfold before my eyes. Surprisingly, despite her rough exterior, I liked her.

I interpreted.

The patient, who went by the name Ryuu Ishii, responded.

"He says he had just finished eating supper at a restaurant called The Flapjack and he was walking off his meal when three men suddenly jumped him from behind."

Detective Ruiz asked, "So, you're telling us you have *never* seen these men before?" She emphasized the word *never*.

I asked Ryuu the question with an emphasis on the word *kesshite*, which, for a moment, I'd mistaken as *shita koto ga nai*.

"*Hai*," he said unsurely, his voice sounding almost crumbly.

Once more, I repeated the question for Ryuu, who, in return, gave me a more confident response.

The two detectives, who knew very little Japanese, understood the word *hai*.

Detective Houser asked, "How long have you been living in the country, Mr. Ishii?"

"He says he's lived in America for around eight months so far—"

Before the detectives could ask any more questions, Ryuu finished the rest of his sentence.

"He says he recently moved from Onaka to the United States to pursue a career in culinary."

"You want to be a *chef* or something?"

"*Itamae*?"

Ryuu nudged his head.

"*Hai*."

He elaborated for the detectives.

I followed Ryuu, "The moment I arrived in San Francisco I fell in love with the city, as well as its people and decided to stay. It was a dream come true. My own American Dream."

"*More like a nightmare*," Detective Ruiz said under her voice. "How do you explain the blood that our forensics team pulled from your clothes and shoes?"

I asked Ryuu the detective's question.

He stuttered for a moment and then hesitantly answered.

"He says he doesn't know what you're talking about—"

Ryuu clarified his answer for me.

"—Everything happened so fast," I interpreted for the two detectives. "One minute, they were all kicking and beating me while I was helplessly lying on the ground. The next minute, they were standing over me and pouring gasoline over my body. 'The one particular man,' he says while striking a match, 'this is what you deserve for killing my father.' The flames engulfed my body." Several of his words get muttered for a moment. "He says all he can remember was the fire and watching it burn right through his flesh. The pain was. . . was *excruciating*. . ."

Overcome with emotion, Ryuu's body jolted forward in a phlegmy cough.

"Can you ask Mr. Ishii if he killed these men out of self-defense?"

I asked Ryuu the detective's question, but all I received in return was another phlegmy cough, this one more violent than the one before.

The burns obviously weren't only on the outside.

His lungs, especially the right one, had sustained significant burns as well.

"Okay, Detectives," Doctor King said urgently as he stepped between the detectives and waved over a couple of nurses to the bed. "That is enough for today. Now please give us the room."

As the doctor and nurses began to work on Ryuu, we were escorted from the room by another nurse.

Outside the room, the two detectives appeared more frustrated, especially Detective Houser, whose once Cowboy ruggedness combined with a cool, charming composure started to slip from his reddened face like a mask.

"He's lying," Detective Houser seethed to his partner.

"He sounded like he was telling the truth," I suddenly chimed in. As soon as the words left my mouth, I knew I was speaking out of place. I was here to interpret Mr. Ishii for the two detectives who were actively working a case and now, I realized how defensive I sounded for a potential suspect in a multiple-homicide.

Detective Houser appeared even redder from my remark.

With his hands worn over his hips and the handle of his service weapon protruding outward along his belt like an erection, Detective Houser squared his body toward me and threw his head in a stiffer nod, "Is that right? And what's makes you so sure, Ms. Spears?"

To my dismay, at that point in time all I could think about was the detective's first name.

I shifted my thoughts toward his question before the red-hot frustration swallowed him whole.

"When Mr. Ishii spoke about the moment before being set on fire," I said less defensively and more detectively, "I could detect fear in his voice, like he wasn't scared of what the men were about to do but scared for what *he* was about to do."

"Have you been watching the news lately, Ms. Spears?"

"I'm afraid I don't have much time for the news," I said, feeling the burn of a spotlight shining down on me. Figuratively speaking, I felt a couple of feet taller than the detective. "Plus, there's enough bad—"

"—Okay. I get it. You're a busy person. We're all *too* busy." The detective was taller, literally and figuratively; in fact, his whole aura was looming over me. "Well, let me fill you in real quick as to what's going on here. I have three men, who were brutally murdered in East Park, and our main suspect happens to be in that room right there. Now, what I need from you is to help us to get to the bottom of what really happened that night. I speak. You translate—"

—*Interpret*, I was itching to correct him.

I retraced my steps and thought about one of the first questions the detective asked.

"Who is Ichiro Higashi?" I asked Detective Houser.

The detective paused for a moment and let his frustration mellow.

"You don't get out much, do you?" Detective Ruiz said with a bad-cop smirk on her face.

I felt as if the question—or statement—needed no response. I wasn't going to give Detective Ruiz the satisfaction.

"*Two years ago*," Detective Houser said as if he was about to tell me a story, "a thirty-one year old named Ichiro Higashi was charged with the murder of Jordan Pruitt but was found not guilty in a court of law due to insufficient evidence. Higashi walked free. Then, last year, Higashi went missing. He was last seen in a small town north of San Francisco, just outside Redwood. A couple months after Higashi's disappearance, the search was called off. Higashi basically disappeared off the face of the earth. Pruitt's son, Evan was his name, a man who was known to wear his heart on his sleeve during the trial, was, of course, the first person who the authorities questioned. It turns out Evan Pruitt wasn't involved in Higashi's disappearance." The detective let out an airy sigh from what sounded like his gut, as if, every time he recounted the story, it had a way of shortening his breath.

Evan Pruitt, I thought to myself.

"*Now*, we have three men found dead in East Park and one of them happens to be Evan Pruitt. However, it gets much better, Ms. Spears. The DNA that forensics swapped from our patient right in there—or this so-called 'Ryuu Ishii' guy whom he claims to be—matches the same exact DNA as. . ."

He paused, as if he was waiting for me to fill in the blank.

"Ichiro Higashi?"

"That's right," Detective Houser said. "I know, as well as you know, that we are certainly not in the business of guessing, but if I *had* to guess, I'd guess Evan Pruitt and his two pals, Cooper Mobley and Brayden Shanks, found Higashi and they bit off more than they could handle."

Detective Ruiz, of course, put in her own two cents: "*Revenge isn't always a dish best served cold.*"

Nice one, Ruiz.

Trying not to display any discomfort in front of the two detectives, I collected my thoughts. It was a lot to take in, so much darkness. Only one question came to mind.

"If you don't mind me asking, how did they die—the three men?"

"All three men were stabbed to death by a wooden blade of some kind. Our forensics found splinters inside several stab wounds. They're still trying to identify the wood. If we found out what tree the blade was made from, then it'll point us in a direction where the blade was made. That's a theory, at least."

Splinters?

"That's bizarre."

Detective Houser let out another sigh, this time short and sharp, like a dart.

"You're telling me."

"So, what now?"

"We wait till our patient can talk."

KAITO

AFTER breakfast, Kaito hops on the Umi Line and rides to the Criminal Investigation Headquarters located in the Chinagwa Ward in Tokyo where yet again he attempts to get a hold of his former colleague, Bunji Kawakami.

As the time before Kaito hangs around the waiting area for hours until *finally* Bunji shoulders through a crowd of plain-clothed detectives.

Kaito! How are you doing, old friend? Already sick of re-tirement? Huh, Kaito?

Pleased to see Kaito, Bunji greets Kaito with an informal bow.

Feeling unappreciated, Kaito barely bows back—more or less, a deep nod.

Bunji loosens the burgundy tie around his collar, pulls out a golden pack of smokes, and offers one to Kaito, who, in return, declines.

No thanks. You know those things will kill you, Bunji.

With a smile worn tightly on his face, Bunji waves off Kaito's comment.

I'll have better luck with the Yoko Clan.

Kaito's emotions slip through as he shakes his head in a ripe disgust.

It's your funeral, Bunji.

As Bunji raises the cigarette up to his lips, his face falls into a slack expression.

You started to sound like my mother, Kaito.

Bunji extends his other hand outward, indicating for Kaito to walk with him down a narrow hallway.

As Bunji lights his cigarette, Kaito contemplates whether or not he should tell Bunji about the reason as to why he's here. Kaito, being the straight shooter, figures he's already pushed past the foreplay.

So what brings you here today, Ka—

—I need to ask you a favor.

Midway through dragging his cigarette, he chokes up from Kaito's response, forcing him to let out a puff of smoke.

Favor? You're in no position to be asking favors, Kaito.

In the case you're currently working, does the manner in which the victims were murdered share any similarities to the Chiaki Case?

Bunji stops in his tracks and squares himself to Kaito.

You know I'm unable to discuss any details of an on-going investigation, Kaito. Commissioner Kamura would have my badge—and my head. Is that why you've been trying to contact me for the past couple of days? Huh, Kaito?

You've noticed, huh?

Bunji takes a deeper drag and smiles out a cloud of smoke.

I didn't join the Detective Unit for my lack of observation.

Ah, so that's why you've been ignoring me.

I haven't been ignoring you, Kaito. I've been busy trying to solve a murder.

Holding out his hands in surrender, Kaito steps closer to Bunji.

Just answer this one question, and I will leave you alone. Was the weapon used to murder the victims made out of wood?

Bunji's eyes widen with what only Kaito can perceive as shock.

Kaito, you know I can't answer that question!

Don't answer. If you don't answer me in the next three seconds, I will know the murderer used a weapon made out of wood. Please, Bunji. This one favor.

Without saying a word, Bunji takes a drag of his cigarette and blows out the smoke. Bunji continues to shoot daggers at Kaito while remaining quiet for three seconds going on four, five, six. . .

Kaito pats Bunji on the shoulder.

Thank you, Bunji.

Relieved from Bunji's answer—or *lack* of answer—Kaito walks off.

Bunji is still left without words.

ZARA
February 14, 2020 9:11 PM

BY the time I prepared a light supper of my favorite "go-to" meal, which was Maruchan's instant ramen noodles, the day was already starting to wear on me. I sat down on the couch and flipped through a five-dollar bin worth of movies on *Shh!* but couldn't find anything decent to watch—or at least, anything that caught my eye at the moment. I took my ramen noodles to the table where I opened my laptop. All I could think about were the three homicides that Detective Houser and Ruiz had been trying to solve for the past few days. No doubt, there was a mystery here, how those three men died, who killed them. Most importantly: *Who is Ryuu Ishii?* I typed his name into Google but didn't find anybody that matched his description. Since he apparently moved to the States only eight months ago, I didn't expect to find much information on Ryuu; however, another came to mind.

With a mouthful of ramen noodles, I googled the name *Ichiro Higashi.*

Sure enough, a slew of information popped up on the popular search engine: articles, blogs, and forums regarding the thirty-three year old's disappearance last July, as well as information on his arraignment two years ago—which seemed to grab a lot of media buzz mainly due to his "undocumented" status in America.

Which, of course you already knew, was a softer word for "illegal."

I pulled up a photograph of Ichiro Higashi, which was taken from a mug shot at the San Francisco Police Department. Excavating the graphic images from earlier today, I pictured his face covered in white gauze. I even ripped out a piece of notebook paper from my memo pad and with the tip of my pen, poked three holes in the paper, two holes for eyes and one for a mouth. I placed the holey paper on top of the photo on the screen. His dark eyes looked very similar, if not the same as Ryuu Ishii's.

I told myself that it could be him.

Could.

About an hour into my search—I lost track of time after skimming through a website on, of all things, hair implants—I came across a questionable link on Jordan Pruitt, a local pediatrician, as well as a cancer survivor whose body was found in a park only a few miles from his house. The link directed me to a sketchy website with a "shocking" headline that claimed Jordan Pruitt was a part of some underground sex cult. Only a few seconds into scrolling through the page, I'm suddenly hit with a spam bomb on my computer screen, the pornographic pop-up ads forcing me to temporarily power off the laptop.

I took a couple of more bites of cold ramen and then tried yet again.

Thankfully, Google was still operable, despite the possible virus—or viruses crawling in my laptop.

Mindful of my overzealous clicking, I googled Ichiro Higashi once more.

28

According to the search results three pages in, apparently Higashi was briefly mentioned in a TV show called *Guilty or Not*, a true crime series which was pulled from the popular streaming service *Shh!* last year due to controversies regarding glaring "inconsistencies" and "exaggerations," in other words, sensational journalism.

On a whim, I pulled up the *Shh!* app on my smart TV and searched for the show but couldn't find any results.

I continued with the search on my laptop.

A few pages into my search, I found a website called "The Leak."

In the back of my mind, I knew it was a bad choice to click on the link. I began to think about how brilliant the Watanabe Brothers' magnifying glass feature was and how much I could've really used it right now while scraping through the scummy parts of the Internet. I braced myself for impact and clicked on the link. I waited a couple of seconds as if I was sitting in the dark movie theater watching a horror movie and I was waiting for our elusive monster to pop out of the screen in the best jump scare only a lowbrow filmmaker could buy. Once I was inside, I breathed a sigh of relief. I was clear of any pop-up ads for online dating, sex pills, magic dildos, or penis pumps—*I mean, guys, is that really still a thing?*

The article was written by Anonymous. Which immediately raised a red flag. Anybody who wrote under the name "Anonymous" was clearly either full of shit or trying to undermine the investigation based out of a personal vendetta.

I read through the article—if that was what you called it. It read more like a whodunit novel than an article written by an on-the-ground journalist, which was about as rare as an endangered species. Most of it was about Jordan Pruitt's murder and how the district attorney, Patrick Winkler, who was up for reelection and ready to hit a homerun with a case that found its way onto a national spotlight and ultimately, pulled on America's heartstrings, overplayed his hand with very little evidence on Ichiro Higashi.

About halfway through the page-scroller, I came across another name, *Kaito Takahashi.*

While digging further into Ichiro Higashi's background, the investigators had no other choice than to reach out for international assistance, starting with the organization, Interpol, which provided them with a "match" in the database.

According to their findings, Ichiro Higashi's fingerprints matched the fingerprints of a former detective named Kaito Takahashi, who died from multiple stab wounds, his body discovered by his only son, Hiroshi, in the Kodama Forest outside Tokyo, Japan on "September 21, 1987."

Takahashi's killer was *never* caught.

I pulled up another window, researched "Hiroshi Takahashi."

Apparently, Hiroshi Takahashi was the creator behind a Japanese anime called ダイヤモンドクロー (*Diamond Claw)*. Hiroshi resided in Tokyo and till this day, refused to speak about his father and the questions surrounding his death.

Dead end.

So, I backtracked.

The location of Kaito Takahashi's death was incredibly significant, considering it was the same area where partial remains of twenty-one year old college student, Sakura Yukimara, were discovered in a shallow grave. With the crime rate in Japan ranking lowest in the world and murders being extraordinarily rare and such a term as police "white paper" putting an emphasis on the word *white*, as in paper was less covered in crime stats, the case was thrust into the national spotlight and had left many of the residents who lived in and around the Kodama region in a state of high-anxiety. The murderer had been popularized as being Japan's very first serial killer, branding the name, "Gravedigger," who was also known to paralyze several of his victims by injecting them with a poison only found in the aconitum—or *aconite*— a plant which was also known as "wolf's-bane."

Kaito Takahashi, who was the lead detective working the highly controversial case which lasted for months, re-

tired shortly after catching his ever-elusive killer: a twenty-
eight year old from Hinshu named "Gaku Chiaki." Takahashi was fifty years of age, which was considered rather
young to retire in Japan or anywhere, for that matter.
Nonetheless, he was considered a legend, mostly for taking
down such an infamous serial killer who went by the name
"Gaku Chiaki." Chiaki, who was responsible for the deaths
of "twelve" victims, all discovered in the Kodama Forest,
which, in a confession, had become his own personal "bur-
ial ground," was sentenced to death by hanging on "July 14,
1982."

When later searching Takahashi's home located in the
mountainous town of Nagamaki, the investigation team
found a prison cell in the shed behind his house and iron-
clad evidence, including hair samples and DNA, suggesting
that suspected killer, Dai Ando, was being held captive
inside the prison cell; however, no body was found, only the
shriveled, warped remains of a decrypted wooden doll with
a bullet hole in its head. The round later identified as be-
longing to Kaito's revolver. As to the doll's significance,
investigators were baffled and had no explanations.

I took a step away from my laptop, took a breath, and
tried to make sense as to what I had just read.

With this mysterious man, Kaito Takahashi, seared in
my mind, I googled his name in the other window. I found
many links directing me to old newspaper articles on the
legendary detective. I decided to click on the images tab
first in order to get a sense of what he might've looked like.
Shockingly, for a woman who spends her days wrapped in
words and translation, I leaned quite heavily toward the
visual side. After all, words were not only verbal, but also
visual.

In a photo gallery, I spotted a Japanese man who, except
for missing the *Pac-Man*-like mole on his right cheek,
looked identical to—of all people—Ichiro Higashi!

I clicked on the grainy photograph, which directed me
to a Japanese newspaper website called Kai Shimbun.
There, I scrolled through a cutout of a newspaper article
from "OCTOBER 1981," written in both hiragana and

katakana, which could be extremely chaotic to any pair of eyes with the main text set to a vertical setting, whereas, the headings, as well as the captions set to a horizontal setting. I translated the article the best I could, which was a statement from Detective Takahashi, who was explaining his account of capturing the ever-elusive serial killer, Gaku Chiaki, to a crowd of news reporters. I wasn't at all interested in the arrest. I was much more interested in Takahashi's "look." I minimized the window and opened yet another window where I had a photo of Ichiro Higashi. I tried to add thirty-some years to Takahashi's face.

Determined to find a much younger photo of the former detective, I kept digging and digging through the search engine until I *finally* found a photo of Kaito Takahashi taken right after he graduated from the police academy.

According to the description on the bottom of the page, he was twenty-seven years old, only four years younger than the photo of Ichiro Higashi, the suspected murderer charged for the murder of Jordan Pruitt but was never convicted, who, as Detective Houser had candidly said, "disappeared off the face of the earth."

As I was about to close the laptop and exhaustedly call it a night, I spotted yet another grainier photograph of Kaito Takahashi in the gallery at the bottom left-hand corner of the screen. Even though the photo was taken when Kaito Takahashi was thirty-three years old—which, bare in mind, was two years younger than Higashi when he allegedly murdered Jordan Pruitt—he appeared much older than the previous photograph. Takahashi was carrying bags underneath his eyes and appeared like a man who hadn't slept in months. I clicked on the link below the photo, taking me to an old *New York Times* article from "June 23, 1964."

The article was about a thirty-three-year-old police officer (Takahashi) who shot and killed a man outside a dojo. The police officer (Takahashi) claimed the shooting was out of self-defense. A fifty-one year old sensei, Fumihiro Hattori, a widely respected teacher and pillar of the close-nit community, was pronounced dead on the scene. Hattori's death sparked much outrage, leaving many of Hattori's students, as well as those in the community, convinced that Hattori was unjustifiably gunned down.

Considering the accusatorial nature of the justice system, Takahashi was later found "not guilty" of the crime and many believed that Hattori's shooter (Takahashi) got off with a minor slap on the wrist and wasn't held accountable.

I couldn't believe the thought actually entered my head. But it did.

And it was all that I could think about.

Forget all about the age difference, *what if Ryuu Ishii is Kaito Takahashi?*

People lied about their ages all the time and with all of those burns covering his face, it was impossible to tell Ryuu's exact age.

Even better, *what if the two were related?*

With both my eyes burning and bloodshot, I took yet another step away from my laptop. My eyelids were starting to curl dumbbells during each blink. In their own subtle way, my eyes were telling me that I needed sleep. More than likely, I was going to have yet another long day tomorrow and if I didn't get at least four hours of shuteye, then I was going to be a straight-up diva.

I closed my laptop, left the dirty dishes in the sink for the morning rise, and headed straight to bed.

Tomorrow hadn't felt so far away.

KAITO
SEPTEMBER 10, 1987 5:08 PM

STARING at the top cabinet above the tansu, Kaito stands motionlessly at the edge of the hallway and mulls over the idea of whether or not he should call upon his old demons that he had locked away so many years ago. Kaito doesn't know if he can become that lone highwayman once again, the one who journeyed down endless stretches of darkness where answered questions led to unanswered questions.

33

With the skies reddening, Kaito decides, once and for all, to confront Dai.

Kaito walks out of the house and with the key that he keeps attached to him as if it's a part of him, unlocks the kura where his enigmatic prisoner is sitting in the corner of the room.

What brings you here at this hour of the day? Past your bedtime, is it not?

Kaito closes the door behind him and walks to the front of the cell.

There, Kaito gets a closer look at Dai's face and doesn't see a face at all—no eyes, no eyebrows, no nose, no mouth, not even the contours of a skull, such as a cheekbone or a mandible, his entire face as blank as a scroll. All of the facial features that any *normal* human would possess are nowhere to be spotted on his face. Kaito reminds himself that Dai Ando isn't human.

Enough playing games. Do you know what's going on?

Startled by a rustling noise of a tree branch, Kaito redirects his attention outside the kura. He turns toward the cut of red sky behind the window and then as he faces the cell, he is greeted by yet another presence, now standing much closer to the cell door. This time, Dai's wearing a different face, a *familiar* face covered in angled shadows.

You're talking about the recent murders, are you not?

Dai's deep, resonant masculine voice softens into a more feminine voice.

Immediately, Kaito detects the tone in his—or her—voice.

Timid by Dai's new appearance, Kaito takes a step back from the cell.

I take that as a 'yes.'

As the prisoner takes a step closer, he reveals himself as a young woman, her eyes glowing like a cat from the angle of the red light reflecting through the inside of the kura.

Even though you have changed over these past few years, deep down inside, Kaito, you're still that same confused little boy who still feels as if the world is out to get him. That *chip* on your shoulder must weigh two tons.

Kaito lowers his head, his brow forming into a letter v.
The colorful glow fades from the eyes of prisoner, Yui *Hattori*. Her eyes, as glossy and glassy as marbles, darken.

You don't know a thing about me.

I know a lot more than you think, *deku*.

Kaito picks up a hint of amusement attached to Yui's voice, causing his eyes to sharpen. His breathing becomes heavier, warmer.

Isn't that what the kids used to call you? Mommy's little 'deku.'

You don't know me.

There's the anger we're all used to seeing. It was that uncontrollable emotion that murdered my husband, Fumihiro.

You think you can fool me, *Dai Ando*. You are not Yui, nor will you ever speak for Yui. You are a bottom feeder who constantly hides behind the faces of other people.

Says the hot-blooded human who shot an innocent man whom he suspected was a pedophile. You know all of that built-up

anger leftover from your crime-ridden days as a young, *confused* teenager who grew up without a father figure has followed you around through your entire adult life. For so long, expressing your anger through violence became customary for you. 'Normal,' some would say. When you entered the real world and realized that you were replaceable, you finally came to the conclusion that your closet-behavior wasn't at all normal. *You* weren't normal. And ever since, you've been carrying around this burden—

With a scowl on his face and his hands balled up into fists, Kaito steps closer to the cell.

Are you involved in these recent murders that have taken place in Aokigatama?

Involved? Is that really why you came to see me? How can I be involved in a murder when I've been locked behind bars for six years, Kaito? Huh?

You must know somebody on the outside. An accomplice who slipped from my reach? An admirer of yours who playing copycat?

With the question hanging in the air, Yui moves from the colder shadows and reveals more of her pale face. Her eyes sharp in a similar fashion as Kaito's.

You know I have *plenty* of admirers, Detective.

Kaito pulls his attention from Yui's face and waits in deep thought.

I'll tell you what, Dai. You help me find the person responsible for these murders and maybe I'll consider letting you go.

Go? Why would I want to go out there when I have you all to myself, Kaito?

Rage fills Kaito. He suddenly lashes out at Yui by striking the cast iron bars with the meaty part of his fist.

Enough! You know something! Don't you?

Now, there's The Kaito who shot my husband.

Beyond frustrated with Dai Ando—Yui or whatever face Dai callously hides behind—Kaito is done with the mind games.

As he's about to reach for the door handle, Dai appears behind the bars. His beard is thin and scraggly. His shit-stained teeth sit along his receding gums like crooked tombstones. His hands spotted with black soil, nails overgrown and dirty as well, appearing like worn talons.

Through the dark cell, Dai points his knobby, veiny finger at Kaito.

Ask yourself, Kaito: Are you any different from all those men and women you locked up behind bars?

Kaito turns away in vexation, opens the door to the kura, and slams the door on the way out.

ZARA
February 15, 2020 7:15 AM

SOMEWHERE between wrestling with damp bed sheets and dozing off in the most uncomfortable position on my bed, I had a dream where I was back at San Felisa Memorial. However, the hospital was much different in structure—at least, it was the little things that dreams tend to alter. The hallways were longer and grimier. The rooms,

TSUIHŌ

as deep as cathedrals. I was standing by Ryuu's bedside. Everything felt as if it was moving in slow motion. With his eyes pinned on mine, Ryuu was unwrapping one never-ending strip of gauze from his head. As Ryuu twirled the gauze around the top of his head, part of his face slowly revealed itself. His skin wasn't burnt, charred, or scarred. Once he finished removing the gauze from his face, I saw Kaito Takahashi's face. He was staring at me with a blank expression. I tried to make sense of the look. But I realized it was just a dream.

And dreams were only extensions from reality.

At least that was what I told myself.

Despite a somewhat decent night's rest, I woke up to the face of Kaito Takahashi still etched in my mind, like a bad song on the radio that I couldn't shake. I checked the time and watched the five turn into a six.

I rolled out of bed and went about my morning routine: coffee, as black as the abyss, toast, a glass of orange juice, a quick recap of whatever show on *Shh!* that I was watching that week, and then checked my work schedule, what clients, locations, times. I cut short my shower in order to squeeze in a few minutes of morning headlines, which was rare for me. In my not-so-distant past, I used to receive a newspaper at my doorstep every morning. While working my way through a second cup of Columbia's Finest, I'd finish reading through the entire paper. For one, it kept me *somewhat* informed—mostly entertained—and had given me the sense of relief knowing the giant rock we lived on was still spinning through a vast universe and that people were still acting like people—I swear, somewhere lost inside my brain, there was a lyric from the Depeche Mode churning throughout that gray matter—and two, which was the most important reason of the two reasons, it was convenient. Yet, over time, it became costly. With more publications winding up on the Internet or the digital newsstands, I didn't see the point wasting the money on something that was eventually going to end up in a recycling bin. In the back of my mind, I was hoping to hear something about those three murders at East Park. Any mention of what

happened at East Park never came up during the broadcast.

Go figure.

Instead, it was Rhodes this or Washington that.

Washington, Rhodes, Washington.

Not in any specific order.

Upcoming elections had a way of putting people in a
tizzy.

I turned off the snooze tube and decided to clean, starting with the bathroom and then moving my way into the
kitchen.

While I was putting away the dishes from the night before, I received a text from Lucy. I was called back to San
Felisa. The text read, "9:00."

I prepared to arrive a quarter till.

On time, I pulled into the parking deck outside the hospital at exactly "8:43," which gave me about five minutes
to primp my hair and adjust my makeup.

Once ready, I made my way to Rothman Burn Center.

The two detectives, Detective Houser and Detective
Ruiz, were waiting next to the front desk as soon as I arrived, which, for a moment, made me wonder how long
they had been waiting. Even though I was ten minutes
early, I couldn't stand being late.

Detective Houser's sharper, cleaner appearance canceled any thought of having to come up with a sorry excuse
as to why I was late. Not to sound like one of those yucky
types who acted as if the world revolved around them, but
I believed he took a few extra minutes from his morning
routine to make sure he looked his Sunday's best. He had a
glow about him, too.

Looks aside, I greeted the two detectives with a handshake.

"Zara," Detective Houser said, "nice to see you again."

"Likewise," I returned. "Have you two been waiting
long?"

Detective Ruiz flippantly shook her head.

"Not long," she said in the same unfriendly manner from
yesterday.

"That's good."

"So," Detective Houser said, his voice louder, "are you ready—"

Before he could finish his sentence, Doctor King showed up.

As before, the doctor escorted us to Ryuu's room.

During the walk, he informed us that our mystery man was doing much better than the day before.

Outside, I witnessed a different police officer sitting in a chair outside Ryuu's room. Apparently, cops had been alternating shifts throughout the day. I didn't know why they were watching Ryuu around-the-clock, considering his condition. Technically, Ryuu was considered a suspect. I guess, in a way, everybody was a suspect until they're deemed not a suspect. To me, though, it was rather strange to watch a man who could barely move an eyelid. But what did I know about being an officer of the law?

Before we entered, I pulled aside Detective Houser and asked him if he knew a man named Kaito Takahashi.

I immediately regretted speaking the name the moment it left my lips and felt as if, somehow, I was overstepping my boundaries.

"Where did you hear that name?" asked Detective Houser.

I was embarrassed to even state where I had heard the name.

"The Internet," I said as if there should've been a large question mark behind my answer.

The detective nearly laughed.

"Right," Detective Houser said with disdain and slowed down his walk. *"The Internet."*

I followed suit, slowed my walk, and hung back while Detective Ruiz and the doctor took the lead.

Detective Houser slipped his hands into his pockets and walked closer to me and said, "Conspiracy theorists dragged along a couple of resentful cops, who had been fired from the force, into their own sick delusions and started up a bunch of rumors that Higashi was somehow related to a man named Kaito Takahashi, a detective who was involved in the infamous homicide case in the early 1980s."

"Gaku Chiaki," I said, not missing a beat. "I've done my homework."

The detective should've been impressed but from the blank expression on his face, I knew it was far from impressed. More like annoyed.

"The story shook Japan like an earthquake. Kaito was one of the detectives who brought down Chiaki. He retired shortly after the case was solved. He was sort of like a legend in Japan. As I'm sure you already *read*, Zara, Mr. Takahashi died thirty-some years ago, which would make it physically impossible for Ichiro Higashi to be Kaito Takahashi."

"So tell me this, Detective," I said, "why did people think Ichiro Higashi was Kaito Takahashi?"

"Why? I'll tell you why," the detective said. "When it came to investigating Higashi, it was some inexperience drone who misread the fingerprints on their side of the pond. Ninety-nine perfect of all screw-ups fall on human error, not the science. The job ain't perfect, Zara, neither is the system. So," the detective said as he held out his hand, "can we continue? Or is there anything else you want to ask me that I haven't already heard?"

"No," I said, struggling to find the words. "That's all."

"Are you two through?" asked Detective Ruiz, as she glanced over her shoulder and gave her partner an eye that rightfully deserved an adjective.

Surprisingly, I felt ill at ease after Detective Houser's poor explanation about Ichiro Higashi and Kaito Takahashi's fingerprints being the same based merely on "human error." Why did I get the impression he wasn't being honest with me?

At this particular juncture, I felt more comfortable redirecting all of my questions toward Detective Ruiz. She struck me as a "no-chaser" kind of gal.

Detective Houser, acting as if he debunked everything I discovered on Kaito Takahashi last night, followed the doctor into the room. Once I entered the room, I first noticed that Ryuu appeared more attentive. He turned his head toward the detectives, his clear eyes acknowledging the detective's presence, then mine.

I greeted Ryuu with a bow.

Ryuu, who remained in a frozen state from the Mummy-like wrapping of gauze around his upper torso and head region, returned with a subtle nod.

"Detective Houser," the detective said, pointing at himself first, then pointing at his partner, "Detective Ruiz. We spoke yesterday."

Ryuu moved his eyes up and down, up and down, as if, in his own way, he was bowing to the detectives.

I interpreted from English to Japanese.

"*Hai*," Ryuu said, his voice less strained.

"How are you feeling?" asked Detective Houser.

Ryuu answered.

I interpreted for the detectives, "Much better than the last time we spoke."

"Okay, well, that's good. Now we're going to make this as quick as possible." I interpreted for Ryuu. "We would like to ask you just a few questions about the night you were attacked." The detective paused, allowing me enough time to interpret.

"*Hai*," Ryuu said.

Detective Houser pulled out a small evidence bag from his pocket, which was holding a bloodstained state ID. He showed Ryuu the ID and asked, "Last night, while I was going back over the crime scene, I discovered this identification card. Can you confirm that this identification card belongs to you, Mr. Ishii?"

I was somewhat baffled by the detective's usage of his name.

Yesterday, he was convinced Ryuu was Ichiro Higashi.

Now, the detective acted as if what he said yesterday came from the mouth of his alter ego.

Talk about déjà vu.

Nonetheless, I interpreted for Ryuu.

Ryuu managed to nod.

"*Hai*."

"Very good," the detective said and placed the ID back in his pocket. "Mr. Ishii, my partner and I would like to know a little more about the timeline of the night of your attack." Detective Houser paused yet again, allowing me plenty of time to interpret. He pulled out his notepad for reference. "Yesterday, you mentioned that you ate supper at a place called 'The Flapjack.' Mr. Ishii, can you recall what you were you doing earlier that day, before supper?"

Once I interpreted for Ryuu, his eyes drifted away from the detectives.

"Can you recall anything for us? Did you run any errands? Did you see anything out of the ordinary?" asked Detective Houser, his once saint-like patience clearly wearing thin.

I shadowed the detective's words.

Ryuu's attention snapped toward the two detectives.

I interpreted, "Now that I think about it, I did see something out of the ordinary. Twice, I saw a red car. Once, outside my apartment building, and then the second time I saw a similar red car parked in a parking lot across from The Flapjack. I remember it was unusual because each time I saw the red car I saw people waiting inside. I couldn't identify who they were. The driver was smoking a. . ."

Ryuu struggled to find the correct word.

"A cigarette?" Detective Ruiz asked.

Ryuu turned his eyes toward me.

Other words, like *shigaretto*, for instance, were used in popular culture; however, I went with the most common usage.

"*Tabako*?" I asked Ryuu.

Ryuu shook his head. He didn't give me a hard "no." Instead, Ryuu verbally danced around the question for a bit and described what the driver was smoking as being the color brown, *not* white. He also remembered the smell in the air and what I interpreted as a rather "sour" or "fruity" smell.

"A blunt?" asked Detective Ruiz.

Ryuu had never heard of such word.

43

She elaborated as if she was talking to an elementary student, "Marijuana?"

I interpreted for Ryuu.

"*Hai,*" he said to the detectives.

The two detectives shot glances at each other as if they knew something that I didn't know. All I could think about—that is, from the expression—was that they ran a toxicology test on one—or all of the victims' blood and they found traces of THC in their system.

Hence the next question by Detective Houser: "By any chance, was this car a Toyota hatchback?" The detective made an exaggerated rainbow-like arch with his right hand—which, I'm guessing was his way of visually describing a hatchback—as if he was hoping animated hand gestures would help further clarify his question.

I interpreted for Ryuu, without the hand gestures.

"*Hai,*" he said.

"Did you get the impression that this red car was following you?" Detective Ruiz asked before her partner could follow up.

I interpreted for Ryuu, then for the detectives: "At the time, I thought it may have been a coincidence." Ryuu returned with the most straightforward question of his own. "Do you believe these men had mistaken me for someone else?"

"We don't exactly know right now," Detective Houser said hesitantly. "According to the evidence we've gathered so far, we're leaning toward the possibility that what happened to you was a case of mistaken identity."

KAITO
SEPTEMBER 11, 1987 11:20 AM

KAITO momentarily drifts off thinking about how the washitsu used to be a room where he and his wife, Manami, would entertain their guests; however, over these past couple of days, the only person whom he entertains is himself.

The sound at the front door pulls Kaito from his deep thought. He places the photo aside and listens closer to yet another noise, this time deeper and hollower, a booming *thud*. He stands up from his kneeled position and cautiously steps out of the washitsu. The knocking at the front of the house becomes clearer.

Feeling the paranoid tightening and rising from his gut, he slides the fusuma, closing the room behind him.

Exercising more caution, Kaito doesn't even recognize his stealthy demeanor until he makes it through the genkan. The praying mantis-like motion, the razor-sharp observation, the manner in which his walk changed from once freely walking flatfoot without the presence of danger to tiptoeing on the balls of his feet, all of these *old* nightly mannerisms overtake him, turning him into a person whom he can only identify as a stranger.

He moves his way toward the front of the house. He peeks out the front window and notices a familiar red car parked in the driveway.

What is he doing here?

After another knock, Kaito exhausts any paranoid left in his system and decides to open the door.

Standing outside is his only son, Hiroshi.

Hiroshi? What are you doing here?

With his face long, Hiroshi tilts his head to the side in confusion.

Nice to see you too, father.

Please forgive me, Hiroshi. I wasn't expecting to see you today.

Surprise.

Kaito steps aside and lets his son inside the house.

Hiroshi hands Kaito two bags, one of them spotted with grease stains, while he removes his shoes from his feet once he enters the genkan and places his shoes inside the geta-bako.

Have you eaten lunch yet, father?

Still baffled to see his son, Kaito hands the two bags back to Hiroshi, who, in return, holds up the one bag, a greasy KFC bag with a box of crispy fried chicken inside.

I'm not that hungry.

Kaito rubs his stomach, as if he has a belly pain. He can hardly look Hiroshi in the eyes when he talks about food.

I brought some KFC from the new store that recently opened next to my studio. You should've seen it, father. There was a line wrapped around the building.

Hiroshi continues to hold up the bag of food as if he's stuck in an American advertisement.

Are you sure? The chicken might be a bit cold, but if you like, I can heat it up in the oven.

Kaito walks Hiroshi to the kitchen, passing the washitsu along the way. The fusuma is partially cracked open, at least three inches, leaving just enough macabre for his son's eyes to see.

What's in the other bag?

The question draws Hiroshi's attention away from the washitsu.

It's a surprise, father.

Surprise? You know I don't like surprises, Hiroshi.

More relieved to arrive in the kitchen, Kaito heats a pot of water on the stove while Hiroshi places the two bags on the counter. Hiroshi opens the other bag and pulls out a pair of binoculars with a red ribbon wrapped around one of the lenses.

Surprise!

What's the occasion?

Hiroshi's brow furrows, his face riddled with shock.

It's a gift.

Spending all of your time in the studio has done quite a number on you, hasn't it? Today's not my birthday.

I know. I saw a pair of binoculars while I was picking up the food. I know how much you enjoy watching birds.

In a quiet, subdued manner, Kaito grabs the binoculars from Hiroshi's hands and looks them over with a hint of misery, as if his son's words had brought back a wave of memories.

Plus, it will get you out of the house more.

A flash of anger comes over Kaito.
"*I get out of the house. . .*" is what Kaito really wants to tell his son and do so in a manner that will earn back his respect.
The thought comes and goes.

Thank you, Hiroshi.

Kaito slightly bows his head.

You're welcome.

So, how's work?

Works going very well. I'm currently working on a new project that I believe is going to be a smash hit.

As the water comes to a boil, Hiroshi grabs the bag of KFC and walks toward the washitsu. Kaito has a snap decision to make: either removing the pot of water from the stove or chase down his son before he reaches the washitsu.

Wait, Hiroshi! Let's eat outside!

Outside? It's rather cold outside, don't you think?

Hiroshi slides the fusuma farther open and only takes a couple of steps inside the washitsu before his body melts with horror. Scattered on the chabudai, as well as hanging on the walls are old crime scene photographs from the infamous Chiaki Case. The photographs appear morbid in nature: CLOSE-UP shots of decayed or decaying corpses, skeletons, bones, body parts, discovered inside shallow graves, as well as protruding from loose soil like roots. Hiroshi himself, an anime artist who constantly fills his day concocting graphic images, albeit fictional, has a hard time looking at the photos.

Two particular photos catch Hiroshi's eye: one photo of convicted serial killer, Gaku Chiaki, hanging out on a street corner and the other, a florist named Dai Ando selling a bouquet of yellow roses to a customer inside his store, both of the photos are private eye-type shots taken from a distance.

As soon as Hiroshi removes the pinned-up photo of Chiaki, he's overcome with sorrow.

You said you burned all of these.

Hiroshi moves his eyes away from the photo and looks at Kaito with an expression of defeat on his face.

The rage climbs inside him.

Why did you lie to me, father? Let me guess. The trees told you not to destroy them or else—

—You're in absolutely no position to be going through all of my personal belongings, Hiroshi!

Kaito charges at Hiroshi and grabs the photo in Hiroshi's hand—or at least, tries to.

Hiroshi recoils and plays tug-of-war with his father until, finally, he releases his grip from the photo.

What's going on here? Does this have anything to do with the recent murders in Tokyo?

Kaito doesn't respond to Hiroshi's question.

Do you not realize what that case did to you? It nearly killed you! And think about what happened to mom?

Don't you dare speak her name, Hiroshi?

I'm your son. I have a right to know.

Kaito points at the front door, his arm and finger as straight as a blade.

How dare you come into my house and question me. I want you to leave right now!

With his eyes widening, Hiroshi innocently points at himself.

Me? Leave? I'm trying to help you, father.

I said, 'Leave.' I don't need your help!

Hiroshi does as his father commands and storms out of the washitsu. He decides to leave behind the food, as well as the gift.

After Hiroshi puts on his shoes, he opens the door and turns back around toward his father, who is still left fuming from Hiroshi's intrusiveness.

I know you don't want to hear what I have to say, father. It's for your own good. *You must move on from the past. Otherwise, the past will become your future.*

Letting out a grunt, Kaito waves off his son and his words.

Hiroshi gets inside his car and drives away, forcing Kaito to vent elsewhere.

Outside, Kaito stands in front of the kura and contemplates whether or not to have a conversation with Dai Ando.

What a terrible idea?

What does he know about being a father?

Kaito, like his son before, waves off the very thought of speaking with Dai.

As he turns around to walk back to the house, he notices the loose soil along the pathway. The soil appears disturbed and dug up by what he can only assume is a mole or the lesser white-toothed shrew that has been causing him great fits as of lately. Kaito leans forward for a closer inspection and comes to the conclusion based on the web-like trenches along the loose soil that a rodent isn't to blame for the disturbance.

Feeling the burden sitting along his shoulders and chest, Kaito makes up his mind by unlocking the kura.

Once inside, Kaito witnesses the path of wet imprints of feet marks leading to the small, crouching figure inside the cell.

A one-eyed child, its eye in the center of its forehead like a cyclops, is sitting with both its knees pressed against its chest in the shadowy corner of the room.

Kaito steps closer to the cell for a better look.

One eye morphs and becomes two eyes.

He looks yet again and recognizes the familiar-looking girl with loose, baggy clothes hanging from her body like torn, raggedy drapes.

Tatsuko?

The great rage swallows Kaito, causing every part of his body to tighten.

How dare you, Dai! Show me your real face!

With a pout on her face, Kaito's eight-year old niece, Tatsuko, takes a step closer to the cell bars, revealing her dripping wet jet-black hair.

If I show you who I really look like, beyond the flesh, you would be too scared to talk to me.

I'm not scared of you.

You should be.

Kaito studies each detail of Tatsuko's pale face. Even her soft, delicate voice sounds the same as Tatsuko's. Surprisingly, the thought of Hiroshi relieves the tightness in Kaito's body. He hangs his head and shoulders in great sorrow.

Hiroshi was right about what he once said to me. I cared more about my work than I did my family.

Hiroshi represents the best part of you. He is an extension of you, but he is *not* you, Kaito.

Kaito lifts his head, his eyes glossy with tears.

Why Tatsuko? Do you really think changing yourself into an innocent girl will make me reconsider releasing you? You are a monster who must suffer for what he has done.

The tears burn his eyes and when they roll down his cheeks, they're warm to the touch. He steps close enough to the cell for Tatsuko to touch him.

Don't you see, Kaito? Even though you may have your free-dom, you've been locked in this cell ever since you failed to hold my father accountable for his actions, or shall I say, lack of action—

—It was an accident! Atsuo was distracted by one of the guests at Tatsuko's birthday party. She wandered off and slipped into the river.

What if my father wanted me to drown? If he cared about me, he would've jumped in to rescue me.

What other reason would he have taken his own life, huh? He was ashamed of himself for what happened to Tatsuko under his watch. He could no longer live with such an incredible burden.

Your emotions blind you from the truth.

You are not Tatsuko! You are a murderer!

I am who you make me to be, Kaito—

—Do you have anything to do with the recent murders in Tokyo? Yes or no?

Tatsuko shrugs her shoulders in similar eight-year old fashion.

I'm afraid it's not a *yes* or *no* answer, Kaito. It's complicated.

Do you have anything to do with the murders in Tokyo?

All of a sudden, Tatsuko's eight-year old innocence melts from her face. She lowers her head downward, both of her narrow eyes glaring at Kaito.

No.

You're lying.

Tatsuko grips the bars of the cell.

Is there any other reason why you came here to talk to me, Kaito?

Wondering whether or not to unburden himself, Kaito loses himself in a long stare with Tatsuko. He opens his mouth, as if he's ready to speak.

Forget it.

Kaito makes his way toward the exit.
As he reaches for the door handle, he hears a strange yet familiar sound behind him. The sound was organic in na-

ture, like hearty fibers twisting and turning and tightening and causing a wrenching effect throughout Kaito's body.

She didn't suffer, if that makes you feel any better.

Immediately recognizing another familiar sound, which is the sonorous voice of Atsuo's voice, Kaito pulls his hand away from the door handle, rotates around, and witnesses his brother, not Tatsuko, standing in the prison cell.

The sight of his brother sends a shiver down Kaito's spine.

Even the words trapped inside his chest are shaky, as if his body is so tight that he has to muscle them out.

How would you know?

ZARA
FEBRUARY 15, 2020 2:02 PM

FOR reasons I couldn't explain, I left San Felisa Memorial feeling extremely depressed after helping out the two detectives with their investigation.

If I had to guess as to why I was feeling so down, I'd say it had something to do with learning that Ryuu had no known relatives or family members. He didn't even have a single friend to visit him over the weekend. According to Ryuu, his background wasn't like any normal child. It was unstable, to say the least. Ryuu was raised in a small town in the valley outside Okugawa called Sayaka, which, I realized, wasn't too far from where Kaito Takahashi lived. Ryuu grew up as an orphan, never knew his parents. Ryuu was discovered by the Nakajimas, Chiyo, a teacher and Kisaku, a local police officer, who ended up taking young Ryuu in after passing through Sayaka. Sato and Chiyo Nakajima lived in the town of Ogata. They had a child of their own, Daiki, and after a year of raising Ryuu, they became his legal guardians. Sato and Chiyo both died in an automobile accident when Ryuu was thirteen years old. He didn't have much of a relationship with Daiki. Eventually, they went their separate ways. Ryuu spent most of his young adult life in Ogata, went to school, and after school, became a police officer after he was inspired by the awe of American television. He got his two hands wrapped around pirated tapes of shows like *Twin Peaks*, *The Sopranos*, *Matlock*, and *Millennium*, which had a way of casting spells on young vulnerable minds.

Even if the detectives found Ryuu guilty of the crime and, based on the evidence gathered from the crime scene, concluded that he murdered those three men not out of self-defense but rather murdered them in cold blood, I couldn't help but sympathize with Ryuu. He was a man living in a foreign land, which he so desperately wanted to call home. I couldn't imagine what it'd be like to have nobody there when I needed him or her the most. I'd even expect Po to stand by my side in a time of need. Despite all of our ups and downs and how alone, how "little" Po made me feel, at the end of the day he still possessed a beating muscle in his chest, which was occasionally mistaken for a heart. I often think about whether or not Porfirio was the same man I married. On the contrary, was he thinking the same about me?

Since my schedule was clear for the rest of the afternoon, I decided to take a late—and well-deserved—lunch.

I found a nice spot next to the Bay called Shuckin' Shack. I ordered a basket of fried shrimp and french fries, which was a popular choice I seemed to gravitate towards whenever I was feeling the blues. I supposed "fried" food was no different than a shot of hard liquor. It temporarily brought relief to whatever ailment, but it was no different than slapping on a band-aid over an infected wound.

It wasn't exactly a working lunch; however, I had Ryuu on my mind.

Since it wasn't crowded at that particular time of the day, I decided to grab a seat outside on the patio. I brought my laptop with me as well. While I was waiting on the food to arrive, I researched "Ichiro Higashi" in the search engine Gumshoe.

I was able to find the same article from before, however, with more conveniency. I found the name of the film-maker, Jatticus Lightfoot, who recently did an interview with Ichiro Higashi days after his acquittal. I tried to track down Jatticus on the Internet, combing through his IMDB page, as well as his social media pages. According to Wikipedia, he lived in Los Angeles. I learned that his real name was Jonathan Lidle and that "Jatticus Lightfoot" was only his stage name. Only one person I knew who was ob-sessed with true crime—I'm talking a full-on true crime buff—came to mind. I hadn't talked to him in two weeks, and I knew calling him up for a favor was not my place. But I had no other choice.

I called up my stepson, Suede.

Clearly, after he answered the phone, he was confused as to why I was calling and not texting him. I completely forgot about the deal we made a couple of months back about the "texting" situation. He was right in the middle of basketball practice and he didn't have much time to talk on the phone. I asked Suede for his opinion about the best means of contacting Jatticus. Suede suggested I "DM" him on Ask™. Which was short for "direct message." Suede acted as if he asked Jatticus questions and received answers on a daily basis.

I took Suede's advice, set up a temporary account on Ask™, and sent a direct message—or DM—to Jatticus on Ask™.

Two beers and four *dings* later, I received a text message from a number with a 213 area code on my phone.

I opened the phone and read the message.

My name is David Henley, Jatticus Lightfoot's agent at CRM. Mr. Lightfoot wants me to pass along a message that he will be in the San Francisco area Tuesday afternoon and is willing to meet with you to further discuss the documentary. I will contact you by tomor-row morning to arrange a meeting with an exact time. If Tuesday is no good for you, please let me know ASAP. Best regards.

Of course, I looked up David Henley's profile on CRM's website.

Sure enough, Mr. Henley represented several well-known celebrities, one being none other than Jatticus Lightfoot.

I matched his phone to the number on my phone.

The phone numbers matched.

However, the phone number wasn't what I was thinking about at that moment in time.

The dates!

Coincidence or not, Ryuu was born the same year Takahashi's dead body was discovered.

Thirty-three years ago.

KAITO
SEPTEMBER 12, 1987 1:03 PM

STANDING in the tokonoma—or *toko*—Kaito holds a clay sculpture of a turtle that his son, Hiroshi, had made when Hiroshi was a young boy. Kaito studies the turtle and its massive hump of a shell. It's quite an ugly turtle, badly misshaped and lopsided; however, it's the ugliness that makes the turtle so special.

Kaito places the clay turtle back in its rightful spot next to an *ikebana* flower arrangement, as well as a *koro* incense burner above the display of a kakemono—or *kakejiku*—hanging on the wall, and saunters back to the washitsu, which now looks more like an art gallery of crime scene photos. He moves toward one particular photo of a dead body with multiple deep puncture wounds penetrating each vital organ. The victim was a local fisherman named Kenji Mizoguchi. His spine was completely shattered, his ribcage as well as most of the bones in his body appeared like broken glass during an autopsy, and it was as if Mizoguchi's body had been dropped from a great height. These trademark wounds remained consistent among other victims and helped back up Kaito's theory that Dai Ando slaughtered his victims from the treetops; however, Kaito's theory had as many holes as Swiss cheese, one of them being the most obvious one: *How could Dai, a man who only weighed a buck-fifty, carry his victims up a tree?*

As Kaito drifts into a trance from the sight of the morbid photo, he recalls the moment he walked into an office supply store and had the original photo from the crime scene photocopied on a Xerox machine. He recalls a young girl walking up from behind him and catching a glimpse of the photocopy. He never forgot such a look and the innocence that slipped right from underneath her feet. He couldn't imagine what it'd feel like to be so young and to have witnessed such macabre.

Left in a state of disgust, Kaito pins the photograph back onto the wall, walks over to the tansu, opens the bottom drawer, and pulls out a gnarly nine-inch piece of jagged wood resting to the right of a leather-bound journal.

The piece of wood is shaped like a sharp blade. And the tip of it is covered in a dark substance that can only resemble blood.

ZARA
FEBRUARY 18, 2020 3:30 PM

AFTER several email exchanges with David Henley regarding Wednesday's meeting, Jatticus made some last minute changes in plans and bumped up the meeting a day earlier. I managed to work in the late afternoon get-together into my hectic schedule—much credit to Hina for being clutch whenever I needed her.

Lucy was clearly aggravated with my recent flakiness; however, I didn't have time or patience to play high school with Lucy.

I arrived right before happy hour at some dive bar called Easy Al's in Hunters Edge, typically a spot in the Bay area one wouldn't find themselves—or, particularly, *herself*—hanging around after dark. Evidently, I wasn't the type of person who followed the news. Although from what I had heard from a few friends, Hunters Edge was considered one of the rougher areas in San Francisco. Which, immediately, had me worried about my meeting with Jatticus or whoever he was. Before leaving the house, I made sure to snap the screenshot of Jatticus on the Internet just in case the person whom I was supposed to be meeting at Easy Al's turned out being a person who looked nothing like the photo on my phone. Hence why I also brought my trusty can of Mace. The last time I ended up using it was a year after my first marriage when I had built-up enough confidence to tryout the dating scene once again. I was thirty-seven years old at the time, rusty yet still possessed just the right amount of quirkiness and wounded desperation to cast a spell on my date, who happened to be, of all the plentiful fish in the Bay, a wedding photographer with a first name easily mistaken for Portfolio and a last name that rhymed with *trap* whose mother was born in Honduras and raised in America where she'd met a respected pianist from Eastback. I just wrapped up my date with a kiss on Porfirio's cheek—which was all the "action" Po would receive in the next three weeks until I finally worked myself up to a dinner-and-movie date with Po where we shared more than a dessert back at his place. Long story short: the first act was much better than the third. I was walking back to my car alone, three glasses of Tanqueray and Tonic making me feel as if I shared a distant bloodline with Princess Diana of Themyscira. As I was about to unlock the car, which was parked in an unlit spot—of all the nights to park, this one particular streetlight happened to be out that night—then a tall, shadowy figure came up behind me, and on instinct, I reached for my purse with that Amazonian blood pumping lightning through my veins, and *WHA-BAM!* I unloaded an entire can of Mace in the young kid's eyes. He had to be no older than eighteen or nineteen, maybe twenty. He was reaching for my purse, maybe more, maybe to cop himself a feel. All I knew was that he went home with an aerosol can of irritant chemical in his eyes. Served him right.

Ten-minutes in, Jatticus was still a no-show. The parking lot was barely half-full and unless Jatticus was driving a

POS or rental, he wasn't here yet. I decided to wait inside my car, my set of keys and Mace within reach. I kept watch for another five minutes until I decided to head inside.

About two seconds later after gathering my things and doing one last primp, a stomach bile-yellow Hummer pulled in the back of the parking lot, taking up two parking spaces. Jatticus and another fellow stepped out of the vehicle—if that's what you want to call it. Tank was more like it.

He looked just like his photo, only "heavier." But it was Jatticus.

As for the other swole guy in the gym suit who looked as if he bench pressed three times Jatticus' weight, he was still a giant question.

I decided to carry the Mace with me inside Easy Al's, which was your typical dive bar with your typical dive bar bartender who looked as if he used to be a professional wrestler in another life. He was carrying a raggedy white towel over his shoulder, which I guessed was kept handy in order to whip away the strays.

Only a couple of people were sitting at the bar watching the news from one of the two TVs on display.

A Rhodes rally and a rerun of 1987 Super Bowl.

The bartender removed a toothpick that he was aggressively chewing on from his mouth and gave me a nod and a gentlemanly "Ma'am."

I smiled back and searched for Jatticus.

I heard a young, shaky voice to the right of me: "Zara Spears?"

Following the voice, I found both Jatticus and Mr. Clean, who had grabbed a booth near the back of the bar.

I returned with a wave.

He waved back.

As I arrived at the booth, the other guy excused himself and took another seat at the bar.

Jatticus pointed at the guy's seat; however, he never called fives on it.

"Don't worry," Jatticus said, following my eyes. "That's Big Rick, aka 'The Brick.' He's my driver. He's harmless, when he needs to be."

I found myself amused by the comment.

Jatticus introduced himself.

I shook his hand, which was smooth and almost lady-like, and went over the basic introductions; however, Jatticus wasn't at all interested in small talk.

"So you have a driver, huh? Must be nice."

"They come in handy in showbiz."

I checked the time of my phone.

"Listen, Mrs. Mapp—"

"—*Spears*. Spears is my maiden name. You can call me Zara."

"Do you not go by Mapp anymore?"

Did I really have to spell it out for him?

"Mapp is my husband's last name."

I wasn't his teacher, even though I was old enough to be his mother.

"Okay, *Zara*," he said, leaning over the table and letting his hands do most of the talking, "I know you came here for a reason. Nowadays, we all have our reasons—and agendas—am I right? So, I'll just make this as short as possible."

He was arrogant. His body language proved to me that he had been raised in a wealthy household that strived off table manners. Yet, he was the black sheep, the one who rebelled against the ritzy lifestyle, rotten to the core. A cartoon character. A manboy who read too many Arthur Doyle novels as a kid and wanted to be a detective but was way too indolent—and privileged—to become a detective that old fashioned way, you know, like going to school or toiling his way through the academy or exhausting hours with on-the-job training or battling hardships or, the most important one, experience, which often times, gave room to compassion and willingness to listen to others.

I liked to thank my marriage counselor, Ivory, for her insightfulness. Lately, I had been spending maybe too much time around her.

Like most opportunists during a time of glorified violence and cut-and-paste whodunits, Baby Sherlock here
decided to capitalize on American's guilty obsessions.

"Please do," I said finally.

"So," Jatticus started, "tell me a little about yourself?
David told me that you do a little interpreting?"

"Yes," I said. "That's right."

"Don't they have an app for that now?"

I didn't know how to respond to Jatticus.

A part of me wanted to hang my head in defeat.

Yes. More than likely they do have an app.

That part of me still living in denial never wanting—
and never would believe any of the above to be true.

Another part of me wanted to punch him in that big
nose of his and watch it split wide open.

"So," he said over my lack of answer, "where you from?"

"I'm from here," I said. "Rock Valley. My mother was
Japanese. My father is American. My grandfather was one
of thousands forced to relocate to a concentration camp
where he was incarcerated after the attack on Pearl Har-
bor. He was a shoemaker who had absolutely nothing to do
with World War II. He was *Nisei* 'second generation' who,
instead of being treated as an individual and most importantly, an American citizen, was treated like the enemy.
After hearing about my grandfather's story, I wanted to
break the language barriers between people of different ori-
gins and make sure everyone had a voice."

"Sad story," Jatticus said arrogantly. "Are you always
this morose with people who you've just met?"

I took a breath.

I wasn't sure what language Jatticus was speaking, but it
was somewhere between asshole and pretentiousness.

"Listen, Jatticus. I think I've told you enough about myself."

"Fair enough." He wasn't the least bothered by my
bluntness. I could tell he had more important matters at
hand. "If you don't mind," he said swiftly, "let me ask you a
question."

"Sure."

"*Why are you so interested in Ichiro Higashi?*"

"I was hoping you could shed a little more light on what happened to him—"

"—Are you a reporter?"

"No."

"Then, why are you interested?"

I shot a glance at Big Rick, who was staring at me from the end of the bar.

"He's a relative of mine."

"Bullshit," Jatticus said bluntly.

"Excuse me?"

"Strike one," he said, calling me out on the lie. "Try again."

I was left momentarily speechless and unable to come up with an excuse as to why I really wanted to see Jatticus. Which had me questioning myself as to why I was really here.

Jatticus made it easy for me.

"Higashi doesn't have any relatives."

"What makes you so sure?"

Jatticus pulled out an old journal from a gym bag on the seat.

Here came the punch line.

"Frankly, I don't care who you are and why you're here," he said seriously, as he looked around the bar in a state of paranoia. "For all I know, you might be a fan who saw the documentary and wanted to, I dunno, pick my brain. David told me that you can translate Japanese. Is that correct?"

"*Kana*," I corrected Jatticus. "Yes. I can translate kana."

"Whatever," Jatticus said and placed the journal on the table. "I've taken this journal to at least a dozen translators in the past month and each one of them gives me the same exact response along with the same exact 'I just-shit-my-pants' expression halfway through translating the journal. They tell me I shouldn't have the journal, that I should put it back where it came from, that it doesn't belong to me. Now, there was this one translator named Miyo, who managed to translate a good portion of the journal before she, like the others, bailed on me."

"What was her reason?" I asked Jatticus.

"It wasn't the journal," he said. "It's what's inside the journal."

Surprisingly, Jatticus had me curious.

I asked, "What's inside the journal?"

"Have you ever heard of the creature 'Ama,' short for Amadoki?"

"Doesn't ring any bells. Why?"

"According to the translations so far, the original owner of this journal writes about an ancient shapeshifting monster called Ama who originated in Japan. Ama can replicate herself by taking the form of as many human beings as she desires. *However*, in order to pull this off, Ama must consume the blood of her victim and only then is she able to shapeshift into anybody—I mean, I'm talking *anybody*." He tilted his head to the side in thought. "Not entirely sure, though, how she reproduces herself." Jatticus started to trail off in his own incoherent rambling, "A *seed* perhaps? Maybe even like a *flower*. . . Whatever the case may be, the owner of the journal writes about this supernatural entity taking the form of Dai Ando. I had my team do some digging on Dai Ando. They discovered that Dai Ando was once a main suspect in a multiple homicide in the Eighties but was set free due to inaccuracies in several witnesses' statements?"

I heard enough.

I let him do his little spiel. But really, it was the word *monster* that ultimately had me throwing in the white towel and sliding from the booth.

Jatticus immediately reached out to me and nearly begged me to hear what he had to say next.

I gave him one last chance.

"About three months ago, I discovered the journal while I was on one of Tokyo's Ghost Walk tours," Jatticus said.

"A what?"

"You know, a Ghost Walk tour," he repeated. "You have this creepy-looking tour guide who's dressed up like a character from a horror movie showing you all of the so-called haunted areas in Tokyo. Most of the tour is a gimmick, a way to take a nice pinch from a tourist's wallet. In all honestly, I'm technically borrowing the journal until I can have it translated."

"So, in other words, you stole it?"

"I'm going to give it back. But that's beside the point—"

"—And what's the point?"

"The point is I believe the owner of this journal knows *what* murdered Jordan Pruitt."

"I thought you said this Ghost tour was all bullshit."

"*Most* of it, but not all of it." He leaned in closer to the table, his voice lowered: "I know what killed Jordan Pruitt." He slid the journal closer to me as if he was making a trade. "The evidence is in here."

"A shapeshifting monster—"

"—Amadoki," Jatticus clarified.

"Okay, so, an ancient shapeshifter who goes after Jordan Pruitt, kills him for no apparent reason. Sounds like a couple of ladies I know."

"So," he said, sitting back, "*she* has a sense of humor."

"Just answer this one question, Jatticus: Where exactly did you *find* this journal?"

"I found it inside the house of Kaito Takahashi," Jatticus said, his face slack. "Now tell me, Zara. Does that name ring any bells?"

KAITO
SEPTEMBER 19, 1987 9:45 AM

KAITO is left surprised by his next customer in the checkout line.

I see you've found yourself an honest job to keep you busy during your retirement. You know I thought they called it 'retirement' for a reason.

What brings you here, Bunji?

With a grin creeping on his face, Bunji places the soda can on the counter.

Hesitant, Kaito grabs the soda can and rings it up.

I came here to buy a drink. What does it look like I'm doing, Kaito?

Bunji pays for the cold beverage and places the leftover change in a bucket with one of those "Feed The Children" signs on the counter.

Will that be all?

No. Actually, I came by here to talk. I stopped by your house earlier, but you weren't home.

Kaito points at the customers behind Bunji.

I'm afraid I can't talk at the moment. I have customers—

—It's about Dai Ando.

The name seizes Kaito's attention, causing him to become quiet and attentive. Trying not to draw any unwanted attention to himself—*too late*—he waves down Hiroyuki, who's mopping up a spill in the back of the store. Hiroyuki stops what he's doing and walks over to Kaito.

Hiroyuki, cover me for a minute, will you?

I'm in the middle of cleaning—

—I said 'Cover me.'

Hiroyuki bows his head.

Yes.

While Hiroyuki takes over for Kaito's position behind the cash register, Kaito walks Bunji outside the grocery store.

Sorry to drag you away from work, Kaito.

No sweat. I can use the break.

Bunji pulls out a cigarette, lights it up, smokes.

We recently pulled a surveillance video showing Dai Ando and Nami Kise outside Okiura, a mile away from where Nami's body was discovered. Based on the timeline of events, we're convinced Dai Ando has something to do with her death.

Are you sure it was Dai Ando in the video?

The department brought in the most highly successful analysts money could buy. They came to a conclusion that the man in the video is, in fact, Dai Ando.

Kaito struggles to look Bunji in the eyes.

That's impossible.

The reason why I'm here telling you this, Kaito, is because you were the only one who originally suspected Dai Ando of the Gravedigger Murders that happened six years ago. Everybody thought you were out of your mind to even suggest these murders were carried out by a man who had been declared dead. Tell me, Kaito. Did we catch the wrong man?

Bunji takes another drag from his cigarette while Kaito looks up at Bunji.

Somewhere behind Kaito's pounding stare, his eyes started to narrow.

ZARA

AT this point in time, I was well beyond sleep.

I rolled out of bed and after spending the last couple of days pecking away at Kaito's journal, I exhausted the next few hours trying to finish the translation for not only Jatticus, but also, personally, to whet my own inexhaustible curiosity into the creature known as Amadoki.

As I documented other translators' notes, as well as translated the rest of the journal into a Word document on my laptop, I found myself turning into Jatticus, going off on rambling fits, and trying to make sense of Ama and the legend of her murdering spree in Japan.

In the journal, Kaito wrote:

The suffering must come to an end.

The final confrontation is upon me.

I typed the journal entry into the document, set aside the journal for the time being, and took a step back from the laptop.

I couldn't help but think about the prison cell that investigators discovered in a storage shed behind Kaito's house.

Who—*or what*—was Kaito keeping locked behind those bars?

As one of the articles explained: a wooden doll.

Whatever the case may be—whether Kaito was writing the truth about holding a man named Dai Ando in his prison cell behind his house and the journal was his own confession or Kaito was simply a man who had gone mad and the journal was his last spat to a close-minded world that had abandoned him—one word was the most prevalent throughout the journal:

Which, in English, translated to the word *tree*.

KAITO
SEPTEMBER 20, 1987 7:32 PM

WITH a lantern in one hand and his revolver in the other, Kaito makes his last trip to the kura while convincing himself over and over that tonight is the night all of the madness ends. The monster has reigned long enough, and tonight its streak of terror finally comes to an end.

He slides open the *shōji* door.

Outside, the *amadoi* gutters carry the heavy rainfall off the eaves and down the decorative *kusari-doi*—or rain chain.

As the rain intensifies, Kaito mentally rallies himself toward the kura, which, of all stormy nights, hasn't felt farther away.

Halfway toward the kura, Kaito stops in his tracks from the sight of the open door!

Startled, Kaito proceeds toward the kura, but this time much slower and cautiously.

Kaito arrives at the doorway and examines the door. He draws his bloodshot eyes toward the destroyed chain, as well as the lock, which has been shattered into many pieces all over the ground. Kaito steps inside the kura and witnesses a short dark figure slumping behind the bars in the cell.

Wringing wet, Kaito extends the lantern closer to the cell and realizes that the man is a disheveled-looking Gaku Chiaki.

Who opened this door?

Clicking back the hammer of the revolver, Kaito inches closer to the cell.

I asked you a question!

Weak and frail, Gaku sharpens the scowl on his face.

You are dealing with a system of forces much greater than you, Kaito, one that constantly requires sacrifice. And you, Kaito, are interfering with her survival.

Kaito steps closer to the cell and holds the lantern closer to Gaku's face.

You're not the only one of your kind, are you?

Gaku gives Kaito a wounded smile.

I see you've been talking to your friend, Bunji.

She could've chose to look like someone else to conceal her cover. Yet, she chose to look like you.

She looks like me because she is me, Kaito — well, *another* me. It's unnecessary for one of us to change the appearance of the body in which we were given because it depletes energy that should normally be used in case of emergencies.

Would you consider our frequent exchanges over these past couple of days an emergency?

Not exactly. I have no other way to entertain myself in here.

How many more of you are there?

Hundreds.

Kaito steps dangerously close to Gaku.

I want a number!

Precisely two hundred and thirty-seven. I'd say it was a rather plentiful spring the day Dai Ando *sacrificed* himself for the greater good. The wars between your species have a way of creating the richest, most fertile soil. Not like I'm complaining. Your species 'divide and conquer' mentality makes it much easier for us. If I may, let me ask you a question: Where do you think the air that you're breathing comes from, Kaito?

Kaito doesn't answer, too enraged by what he's hearing.

Whether you like it or not, you must understand that you're a part of an organic network that serves both man and nature—

—You believe by killing innocent people you're sustaining the survival of the earth?

And there lies the contradiction, Kaito. Humans slaughter and eat the flesh of animals as their own means of survival. You actually thought that your species had rightfully declared its spot on the top of the food chain? I have news for you, Kaito. We owned the food chain.

You killed innocent people!

Like you should know a thing or two about killing *innocent* people, Kaito.

In the most animated way possible, Gaku acts out his final moments before the other Gaku—the real one that is—was executed. He lifts his left arm directly above his head as if he's grabbing onto an invisible rope. Then, he makes a loud *whooshing* noise with his mouth. His arm drops to his side like dead weight.

Next to drop is his head and it does so quickly and violently, like a *snap*, breaking his neck.

They say 'death by hanging' is considered one of the quickest deaths. But what they don't tell you is that not *all* hangings are always successful.

With his head flopping and rolling around like a ball and chain attached to his loose neck, Gaku displays a wide, devilish grin for Kaito.

Gaku Chiaki was a low life, career-criminal who deserved to die. But *you*, you don't deserve to die. You deserve to live the rest of your existence in a jail cell.

Soon, you will get your wish, Kaito.

Gaku's head remains hanging loosely on his neck, his voice muffled from the weight of his chin pressing against his windpipe.

Without the light, I've been bound to darkness. You and I both know that life cannot survive long in the dark. Life needs light in order to thrive—

—You will die before you ever *thrive* again.

You're right, Kaito. Eventually, this body will die and life will go on. We were here long before your species and we will be here long after your species. We will survive. Out of the ashes, another species will rise.

Kaito bangs on the bar with the butt of the revolver, causing Gaku's head to slowly yet mechanically lift upward. Dai Ando no longer wears the face of Gaku. Yet, Dai appears as Kaito's ex-wife, Manami.

It was the job that ended your marriage. Wasn't it, Kaito?

You think that you can get under my skin by pretending to be the people from my past? You're wrong, *Ama*. I've figured you out. I'm done playing your cruel game.

Like the bud of a flower blossoming in the matter of milliseconds, Manami's face shapes into multiple other faces, including Yui Hattori and his eight-year-old niece, Tatsuko, before ending up in the form of Dai Ando, Ama's *first* form.

How about the people from your future?

All of sudden, Dai uses his last bit of energy to shape-shift into Kaito.

The sight of staring at his own reflection in the prison causes Kaito to take a step away from himself.

Unlike your species, Kaito, we stick together. We do not abandon each another based on our differences. After all, it's our differences that bind us. Like different pieces that fit together. Earth's own Jigsaw Puzzle.

Dai Ando—Kaito—interlocks his hands together.

Now that you have confronted yourself, Detective, it's time for you to confront who you are meant to become. *Ama* requires a sacrifice. And she has chosen you, Kaito Takahashi.

Ama, huh?

Kaito glances at the revolver in his hand. He draws his narrow eyes back on the reflection of himself, the "version" of himself standing in the prison cell.

Why don't you give Ama a message for me, huh?

ZARA
FEBRUARY 21, 2020 4:17 PM

AFTER having finished translating the journal, I had Lucy find another interpreter for my three o'clock located all the way across the city in Castro Valley and paid one last visit to Ryuu at San Felisa Memorial.

When I arrived, a shady-looking crowd of people was gathering around the front entrance of the hospital.

I detoured away from the parking deck and decided to take a closer look. At least three news vans from three local stations with the word *Channel* followed by (enter any number here) were parked within an inch from each other alongside the hospital.

The crowd of people turned out to be not your ordinary crowd of people but rather an antsy mob of news reporters and cameramen with itchy trigger fingers. All I could think about was Ryuu, his safety, and how his soon-to-be story made it to the news to be picked apart, manipulated, tweaked, and ultimately, used for political purposes—of all places to have one's story broadcasted to the world.

Based on the constant surveillance, reporters appeared to be primed to snatch a detective or police officer in order to wring out a juicy sound bite for their evening broadcast. There were some stories that you couldn't bury. With that said, I knew it was all over as soon as I saw the phones come out.

KAITO
SEPTEMBER 21, 1987 11:12 AM

AFTER knocking several times on the front door but receiving no answer, Hiroshi enters Kaito's house.

He removes his shoes, places them in the getabako, and proceeds inside. He stops by the washitsu where he finds crime scene photographs strewed all over the floor. He comes across a set of weapons laid out on the table. Immediately, Hiroshi notices the katana missing from the set.

On the kitchen counter lies a black and white photograph of a crime scene—in fact, it happens to be the location of the very first murder in the Chiaki case.

Kodama Forest.

Lastly, Hiroshi finds a journal next to the photograph.

He opens the journal and reads the last line of the last entry:

Today, I will kill the *final boss* once and for all.

After reading through Kaito's journal, Hiroshi knows the whereabouts of his father. He decides to take the journal into the hallway where he pries open one of the loose planks in the hardwood. He hides the journal underneath the floor and places the plank of hardwood back over the journal, making sure to seal it tight.

ZARA
FEBRUARY 21, 2020 4:23 PM

AFTER I parked my car in the parking deck, I took the elevator to the Burn Center.

The same young police officer, Officer Drewby, "Ronald," was the name that slipped from his mouth toward the tail end of our pleasant conversation the other day, stood guard outside Ryuu's room. I felt somewhat relieved from the sight of Officer Drewby, or Ronald.

Once Ronald's eyes crossed mine, he lit up with surprise.

"Zara?" he said, his voice drawn out like a single-word question. "What are you doing here today?"

"Hey, Ronald—"

"—You remembered my name."

Ronald made it easy for me. Plus, I didn't feel like removing that pistol from his holster and thumping him over the head with it. He was a good kid, flirty too. I played the part.

"How could I forget?" I let my eyes fill in the rest of the sentence. He struck me as someone who often drifted in fairy tales and dreamscapes. It beat staring at walls for eight hours.

An awkward silence crept between us. Which was the whole point.

The color in Ronald's face throbbed.

"So, where's Detective Houser or Ruiz?" asked Ronald.

"Houser didn't tell you?"

"Tell me what?"

"That he was running late?"

Like a child trying to decipher a code, Ronald eye's scrambled through each thought.

"No," he said dumbly.

"He told me to keep the patient company while I wait."

"He did?"

"Yes."

With a sense of urgency creeping into the situation, I looked around the hallway, scanning for other cops, doctors, or nurses, anyone who would deem my unannounced visit as roughish. My eyes crossed a janitor's closet behind me. The door was cracked open—except for the hospital rooms, hospitals *never* kept doors open, especially ones with signs that read "Hospital Staff Only" on them. There weren't any janitors, employees, or hospital staff in the vicinity. A thought came to me, and I wanted to open that door and flip on the light switch. I didn't exactly know why my attention was drawn to the janitor's closet—maybe I had picked up on the ability after spending a few days sharing the same air with detectives—but later, I would kick myself for not following through on what Detective Ruiz referred to such talent as a good ole "hunch."

"But Zara," Ronald said, seizing my undivided attention, "you know I'm not supposed to let anybody in this room unless they're wearing a badge. That's the rules."

I reached into my purse and pulled out a plastic visitor's badge that I had kept from last year's MangaCon where I interpreted for a couple of well-known Manga artists.

I read him the label on the badge.

"See," I said, "*Interpreter*."

"A police badge, Zara."

"I just need to ask Mr. Ishii a couple of questions—"

"—I'm sorry," Ronald said, holding out his firm hand like a street cop. "It's against my orders."

I didn't want to reduce myself to an object, but Ronnie Boy here wasn't giving me any choice.

Before I could change my face, Ronald burst out laughing.

"I'm just messing with you," he said, waving off the previous comment. He stepped aside, even held the door open for me. "Go right in. . ."

I didn't know what to think or do. Should I step inside? Should I wait for the punch line? Initially, I thought he was *joking*, and that he was going to slam the door right in my face as soon as I made a move inside the room.

I found myself mimicking Ronald.

"Thank you?"

"No problem," he said, more charmingly.

Ronald closed the door behind me.

I walked to Ryuu's bedside. I couldn't help but peek over my shoulder where Ronald took one final glance through the window on the door before he sat back down in his chair.

Ryuu woke from my presence, his beady eyes turning toward my direction.

Hello, Zara.

I stood by Ryuu's bedside.

Hey.

Despite the fact he could hardly move an inch from his burns, Ryuu was keen enough to pick up on my paranoia.

Where are the two detectives?

It's just me.

Won't you lose your job if they find out you were here talking to me —

Naturally, I let out a sigh that didn't go unnoticed.

I don't care.

Tell me, Zara. Why are you really here?

I want to know why you quit your job as a cop.

Ryuu moved his eyes away from me.

You came all the way here just to ask me why I stopped being a cop?

Yes.

Ryuu was rather intuitive. I knew that he knew the question was only a precursor toward a greater question. I still hadn't worked my way up to asking him yet.

I was sick and tired of policing the public. After spending years being raised by a family that provided me with the love and nourishment that every child deserves, yet, at the same time, having a family that followed rules that were enforced and handed down by their ancestors, I wanted to live a life where I created my *own* rules. So, I did. And I started to look at the world much differently. Once I removed the distractions that were holding me down, the world opened up to me and showed me the beauty she had to offer. I *saw* the universe in the eyes of every individual. Stories that connected each and every one of us.

I stepped back from Ryuu's comments, digested them, and said to myself, "I wish I could look at the world that way."

"*You can*," Ryuu said, the sound of his perfect English momentarily stealing the air from my lungs. "It doesn't take a *wish* to be able to look beyond the artificial world."

I looked back up at Ryuu and his eyes were pinned on me.

"This whole time, you could speak English?"

"*Yes.*"

"Then why'd you act as if you didn't in front of the hospital staff? In front of those detectives?"

"If they knew that I understood them," Ryuu said, "they wouldn't have called you, would they? It's nice to share company with someone who sees you."

"You don't know me."

"*I know* you wear the burdens of your relationships, both past and present, on your shoulders as if they define you. *I know* by the way you often rub the side of your ring finger you miss wearing the ring that was given to you by someone who once cared about you. I *know* you look at other people with a sense of superiority. *I know* you're trying to regain control over your life and prove yourself worthy to those who abandoned you. What other reason would you risk everything to come here and ask me questions that you already know the answers to?"

I found myself backtracking as if I was playing mental gymnastics by flipping the right words in order to defend myself. The chink in my armor was pried wide open, exposed. The heat inside me, snuffed out.

I finally asked Ryuu, "Are you Kaito Takahashi?"

"What makes you so sure I'm not who I say I am?"

"I don't know," I said, losing confidence. "A hunch, I guess—"

"—No," Ryuu said. "I'm not Kaito Takahashi."

I sort through my thoughts, digging for another question to ask.

With the idea that, at any moment, the door could open and a nurse or doctor could enter the room, I forced myself to glance over my shoulder.

In my brief survey, I saw that Ronald was no longer sitting in the chair.

Which was cause for alarm.

"Why does my answer disappoint you, Zara?" asked Ryuu.

I drew my attention back to Ryuu and wrapped my head around the question.

"I don't know. I just. . . I thought you. . . Never mind." The silence between us tempted me to share what was on my mind, in fact, an issue that had been on my mind ever since Po and I separated. "Do you believe things happen for a reason?"

"It doesn't matter what I believe—"

"—Yes or no?" I said.

"Belief isn't always a yes or no street, Zara. Over time, a person's beliefs can evolve."

I regretted even asking the question.

"Forget I asked," I said with a hint of hostility in my voice.

"Yes," Ryuu said over the forming tension. "I do *believe* people possess an uncanny ability to subconsciously put themselves in certain positions which reinforce their self-interest."

His face surfaced in my mind again.

"Po would've said the opposite."

"Who is Po?" asked Ryuu.

"He's my husband—well, we're currently separated. He once told me things don't happen for a reason and that 'people have to make the best with what they have.' He was more pragmatic than me. Which completely contradicted what he did for a living."

"What does Po do for a living?"

"He's a wedding photographer. He gets to capture a moment in time that two people will remember forever—" I said in side-thought, "—Po didn't believe in soul mates. He believed love was no different than a job. The more you work at it, the better you are. Considering he's fifteen years younger than me, he's much wiser than his age, 'an old soul,' which was what my mother called him before she passed away. Over time, I stopped working—with him, that is. Simply, I got lazy. Consequently, instead of resolving my own issues, I looked elsewhere and pointed the finger at the first person I could blame. Po's relationship with his father, Oscar, was complicated, to say the least. They never spoke to one another and whenever they did, it always started with Oscar asking a question. He did so with a tremble in his voice. He was scared of Po. You could run through a list of reasons as to why a father would be scared of his own son. I believe he saw himself in Po and felt bad for the misery that awaited him. Eventually, Po started to turn into his father. He brought that *self-pity* into our relationship and over time, he broke me down. Over time, I lost all confidence in myself. I stopped enjoying life. Work, *this job*, it was all I had left. The fact of the matter is I don't love him anymore. Yet, I can't let him go."

I paused, waiting for Ryuu to give me something, advice, anything. He gave me nothing, only his ears.

"Even though we're separated," I said to Ryuu, "I still keep him around, constantly check up on him, ask him what he's up to. In a way, I'm punishing myself for reasons I still can't explain. I'm *trapped* in a prison that I created for myself."

I broke down in front of Ryuu. Tears fall from my eyes. I quickly wiped them away before I could taste them.

"Listen to me going on and on like this," I said, my voice starting to crack a bit. "Sorry for all of my moaning. You're lying there, looking like the Mummy, and my problems must seem so trivial to you."

"There's nothing trivial about love. Love is everything, Zara. Without love, *we* wouldn't exist."

Parts of the room suddenly shook. I heard a couple of *thuds* and thunder-like rumbles coming from outside the room.

I stopped, sobered, and shot a glance over my shoulder.

Still no sign of Ronald.

"Expecting somebody?"

Feeling the anticipation building inside me, I turned back around to Ryuu.

I pointed at the white gauze wrapped around his face.

"May I?"

You still don't believe me, do you?

"I just want to see with my own two eyes."

Ryuu blinked his eyes, as if he was giving me the go-ahead.

Making sure to breathe, I carefully peeled away the white gauze. Ryuu made it easier for me by slightly raising his head.

I peeled the gauze from his face until the burns were revealed. Most—if not, all—of his face was covered in third-degree burns.

When I examined his face, I didn't see Kaito Takahashi. I didn't see anyone. Before me lay an unrecognizable man with an unrecognizable face that had been completely burned away and all that was left was tissue and bone. Underneath all of that red, I saw Ryuu.

"That bad, huh?" said Ryuu.

Before I could answer Ryuu, I heard another sound coming from outside, the sound of people talking. I attempted to wrap the gauze around Ryuu's face.

He grabbed my wrist before I could do so.

"No," he said. "Leave it."

"I can't leave you like this."

"Yes. You have to. Trust me."

"Who can you trust these days?"

"Yourself," Ryuu said. "You can trust yourself."

Outside, I heard a man, who sounded similar to Detective Houser, talking to a woman whom I could only imagine was one of the nurses.

Since exiting through the door was clearly not an option, I looked around the room for a place to hide. I found a dark bathroom across from Ryuu's bed. I decided to take cover behind the door; and through the crack of the door, I witnessed Ryuu's face *changing*. For a moment, I thought I was hallucinating. Maybe I had ingested a drug during lunch, possibly poisoned, and now, I was starting to feel its effects. I peered closer and rapidly blinked my eyes into focus. Ryuu's face was violently shaking and appeared like the ghosting effect of a photograph.

Throughout a blurry twister of flesh, I witnessed part of another face emerge.

I had seen the face before.

However, I couldn't pinpoint where I had seen the face.

All of a sudden, the door opened!

Ryuu's face returned back to the same way it appeared moments after I removed the gauze, red and gory.

Detective Houser, who was dressed in a pair of blue jeans and a black sweatshirt and looked as if he was off the clock, stepped into the room. A young nurse followed behind him.

I brought my attention back to the detective's clothes, in particular, his blue jeans. They appeared as if they were two sizes too small.

The two moved with a sense of urgency, as well.

The nurse was first to notice the bloody, pus-spotted gauze lying to the right of Ryuu's right shoulder.

"What in the world happened here, Mr. Ishii?" asked the nurse.

"Looks like he had an itch," Detective Houser said.

I couldn't tell whether or not the detective was trying to be cute; nonetheless, the line—as innocent as it came across—sounded out of character.

The nurse examined Ryuu's face.

Then, once she knew he was all-good, she leaned closer and spoke to him as if she was talking to a senile man who had trouble hearing.

"Mr. Ishii, did you remove these bandages from your face?"

All wide-eyed and slack faced, Ryuu stared back at the nurse.

I don't understand.

Except for the basic greetings, neither the nurse nor Detective Houser understood a word of Japanese.

"Let me go grab Kerri. She might be able to help us out here," the nurse said and exited the room.

Detective Houser stayed by Ryuu's bedside.

I couldn't help but notice his quiet demeanor. Normally, the detective was a chatty man who often used communication as a means of warding off any nerves. He appeared rather comfortable around Ryuu, perhaps too comfortable.

Also, *what was he doing here*, for one, *without an interpreter?* And two, *why was he dressed in casual clothes?*

Detective Houser touched Ryuu on the shoulder.

Ryuu, in return, gently raised his wrapped arm and held out his stiff hand.

The detective grabbed Ryuu's hand in what I could only describe as a tender moment of affection.

At that moment, my insides started to bake.

With only an inch-long gap to look through, I shifted my head slightly to the left, hoping it would give me a better angle at the detective's face in order to confirm that he was, in fact, Detective Houser and not an imposter.

The detective turned his head, giving me a decent profile. He was Detective Houser—as God is my witness, I was sure of it!

I couldn't quite make out what the detective said to Ryuu; however, the only words I caught were the words *hang* and *on*.

"Hang on."

The detective hurried from the room.

I found the right—and perhaps the only—opportunity to make my move.

Carefully and cautiously, I snuck out of the bathroom and moved like a ghost toward the exit.

I stopped at the doorway and once more, glanced at Ryuu.

I gave him a nod of the head.

He nodded back, as if we both had an unspoken understanding.

I poked my head from the room.

Like crossing a busy intersection, I checked both directions, first looking to my right, then my left. Next to me, the chair was vacant. Ronald was nowhere in sight. Neither was Detective Houser.

I slipped out of the room, quickening my pace. Occasionally, I looked over my shoulder; however, I tried not to draw too much attention to myself.

As I made it to the end of the hallway, I glanced over my shoulder yet again and as soon as I turned back around, a dark figure filled my range of vision. The blood rushed through my veins from both the collision, as well as that tricky element of surprise.

Before me stood Detective Houser. Detective Ruiz was standing to his right. To his left was Rie Cronjager, an interpreter whom, except for her being half-and-half like me, her mother Japanese, father something else, I barely knew.

With the startle aside, I drew my eyes back to Detective Houser, particularly his clothes. He was sporting a beige trench coat, khakis, a red collared shirt, *not* blue jeans or a black sweatshirt. The sight of the detective left me searching for words inside what felt like an empty, bottomless bucket.

"Zara?" he said, clearly confused to see me. "What brings you here?"

I gave myself time to think of the answer by mumbling a couple of "I's" and "uhs" until finally the words exploded from my lips: "Did you change clothes?"

The confusion spread along Detective Houser's face.

"You know you're the second person to tell him that," Detective Ruiz said.

Detective Houser teased, "I must have a twin walking around here." The detective's face changed yet again, this time more serious, business-like. "So, what are you doing here, Zara? You know you're not supposed to be here without one of us. . . "

I played the ditz.

"I was told to meet you here," I said nonchalantly. "Did you not receive my message?"

By his facial reaction, he clearly wasn't buying whatever I was trying to sell.

"There must've been some kind of miscommunication—"

"—Lucy said you were unavailable," Rie said, backing up the detective.

"Lucy said that?"

"You weren't available, so they called me."

Bullshit.

Either Rie was lying—for whatever reason, I still couldn't explain—or Lucy was screwing me over and I just moved up on her own personal shit list by declining that job in Castro Valley.

Or, the detectives wanted another interpreter because they thought I was getting too close with Ryuu. Detective Houser even said so the last time I saw him.

"Well, I'm here now," I said while I stood my ground. "Do you mind if I tag along with you guys?"

"I'd let you," Detective Houser said, "but Mrs. Cronjager was here first."

"No offense, Rie," I said to Rie, then turned to the detective, "wouldn't Ryuu feel more comfortable talking to me?"

I realized I put the detective in a position that he preferred to avoid.

"I'll tell you what?" He pointed at Rie and kept moving along. "Take it up with Mrs. Cronjager. If she doesn't mind, then I don't mind."

"Rie?"

"I don't mind."

She did.

Said the color rising in her face.

As I followed the detectives through the hallway, I witnessed a couple of security guards, as well as nurses gathering outside Ryuu's room.

Once one of the head nurses spotted the detectives, she waved them over.

"The patient is missing!" she was yelling out.

The two detectives rushed over, Rie was slow to follow.

I hung back while commotion grew outside Ryuu's room.

I knew that Ryuu's disappearance had to do with Detective Houser—or some look-alike who was posing as Detective Houser.

A couple of rooms down from Ryuu's room, rays of sunlight caught the corner of my eye. I turned toward the sunlight, directing me toward another hospital room where I witnessed an empty wheelchair, which appeared as if it was deliberately parked in front of a window. The front casters remained in an askew position. The front right rigging along with the footplate was open and loosely hanging from the side of the wheelchair like a dead limb. The curtains had been pulled all the way open, and the sun was blasting through and casting quite a glare over the slick tile floor. Next to the wheelchair were a couple of drops of blood.

While the detectives searched Ryuu's room, I went inside the other room. I inspected the wheelchair first, then the evidence around the wheelchair. Smudges of blood and flakes of dried, dead skin were scattered along the armrest, as well as the seat upholstery. The skin, however, was much darker, like ashes. The air also carried a strange odor underneath all of that sterilized cover-up of chemicals and aerosols. The smell was faint yet striking for it was one that was all too familiar. *It was happening again*, I was ready to tell myself. Besides the recent drought, it was highly unusual for this certain time of the year. Although over these past couple of years, it had only become customary to catch such a potent stench at *any* time of the year. *Maybe there was a house fire nearby*, I wondered, *and someone at the hospital had left a window open.*

Below the wheelchair, strips of white gauze were piled over the tile floor like a snake's skin that had recently been shed.

I poked my head outside the room and searched for Ryuu; however, I wasn't looking for Ryuu Ishii, per se.

If Ryuu was *what* I thought he was, then he could've been anybody—a nurse, an orderly, a security guard, anybody!

How about Rie, I thought to myself, *what if she was Ryuu?*

I stepped out of the room.

As the two detectives followed the nurses down the other end of the hallway in search of Ryuu, Rie shot a glance over her shoulder. We both made eye contact. Without saying a word, she followed the detectives.

I thought again, canceling all doubts: *He wouldn't have been able to change so fast.*

I went the other direction and walked back down the same way I came in. I took an elevator and pushed the first floor button.

As the doors were about to close, Doctor King appeared on the other side.

He lifted up his hand.

"Hold the door please," he said.

At the last second, I extended my arm outward and slid my hand between the two doors. The doors slid back open.

"Thank you," the doctor said, out of breath.

"No problem," I replied.

Doctor King stood at the other side of the elevator, not uttering a word about where he was going.

"What floor?" I asked.

"First floor," he said.

The button was already pushed, so I left it alone.

The doors closed, and we both waited in a silence that carried a weight to it.

From Doctor King's expression—or lack thereof—he appeared as if he didn't know me. Either that, or he wasn't in any mood to strike up any conversation.

In a blurry reflection of the elevator's mirrored walls, I couldn't help but notice a red spot on the doctor's white cuff. I moved my eyes downward and confirmed that the red spot was either blood or ketchup. I told myself over and over that it was ketchup. The doctor took a late lunch or early dinner in the downstairs cafeteria and dipped his sleeve in ketchup while he was dipping his french fry. I noticed another red spot on the collar of his white coat.

How in the hell did ketchup wind up all the way up there?

I clammed up.

Realizing that the person—*or thing*—standing to the right of me wasn't Doctor King at all but rather an entity wearing the face of Doctor King, I found myself gradually stepping away while moving the purse toward the front of my body. Right then and there, I put the two pieces together, and I knew exactly where I last saw his face—at least *part* of his face.

As soon as I was about to speak his name, I heard the *ding* of the elevator.

The doors opened.

Not wasting anytime, Doctor King exited the elevator.

I stood in a state of disbelief.

It wasn't until the doors started to close that I finally exited the elevator.

I followed the doctor outside; however, I made sure to keep my distance from him. He dodged the news reporters in front and walked around the hospital.

Once I found more space between us along the side of the hospital, I called to him, "Ryuu!"

Doctor King stopped in his tracks and after a couple of tense seconds, finally faced me. He was no longer wearing the doctor's squared, scruffy face. Instead, he was wearing the face of a man who had haunted my dreams for the past three nights. The resemblance to Kaito Takahashi was uncanny.

Not too far away emerged another man who looked identical to Ryuu. It was the clothes that gave him away. He was wearing the same casual clothes that Detective Houser was wearing—the first Detective Houser. He had a dark, indistinguishable mole on his right cheek.

Higashi?

As Ryuu was caught in the middle of me and Ichiro, he turned to Ichiro, who, in return, threw his head in a nod, as if he was motioning for him to follow along.

Ichiro went ahead. I lost him in a crowd of pedestrians walking on the sidewalk.

Ryuu made an attempt to walk away.

I called out to him once more, forcing him to confront me.

Ryuu stopped, turned around, and faced me.

"Where will you go, Ryuu?" I asked him. "The cops will be looking for you. You really want to be looking over your shoulder for the rest of your life? That's no way to live. . . " I begged, ". . . Just come back with me, Ryuu, and we can sort out this whole thing."

"One day," he said plainly.

Before he could walk away, I shouted out, "Only a guilty person would run."

I'm not running.

Ryuu spoke what he had to say and walked away into the crowd.

Later that night, I watched a news report on the TV stating that police officer, Ronald Drewby, as well as a civilian named Douglas Trumbull, were discovered inside that very same janitor's closet. The two men had been both drugged, which left them in a temporary state of paralysis. Their clothes were missing from their bodies. But they were okay.

As for Doctor King, he was still reported missing.

KAITO
SEPTEMBER 21, 1987 2:03 PM

WITH labored breath, Hiroshi treks up the steep slope in Kodama Forest and approaches the site where the first crime in the Chiaki Case took place.

Dad!

Stopping to listen to the feedback of his voice echoing throughout the forest, Hiroshi hunches forward to catch his breath.

Sticking out of the weeds and thick vegetation along the ground, Hiroshi locates a shoe. Hiroshi picks up the shoe, holds it close, and concludes that the shoe does, in fact, belong to his father.

Dad!

Hiroshi pushes forward.

He makes his way around a knobby sugi tree, only to find the aftermath of a battle scattered before him: several pieces of severed branches, as well as torn articles of Kaito's clothing randomly pepper the forest floor.

The sun hits the blade of the katana resting on the ground. The glare catches Hiroshi's eye.

As with the shoe, he leans down and picks up the katana by the sharp end. A severed hand is revealed underneath a thin blanket of leaves, the hand still tightly gripped over the handle.

Horrified from his discovery, Hiroshi backs away and trips over a protruding root along the ground. The roots are swollen, Hiroshi realizes, and throbbing like a pulse. Along with the web of branches above, the entire tree is pulsing as if it's alive!

Covering the fertile ground around the base of the tree is a patch of *torikabuton*—or aconite "wolf's bane"—all in full bloom with their purplish-blue helmet-like hoods bright and brilliant.

After a thorough study, Hiroshi is taken aback from the sight of the massive tree—most importantly, the shape and texture and color of the tree. It's sugi, but, after another vigilant survey, Hiroshi realizes it's *not* sugi. It's much paler than a sugi tree, and the texture of its bark is coarser yet thinner with deep, dark trenches running along the base of its crooked trunk.

Hiroshi draws his eyes farther upward, studying each bend and bump in awe.

That awe soon turns to sheer horror.

Above, hangs Kaito, his body suspended upside down and held up by the tree branches, which have penetrated all of his major organs. His neck is slit open and most—if not, all—of the blood in his body has been drained.

Only a couple of droplets of blood drip from his head, as well as his dangling arm, which has been severed by one of the many jagged, gnarly, sword-like tree branches. The soil below Kaito's body, still dark and soggy with blood.

As Hiroshi looks closer at his father, he hears a sudden *thud* next to him!

He turns to the sound, only to discover a tree nut the size of a chicken's egg with its shell having the veiny, bumpy texture of a peanut or pecan; however, its exterior texture is as tough and leathery as an acorn with a fist-shaped cupule covering the top of the nut.

As he takes a step closer to the tree nut, another one falls from the tree.

Hiroshi picks up one of the tree nuts from the ground and holds it in his palm. The tree nut isn't as light in weight as any other tree nut Hiroshi had held. Yet, it is rather heavy, weighing approximately ten pounds or so.

The tree nut suddenly vibrates in his hand!

Hiroshi can feel something moving inside. . .

As he holds the tree nut closer, the shell suddenly cracks open!

A black, gummy, spider-like creature emerges from the tree nut, causing Hiroshi to drop the tree nut to the ground.

The same creature emerges from the other tree nut.

Together, the two creatures scurry away into the Kodama Forest, leaving Hiroshi at a loss for words.

ZARA
MARCH 20, 2020 10:01 AM

WITH everything that happened over the past month, I cut short the workweek and took the weekend off for what I liked to call a little "me time" and traveled north of San Francisco to Redwood Park.

I spent the late morning hiking through the park, mostly sightseeing and taking photographs of the nature around me. I ended up taking a lot of amazing photos, one of which I planned to frame and hang on my office wall.

A few hours in, I decided to call it a day and head back to my car. For one, I needed to rest my legs. And two, I was starving. The plan was to grab lunch at a new restaurant called The Rolling Boulder Café that had recently opened up a few miles from the park.

With food on my mind, my walk felt faster; however, I told myself over and over that it was the food driving me.

But it was something else.

Not something I couldn't see but something I could feel in my bones.

With the panic creeping in, I caught a metallic object glistening in the corner of my eye. I knew, from first glance, it had no earthly business being there.

My guard was up. Senses heightened.

I crept closer to the strange object, which was lying in a dark area underneath a pale-looking tree that looked dead—or decaying—from second study. Unlike the redwoods, its bark had a grayish-brown tone and like the object, looked as if it had no earthly business being there.

I kneeled down, pinched off a couple fingers-worth of moist dirt, and rubbed it between my fingertips, which left a bright red ink-like substance along my skin.

I brushed aside the dirt and found a wedding band half-buried in the ground.

In hopes that I might one day find the owner, I decided to pocket the ring.

While doing so, the tree branches above me suddenly stirred and rustled.

Startled, I looked up at *still* branches.

I told myself, "It's just the wind, scaredy-cat."

But, I knew, I was partly lying to myself.

THOSE who managed to survive the Cherry Grove Road Massacre will look back at what happened during that awful night of May 5, 2020, and wonder how a species was capable of committing such inconceivable violence. One would say, without hesitation, that this was where it all started, the "beginning of the so-called 'end,'" while another: "They simply learned it from watching us."

Or, there was a possibility: "Nobody had a fucking clue what they were talking about."

SINCLAIR LEPRIEUR, LOUISIANA
OCTOBER 5, 1979

ANASTASIA was out cold well before "Mr. Johnny" came on when her seven-year-old boy, Wyatt, shook her shoulder to complain about some strange noise that he heard outside. Now, Wyatt knew not to wake his poor mama, but the noise was unlike anything he had ever heard before; and Gramma Eunice, who was often referred to as the "Unit"

97

for her burly size, was beyond interruption. Even so, young Wyatt knew for sure not to ever disrupt his gramma from catching sleep; otherwise she'd turn into one of them evil characters his mama occasionally read to him right before bedtime. From the crack of the guest bedroom door, the boy saw the good side of her playing Beethoven's Symphony No. 9 with a kazoo of a nose; both her arms crossed over her chest like Dracula, while one of her legs dangled over the side of the lopsided bed like a broken tree branch. He thought she made the funniest sound when she drank the special "medicine" with his mama.

Once more, Wyatt heard that strange guttural sound coming from outside the window, immediately prompting him to give his mama another shake on the arm.

Anastasia shrugged off Wyatt and rolled over on her side, letting out a couple of farts that could pass as door squeaks. Wyatt clung to his mama's meaty wrist, tugging and yanking at it as if he was trying to pull her from dreams that had swept her away. It was the medicine, he knew. *Yep*, that good ole medicine.

While Anastasia stirred in the raggedy recliner, she let out a groan and jerked her arm away from Wyatt's clammy grip.

"*Leav'me 'lone, boy*," she said, her voice still wet with booze. "Go'sleep."

"But Mama. . ." Wyatt pouted.

"Go on now," Anastasia said demonically, which caused Wyatt to back off.

Wyatt didn't know what was more frightening: the strange *clicking*, *hissing*, guttural-like noises coming from the night darkness outside the cracked window or that food demon inside his mama's belly emitting what Wyatt could only imagine as foul toxic gas from every orifice of her body as if it was some kind of defense mechanism.

As Wyatt backpedaled, his heel stepped on the TV remote lying on the floor, causing the channel to switch from the local programming where a meteorologist was detailing the latest update on Hurricane Orson, which had weakened substantially from a CAT 1 hurricane to what the meteorologist called a "rainmaker" of a tropical depression stalling over Nashville, Tennessee, to the late-nite show airing the band Raydio's latest music video for the song, "You Can't Change That."

With eyes glued to the screen, Wyatt ignored his mama and sauntered toward the TV where he stood in fascination by what his Gramma Eunice once called the wages of the devil's workshop. Wyatt didn't know anything about that, nor was he at all interested in Gramma's prejudices. But what he did know for certain was that he liked the sound; in fact, it was the music that helped lessen the fear inside him.

Behind him, he heard his mama humming the lyrics of the song; however, it was clear to Wyatt that it wasn't his mama that was singing in her sleep but rather that "medicine."

He smiled at the sight of his mama, who, soon after, let out a couple of more airy farts through her blowhole, as if she was tooting her horn along with the melody of the song.

The smell alone forced Wyatt to pinch his nose and seek fresh air elsewhere.

From the other side of the room, Wyatt heard yet another noise, but this time the shriek of a man's scream cutting through the woods.

With his seven-year-old mind trying to match the scream to the lips of each one of the singers on TV, Wyatt focused his eyes and opened his ears. He heard the same scream once more; however, the scream wasn't coming from that glowing box in front of him, Wyatt concluded. It was coming from outside.

That wide-eyed curiosity drove Wyatt toward the back door.

Without wasting anytime, he opened the door and looked back at his mama, who was as still and silent as a corpse.

Cautiously, he closed the door behind him as if he had snuck around a few times before.

Next to Wyatt the day's labor was scattered around the house: a neat pile of fallen tree branches stacked on top of a blue tarp; an axe perched along the side of the house was sticky with tree sap and covered in flakes of wood; next to the axe, the teeth of a chainsaw were clogged with chewed-up bits of wood; least a dozen tree trunks had been cut into manageable logs and lined up on the back lawn like soldiers. The ground was still soggy from the past few days of heavy rain. The air, however, was clean and remarkably crisp with a fall breeze providing enough chill to make the night less tolerable. The night sky was as nearly as bright as the day's.

Wyatt shot his wide eyes toward the full moon above and basked in its lure.

Beyond the moonlit woods, the trees spoke with snaps and distant *pops* as the wood started to dry out.

Once more, Wyatt heard the shrieks of a man in danger; however, it sounded more distant and trailing away. In those screams, he caught the word *Help!*

Wyatt disobeyed everything that his mama—and most importantly, Gramma Eunice—told him about the nights, the dark woods, and specifically, the night of the full moon where the "Swamp Devil" feasted on young boys who misbehaved. Somewhere among the disarray of thoughts, Wyatt recalled his mama mentioning the wildlife while chopping through wood with an axe and how the past storm had drove most of the animals away. "Yet," Anastasia said with a curl in the corner of her lip, as she rested for a moment to catch a good look at a shirtless man named Tyde, who was running a chainsaw through the oak tree that had fallen across the neighborhood street, and the thinner, more attractive neighbor Marie-Rose trying to flirt her way directly into Tyde's breeches, "it had a particular way of attractin' dem *different kinds* of animals."

And monsters.

Of course, Wyatt had absolutely no idea what was going through his mama's head when she spoke those words with such loathing nor did he understand at all what she meant by a storm attracting a different kind of animal for it was best left up to adults to squabble about; however, what he knew was certain: someone was out there.

A man.

In danger.

Possibly in need of his help.

However, Wyatt wasn't at all interested in the "help" part.

He just wanted to know what the fuss was all about.

Determined, Wyatt set out through the woods while occasionally he was distracted by surprising yet welcoming sounds of frogs or crickets.

Wyatt tracked down a frog and snatched it in his hands. He kept it concealed in his palms and wandered through the moonlit night, rerouting and taking minor detours around uprooted trees and flattened vegetation.

As Wyatt approached an "off-limits" area, which was considered dense wetlands where dangers weren't too hard to find, he heard that same man again. His screams were more urgent, closer; however, as the harsh screams intensified, they were suddenly squelched, leaving room for much concern.

Silence throbbed. Crickets, frogs—even the one Wyatt carefully nestled in his two palms—any sound of nature for that matter came to a blistering halt, as if someone had switched it all off, like a TV set.

Once life thriving, then death approaching.

And approaching fast.

To the right of Wyatt, the footsteps quickened. Tree branches and overgrown shrubbery whistled and rustled. The wheezing breath of a man taking in gulps of air was the most evident.

Wyatt braced himself so hard and tight that he smothered the frog in his two hands. Slimy frog guts and blood oozed from the cracks of his fingers; however, that was the least of Wyatt's concerns. His eyes were pinned on a tall dark figure cutting through the woods like a swinging machete.

All of a sudden, the same man whose screams hadn't gone unnoticed charged through a thorny brush and barreled into Wyatt, who took the brunt of the man's leg, knocking him flat on his back. The panicky, out-of-breath man tumbled over Wyatt and rolled to the ground.

As soon as the man witnessed Wyatt, the man's face lit up with both surprise and terror.

"You have to get outta here, kid," the man urged.

Wyatt heard a familiar noise behind him; in fact, it was the same noise that had initially waken him up from deep sleep.

"It's... coming..." the man said to Wyatt. His parched throat from sucking in air, as well as his labored breath made it harder to speak.

It was at that very moment when the man reached out to grab Wyatt's hand that Wyatt witnessed the man's injuries.

First, he saw the blood all over the man's right hand.

Then, his other one, the left arm which he nursed like a chicken wing against his body, was missing.

Gone. Not cleanly severed but torn off brutally and violently. Strips of loose flesh and tissue hung from his bicep like shredded meat. Deep gashes ran up the side of his shoulder and back. Part of the humerus bone was visible underneath all of that blood and gore.

But no hand.

No forearm.

Nearly the entire arm, gone.

As Wyatt waited in shock, the man waved Wyatt closer.

"Com'on, boy," he urged in one breath. "We have to get outta here..."

Wyatt reached for the stranger's hand; and as soon as both of their two fingertips grazed one another, a darker, much larger figure leaped over Wyatt.

The man's slack, pale face was like a still image in the boy's head.

All he could think about when the creature clamped its powerful jaw around the stranger's neck was that it was the same mythical beast that his gramma often used to scare him—the "Swamp Devil." The spiky, lanky, long-limbed creature, which bore a Afro-like mane similar to his own, stabbed the man in the side with its sharp, scaly tail and held the man up in the air as if he was a lollipop and licked and slurped up all of the blood gushing from his gaping neck, which had been bitten open.

The man was dead—clearly, his head was attached by a couple of strings of cartilage—when the red-eyed creature lay down the body and moved its way toward the guts and internal organs, as if they were the main entrée.

Wyatt backpedaled from the creature. His heel stepped on a twig, causing it to *snap* in two. The sound drew those red eyes to Wyatt, who immediately froze.

From a distance, Anastasia yelled out his name, "Wyatt!"

The creature poked its head up, its snake-like tongue licking the breeze as if it used its tongue as both ears and eyes.

As Wyatt's mama continued to call out her boy's name, the creature grabbed the man by the leg with its mouth and dragged the body away in the swamps.

Wyatt was unable to move.

All he could remember after sneaking out of the house was standing slack-jawed on the back porch with a blinding floodlight beaming directly down on him and Gramma Eunice swinging open the backdoor and grabbing him and pulling him straight into the house while his mama was at the front door talking with two deputies who were jotting down Wyatt's description.

Anastasia nearly fainted from the sight of her boy.

VANCOUVER, CANADA
APRIL 14, 2016

BEXLEY sat next to her longtime video editor, Nickle, in a dark editing room about the size of a walk-in closet and meticulously went through each video on two 27-inch monitors by helping Nickle with the editing—or "cutting," as Nickle so flippantly put it—of several B-rolls, as well as long-winded and occasionally tedious interviews with local fishermen and tourists during her latest trip to Archipiélago de Colón—or better known as the "Galápagos Islands."

Nickle pulled up a bin folder labeled "Interviews" and scrolled through each video of local fishermen, starting with one particular fisherman named Fernando, who moved from mainland Ecuador to the islands for work, and played the audio for Bexley.

"Wait a sec," Bexley said after sipping from her third cup—or fourth, she lost track after combing through silly videos of sea lions and giant tortoises. "Can we do a soft pan from right-to-left?"

"We can indeed," Nickle chirped.

"Start at the center of the pier and then pan toward the beach where—"

Before Bexley mapped out the direction of the pan, Nickle was already two clicks ahead of her with one of his many "stocked" pans that Bexley used often in her show.

"*Beautiful*," she said, as Nickle played the clip, now with a soft pan.

Fernando's English was poor and more than likely, subtitles would have to be inserted at the bottom of the screen—that is, if the interview made the final cut; however, Bexley found the interview extremely enlightening, especially about the part where Fernando talked about a host of many illegal activities such as the cutting of shark fins, including hammerheads, and selling them on black markets and how, over two to three decades ago, fishermen would kill, literally, to obtain *sea cucumber*, even hold members of the National Park Service hostage in order to cut deals for higher annual quotas on the sought after marine animal.

"That's the cue," Bexley said urgently. "Let's throw in some of them clips of sea cucumbers while Fernando is talking."

Fernando wasn't exactly telegenic. He had a disheveled appearance and the thought of a local fisherman stealing the show with his quirky mannerisms and his wild eyes unclothing Bexley. There was only *one star of this show*.

But most importantly, Bexley knew that people, like them or not, were visual creatures. Most people didn't want to watch someone talking. They wanted images to go with the talking, to keep them engaged, so she thought.

Nickle scrolled through the bins until he found the one that read: "Deep-sea diving."

"Who'd ever imagine that sea cucumber was such a hot item."

Nickle clicked on the video bin and scrolled through a bunch of clips of Bexley swimming underwater.

"You serious? It's an Asian delicacy, *very* expensive."

"Have you tried one before?"

"Me? Eww. Hell no."

"Let me guess, it's the slippery texture. . ."

"That, and the fact it's basically a sea worm."

"Not a fan of worms?"

"And you are?"

"Me? I love worms! As a matter of fact, I can't get enough of them!"

Nickle's jab at Bexley prompted her to smack him on shoulder.

"Trust me," she said, laidback. "In all of the years I've been traveling around the world, you know what the one thing is I've learned?"

Nickle asked, "What's that?"

"Bring your own food."

"Not a food taster, huh?"

"I am, but I ain't eating sea worms. No, thank you. I'll pass."

Nickle laughed.

"You're a trip, Bexy," he said and found a couple of decent clips of Bexley studying sea cucumbers along the ocean floor worthy enough to work into the interview. He stopped cutting for a moment, tilted his thought, then turned to Bexley. "I wonder what they taste like. . ."

"I heard they taste like squid."

"Hey," Nickle said suddenly, his face lit up, "maybe you can incorporate the local cuisine into the show. I don't know what it is. But people, for some reason, like watching other people eat."

"Sorry, Nicky Boy," Bexley said, her voice flattened as if she was turned off by Nickle's suggestion, "This isn't *that* kind of show and as long as I'm host, it never will be. I'm a biologist, *not* some foodie trying to make a quick buck."

The spongy marine animal that acquired its name from a fruit that most of us humans ate pickled or in a salad, as well as its complex yet supernatural-like defensive system was far more intriguing to Bexley, than, opposed to, you know, the thought of actually eating one. She said more defensively, "Believe it or not, like all echinoderms, a sea cucumber embodies features that, from a human's perspective, would be considered physically impossible. Get this," she said in a state of exhilaration, "in order to defend themselves from predators, the sea cucumber expels what are called *cuvierian tubules*, which contain *holothurin*, a toxin that can be toxic to humans if high amounts are ingested; however, what makes these clusters of fine, tensile-strength tubes so fascinating is that they're able to elongate up to twenty times their original length once expelled from their anus." Bexley made sure to put an emphasis on the word *twenty*. "These sticky threads can also become extremely adhesive when touched by an object. It's pretty amazing, if you think about it."

"Sounds like ah, like a spider web."

"Sort of, yeah," Bexley said. "The concept is vaguely similar, which is to entangle predators. However, for a spider, it's more about catching its meal rather than defending itself. The main difference is an autotomic process known as *evisceration*."

"Please tell me more, Doctor Hun."

Once more, Bexley played off Nickle's obvious sarcasm with a lighter smack on the shoulder.

"These creatures literally expel part of the gut in order to defend themselves. I mean, how freaking amazing is that?"

Nickle mumbled from the corner of his mouth, "Talk about scaring yourself shitless."

"And that's not even the coolest part. They're able to regenerate their internal organs, the *viscera*, within several weeks."

"That's something," Nickle said, his eyes lighting up from another thought. "Say, that reminds me, have you heard the one about the flatworm—"

"—You must be talking about the planarian flatworm," she said over Nickle. "It has the ability to regenerate itself into one complete organism."

"Like a lizard growing back its tail?"

"No. Not exactly," Bexley said. "Most lizards shed their tales as a decoy to distract predators, which allows them enough time to flee while the detached tail is able to writhe. They're able to *partially* regenerate their tails. However, say, if you cut a lizard in half, then obviously, you will kill a lizard. *But* with the planarian, if you cut it in half—or even cut it into pieces—then it's able to regenerate its entire body from those pieces."

"That's insane."

"Well," Bexley said. "Not really. It's nature." The sudden pause in the conversation forced Bexley's eyes back on the monitor. She said to Nickle, "Let's do a dissolved transition from Fernando to the wide shot of Wolf Volcano."

Nickle pulled up the video bin with the label "Isabela Island."

As Nickle searched for the volcano clips, Bexley's phone rang. She placed the coffee aside and noticed the Los Angeles area code first, then checked the rest of the phone number. Instant disgust on her face.

"Ssshit," she hissed under her breath, as her stomach twisted in knots.

Nickle immediately picked up the change in Bexley's behavior.

"Who is it?"

"Who'd you think?"

"Again? What's his deal? Lemme guess. The studio execs?"

"You know how pushy Pat is every time we get back from a shoot," she said.

"Well I'm working as fast as I can, Bexley, and him calling every ten minutes doesn't help the process at all—"

"—I know, I know. It's not your fault, Nick."

"If he really cared about *your* show, then he'd be here in person and not back in his cozy little palace—" Nickle glanced over his shoulder and whispered, "—Don't tell him I said that."

"I'm not."

She held up the phone, which was still ringing.

"You mind?"

Nickle turned his focus back on the monitor and the Bexley Hun who Americans knew and loved.

"Good luck," he said dismissively.

Bexley exited Suite B, stepped out into the hallway, and finally answered the phone. During the entire phone call with the show's producer, Pat German, Bexley could only muster out a couple of words, mostly sounds or attempts at uttering a follow-up questions.

After Bexley hung up with Pat, she poked her head back in the editing suite.

"Hey, Nick," she said shortly, "let me bum a smoke from you."

Not a question, but more of a stern demand.

"What about your streak?" asked Nickle.

Bexley didn't even respond to Nickle. Instead, she displayed a look—or lack of a look—on her face.

Nickle took the look as a warning, more or less, one that warranted obedience and an even temper. He reached for a pack of Marlboro Lights next to the mouse and glanced at the three remaining cigarettes inside.

As he handed Bexley the entire pack, Nickle asked, "Is everything okay?"

"Not now," she said, her face and the voice that came out of it wounded.

Nickle kept quiet and continued to work as Bexley stepped outside the building for a smoke.

All she could think about were Pat's words, especially, after two seasons and a growing and unarguably loyal fan base, his audacity to speak about the show in such a negative light that had cast so many doubts regarding his true intentions: *You*—not we—*are turning into the typical cut-and-paste explorer show that any Joe Schmoe can find while flipping through cable TV.* Nothing at all had changed in the footage Bexley had sent Pat and the studio hounds. For the past two years, Bexley pretty much stuck to the same format with her arriving via an airplane—or boat—to your exotic (fill in the blank) location, then talking to locals, then jumping right into the exploration of rugged and perilous landscapes, mostly uncharted territory, and learning about the creatures that inhabited the land, water, or wherever the adventure had taken her. It wasn't good enough, not anymore. The suits were craving a more "daring" Bexley, one who risked life or limb for the sake of a *click*. From the moment Bexley's agent, Wayne Shivers, arranged a lunch meeting with Pat German to discuss the inception of the show, Bexley specifically told Pat, as well as the other producers that she or her team wasn't at all interested in making a fool of herself in order to win over viewers. The whole premise of the show was to take the viewers to places where he or she had never been before from the comfort of their own home while, at the same time, provide them with education one couldn't find in any book; the times were changing, though, maybe too fast for Bexley to keep up. And everybody wanted Bexley 2.0.

Not only that, the thought of having to book another trip back to the Galápagos Islands and basically scrap everything and re-shoot the entire episode in three days so that the show wouldn't "go under," as Pat put it lightly—which was another way of saying that he was no longer going to fork out the money to keep the show running—made Bexley sick to her stomach.

While pacing around the sidewalk, Bexley pulled a lighter out of the cigarette pack and lit up the Marlboro.

She couldn't help but draw her attention to two kids, probably no older than fifteen or sixteen, waiting outside a deli shop, Ruffio's, next door. It was not only what the kids were watching, but also what they were watching it on.

Bexley crept closer for a better look.

On the phone screen was a video of a white van deliberately mowing through two tents, as well a crowd of people who appeared to be attending a barbeque festival. Over a dozen of people were violently flung in the air like rag dolls.

The two kids suddenly burst out laughing from the initial impact of grill and flesh. Then carnage.

One of them rewinding, then slowing down the video, and saying more hysterically, "You see that one dude?"

Referring to the one "dude" who was flipped over the hood of the van, which hurled his body in the air, causing him to land headfirst directly on the pavement of the parking lot.

The "10-point" landing receiving the most laughs—and likes.

The sight of the two kids finding pleasure at the expense of others, who, more than likely, resulted in the loss of their own life, had Bexley turning her thoughts inward to dig up for the better parts of humanity, not the worst.

Blinded by the rage, she found nothing with any substance or meaning.

Yet, only a distant shade of what mankind once was before clouded over by a digital storm destined to rewire and reshape day-to-day life.

And lately, the very thought of who naturally thrived in a constantly checked world before her time made the evolution of mankind seem like a wicked experiment run by those who only spoke in code.

BATON ROUGE, LOUISIANA
JUNE 17, 2019

THE once wild crowd outside the local dive bar called Suck The Head, which was known for their famous crawfish boils every Sunday afternoon, thinned out dramatically as the night regressed to a gassy lull.

Sunday's leftover stragglers, who had been hanging around the bar well past last call, sashayed outside like weary ghosts on a haunt binge. A round bouncer named Hunchback directed stragglers toward the parking lot.

Five of them altogether, three guys in their late twenties—one of them named Tad who was powering forward as if his head weighed twice his body weight—two females who were running wet off the sauce. The two were college-age, their summer attire rather skimpy with a figurative neon pink bar sign that read "Open for business," and "thick" too, as one of the guys, Beaux, described the two chicks to his drunk buddy, Geraldo, who teased, "more cushion for the pushin'."

"Where y'at?" asked Hunchback, clearly concerned for the well-being of the one guy named Tad, who couldn't stand up straight and looked so wasted that the next few hours entailed an emergency room visit at the hospital where he was going to get his stomach pumped.

Beaux, the most sober one who clearly had taken the role as the alpha of the trio, gave Hunchback a thumb's up and said, "He's good. We'll take care of him."

"You sure?"

"Yeah, yeah," Beaux said coolly. "My boy here gets like this all da time."

"Well, make sure he don't puke all over the parking lot."

"Yeah," he said, moving away from Hunchback. "Gotcha."

Beaux, who had been hounding the two women all night and wasn't going to let Tad's intoxicated state ruin the after party, which, for Beaux, was considered the only true party, hung back while Tad and Geraldo proceeded toward Beaux's black Dodge Durango, which was parked in the back of the parking lot.

"A'ight, Cher," Beaux said to Missy Landry, the more talkative and blonder of the two. "Where da party at?"

Missy couldn't help but glance back inside Suck The Head at the older lady with greasy, wiry, uncombed hair, and dressed in a black duster that hung down to her ankles, and whom Missy commonly referred to as "super creepy," sitting at the far end of the bar and *still* pounding away booze like no tomorrow, despite the slow rush of stragglers oozing from the bar.

Everything about Missy changed, her face, even the tone in her voice.

More uncertain, Missy faced Beaux.

"I dunno," she said unsurely. "I think we gonna call it a night."

"What! No way!"

"But your friend's obviously messed up—"

"—Who? Tad?" He waved off Missy's concern for Tad. "He'll shake it off. Trust me," Beaux said with a twinkle in his eye. "Once Tad gets some chow in him, he'll be doing cartwheels." He leaned in closer to Missy and in a subtle way, started to beg, "Come on. Let's hang out. I promise it'll be fun. We got plenty of food back at the house—that is, if you two ladies are hungry."

Missy turned to her shy friend, August, for approval.

August gave a half-shrug.

Her stomach did most of the talking.

"Sure."

"Good 'cuz I'm starving actually," Missy said in return. "Plus, I don't have anything to eat back at the house. End of the month, you know?"

"Awesome! You two drivin'?"

"Nah," Missy said. "We took Uber."

In Beaux's mind, he started to judge. *She had enough money for booze and a ride. Yet, she doesn't have any food at her house.*

He already had them in his pocket, though, and no longer needed to convince them how gorgeous he thought they were.

"Screw that," Beaux said merrily. "I've got plenty of room in my car."

Before Beaux escorted the two women toward the car, Missy grabbed August by the arm.

"First, I have to seriously pee," Missy said to August, as she tiptoed in place, "like I'm about to pop."

"Just hold it," Beaux demanded and without even realizing it, started to push his luck.

Missy rolled her eyes at Beaux and gave him a "Are you for realz?" kind of expression that had him regretting what he said.

"You can always pop-a-squat?" said August.

"Shoot. I ain't pissing out here." She looked at August with a wide-eyed expression, as if she had to tell August something personal but didn't want to say it in front of Beaux or in front of any man for that matter. She waved down Hunchback, who was standing guard by the entranceway. "Can we use the ladies room? We'll be real quick. . . "

"We're closed."

"Pretty please, Hunchie Baby," Missy said, anxiously tugging at her friend's arm. "We'll only be a second. . . "

"I can't. Sorry."

"I'm going to piss myself, Hunchback!"

Missy sold it by squirming back and forth and plugging herself as if her index finger was a cork.

Hunchback finally gave in and opened the front door for Missy and August.

"I'll just pull the car around," Beaux said, his voice trailing off as if he was losing confidence by the second in tonight's easy score.

For a moment, he even questioned himself: *What I am doing?*

I can pull much better tail.

The thought came and went and Beaux directed his attention back to Geraldo and Tad, who were nowhere to be found. He figured they were already in the car, but the car was empty.

Maybe they were taking a piss behind a bush or something.

Speaking of taking a piss, Beaux had to go himself; however, he wasn't in the mood to walk back to Suck The Head where he could potentially blow it with the two chicks. He found a bush along the side of the building.

While draining his lizard, he said to himself, "*Laissez les bon temps rouler.*"

Which was a popular expression in Louisiana—especially around the time of Mardi Gras—which was French for "Let the good times roll."

As he zipped up his khaki shorts, he caught a small, dark figure in the corner of his eye. He turned his shoulder and saw Tad, who was on his hands and knees and puking all over the place.

"For fuck's sake, Tad," he said, rushing over to a dazed Tad, "where da hell's Geraldo?"

As Beaux turned a murmuring Tad on his side, his hand slipped over his slick arm. He immediately thought it was vomit. With disgust, he raised his arm in the air and held it away from his body as if it was covered in a contagious disease.

Intrigued by the color of his arm, Beaux carefully peered closer.

"Blood?"

Either Tad was puking up blood or. . .

Beaux tended to Tad, who had a massive laceration across his entire chest. It looked as if he had been diagonally slashed across his chest by a machete. Either that, Beaux thought, or the other possibility, the one being that his drunk ass cut himself along a sharp object, like a metal rod along the side of the dumpster, during a fall or stumble. He hoped to God Tad got his Tetanus shot.

Considering Tad was numb from a day's worth of alcohol consummation and more than likely couldn't feel a damn thing below his ears, Tad had absolutely no idea where he was, what had happened to him, or even if he was trapped in a horrible nightmare.

"Dude," Beaux examined Tad's injury, "you're bleeding."

He was bleeding bad, too; in fact, bleeding out.

"What happened?" asked Beaux. "Tad, who did this to you?"

He couldn't find the words and even when he did, he was slurring his speech.

"Tad, who did this to you? Where's The Chair?"

Which was the nickname that was branded to Geraldo.

He heard a response but not from Tad, who was too inebriated to even coherently speak his name.

To Beaux's left, he heard—or at least thought he heard—a groan followed by the sound of his name coming from the edge of the woods behind the bar.

Beaux instructed Tad to apply pressure to the wound. He did, but only momentarily. His arms went limp like wet noodles and flop away from his body. He slapped Tad in the face and once more, told him to apply pressure. Tad did.

"Geraldo?" Beaux said, turning his focus to the direction where he last heard the sound.

All of a sudden, a loud scream—possibly Geraldo's—cut through the darkness of the woods!

The trees violently shifted and shook and left a disturbance along its wake.

Heavy footsteps fleeing deeper in the woods.

Beaux was positive he heard Geraldo's scream for he had heard the scream so many times while goofing off or pulling "bro" business and pranks or wrestling or screaming for the sake of screaming.

The scream was cut short, though, faint and muffled, as if whoever was doing the screaming had something obstructing his windpipe.

Regardless, Beaux knew it was Geraldo.

The Strawberry Moon was full and bright and cast enough light for Beaux to locate a trail in the woods.

Before entering the woods, Beaux noticed the ground and how the grass before the woods was flattened. With his eyes, he traced the fresh trail back up the soft incline which lead up to Tad, who appeared unconscious next to the dumpster behind the bar.

Guided by pale moonlight, Beaux crept farther into the woods, making sure to watch his step. Even the very notion of getting laid tonight was still bubbling through his mind, despite the blood running cold in his body. He'd find out the person—or persons—responsible for slashing Tad and then, he'd kick the shit out of them and then tap some ass and then sleep like a baby.

Strangely, the woods turned silent all of a sudden.

With the thought of the two chicks waiting around—and possibly catching an Uber back home—Beaux quickened his pace.

"Geraldo, dude, this ain't funny, man. Someone fucked with Tad. Now, quit you're fuckin' around. Geraldo? You there?"

Finally, a response but not the kind Beaux was expecting.

Beaux rushed over to Geraldo, who was lying behind dense vegetation. After clearing away the weeds and branches, he found Geraldo in such an incapacitated state that he was afraid to touch him. He had similar lacerations running along the side of his face but much deeper than the one on Tad's chest and underneath all of the gore, he witnessed one of Geraldo's glossy dark eyes that was glistening in the pale moonlight staring up at him like a doll. Both of his arms, as well as his legs were positioned in angles, which contradicted the normal flexibility of any arm or leg. The jagged, curled bones from his ribcage were broken and protruding from the side of his body. His guts were exposed as well and draped over both sides of his body as well as intertwined around his hands as if, for a moment, he tried to stuff them back into his body but didn't have the strength.

"Who the fuck did this to you?" cried Beaux, the couple of beers from earlier that day bringing out a bottled-up kind of rage that he had on reserve for moments such as these. He was still young, after all, and he could easily call upon such aggression.

With his fists clenched tight, Beaux Dumas, whom his friends enthusiastically called "Chevy" because he was built like one, despite having rhymed with a word that every single Louisianan knew all too well over these past few years, was ready to throw down, ready to take on, and conquer, whatever person or animal had torn through his friend—at this point, the line separating man and animal no longer existed and for Beaux, the two were the same.

As Geraldo took his final breaths, all of Beaux's answers came in the form of a bloodcurdling hiss directly over his shoulder.

Back at Suck The Head, Missy and August stepped out of the bathroom and were both greeted by the sounds of the song "Baker Street" by Gerry Rafferty.

The clownish bartender, "Swerve," who had been growing out a mustache for the past three months for an upcoming role on a local TV show *Only One Life To Live*, was playing the air saxophone while, once more, Missy's eyes turned toward that same creepster, who was sipping on the tall glass of an IPA.

"Ready, ladies?" Hunchback said from the open doorway.

Missy and August walked outside.

On the way out, she glanced over her shoulder at the older lady, who, in return, acknowledged Missy with a subtle wink of the eye.

"Let's go, ladies," Hunchback said, winding his hand like a reel.

Missy faced forward and said to Hunchback, "So, does it always get like this lit after closing?"

Hunchback rolled his eyes at the bartender Swerve's nightly routine and said with a mild disgust to Missy and August, "Freakin' Swerve and his Eighties music. He does this every night after we close. Dude's still living in the past."

"Seventies, *not* Eighties," Missy corrected, as she drew a confused expression from Hunchback. "My dad, he listens to this shit all the time."

Swerve pulled one of the waitresses from counting tonight's tips and started dancing with her.

Missy modestly shrugged.

"But hey," she said, "fuck 'adapt or die.' Ain't a goddamn thing wrong with livin in the past, right?"

"Good night, ladies," Hunchback said, as he directed the two women toward the parking lot.

Missy caught half of a circular tattoo, which appeared to be a serpent, above a barcode tattoo along the underside of

Hunchback's wrist underneath the sleeve of his wind-breaker.

In her slightly drunken daze, she drifted off and got hella-deep while thinking about that tattoo—the barcode, that is. Maybe it was a sweet perfection of Jello shots and draft beer that had forced Missy into a more critical think-ing stage. Or, maybe she was coming off a buzz. Whatever the case, her mind raced, each idea running like a current of electricity through a wiry mess of thoughts and coming close to pinpointing exactly what would possess someone, *this here man*, to wear a fairly common identification as a tattoo on his wrist. *Was it something symbolic?* A barcode represented a product. She wasn't into symbols—or flags for that matter. Symbols were only for the symbol-minded.

As Missy shrugged off her theory and stepped outside, she swore she heard Beaux screaming over the blaring mu-sic.

She turned to August, "You hear that?"

"Hear what?"

Missy scanned the parking lot until she spotted Beaux's Durango.

With a blank face, she faced Hunchback.

"The guys we were with, did they come back inside?" she asked Hunchback.

Hunchback shook his head.

"Nah," he said, folding his arms across his chest.

Missy was expecting more from the bouncer, like a more detailed answer, but all he gave her was a similar look her father would give her whenever he was disappointed.

"Just call him," August suggested.

"Right," Missy said and scrolled through the contact list on her phone while venturing out into the parking lot.

"You find him?"

She found one contact that looked newer.

"Red Shirt?"

"Is that a name?"

"Who the hell is Red Shirt?"

Missy read out the number. It was local.

"Red Shirt," August said. "He was wearing a red shirt."

"Why in the world would he *not* put his name in my phone?" asked Missy.

"I dunno," August said. "Looks are easier to remember than names."

"That's ridiculous—"

"—He's a guy," she said. "They're weird like that. I mean, how many times have you forgotten a guy's name?"

"So, I'm weird?"

"No," August said, her cheeks clouding red. "I'm just saying that I don't recall him saying your name throughout the entire night."

Missy had nothing.

Because, for once, August was right on this one thing.

"I tell you what, Missy," August said playfully. "How much you wanna bet he didn't remember our names?"

She pulled out her purse and dug through her wallet.

All she had was a five and some change.

"Five dollars?" asked August.

Missy shook August's hand.

"You're on."

Inside Suck The Head, Swerve directed his attention toward one of his most loyal customers who was sitting at the bar.

"You're scaring away the customers," he said jokingly.

The older lady whom Missy had been carefully eyeballing from a distance all night looked around the bar, snorted.

"You ain't got no customers," she said grumpily.

The next track "Right Down the Line" came on but only played for a couple of seconds before Swerve first caught a glimpse of those beady eyes, which were burning a hole right through him, and then the slack-jawed, loosey-goosey gawk of a dead woman. He paused Gerry Rafferty and searched for a more fitting song to play in the bar. He came across Mötley Crüe's "Shout At The Devil," but she appeared as if she had already been shouting out at her own devils.

While he scrolled through a playlist of Seventies tracks on a digital jukebox called Touch-a-Tune, the older lady threw her head in a nod.

"Hey, Swerve City," she slurred, "mind taking one last request before I call it a night?"

"The stage is all yours, Mama." The bartender spun the towel until it was as tight as a rope and flung it over his shoulder. "What will it be, Ms. Necro?"

Swerve reached into his back pocket and pulled up the relatively new Touch-a-Tune app on his smartphone.

"Mind?" the older lady known as "Ms. Necro" said and held out her knobby left hand.

Swerve placed the smartphone on the bar in front of Ms. Necro. All five of her gnarly fingernails were the color of aged wood and she ended up using the flat part of her finger to scroll through the list of songs. She pulled up the Seventies, *not Eighties*, Hits: first starting with Seals and Crofts, Carole King, Jigsaw, Heart, Starbuck, Harry Chapin, England Dan, John Ford Coley, Carly Simon, and then, finally. . .

Swerve said impatiently, "While we're young."

Finally, she played Barbra Streisand's "My Heart Belongs To Me" from the album *Superman* and handed the smartphone back to Swerve.

"There," she snapped, as she took a sip of her IPA. "You can have your little toy back."

"You know how to chose 'em, Mama," he said, pocketing the phone.

Ms. Necro couldn't tell whether or not Swerve was being sarcastic; nonetheless, she smiled, displaying her yellow-stained teeth.

During the song, the smile slowly faded from her face. She sat quietly at the bar, not saying a word, not even moving a muscle. She had completely zoned out, her eyes watering from the very thought of a past love.

Once the song was finished playing on the digital jukebox, Swerve planted his hands along his hips, tilted his head to the side, and stared at the sad drunk at the bar, as if, in a way, he was phrasally looking down on Ms. Necro.

"Where y'at, Necro?" asked Swerve.

He was asking her not where she was at—obviously, at Suck The Head—but where she was at, mentally that is.

Ms. Necro snapped from the wet memory.

"Huh?"

"That's fuckin' depressing," Swerve said to Ms. Necro. "Now, if you'll excuse me, I'm gonna go home and slit my wrists." He whipped out his phone yet again and searched for yet another song. "Got something you might like," he said and played the track "More Than a Feeling" by the band Boston.

Ms. Necro shrugged.

"Yeah," she said. "They're a'ight."

Outside in the parking lot, Missy decided to send Red Shirt a text after checking the inside of the Durango and coming up empty.

August tilted her head slightly and listened carefully for a ring tone.

Over Boston, she heard a *da-ding* sound coming from the woods.

"Wait," August said. "I thought I heard something. Text him again."

Following her original text "Where r u," Missy texted: ????

August heard the same *da-ding* coming from, of all places, the woods.

Inching away from the parking lot to the woods, August said, "Again."

Missy sent the same "?" text.

"Any response?" asked August.

"Nope."

"Hey, Red Shirt!" August shouted out. "Quit fuckin' around! We're ready to leave now!"

August didn't get any response.

"Just call the fool," August suggested.

"Good idea," Missy said and called Red Shirt.

In the dark woods, a phone started to ring.

"There," August said, pointing in the general direction of the sound.

Missy followed August toward the woods.

"Are you sure about this, August?" asked Missy, still skeptical about entering the woods.

August waved in Missy.

"Why don't we go get Hunchie Boy?"

"Forget it," August said, as she took a step into the woods. "He's probably taking a leak. You know how some guys get stage fright."

Again, Missy didn't budge.

August slumped her shoulders.

"Are you coming?"

"I'll just wait here—"

"—Really? You're gonna let me go into the dark-ass woods all by myself?"

"A'ight, geez," Missy said and followed August into the woods.

As the two got closer to the sound of the phone ring, August stopped in her tracks and shouted out, "Hey, Red Shirt! Where are you?"

Nothing.

"We're close," Missy said, her voice trembling. "Really close."

While hunched under a tree branch, August surveyed the surroundings and strangely, coming from the opposite direction in which the phone was ringing, she witnessed the pale glow of a smartphone on the ground.

"There!" she pointed.

She hurried over to the phone, Missy staying close to her friend, who acted as if she had taken over the role as leader.

August picked up a smartphone, which was covered with blood. She silenced the phone with a swipe left, which left behind a streak of blood along the screen. She ignored the blood all over her hand and used the phone's flashlight to inspect the area.

"Where is he?" asked Missy while clinging to August.

Missy's question was answered as soon as August shined the flashlight on the frozen ghostly face of Beaux, who was lying lifelessly on the ground.

August tracked the light below his face.

All she saw was red everywhere.

And it wasn't just his shirt.

August's scream was contagious. The scream spread to Missy. Then, Missy took off first. August closely followed. Screaming and waving their arms around in the air as if they were batting away mosquitoes, the two ran back the same way they came. They followed the hook of ABBA's "SOS."

SINCLAIR LEPRIEUR
PRESENT DAY

EVERY first Thursday of the month a group of botany students from Churner College led by college professor, Dr. Martello Gooch, made an afternoon road trip to the Wyatt Whyte Park, a fairly new edition to the parish which had a six mile long greenway that circled around Lake Wilshire where gators were known to frequent, as well as turtles and white cranes, to observe and study the native orchid, as well as other rare species along the wetlands.

On arrival, Dr. Gooch couldn't emphasize enough about watching where his students stepped and making sure to avoid walking too close to the plants in order to prevent not only trampling any of the seedlings, which they may not be able to see with the naked eye, but also smothering the roots that the plants needed to survive. Each group separated, spread out, and followed the universal "buddy system," which was never wander alone.

Wearing rubber knee-high boots to stomp through bogs, two students, Faith and Jed, were on the lookout for an elusive *Platanthera integra*, also known as the "yellow fringe-less orchid," due to its bright yellow flowers.

Jed briefly strayed away from Faith's reach and came across a small walkable embankment along Lake Wilshire.

In between thick, swollen roots along the base of a *Nyssa biflora*—or swamp tupelo—perched a pink *Pogonia ophioglossoides*, a species of orchid normally found in wet pine savannas or among wiregrass and longleaf pine in stretches of flatwoods. The sight alone of the flowering plant, which was commonly referred among the botany community as the "snakemouth orchid," warranted Jed's attention. Jed could've stayed safely on dry land and avoided dipping his legs into the water altogether; however, the snakemouth orchid was on the water-side of the tree and there was very little ground to stand on.

As Jed eased deeper into the water and walked along the side of the swamp tupelo facing Lake Wilshire, his mind ventured off somewhere for a moment and he started to wonder how a flower, like the snakemouth orchid, wound up in such an unusual place, which provided very little ground to thrive. Flowering plants, ones whose pollen was often spread through the travel of bees, had a strange way of winding up in spots where one wouldn't normally find. And the thought alone excited Jed.

"Hey, Faith," Jed hollered out, as he sloshed his way through the murky water. "Come quick!"

In no time, Faith stopped jotting down notes on her clipboard and rushed over to Jed, who was only a few steps away from the snakemouth orchid.

"What is it?" asked Faith, relieved to find Jed in one piece.

From the tone of his voice, the first thing that ran through her mind was gator. Even though she proudly wore her green thumb on her sleeve and so desperately wanted to be a part of a tedious profession where you were often left at nature's mercy, the idea still disturbed her.

"Snakemouth—"

"—Did you say snake?"

"No. The plant."

"Where?"

Out of breath, Jed pointed at the orchid sticking out of the base of the swamp tupelo.

"Right there," he said and arrived at the base of the tree.

As he leaned in closer for a better look at the snakemouth orchid, he suddenly felt something poking him along the side of his thigh. He redirected his attention downward and saw what first looked like an old, dirty ball bobbing in the murky water.

"Jed?" Faith said, her voice trembling. "What'd you find?"

"I dunno," he mumbled.

Jed reached down and poked at the ball and immediately realized, as soon as the other side of the ball presented itself, that it was no ball. His eyes locked into the two gaping black holes as well the teeth, which were still intact and appeared like tiny, crooked woodchips.

Twitching in a seizure-like pace from the sight of the human skull surfacing from the lake, Jed grabbed whatever he could find, which happened to be part of a root above him, and frantically pulled himself from the water.

With his skin turning as white as milk, he stumbled over to Faith, who tended to him.

"Jed, what'd you see?" asked Faith.

Jed was shaking, his eyes still and wide.

"Jed?"

With his face long and slacked, he turned to Faith.

"You look like you just saw a ghost," Faith said, acknowledging the color—or lack of color in Jed's face.

Once more, Jed tried to find the words.

But even something as common as speaking felt like a task in itself.

✳

TEN minutes later after the shocking discovery at Lake Wilshire, the Calssier Parish Sheriff's Office received a telephone call from Dr. Gooch.

It wasn't exactly considered a slow day, more like a "when-duty-calls" kind of day.

"You found *what*?"

As though Deputy Scooter Twiggs was hard of hearing, he had the professor repeat his explanation.

The deputy finally registered what he had heard and told Dr. Gooch to wait on the line for a second while he grabbed the sheriff.

Deputy Twiggs removed his feet from the top of the desk and spun his chair around toward Sheriff Donovan Barbee, who was brewing himself a cup of afternoon coffee by the open break room, which happened to be a small recess with a fridge, a microwave, and a countertop, than an actual room per se.

From the exhaustion worn on his face, the sheriff was experiencing what was commonly known around the office for those who worked first shift as that "three o'clock feeling."

"Donnie," the deputy said with the telephone draped over his shoulder, "you won't believe this. . . "

Donovan planted a hand over his hip and shifted his weight to one side of his body.

"Now what, Twiggy?"

N

NOT too long after the call, Sheriff Barbee and Deputy Darlington Afolabi, whom the sheriff had specifically chosen due to his more reserved temperament which was best suited for handling more "sensitive" situations, arrived at Wyatt Whyte Park where several deputies, who were patrolling the area at the time the call was made, gathered statements from students. The two main stars, Jed and Faith, who were receiving the most attention from other students, kept mostly to themselves, despite nagging questions coming from the class clown, Chaz, who often acted as if taking Dr. Gooch's course was based out of spite for his parents and was two awkward racially-sensitive jokes away from being kicked out of the class. One of the students held his stiff arm outward, shielding Faith like a parking gate, and told Fuzz to back off "or else." From the redness clouding in his cheeks, it was clear that the nickname never quite sat well with Chaz.

Chaz threw up his hands and finally, backed off.

One of the deputies escorted Dr. Gooch and his two students, Faith and Jed, to the sheriff and his deputy.

Upon greeting, the sheriff turned to Deputy Afolabi, and in a spur of the moment, asked, "By the way, I was meaning to ask you, Darlington: How's ya mama holdin' up?"

"Better now," he said, "after she finally received treatment."

"Still don't know the identity of Mister Anonymous who paid for her treatment?"

Deputy Afolabi shook his head.

"Nope," he said.

"Well, she got herself an angel lookin' after her."

"Or someone who thinks he's an angel," the deputy said grimly.

"Thanks for coming, Sheriff Barbee," Dr. Gooch said after the deputy spoke freely. Dr. Gooch shook the sheriff's hand; and when it came time to acknowledge his deputy, he only gave him a timid nod of the head. "Darlington," he said, his demeanor turning way more serious in nature yet remaining civil, "good to see you as always."

The deputy nodded back.

"Sir—"

"—So, what we have here?" asked Sheriff Barbee.

Dr. Gooch acknowledged Jed, who was still shaken up.

"Jed here was the one who found the remains," Dr. Gooch said in a fatherly way, as his voice sounded like a gentle touch.

"How you doing, son?" asked the sheriff.

"Despite the fact that I'll probably like never sleep again. . . fine, I guess."

"Well, that's why man invented Ambien."

It wasn't actually a joke, but it came off as one.

The mood was way too tense.

"Jed," Dr. Gooch said, remaining calm, "if you can, please tell Sheriff Barbee what you told me."

"Yeah, right," Jed said, sighing and running his hand through his hair, "I was over there." He pointed to the crowd of deputies who were marking off the scene with yellow caution tape. "I saw a snakemouth orchid along the water. So, I decided to climb down into the water. That's when I saw. . . you know. I remember stepping on something hard below the water, like maybe a tree branch, so I didn't think anything of it. . . "

The thought alone of stepping on a bone, possibly an ulna or femur, stole the words from Jed's mouth.

"What compelled you to get in the water?" asked the sheriff.

"Like I said, I saw a rare snakemouth orchid," Jed said, the panic creeping in. "I thought if I could reach the orchid from the other side of the tree, then I get a better look at it." His eyelids fluttered, his eyeballs bouncing like pinballs along the sides of his sockets. He looked up at the sheriff with wide glossy eyes.

Dr. Gooch consoled Jed before he broke down yet again and faced the sheriff, who, in return, gave the doctor a nod.

"Are we through here, Donovan?" asked Dr. Gooch.

"Yeah, we're through," Sheriff Barbee said. "If you need anything, just let us know."

Dr. Gooch walked Jed and Faith back to the other classmates.

"Poor kid," Deputy Afolabi said to the sheriff.

"Well," the sheriff returned with a sigh, "let's see it, shall we?"

The deputy walked Sheriff Barbee to the site where the human remains were discovered.

As soon as Sheriff Barbee witnessed the human skull with those two black empty sockets directly staring back at him, as well as other skeletal bones entangled and wrapped around wiry roots and vegetation, he turned to his loyal deputy and keeping his composure, said, "Call up Ronnie, will ya? Let's get some divers down here ASAP."

"Yes, sir," Deputy Afolabi said and stepped away to use the phone.

Sheriff Barbee rested both hands along his hips.

He thought about how much he could use another cup of coffee.

N

SINCE Ronnie only lived a few minutes from the park, it didn't take long for him and his two-man diving crew to show up in their truck that was hauling a boat on a trailer.

Without wasting time, they suited into their diving equipment and pulled the remains from Lake Wilshire and laid them all out on a blue tarp on the grass.

Ronnie noticed what looked like a large fang-like tooth about the size of an average human pinkie finger wedged along the base of the skull.

"Hey, Donnie," Ronnie said, pulling the goggles from his face, "you might want to take a look at this."

With his gloved hand, he held up the tooth for the sheriff to see.

"Gator?" said the sheriff, the sides of his face wrinkled in perplexity.

Alligator was probably the last animal on Ronnie's mind.

"Doesn't look like it," he hesitated.

Then, clarified, "Whatever it is, it's big."

N

LATER that evening, after all of the remains of the unidentified body, which were collected at Wyatt Whyte Park and transported to the Crime Lab, Sheriff Barbee, who hadn't taken a break all day, not even to eat, met up with seasoned coroner Susanne Gloss. Susanne, who hadn't seen the sheriff in quite some time—in fact, she couldn't remember the last night she saw him—went over the basic greetings, asking about the sheriff, his family, asked him how his daughter, who was away at an out-of-state college somewhere in the heart of Texas on a full ride from an athletic scholarship (apparently, she was *that* good at volleyball, like the kind of good that lead her high school team to the State Finals), was doing, as well as the missus, which received the same answer as the last time the sheriff saw Susanne. "She's hanging in there," Sheriff Barbee said, immediately searching for another subject. He found one, a sparkling gold one that looked as though it cost about as much as a car on Susanne's wrist. "That's a nice bracelet. New?" he asked, nodding at the piece of jewelry on her wrist.

"Oh," Susanne said, holding up her wrist, "*this*? Landon received a nice bonus this year. Plus, we got a lot of money back in tax returns. Let's just say that Uncle Sam was good to us this year."

"Every single time I scrounge up enough money to buy Cheyenne something nice for her birthday, she's always telling me to take it back where I got it and for me save the money for something more important."

"Well," Susanne said, shrugging, "she sounds like a smart woman."

"Yeah, well," the sheriff trailed off, hanging his head and losing confidence. "I reckon so. So, Twiggy said you found something. . . "

"Right," Susanne said with perfect timing. "As a matter of fact, I did."

After Susanne slipped on a pair of plastic gloves, she handed the box to Sheriff Barbee, who, in return, slipped on a pair as well.

Susanne carefully pulled the white sheet from the scattered bones, as well as the skull, which were lying on a metal table.

"For starters," she said and showed Sheriff Barbee one bone in particular, the humerus, "the lower part of the humerus was completely shattered."

"The kid who found the bones said he thought he stepped on a branch while he was walking through the water."

"Unless he weighed a ton, this wasn't broken by someone stepping on it."

"What are you saying, Susanne?" the sheriff asked, more serious.

Susanne picked up the humerus and held it underneath the light for closer inspection.

She pointed out for the sheriff, "You see the indentation along the break?"

Sheriff Barbee followed the tip of Susanne's index finger. "I think so."

"Now," she said, placing aside the humerus and picking up the skull, as well as the strange tooth, "look at the back of the skull." She turned the skull over and showed the sheriff a similar indentation along the base of the skull. Then inserted the tooth inside the marking. The tooth fitted perfectly, like a piece of a jigsaw puzzle.

"So, what are you saying, Susanne? The arm was bitten off?"

She placed the humerus back underneath the scapula and pointed at the vacant spot on the table.

"Hence why the rest of his left arm is missing," she said and took a moment to gather her thoughts. "Don, this man's bones are completely riddled with bite marks. I found several cracks in the ulna and radius of his other arm, which appear to be defensive wounds."

"Who was he?" asked the sheriff.

"We're looking at a male possibly between his thirties and forties. Based on the condition of the bones, I'd say the remains are at least thirty years old."

"You're telling me they've been lying out there for that long and nobody has seen them?"

"You know I don't like to guess. But if I had to, I'd say the boy who found these disrupted the environment around the remains, causing them to surface—"

"—What about the tooth?" asked Sheriff Barbee.

"If you're wondering if the tooth belongs to an alligator," Susanne paused for a moment as if she was choosing her next words carefully, "my answer is no."

"No?"

For a while now, Sheriff Barbee had gotten so used to hearing that an alligator was responsible for possible animal attacks that anything other than an alligator raised alarm.

"In fact," she said, grabbing hold of her bracelet, "this tooth doesn't belong to any species that I've ever seen or heard. . . " Susanne could barely muster out the word *heard* from her lips. She hung her head and struggled to look the sheriff in the eye.

Sheriff Barbee knew a woman like Susanne Gloss, a woman who had fought overseas in Iraq, who had laid her body on the line in order to protect her country and in doing so, was riddled with shrapnel from a roadside bomb, resulting in the removal of her left kidney—whenever thanked for her brave service, Susanne always lightened the mood by joking that you only needed one anyway. Considering her background and how she spent most of her time surrounded by The Dead opposed to The Living, it was fair to say that Susanne wasn't the type of person who got easily rattled as most people. But she was petrified.

Not only could the sheriff see it on her face, but he could also sense it, as if the fear in itself was a singular entity that made tenacious women such as Susanne Gloss tremble at the knees.

"Is there something you're not telling, Susanne?" asked the sheriff.

Susanne started to talk, then shook her head and blushed.

"Forget it," she said, as if laughing would remove such suspicion. "It's nothing."

Sheriff Barbee, who wasn't laughing, said, "Tell me."

"It's nothing, really."

"I've known you for too long, Susanne, to know when something is bothering you."

Once more, Susanne struggled to look the sheriff in the eyes. The redness in her cheeks brightened. She did this back and forth thing where she'd look up and then hang her head and try to laugh away the awkwardness, as if the thought alone was greater than any punch line.

Susanne could feel the sheriff's gaze pounding down on her.

"Okay," she said, holding up her hand. She gathered herself, her thoughts.

"Remember, Susanne. I'm a friendly."

"I know you are."

"Whatever it is you have to tell me—"

"—When I was a little girl, my grandmother used to tell me about a creature that lived in the woods behind our house called the Shadow Monster—*Monstre de l'ombre*, she called it. I remember her telling me that this Shadow Monster came out every full moon to feed."

"What?" Sheriff Barbee said amusingly. "Like a were-wolf?"

"Sort of. I believe it was her way of telling me to never go out in the woods alone, to scare me. I was a tomboy, and like all tomboys, I had a knack for sticking my head in places where it didn't belong. For me, it was the wetlands gathering insects and whatnot. My grandmother, however, did not approve of me going into the woods, especially alone. So, I believe, she created a monster in order to strike fear in me. For a while, I actually believed that there was something in the woods, something larger and deadlier than any man or woman."

Susanne's eyes drifted in thought. She specifically remembered a time when she was nine years old standing at the edge of her backyard and staring at the dark woods. It was twilight and the sunlight hadn't quite faded into darkness and there was still enough light shining through the trees to cast out the silhouette of a massive creature lurking behind a bush. She specifically remembered the two narrow red eyes of the Shadow Monster staring back at her. *Those red eyes*, she thought.

Till this day, she questioned whether or not the eyes were real or if it was just the imagination of a nine-year-old flaring through her growing mind.

Why is it that the moments spent with grandparents—in this case, Susanne's grandmother—*are ones that stay with you the most, even as a grownup?*

"What are you getting at, Susanne?" asked Sheriff Barbee, his words cutting through the silence.

Susanne snapped from her trance.

She said with a straight face, "I'm saying it could be anything."

N

THE following morning Donovan was up and about earlier than usual to prepare breakfast in bed for Cheyenne, whom he had been married to for forty-two and a half years with an emphasis on the *half*. He skipped breakfast himself and settled for only a couple of bites of dry toast and then he was ready to carpe diem.

As Donovan did every single morning, he kissed his wife on her forehead and told her he loved her more than the world itself. He ran his coarse hand along the top of her smooth scalp. The hair was punk-rocker short—or what boomers like Barbee would refer to as your classic "buzz cut"—and was starting to fill in rather nicely, two months after having stopped her second round of chemotherapy treatment that nearly killed her this time around. Regardless of the minor setback, his Anne was cancer-free—in fact, she kicked cancer's ass back to the Stone Age. In a way, Cheyenne was starting to dig her new increasingly fashionable do, which complimented her face and made it look at least ten years younger.

As for Donovan, deep down inside he missed his wife's lush brunette hair.

Not like he had any say-so in the matter.

He preferred to sleep in a bed, opposed to the alternative.

Which was more than likely the couch.

A much softer word that often replaced "dog house."

N

WALKING toward the office, Donovan ran into Sinclair Leprieur's mayor, Audire Debose, as well as the billionaire investor Kenneth Satterwhite, who contributed a good chunk of his wealth into rebuilding and revitalizing Sinclair Leprieur.

Satterwhite was wearing a navy blue sweater over a plaid collar shirt, which, except for the collar, never saw the light of day.

Despite having a net worth of somewhere between ten and twenty billion, he dressed no different than any white collared man. The word on the street was that Satterwhite made his first million at the age of twenty-nine. Satterwhite was only a decade younger than Donovan. Yet, throughout years of constantly watching the stock market rise and fall, then fall dramatically during the last administration, clearly took a toll on his body. He had a much older face, too, more wrinkles, deeper and longer crow's feet, and skin as tough as old leather. He had both of his hands in his pockets and was glancing around Main Street as if he was mentally playing a wicked game of *The Sims* inside his head, moving around and adding to older structures that had been here ever since Donovan was a young boy. Those same structures that were a part of Donovan, structures that held him back or helped him grow, structures that shaped his arduous journey to becoming the sheriff of Sinclair Leprieur.

The two men appeared casual yet *highly* motivated. From the way the mayor, a short man who made up for his small, well-below average size with his big gulp size of a mouth, pointed at the various older—which was a more polite version of saying old and rundown—buildings along Main Street, it was evident to the sheriff that Kenneth Satterwhite was planning to what the socially-aware, mostly considerate yet, at times, foxy beings of society called "gentrify" the rest of Sinclair Leprieur's downtown. He already turned South Dock into a consumer's paradise, which had brought in more shopping malls over shopping malls of outside corporate businesses and interests, which drove away a lot of the local, family-owned businesses.

The mayor's main focus remained on the Old Mill at the edge of Main Street. Rumor had it that Satterwhite was planning on buying the property and flipping it. There had been some chatter that he was going to turn the Old Mill into a bowling alley. There was another rumor floating around the town that he was going to tear down the Old Mill and replace it with a huge entertainment center, including an arcade for adults, as well as clearing the land behind the Old Mill to put in affordable yet "luxury"-style lofts and condominiums, which would help attract a much younger demographic, mostly young professionals and whatnot, to the area. Like many of the locals who stayed in Sinclair Leprieur during this so-called transition, Donovan had his opinions about the idea but never voiced them.

Donovan still couldn't—and didn't want to—believe that a town such as Sinclair Leprieur, a place he rightfully called "home" for sixty-six years and counting, was about one or two big-box stores away from becoming another one of those towns like so many he and Cheyenne often passed on I-10 while driving to Panama City, Florida, every Thanksgiving to visit Cheyenne's folks, who had lived in Jackson, Wyoming, for most of their lives before they came down with what Cheyenne's father called the "Florida Itch." It was only a matter of time before statues of Satterwhite started popping up around town, in front of town hall or the library, even next to the park benches where he and Cheyenne shared kisses and past high school dreams at the City Loop. Eventually, Satterwhite was going to buy Sinclair Leprieur—if he hadn't done so already—and name it after himself.

As soon as the two men stopped talking to one another on the sidewalk, the same one that led directly toward the office, and redirected their attention toward the sheriff, he had no other choice than to drop a line.

"Good morning, gentlemen," the sheriff said respectfully.

"Sheriff Barbee," Mayor Debose said merrily.

Satterwhite needed no introduction.

"Mayor Debose," the sheriff said and nodded at Satterwhite, "Kenneth."

"The mayor here says that you guys had quite an interesting day yesterday at Lake Wilshire," Satterwhite said, as if he was trying to strike up small talk with a sheriff who had very little time for small talk.

"Guess you can say that," the sheriff said hesitantly. "But, don't worry, we'll get to the bottom of what happened. It's our job. Right, Mayor?"

"That's right." The mayor showed off the sheriff to Satterwhite, as if he was for sale. *Go ahead and just name a price, you rich asshole.* "Sheriff Barbee was born and raised right here in Sinclair Leprieur and if there's one man you want on your side, you're looking at him."

"I don't see how you guys do it," Satterwhite said. "Me, I have a tendency to faint from a paper cut."

Sheriff Barbee could barely bring himself to laugh at Satterwhite's joke—and a poor attempt at a joke, it was.

"Well, nobody ever said it gets any easier," Sheriff Barbee said humbly, as he started to make his way toward the parish office.

The sheriff excused himself from the two men; however, from Satterwhite's interest in the sheriff, he appeared as if he still had a lot to talk about with Sheriff Barbee.

For now, it had to wait.

Once the sheriff walked into the parish office and greeted several of his fellow lawmen, Deputy Twiggs, who had not only been skimming over the details of yesterday's report behind the other deputies' backs, but also driving Deputy Afolabi up the wall with his gazillion questions about the corpse found at Lake Wilshire, was swift to make a suggestion.

"You know, Sheriff," he said, "I had some ideas about the remains you pulled from Lake Wilshire."

On a corkboard behind the deputy's desk, he had four hand drawn, dark and heavy graphite sketches of serpent-like "upright" creatures that looked as if they had been drawn by four different amateur sketch artists who couldn't draw a single straight line to save their lives.

"What now, Twigs?" Deputy Brown said foolishly from the other side of the office. "It was the *Swamp Thing*."

"How about that one creature, the one from Black Lake?" other deputy said, as if Deputy Brown's comment made a ping-pong effect.

"Black Lagoon?" Deputy Brown corrected. "It's the *Creature from the Black Lagoon?*"

"We have a busy day ahead of us, Deputy," Sheriff Barbee said, as if he was already losing his patience with not just the one deputy but *all* of his deputies. It wasn't even noon yet, either. "Let's not get ahead of ourselves, all right?"

"You know who could help us out on this one?" Deputy Twiggs pronounced, which drew more silence and empty faces around the office. "This is right up his alley. Considering those remains were found at a park named after his father, the least we can do is reach out to him."

"No way," the sheriff snapped. "Not gonna happen."

"Zip knows all about these things—"

"—I don't even want to hear that man's name in my office, you got that?"

"But Sheriff, Zip could give us a hand—"

"—Saying his name three times ain't gonna make him magically appear. I'm not wastin' my time with that man. Understood?"

"But Sheriff. . . "

"You gotta be shittin' me, Twiggy," the sheriff said, his face reddening. "After what that goddamn jester did to one of my patrol cars?"

"The man was intoxicated, clearly."

"It was deliberate."

"But Sheriff, you know he can point us in the right direction."

Sheriff Barbee stopped, which caused Deputy Twiggs to stop walking along side him as well. The sheriff didn't say a word in return, didn't have to. All he did was give Twiggy a mean look that had him taking a step back.

Over the tense silence, Deputy Brown said tenaciously, "What about Bexley Hun?"

The name caused the sheriff's face to pucker in several different emotions.

"Bexley *Who*?"

"Hun," Deputy Brown said, her voice drawn out like a question.

"Excuse me."

Sheriff Barbee wasn't quite sure whether or not Deputy Brown was addressing him by the name "Hun." The notion alone disturbed him.

"No," the veteran deputy said. *"Hun.* Her last name is Hun."

"You know," Deputy Afolabi said, who was standing the closest to the sheriff, "the one from TV?"

"You know I don't watch TV."

"Think of her like Indiana Jones meets the Crocodile Hunter," Deputy Brown said to the sheriff. "She was involved in a terrible car crash about two years ago, but that didn't stop her from continuing her show—"

"—I heard about that."

"Woman's legit."

"Yeah. If only I had her drive. . . "

Deputy Brown drifted off for a minute as if she was thinking about all of the professions that she could've chosen and none of them involved being a cop.

"Right," Deputy Twiggs said from the corner of his mouth. "If you had her drive, Pamela, you climb Mount Everest—"

"—Funny."

Deputy Twiggs teased to the others, "Just imagine if *the* Bexley Hun came to Sinclair Leprieur?"

From Satterwhite determined to take over Sinclair Leprieur with his wallet to Twiggy and his Bexley Hun obsession, Sheriff Barbee was at his wits' end.

"Are you through?" asked the sheriff with that same look on his face.

The office got quiet again.

"Get back to work," Sheriff Barbee said and walked to his office. "What the hell did this world come to?" he mumbled to himself, as he closed the door behind him. He threw his jacket along the back of a chair, opened the blinds, sat down at his desk, and leaned back in his chair while staring at the parking lot outside the office. He couldn't help but contemplate the deputy's suggestion from the sight of what looked like two perfect strangers starting up a conversation as they passed by one another in front of the office. One of them, a recently widower in her sixties—"Ms. Cantberry," was her name and all he knew about her was that she recently retired a few months ago, a former algebra teacher turned grouchy civilian who made it her mission to complain about anything and everything, while, the other one, a laidback middle-aged man who was walking his Pomeranian, a yappy little thing—Donovan had only seen him a handful of times but he knew he was about to receive an ear load from the angry old bitch— couldn't have been more farther apart in personality; yet, as they continued to talk, the two appeared to enjoy each other's company.

On a whim, the sheriff sat upright, closed the blinds, and awakened his computer with a shake of the mouse. He typed in his seven digit password, which was Cheyenne's birthday, and gumshoed the name "Bexley Hun" in the search engine.

Pages and pages of TV celebrity Bexley Hun popped up on the screen.

He clicked on the VIDEOS tab and watched the first video that he could find, Episode 39 "The Legend of the Pango" from Season 3 of the hit TV show called *Unleashed: The Bexley Hun Show.*

In the video clip, Bexley was tracking down the mysterious Pangoliath—or "Pango"—a scaly cat-like nocturnal creature only found exclusively south of the Serengeti plain in the Udzamrundi Mountains, which was located in the United Republic of Tanzania, or most commonly known as Tanzania. The elusive Pango was said to be on the verge of extinction due to poachers hunting down the rare species for its plate-like keratin scales, which were in high demand among Chinese black markets. The scales were believed to have medicinal properties, from curing cancer to treating asthma. Back in the medieval times, the Pango's scales were used as protective coats of armor made from gilded scales.

With only a machete in her hand and the circular light from the camera acting as her only source of light, Bexley stomped her way through a dense tropical rainforest. The beam of light created a horror movie-like tension and the environment surrounding the light was covered in night darkness.

Bexley stopped chopping through thick vegetation and shrubbery and heard a *squeak*-like noise coming from inside a burrow. She threw up her hand, signaling in military-like fashion for her team to stop. She rotated around toward the cameraman, who, in return, switched off the light, which created a domino effect, cuing another cameraman, who, in return, switched on an infrared camera.

As Bexley crept closer to the burrow, she heard yet another sound, a rustling. Then, tiny footsteps. Another heat signature bloomed over the camera, one being Bexley's heat and the other, which was a smaller creature about the size of a cat, stalking closer to Bexley. Dropping her machete to the ground and showing the Pango that she wasn't a threat, she kneeled down to the ground. The Pango approached Bexley, skittishly at first, then once realizing she wasn't a threat, walked up to her. The other cameraman switched on his light, first shining it over the forest floor, then slowly bringing it to Bexley and the rare Pango.

In the "money" shot, Bexley was doing something that no human being had ever done to a Pango.

She was petting it.

Donovan was shocked by the video, not by Bexley's ballsy behavior, but by Bexley's appearance. She reminded him of his wife, either she was Native or had a parent or relative who was Native. *She looked just like Anne but much younger.* Both her dark, hazel eyes, like Cheyenne's, sat much farther apart on her face and looked non-Western, opposed to Donovan who looked as if he was one of many stylized versions of the Western look: rock-solid chin, sharp jawline, high cheekbones, fair skin, hair as red as hellfire. He couldn't help but click on other videos of Bexley going on adventures, including Bexley and crew filming a "Saq-uangi," which was also known as the elusive "Japanese Unicorn" based on its rarity and gentle nature or Bexley chasing after the "neon frog" in the Western Ghats, Sahyadri, along the southern coast of India, which looked more like a lighthearted episode due to Bexley's many failed attempts at catching the slick creature or signing with a charismatic, highly intelligent Minean Orangutan, which, according to

conservationists, was considered endangered due to defor-
estation, off a spit of an island of Mineo located in the
Philippines.

After spending at least an hour watching random episodes of *Unleashed* and learning about species that he had
never heard of before, like the Elephant rat, the Arabian
Eagle, the red-hooded mallard, the Colombian lion spider—which really made his skin crawl—or that ever so
adorable yellow-footed rhinoceros, Donovan couldn't believe where the time had gone.

He decided to stretch his legs by pacing around the office. He cracked open the blinds, which provided more
light into the office. He walked back to his desk and
opened the top drawer where he kept an evidence bag of
the strange tooth that was found at Lake Wilshire. He
held up the evidence bag in the rays of sunlight and started
to question whether or not Susanne was telling the truth.

In the back of his mind, there was always a *"what if"*
scenario.

Having given his blood, sweat, and tears for forty-three
years toiling away at a profession that strictly revolved
around facts, not theory, Sheriff Donovan Barbee—of all
people—knew that two words didn't exist in his line of
work.

MANHATTAN, NEW YORK

FACING the Hollywood-style vanity mirror in the open
wardrobe department while the lighting guys were adjusting their equipment, Bexley sat in a director's chair with
HUN written on the backrest.

Bexley zoned out as one of makeup artists patted away
the beads of sweat with a chemical-free, fragrance-free,
lint-free cotton round while another makeup artist, who
hadn't smiled or even batted a single eyelash ever since
Bexley arrived at the photo shoot, touched up Bexley's
foundation. She looked over the makeup on her face, the
mascara, the eye shadow, the lipstick, particularly the

shade of the lipstick—Bexley wouldn't be caught dead wearing that color, a bluish purple lipstick, out in public— all of it worn like a heavy mask covered in thorns. She felt nothing but antipathy toward her dolled-up appearance. She turned her eyes elsewhere and ran her fingers along the material of a colorful peafowl-like dress, which she was going to be wearing on the front cover of the upcoming controversial issue of the magazine BOLD &.

One of the wardrobe ladies, Corolla, who was adjusting the bluish-green bodice to cover up the wicked scar running along the side of her ribcage, noticed the nicotine patch on the side of Bexley's arm. She was tempted to ask her where she had gotten the scar, not the patch, if it was from the accident—where else would she have gotten such a nasty scar—but, considering she was on the clock, decided it was best left alone, a wrong place-wrong time sort of deal.

"I know what you're going through," Corolla said, her raspy voice making it abundantly clear to Bexley that she didn't have a cold. "Been there. Done that."

"Excuse me?"

She pointed at the patch.

"Right," Bexley said.

"I'm going on five years now with a cigarette."

"You miss it?"

"Only when I drink."

With her red-framed glasses worn at the tip of her nose, Corolla lowered her head and looked at Bexley with her natural, undressed eyes and smiled.

"I can take it off," Bexley suggested.

Corolla waved off the comment,

"No need," she said. "I can cover it up with the dress."

"Thanks."

"That's why I'm here, right?"

Bexley ignored all of the adjustments to her face and outfit and stared in the mirror. She didn't know the person who was staring back at her. In some way or another, she was locking eyes with a stranger in the reflection. The same stranger whom she swore she'd never ever become.

She didn't blame herself, though. Throughout the four years of stardom, not once did she point the finger at herself. She blamed "them." They were the ones who turned her into the person whom she so desperately loathed.

One of *Unleashed*'s several producers, Kristine Noakes, approached Bexley from behind.

"How's the shoot going so far?" asked Kristine, as she lowered her head into Bexley's range of vision.

"It's going," Bexley said to Kristine's warped reflection.

"Say, I was meaning to tell you earlier," Kristine said hesitantly over a pause, her voice sounding more serious. "After our last conversation, I got an interesting call from a sheriff named Donovan Barbee. He lives in a small town in Louisiana called Sinclair Leprieur. Ever heard of it?"

"I don't think so."

"Well, anyway, he wanted to know if you were interested in filming a show in Sinclair Leprieur. Apparently, there have been a lot of 'questionable' deaths in his town. He believes these deaths may be linked to a strange animal, a *mythical creature*—which was the word he used."

"Mythical creature, huh?" Bexley said, eager to roll her eyes.

"I'm going to send Gorg and Kopeck down there and see if it's worth looking into. If we can get the film permits—and that's a big IF—it could make for one heck of an edition to our next season 'America's Myths and Mysteries.'"

"You like saying that, don't you?"

"Well, it was *my* idea," Kristine said in a sort of pseudo-arrogance. "But hey, at the end of the day you have to give the audience what they want. What do you say?"

Bexley carelessly shrugged.

"Sure," she said. "Why not?"

"Thanks, Bex," Kristine said shortly. "By the way, you look fantastic."

Before Bexley had a chance to pull more information from Kristine, let alone thank her, Kristine already stepped away and started to mingle with other producers hanging around the set, which was made to look like an All-American backyard with real tall fescue grass, which had been shipped in all the way from Charlotte, North Carolina, an above-ground swimming, a Char-Broil grill, a patio with outdoor furniture, including a lawn chair and umbrella, a lawnmower, as well as various outdoor hardware.

Bexley pulled out her phone and gumshoed the name "Sinclair Leprieur."

In the results, she found a Wikipedia page. Then scrolled through pages and pages of links to articles on "Missing Children" from the 1970's to the early 80's.

Finally, she came across the town of *Sinclair Leprieur* highlighted in a book that was written by Wyatt Whyte III (*The Third*), who happened to be, based on photos of him taken at bookstores, events, and fundraisers, a local celebrity.

The book was about a creature—possibly the same mythical creature Sheriff Barbee spoke of—known as a werewolf snake. It had other names as well.

Such as "Swamp Devil."

Immediately, Bexley was interested in learning more about the creature.

Inside Bexley's head, a plan started to materialize.

For once in her life, she was able to take a step back to see the bigger picture.

And finally, everything started to make sense.

SINCLAIR LEPRIEUR
LATER THAT NIGHT

WHILE lounging in her burgundy La-Z-Boy, which had been with her ever since the turn of the century, Ms. Necro was watching *The Evil Dead* on a scratch-laced DVD that she bought from a bootlegger who ripped the movie from the Internet.

Within only the first ten minutes of the movie, she munched her way through an entire family-sized bag of Cheetos as well as pounded down nearly half a liter of Pepsi. She left behind cheesy fingerprints on everything she touched: the white cap along the top of the Pepsi; the sides of La-Z-Boy, the handle; a TV remote the size of one of those cop flashlights, which controlled the boxy, out-dated TV that was destined to live out the rest of its days on a dusty shelf in the very back of a Goodwill store before the inevitable haul to the dump where it would ultimately be picked apart by junkies and scrap dealers.

After she killed the Cheetos, she worked her way through a pack of Reeces—something about cheese and peanut butter that tasted nicely on her palate.

As Ms. Necro stuffed the whole Reeces cup into her mouth, the doorbell suddenly rang.

She paused midchew, the right side of her cheek bal-looning outward.

"Perfect timing, you slippery fugger muffin," Ms. Necro murmured to herself in annoyance. *My favorite part*, her favorite part of the movie which happened to be that con-troversial tree-rape scene.

Ms. Necro retracted the recliner and slammed the foot-rest back into the chair, making a loud *thu-chunk*. She sat up and stood to her feet, leaving behind an imprint of her petite body that, over two decades of heavy nights of lei-sure, had been molded to the seat. She reached across a junky coffee table and turned down the volume, leaving behind a cheesy, orange thumbprint on the down arrow button.

With the TV unsteadily screaming at a much lower vol-ume behind her, Ms. Necro used the most extreme precau-tion by grabbing a tiny squeaky toy from the bottom shelf of the side table.

All it took was one squeeze of the spiky hedgehog toy and Bubby would be on any intruder like white on rice. Beat carrying around a gun. After all, she had heard horror stories of past relatives accidentally shooting themselves in the face with a gun. The last thing she wanted was for his-tory to repeat itself.

With squeaky toy in hand, Ms. Necro answered the door.

The front porch light was out and all she could see was the tall unmoving but breathing silhouette of a man stand-ing before her.

She started to slowly make a fist over the squeaky toy no differently than an index finger tightening over the trigger of a pistol.

Satterwhite took a step forward into the flickering glow of the TV. The horrific screams of the young woman on TV came in and out due to a scratch on the DVD.

Ms. Necro relaxed her hand over the squeaky toy. She thought, *If scrotum-face here hadn't revealed himself a second sooner, than he would've been roadkill in the blink of an eye.*

"*You,*" Ms. Necro said, repulsed by Satterwhite's untimely appearance.

"I thought I told you I was coming by."

"You did," she said impudently.

Fugger muffin.

"Excuse me?"

Ms. Necro's eyes widened.

"Did I say that out loud?"

"Say what?"

"I forgot."

"Forgot what?"

"I forgot you were coming by."

Lackadaisically, Ms. Necro walked back inside and left the front door open for Satterwhite to enter. He barely took a step inside.

"Well, you just gonna stand there or you gonna let the bugs in?" asked Ms. Necro in a tetchy manner. "And close the door behind you!"

Satterwhite cautiously stepped inside the house and acted as if the floor was made of broken glass. Eventually, he closed the door behind him. Yet, he didn't bother walking any farther into the house than he needed to; instead, he remained suspiciously close to the front door.

"So, Mr. Fancy Pants," Ms. Necro said and left yet another cheesy fingerprint on the pause button, "wanna tell me what you doin' here?"

"I just wanted to make sure it was ready for tomorrow night."

"It?" Ms. Necro snarled. "What you mean 'It'?"

Satterwhite crept closer to the door as if he was planning a quick escape.

"Well, whatever it is," he said, his voice slightly trembling.

"*Well*, 'It' has a name, you know?"

"I wasn't aware."

"And it's a he."

"A 'he,'" Satterwhite said amusingly, slipped his hands into his pockets, and leaned back on his heels, as if, for a moment, he was listening to a child prattle on about imaginary witches and dragons. "I see. So, is he going to be ready for tomorrow night—"

"—Bubby," Ms. Necro said, as she grabbed the litter of Pepsi from the floor.

"I'm sorry."

"His name is Bubby."

"And will Bubby be ready for tomorrow night?"

"Ready?" Ms. Necro pinched her face, the bridge of her nose crinkled like a crumbled up piece of notebook paper. "You kiddin' me? Bubby's *always* ready; in fact, Bubby's ready to go right now." She took a swig of the Pepsi, savored it, then let out a burp. "That reminds me, Mr. Fancy Pants: Next time you decide to pop in, you might wanna give me a call beforehand like when you're on the way."

Satterwhite narrowed his eyes at Ms. Necro, who started to sound like a frog as she let out a series of burps and farts.

"I'll keep that in mind," Satterwhite said, holding back his disgust.

"Good," Ms. Necro chirped. "We wouldn't want Bubby mistaken you for an intruder. Now, would we?"

"No," he said. "Certainly not."

"Give me a sec, will you?" Ms. Necro said, walking away. "Lemme just grab a lil' snack from the fridge and then I'll take you to my Bubby."

A snack? Satterwhite furrowed his brow. *Is this bitch for real?*

"Not for me," Ms. Necro hollered out, as she walked into a kitchen covered in grime and a sink full of unwashed pots and pans, "for Bubs."

Ms. Necro stood in front of the fridge and washed down the leftover crumbs wedged between the back of her teeth with another swig of Pepsi. Along with all of the other trash and junk food wrappers scattered about, she tossed the bottle on top of the overflowing countertop and opened the fridge door.

Even across the living room, Satterwhite could see the odor emitting from the fridge. The odor was strong enough to force him to cover his nose and take small gulps of air through his mouth.

Ms. Necro reached inside the fridge and grabbed a cow's leg—still as raw as the day it was butchered—from the bottom shelf of the fridge.

"Should be thawed out by now," Ms. Necro mumbled to herself.

She removed the damp sheet of newspaper from the leg and held the hunk of meat up to her nose, gave it a whiff, and let out an innocent "Meh."

She closed the fridge door and exited the kitchen.

"What's the meat for?" asked Satterwhite, sounding more amused than concerned for his own safety.

Ms. Necro approached Satterwhite.

"It's either this or *the alternative*," she said and gave Satterwhite a once over as if she was suggesting that "he" might be that alternative.

The thought alone of being a menu item made him rethink the very notion of coming here in the first place. He canceled the thought and remained confident.

Ms. Necro flipped a light switch, which turned on a floodlight along the side of the house.

"Shall we?" said Ms. Necro, as she pointed at the door behind Satterwhite.

"After you," he said and opened the door for Ms. Necro.

"Such a sweetie," Ms. Necro said, smiling like a schoolgirl at Satterwhite as she passed by him.

Satterwhite followed Ms. Necro outside in the night darkness. They walked around the front of the house in the dark. The floodlight exposed some of the off-white, dirty, loose siding along the house. The front yard had weeds as tall as the average man and thick enough to get lost in. Satterwhite's fully loaded, midnight blue Beamer with what the dealer described "those neat little sensor thingies on the side view mirrors" was parked at the very edge of the gravel driveway, which was surrounded by woods. A place which was considered by most as being "out there."

The Beamer caught Ms. Necro's eye.

She was struck by a momentary ripple of disgust.

"Nice whip," she said. "You know, I've always fantasized about drivin' one myself."

"There's a lot of money on the line, lots at stake. If everything goes to plan," he said and stopped with Ms. Necro, "then soon that fantasy will become a reality. Believe me. You'll be swimming in wealth and be able to buy seven of these puppies, one for each day of the week. And that dark horse of ours will be living high off the hog."

No amount of money on the earth could buy her Bubby. That, she damn well knew. Satterwhite's choice in wording, particular that one word, *ours*, he used to convey the importance of the deal, caused Ms. Necro's lip to curl with rage.

"He don't particularly like swine," Ms. Necro said, once more eyeing Satterwhite from head to toe. "I'm trying to get him on a leaner diet, if you know what I mean."

Ms. Necro pulled her eyes away from Satterwhite and turned to the Beamer. Tickled by the very idea, she bit the corner of her lip.

Soon, the excitement wore off her face, unveiling a deeper sadness. Her eyes started to water. The cow leg nearly slipped from her grip.

"Is something wrong?" asked Satterwhite.

She ignored Satterwhite, caught the tears before they could reach her eyelids, and proceeded toward the shed behind the house.

As soon as Ms. Necro opened the door to the shed, Satterwhite was hit by yet another stench, one far worse than the one inside Ms. Necro's house.

He knew exactly what the smell was for he had smelled it before.

Forget "whoever smelt it, dealt it."

In this case, it was the smell of death.

Ms. Necro walked Satterwhite into the open shed where the walls were lined with rusty outdoor equipment and tools, such as axes and shovels.

In similar fashion as before, he stood close to the doorway while Ms. Necro walked closer to the middle of the room where a wobbly canned light hung over a large well-like structure made out of pewter-colored stone.

Satterwhite actually could hear it—or Bubby—moving around below.

"Don't be afraid," Ms. Necro said sneakily. "*It* won't bite."

Ms. Necro walked to the pit, which had a diameter of at least ten feet and had to be between two to three stories deep.

After receiving a nod from Ms. Necro to come closer, Satterwhite eventually stepped forward and approached the pit.

Once more, Satterwhite could hear Bubby sliding around the dirt, kicking up tiny dust clouds. The sound of the scales rubbing against each other reverberated throughout the inside of the shed.

Finally, Satterwhite made it to the pit and stood by Ms. Necro's side.

The stench had also brought yet another nuisance.

The flies.

They were everywhere.

Trying not to draw much attention to himself, he waved away the flies from his face.

"I wouldn't do that if I was you," Ms. Necro said, reshaping her glare at Satterwhite.

"Do what?"

Satterwhite continued to shoo away the flies.

"That," Ms. Necro said, her eyes widened.

Satterwhite stopped waving.

The sounds below him intensified and among those sounds he heard a couple of booming *thuds*.

Ms. Necro tossed the cow's leg into the pit.

Among all of the coiling, shiny blackness below Satterwhite witnessed a head with two dull red eyes emerge. Bubby's two furry hands were next to emerge as each one grabbed a hold of the cow's leg.

Strangely, the sight of Bubby wrapping its row of massive fangs around the leg of a cow, as well as those wet, gummy sounds of the creature chewing through meat and bone, aroused Satterwhite.

As Bubby chewed, gnawed, and sucked on the bone, the plump, pink stuffed animal of a pig that Ms. Necro won at one of those Whack-a-Jester events during last year's Mardi Gras surfaced from the center of Bubby's coiled tail. The scaly tail tightened over the stuffed animal, as if, in a strange way, it wasn't strangling it but rather hugging it.

Satterwhite glanced into the pit and asked Ms. Necro, "What do you want?"

The sound of the stranger's voice above caused Bubby to let out a stingy hiss that excited Satterwhite.

A couple of fistful sizes of cotton balls fell from the torn stitching along the back of the pig.

"I'm not talking about the money and the *toys*," he said, referring to his own Beamer as one of his many toys. "After all of this is said and done, what do *you* want?"

Ms. Necro thought carefully about the question.

Then, answered with a slack, expressionless face and what he perceived as a sparkle in her eye, "I want to be remembered."

"Don't we all—"

"—No," Ms. Necro snarled again, drawing yet another *hiss* from Bubby. "I want people to know my name."

"Well," Satterwhite said, slipping his hands into his pockets, "given the time, I'm sure everybody will know your name." He looked down in the pit and flicked his head in a nod and asked quietly, "What's up with the doll?"

"At the end of the day," Ms. Necro said motherly, "he's a big baby."

"Yeah, a big baby that would bite your head clean off."

Ms. Necro laughed a phlegmy laugh and hollered at Bubby below.

"He's my big baby," Ms. Necro said in a schmaltzy kind of way, "aren't you, Bubby? You're a big baby. . . "

She leaned down, rested her hands along the top of her knees, and puckered her lips as if she was blowing kisses at Bubby below.

In return, Bubby let out a rattling noise that sounded like to Satterwhite as a purr.

Again, Satterwhite couldn't help but redirect his attention toward that stuffed animal, as well as the balls of cotton bleeding out of it.

In that moment, he found himself smiling.

SOMEWHERE OVER BATON ROUGE
TWO WEEKS LATER

WELL-known for his documentary-style shooting, director Floyd Bivins, who had been with *Unleashed* ever since the first explosive episode of Season Three when new producers came abroad and started to "ruffle some feathers," Bexley's longtime friend and one of the show's cameramen Julien "Jewels" Etheridge, who had been with the show ever since the pilot, as well as several other crew members, tagged along with Bexley on Kristine's private jet which flew straight from Hollywood Burbank Airport to Lafayette Regional Airport, stopping once to refuel in Fort Worth.

Once they landed in Louisiana, the crew hoped aboard a helicopter and flew around Baton Rouge, as well as Sinclair Leprieur, mainly for B-reels.

Seated in the passenger seats of the helicopter, there were five of them altogether, Floyd, the director of the show, Julien, the cameraman, "Ashley the Audio Guy," a boom mic operator who had been with the show for only two years after the man he replaced, Marlow Crane, suffered what the doctors called a "massive coronary" and had no other choice than to step away from the show due to medical reasons, one of the producers, Bill Kopeck, who spent the last two weeks with cinema photographer, Tobin Schumacher, scouting out locations in Louisiana and had been waiting for the crew when they landed in Lafayette, and then last but not least, the star of the show, *the* Bexley Hun.

While flying over a residential area in Baton Rouge, Floyd, who was notoriously known for his off-the-cuff, often "gorilla" style filmmaking, made a suggestion to Bexley that the helicopter ride over Baton Rouge would make for an ideal shot to start the show. "To heighten the anticipation," he explained.

Bexley couldn't agree more.

And so the two riffed off one another, shooting out one idea after another.

Floyd first started by directing Bexley to look down at the city below while she flew over the city like an owl through the night.

Julien, who had worked with Floyd for some time now and basically shared his same headspace, positioned his camera lens exactly where Floyd wanted and filmed Bexley.

"More serious," Floyd directed Bexley, who, in return, sharpened her eyes as she looked down at the city below. "*Purrfect*," he said.

Floyd patted on Julien's shoulder and pointed at Bill, who was seated across from Bexley.

"Now," he said, "let's get Bill in the shot. Bill, I want you to look extremely nervous."

"Nervous?" Bill repeated, his face ghostly white. He let out an anxious laugh as if it was his way of releasing the nerves. "I think I'm about to shit myself over here."

The comment drew a couple of laughs from the others, *except* Bexley.

Julien moved the camera toward Bill, who couldn't have acted more spot on.

"Fantastic!" Floyd said proudly.

Julien moved the camera back to Bexley and caught a glimpse of a smirk on her face.

"Zoom in, Jewels," Floyd directed. "Slowly."

As the camera started to *slowly* zoom in on Bexley, she found herself getting lost into the character, even though the one whom she portrayed on the show was probably the closest portrayal of herself. She focused her eyes on a sea of lights below. She could even see the soft blue glow of televisions flickering through the windows of each house, watching her, binging each episode of *Unleashed*, waiting for the new season to arrive. Her thoughts turned dark and spread to her face, then those keen eyes. She mentally told herself that this trip might possibly be her last. She was determined to make it count, though. And all of those thousands of people, who were caught in a trance by the TV, had no idea of what was coming their way. And the thought alone excited her.

Yet, at the same time, Bexley was also terrified.

But one would never know.

She wore a great poker face.

SINCLAIR LEPRIEUR
MORNING

DONOVAN was woken up at ten minutes till six by a phone call from an unrecognizable number with a 213 area code.

With one eye open, he glanced at the area code and mentally tried to pinpoint its origin through the visual, chaotic fallout of a past nightmare involving snakes.

"You got to be shittin' me," Donovan said, as he sat up along the edge of the bed and contemplated answering the phone call.

"You gonna get that or not, Donnie?" groaned Cheyenne, who was lying on her side with her back facing her husband. "It's probably that producer. . . " her voice was clearer.

"Yeah," Donovan muttered, as his stomach stirred.

The past two weeks of search parties and questions, so many damn questions, most of them unanswered and laced with speculation, rumors and conjectures, had clearly done quite a number on the sheriff's body, particular his stomach. He had already lost over six pounds. He could hardly eat a complete meal. Whenever he did manage to eat, it was like the food went straight through him, as if his gut had turned into one fatly meat grinder that had sprung an awful leak.

After embracing a deep inhale through his nose and then holding it inside his lungs for three seconds before exhaling, Donovan answered the call.

From Cheyenne's perspective, all she could make out was several uh-huh's and yep's and two you-got-it's from her husband. He didn't sound like his usual self, Cheyenne knew.

Donovan wrote down a couple of scribbles on a 3 x 5 inch memo book on top of the nightstand and finished the call by saying, "See you soon."

"What now, Hollywood?" Cheyenne said, as she rolled over on her side.

"That was Makana Gorg."

"*Makana*, huh?" Cheyenne thought more about that name, since it had been on her mind for the past several days. She suddenly realized where she had heard the name before and how, when she was much younger, she used to have a friend of the same name. "The producer lady?" she said, as she quickly dismissed what she would call a "senior moment."

"Yep."

Cheyenne let out a sheltered sound from her closed mouth that struck Donovan the wrong way.

"Jealous, are we?"

"I'm not jealous," Cheyenne said defensively. "It's just not you."

"Opportunities like this are rare, Annie."

"Okay," Cheyenne said shortly and sharply, more or less, a familiar tone that was a precursor for an argument.

Donovan turned to his wife.

"It's a bad idea, isn't it? Me doing this show when Guidry's been missing for two weeks? People are gonna start talkin—"

"—Then let 'em talk. If you think she can help with the case. . . "

"I dunno. Maybe." He let out a sigh, as if lately he was full of sighs. "Right now, what do I got to lose?"

"For one," Cheyenne said bluntly, "your job."

The comment cut right through Donovan. He was in no mood to argue with Cheyenne. Not today. Of all the days, *not today.*

He rolled out of bed and raced around the bedroom for a clean white shirt to wear underneath his uniform, first by checking the wad of clothes on the chair and then digging through the chest drawer.

Cheyenne couldn't help but watch her husband from the comfort of her bed. She hadn't seen him this nervous— and excited—in ages.

Finally, Donovan found a clean white tee shirt and gave it a whiff.

He turned to Cheyenne and flashed his brow.

"Showtime," he said.

Somewhat amused yet taken aback by her husband's out-of-left-field boyish behavior, Cheyenne shrugged it off and said, "Break a leg, will ya?"

✦

WHEN Sheriff Barbee arrived at Lake Wilshire, Spoiled Monkey Production had already started to set up cameras and lights around the location where the skeletal remains were discovered.

The two producers from earlier, Makana Gorg and Bill Kopeck, were hanging around a small crowd of people next to a tent while the assistant director Brice Shuffly, or better known around the set as the "AD," was animatedly instructing a handful of extras—the background—where to stand, what to do, and how to act.

A hazel-eyed twenty-something brunette named Posie was first to greet Sheriff Barbee. She couldn't have been nicer, as she pointed at a table of refreshments to the sheriff. She mentioned the word *coffee* somewhere in her fast-paced spiel, which immediately piqued the sheriff's interest; however, the last perk the sheriff needed right now was a beverage that normally heightened his senses—and stomach. He was already awake and running off a fantasy camp-like enthusiasm; and for the sheriff, being nothing short of awake was good enough.

Sheriff Barbee declined.

"I'm good," he said kindly. "But thank you. . . "

"Posie," she said ecstatically. "Posie Rodgers."

The sheriff pointed at the other crewmembers on set.

"So, what's your role in all of this?" asked Sheriff Barbee.

"I'm the show's PA—or 'wrangler'—but I prefer PA," she said speedily. "I think it sounds better."

"PA? What's that?"

"Production assistant."

Donovan thought, *Don't ask questions like that when you're on set, you idiot.*

"You're nervous," Posie said. "I can tell."

"You can?"

"Yeah," Posie said innocently. "Don't be."

"Easy for you to say."

"So, is this your first time in front of a camera?" asked Posie, as if she was genuinely interested in what he had to say when, in fact, to the sheriff, Posie came off as someone who was trying to chummy her way to the top.

The notion that the young lady had taken an interest—fake interest or not—in the sheriff made him feel, dare he say, confident again.

"Not exactly." Hoping to relieve any leftover nerves, he poked fun at himself, "Normally, whenever I find myself in front of a camera, I'm answerin' questions by a couple of our local reporters who act like it's their life's mission to twist my words around to protect their own self-interests." The sheriff said more lightheartedly, "That is why, every now and then, I like messin' with reporters by giving them enough information to have them fillin' in the blanks. I'm like a tease. They even have a name for me, you know?"

"What's that?"

"Sheriff Tricks."

They didn't. It was a lie.

"That's right," Posie said, more foolishly as if she caught herself in a sudden "duh" moment. "Sheriff."

The sheriff liked Posie. She reminded him a lot of his daughter, only without the fakeness.

As soon as one of the producers, Makana, spotted Sheriff Barbee approaching with Posie, she stopped whatever it was that she was doing—or saying—and acknowledged the sheriff.

"Glad you made it," she said, stepping away from the crowd to shake Sheriff Barbee's hand.

"Quiet a lil' production ya' got here," Sheriff Barbee said, as he surveyed the film crew, which was much larger than he intended it to be. On top of the fearless five, there were a handful of rough-looking guys from the lighting department, a makeup artist, as well as two ladies from wardrobe, who looked as if they were all waiting for their cue to pounce on Sheriff Barbee, two guys from grip, who were moving around and adjusting camera equipment. Other than that, even though to the sheriff it might have looked like a fairly large crew—much larger than any TV news crew he was used to seeing—in actuality, it was quite a skeleton crew compared to other big budget productions.

Among those fearless five, a familiar figure revealed herself in the corner of the sheriff's eye. First, he heard her distinguishable laidback voice. He immediately recognized that voice, especially last night after spending several hours sitting slumped over the kitchen table in the dark with his laptop screen only inches away from his face while watching her face on the YouTube when Cheyenne was sleeping upstairs. He spent the night constantly listening for a *creak* in the hardwood floor or glancing over his shoulder as if he was watching something that he wasn't supposed to be watching, like porn. Secondly, he turned toward the back of the tent and saw the back of her head. Her hair was deep and dark and shined brightly along the areas where the sun hit it.

"You haven't met Bexley, have you?" asked Makana, as she poked Bexley's shoulder.

"Yes?" Bexley, who was sipping from a small Styrofoam cup of coffee, spun around and faced the sheriff. Her face, as well as her eyes, lit up from the sight of Sheriff Barbee. "You must be Donovan," she said, carrying that same exact glow that Cheyenne wore the day he met her.

"I am," he said somewhat bashfully and soon realized how much he sounded like dry toast. He straightened up his act and put on his professional-looking face. "Sheriff Barbee," he said, more dourly.

"Of course," Bexley said, keeping her smile. "I'm Bexley Hun."

"I know." The sheriff naturally flashed a smile. As soon as he found himself staring and smiling at Bexley, he remembered to stay professional. And so he did exactly that. Before any unwanted awkwardness set in, he said straightforwardly, "I watched a couple of shows last night."

"You did?" said Bexley. "What'd you think?"

"It was very interestin'—and quite enlightenin', to say the least," he said.

"That's what we enjoy doing on *Unleashed*," Bexley said humbly. "We like to keep our audience engaged. Yet, at the same time, our goal is to have each one of them leave the show with something they've never seen before."

"Sounds great," Sheriff Barbee said and reached out his hand to shake Bexley's hand. "It's a pleasure to meet you, Bexley."

At first, she was reluctant to shake his hand since it had come a few lines into the initial greeting; however, once she saw his hand hanging there in the air like a turn signal, she eagerly shook his hand.

"Likewise," she said with a firm handshake. "So," she said, letting out a sigh of relief, "are you ready?"

"I guess so," the sheriff said. "Have any pointers for me?"

Bexley said in a soft, soothing tone without missing a beat, "Just be yourself. Our show thrives off authenticity."

Bill Kopeck said from the side, "That is why we are one of the most popular shows on TV right now." He nodded at the sheriff and held out his hand. "Sheriff Barbee," he said and shook the sheriff's hand, "nice to see you again."

"Bill, right?"

"You got it," he said with his mellow California-like aura.

The sheriff thought he looked stoned, but it wasn't his place to voice it.

"Also," Bexley said, "never look at the camera unless Flo tells you to." She turned to the forty-something year old man who was talking to one of the lighting guys. "Speak of the devil—no pun intended—this is our director Floyd Bivins."

Floyd turned around and had that same light bulb-flash of a look once he saw the sheriff.

"Are you the sheriff?" asked Floyd.

"Sheriff Barbee," the sheriff said and shook Floyd's hand. "Pleasure."

Floyd gave the sheriff a thorough once-over, his queer eyes marveling at the sheriff's broad-shoulder physique.

"The pleasure is all mine, Sheriff Barbee." He turned toward Bexley and said arrogantly as if the sheriff was no longer standing directly in front of him, "He's much taller than I hoped for." He glanced him over yet again, but this time with a keener eye. "The jacket might be an issue. Could cause some reflections with the lightning."

"Is there a problem?" asked Sheriff Barbee, who was eternally turned off by the director's impertinence.

Do they teach you people any manners in California?

He held his tongue.

Man, was he glad he held his tongue!

The director gave the sheriff a soft touch along the shoulder.

"Nothing we can't fix, Sheriff," he said nonchalantly. "We may have Ronda from wardrobe swap out your jacket for one of our own." Floyd squinted one side of his face when he emphasized the word *may*. "May," he reiterated.

"What's wrong with my jacket?" asked the sheriff.

"It's just the material," he said shortly. "It tends to give the lighting department headaches every now and then. But thankfully," Floyd pointed above at the overcast sky, "mother nature is on our side today. Besides," he said, "it's going to be as hot as balls today. We might want to *lose* the jacket—I mean, if that's okay with you."

"Sure," the sheriff said. "It's your show."

While Floyd excused himself for a moment to talk with other crewmembers, Sheriff Barbee looked down and ran two fingers along the smooth polyester material of his sheriff's jacket and was left baffled.

Before the sheriff could put any more thought into the matter, Bexley pulled Sheriff Barbee aside.

"It's a lot to take in, I know," she said. "But trust me. You're in good hands, Sheriff Barbee."

"Donovan," the sheriff said, as the nerves started to ease away. "You can call me, Donovan."

"Not a problem, *Donovan*," she said before a silence could form. "We really appreciate you doing this. I'm aware we may seem like a fifth wheel around here. If it makes you feel more comfortable," she said warmly, "just pretend we weren't even here. After all, we're here to help you."

"That's gonna be quite a challenge," the sheriff said unsurely, as he glanced around at all of the chaos around him. Every single one of the crewmembers was moving like a colony of ants. Each one had a specific role, a specific task.

"Yeah. It's pretty amazing," she said, following the sheriff's eyes. "As you can tell, we don't waste anytime. They've been here since five o'clock this morning setting up everything."

"I don't see how y'all do it."

"Do what?"

The sheriff nodded at the cameras.

"*This*," he said. "It's a little nerve-racking."

"Well, you get used to it."

"I don't see how."

Bexley touched the sheriff on the side of the arm.

"You're going to be great," she said.

Her words gave Sheriff Barbee not only more confidence, but also gave him a sense of comfort, as if, in a way, he was, in fact, in good hands.

Great hands, actually.

The sheriff returned with a closed smile while Bexley, who had an uncanny way of relieving tension or any soon-to-be awkwardness, said suddenly, "You'll soon find out Flo likes to keep things moving."

"Okay, okay," Floyd announced while clapping his hands. He made his way toward the sheriff and Bexley. "Ladies and gentlemen," he said to the crew, "start your engines."

Bexley glanced at the sheriff in the corner of her eye.

Bexley turned to Sheriff Barbee.

"Told you."

"Okay, now," Floyd explained to Sheriff Barbee, "in this scene, you're going to walk Bexley to the site where the remains were discovered and along the way," Floyd said, as he escorted both the sheriff and Bexley toward the spot where the remains were originally discovered, "if you would, please walk with me." Both the sheriff and Bexley walked with Floyd, both of them watching and listening to him with a pinpoint focus. "Bexley is going to ask you about the remains," Floyd listed off from each one of his fingers, "who found them—you don't have to give a name; in fact, it's best that we keep his identity concealed—" he said before the sheriff could interject, "also, what condition were these bones in," another finger, "has there been any other discoveries of human remains," then another finger, "if so, when," he was running out of fingers, "—also, it's important that you describe this unusual tooth that was found inside John Doe's skull. Essentially, this scene will flow right into the next scene, which will take place at the Crime Lab where you will unveil the tooth."

Sheriff Barbee was slightly at a loss of words.

As Bexley had pointed out earlier, it was a lot to take in for the sheriff.

"Remember, Sheriff Barbee," Floyd said charmingly, as he stopped walking and squared himself toward the sheriff, "*just be yourself.* Okay?"

"Got it," the sheriff followed. "Just be myself. Easy enough, right?"

So he said.

※

THEY were nearly finished shooting the LAKE WILSHIRE SCENE when Sheriff Barbee heard the numbing *ring* of his flip phone, which most kids nowadays would respond with a puzzled look or a speedy gumshoe on the phone or a questionable response such as "What's that?" Everybody back at the Sheriff's Office knew *not* to call him unless it was an emergency, which made the sound of his phone ringing that much more unsettling.

Considering Sheriff Barbee was still the sheriff and had a duty to his town, he excused himself for a moment and answered the call.

Without the sheriff aware, Floyd made sure to keep the camera rolling.

Sheriff Barbee did very little talking over the phone.

Instead, he mainly followed with several heads nods.

"Shit," Sheriff Barbee said finally. "I'm on my way."

Somewhere, in the conversation, Bexley heard the name "Zargarpour."

He hung up with Deputy Afolabi and turned to Bexley, who was also wearing a look of great concern on her face, as if she could see right through Sheriff Barbee's hardened gaze.

"A body has been found a few miles from here," Sheriff Barbee said gloomily. "From what my deputy told me, the markings are the body appear to be suspicious by nature."

"Suspicious how?" asked Bexley.

The sheriff said, "He *thinks* they may be from an animal."

N

AFTER very little convincing—after all, Donovan thought to himself, it was not only his responsibility, but also his duty to look after the crew during their stay in Sinclair Leprieur—Bexley, Floyd, and Julien tagged along with Sheriff Barbee.

Bexley rode shotgun while both Floyd and Julien, who set up a camera for an over-the-shoulder shot, sat in the backseat.

On the way to the crime scene, the sheriff drove past an old truck, which was hauling a dead alligator in the back. A gray tarp was concealing part of the gator; however, Bexley knew it to be dead from the fresh blood covering the tailgate, as well as the gator's tail lifelessly hanging from the truck.

"I can imagine some of the townspeople must be extremely panicked by what happened," Bexley said, as she turned her eyes toward the sheriff, who acted as if his constituents hauling around dead gators were the least of his concerns.

"Not all of them," he said, glancing at the red light on the camera through the rear view mirror, and returned with a question for Bexley, "So you have any theories about what might've killed our John Doe?"

"Well, until I'm able to examine the remains, I can't make any determination what it is. *But* based on my gut as well as the statement Thaddeus Hoper gave last year after he was attacked on the night of June Seventeenth, it sounds to me like we are dealing with the legendary steckophorus, 'Phoenix Snake'—or as you've heard it mentioned around town, a 'werewolf snake.'"

"More than I'd like," Sheriff Barbee said defensively to Bexley. "But truth is we won't know what we're dealing with until we can get eyes on it."

"We have eyewitnesses to prove it. And soon, we'll have evidence."

The sheriff turned his shoulder and asked Floyd if he could turn "that" off for a sec—*that*, referring to the camera.

Floyd nudged Julien on the side and told him to do as the sheriff asked.

"That boy you're talkin' about—'Tad'—on the night he was attacked, he had enough alcohol in his body to take down King Kong. Doctors even had to pump his stomach. Now, you're gonna believe some guy like that, a guy who wasn't in his right state of mind?"

"As we're probably aware of, Bill has arranged an interview with Tad tomorrow," Bexley said.

"Have at it," the sheriff said with frustration, as he started to mentally question himself why he even agreed to be a part of this show in the first place. "*But* I tell you right now: You ain't gonna learn anything that hasn't been said before."

"Let's just try to keep an open mind, Sheriff Barbee," Floyd suggested from the backseat.

The sheriff moved his eyes up at the rear view mirror and met Floyd's beady eyes in the reflection.

∕

ONCE they arrived at the crime scene on a stretch of dirt road surrounded by dense woods, Sheriff Barbee specifically ordered Floyd and his cameraman, Julien, to stay put for the time being, which was met by immediate protest by the director.

When questioned, Sheriff Barbee's reason was that it was still an active crime scene and except for Bexley, who, based on her expertise, was the one of the three qualified to join the sheriff, no other crewmembers were allowed beyond the caution tape in order to protect the integrity of the crime scene.

The sheriff's demands didn't sit well with Floyd.

"It's okay, Flo," Bexley said patiently, as she tried to calm down Floyd. "We have to respect the sheriff's demands. Let me check it out." Floyd had nothing in return, only a face that screamed traitor. "I won't be long, okay?" Again, she received nothing of reassurance from the director. "Okay?"

"This is bullshit and you know it, Bex," Floyd said, his teeth barred. "This is not—"

"—Floyd," Bexley said over Floyd and without the sheriff knowing, flicked her eyes toward a narrow trail along the side of the dirt road, "have patience. The shots will come. We just have to think outside the box."

As Bexley and the sheriff made their way toward Deputy Twiggy, who was waiting between two patrol cars in front of the caution tape, Floyd tapped Julien on the chest and said, "She just gave me a brilliant idea, Jewels."

"Oh, yeah," Julien said, losing confidence. "What's that?"

He nodded toward the trail to his immediate left.

"We'll get a better angle at the crime scene," Floyd said and walked toward a trail that led into the woods. "Besides, Jewels," he waited until nobody was looking, entered the trail, then spoke over his shoulder, "we didn't come all the way out here to sightsee. Bring the cammy."

Julien walked back to the sheriff's car, left behind his camera, which tore him up inside to leave behind considering the thing cost more than a cop's salary, then grabbed a more inconspicuous handheld camcorder, which he kept with him for those intimidate "off-the-cuff" shots, and closely followed Floyd into the woods.

While Floyd and Julien were off searching for that "perfect shot," the sheriff introduced Bexley to his deputies, Deputy Afolabi and Deputy Twiggs, and did so with slight constraint, mostly directed toward Deputy Twiggs in particular, talking to him the same way a parent would talk to their child.

"Deputy Scooter Twiggs," the sheriff said, "this is Bexley Hun. She flew in all the way from California to assist us with the case at Lake Wilshire—"

Deputy Twiggs shook Bexley's hand before the sheriff could finish his sentence.

"It's a pleasure to meet you, Ms. Hun," the deputy said giddily while shaking Bexley's hand. "We watch you every Friday. My two girls adore you."

"That's sweet," Bexley said, as she pulled her hand from the deputy's. "How old are your girls?"

"Seven and nine," he said.

The age of both of his girls was somewhat disturbing to Bexley, considering the often-graphic nature of her show.

"I see."

"What'd we talk about, Twiggy?" the sheriff asked, as the disappointed father in him came out through the creases of his face.

"I can't believe I'm talking to *the* Bexley Hun."

The sheriff leaned in next to the deputy.

"Get a hold of yourself," Sheriff Barbee said in a ventriloquist-like style.

Deputy Twiggs backed off, redirecting the sheriff's attention toward his other more professional deputy.

"Deputy Afolabi," the sheriff said.

Bexley reached out her hand and cordially shook the quiet deputy's hand.

"Bexley Hun."

"Pleasure to meet you," said the deputy.

"Likewise."

On the other side of the patrol car, Deputy Brown was talking with two men who found the body.

One of them, a burly man with a five o'clock shadow who was decked out in orange cameo, hollered at the sheriff in his thick Cajun accent, "Come see, Sheriff Barby!"

The sheriff gave Deputy Twiggs a "you-behave" glare and excused himself.

Bexley drew her eyes toward the crime scene along a dirt road that looked as if it hadn't been driven on since Hurricane Orson. Not too far away, the front end of a rust-colored truck was stuck in a ditch along the side of the road. Pebble-size pieces of glass were scattered along the road. The driver's side window appeared shattered. Several web-like fractures covered the front of the windshield.

While the sheriff was away, Deputy Twiggs sneaked in a comment to Bexley, "I'm just curious. How in the world did you manage to tame an Arabian Eagle? You have to tell me. What's your secret?"

"I'd say it's part luck, part patience," she said. "You wouldn't believe how many takes it took for me to get that eagle to land on my arm."

"I'm surprised it didn't rip ya face off."

Bexley teased, "That would've been something, wouldn't it?"

A grin stretched along the deputy's entire face.

"I know, right? If that was me, I'd shit my pants."

The sheriff was back before he could lose control over his deputies—or better yet, deputy.

Bexley acknowledged the stern sheriff, "Who were those men?"

"Two swampers who were tracking down one helluva big mamou when they came across the body—"

"—What's a mamou?"

"Mother," the sheriff corrected. "Just an expression."

"Right," Bexley said. "Forgive me. I'm still trying to get used to the expressions around here."

"Well, we got plenty. *Anyway*, every now and then they come out here to kill 'gators' in order to help control the population. For some, it's their only way of makin' groceries. As of lately, though, like most in Sinclair Leprieur, they've had other reasons."

"What reasons are those?"

The sheriff paused and exaggeratedly remoistened his lips, as if he was lubricating the soon-to-be words.

"In my honest opinion," Sheriff Barbee said, "I believe there are people out there who *still* think we didn't catch the one responsible for those two boys' death last year. They'll never tell you that, though."

"You're talking about Beaux Cormier and Geraldo Vosper," Bexley said, yet her comment came off more as a question.

The sheriff didn't give any verbal response. Yet, with his tongue rolling over his bottom gums, he nodded his head.

The thought alone of the two men killing alligators in their natural habitat had pissed off Bexley something awful. What made her even more pissy was the idea that these two men had been possibly duped by the one emotion that turned decent men into rabid dogs: fear. She kept it all in, though, the immediate emotional response to lash out at the men. Bexley figured it wasn't her place at this particular juncture. After all, she wasn't here to lecture. Most importantly, it was a mayor's job to keep people from acting out of fear, not an outsider who came from a place in which locals commonly referred to as "La-La Land."

"So, where's the body?" the sheriff asked, nodding at Deputy Twiggs.

"Just follow the smell," he said.

As soon as Bexley heard the word *smell*, she picked up the smell. She sniffed deeper and immediately knew the smell.

"This way," Deputy Afolabi said, nodding his head toward the woods.

The sheriff held up the caution tape for Bexley as if he was helping her into a ring. Bexley thanked the sheriff for his southern hospitality and followed the two deputies to the truck, first, where she inspected the inside compartment as well as the old, dried blood caked over the seat and door, prompting a response from Bexley, "It looks like the driver was pulled through the window." With a keener eye, she inspected the brown blood on the tiny pyramid-like pieces of glass along the lining of the window.

"It gets better," Deputy Twiggs said, as he pointed toward the woods.

As they crossed the ditch, Bexley tracked the blood trail along the ground, as well as the overturned vegetation where a body had been dragged.

About twenty yards ahead, two forensic investigators were snapping photos and marking the area with yellow markers. Next to them were the two lead detectives, Detective Ram Zargarpour, who was inspecting the body, as well as Detective AT Harlem, who was towering above and studying the surroundings.

Bexley passed a yellow marker with the number eight next to a wristwatch on the ground.

"Over here, Bexley," the sheriff said while standing with the two detectives, who were giving Bexley a look that suggested that they both didn't want her here. It wasn't the first time she received such disparaging looks. He pointed at the Indian man first with a uni-brow. "This is Detective Zargarpour." Then, the bald-headed man whose head was shaped like a Ninja Turtle, "Detective Harlem."

The detective barely acknowledged Bexley upon greeting. The only one, AT Harlem, was civil enough to give her a nod, then a "Nice to meet you."

Shooing away flies, Bexley arrived at the body. The smell was gagging and caused Deputy Twiggs to cover his nose. Deputy Afolabi didn't even bat an eyelash. Yet, he wrinkled his nose and made a sour face.

"Gentlemen," the sheriff then said to the investigators, "this is Bexley Hun."

The investigators, who were busy taking photos, gave Bexley a nod of hello.

One of them gave Bexley a lecherous gaze.

"How long has the body been here?" asked the sheriff.

One of the investigators, Chucky was his name, lowered the camera, pondered for a moment, and then said, "Based on decomposition, the body has been dead for a while. A couple of weeks, maybe a month?"

Bexley glanced down at her phone and read from a moon calendar.

"Two weeks," she said confidently.

"How'd you know that?"

She showed them the date on her phone.

"It was a full moon two weeks ago," she pointed out.

The sheriff asked, "What does that have to do with anything?"

"Werewolf snakes are more active during full moons," she said. "However, they have been known to feed more during warming conditions such as the spring or summer."

"Hold up. Werewolf snakes?" the other investigator said, sneering. "Is she for real?"

Then, came the attacks.

One of the two detectives, Zargarpour or Harlem, Bexley couldn't tell which, chimed in: "Think someone's been reading too many Wyatt Whyte books."

With his eyes directed at the sheriff, the investigator was pointing at Bexley, speaking in the most conceited way possible: "Who is this again?"

"*Bexley Hun*," she said clearly before the sheriff could speak for her.

Chucky said under his breath, "You certainly know how to pick 'em, Donnie Boy."

Trying to keep the peace and order, the sheriff intervened, "She's a biologist. I called her in to help us with our situation. Now, if that's going to be a problem with you, Talbot, I suggest you step aside. Otherwise, you can save your smartass comments to yourself."

"You got it," the investigator said, holding up his hands. "No problem. All I'm saying is that I'm pretty sure Lil' Skid and Big Dave would've been glad to help you out in that department. Who else knows these swamps better than those two?"

"Lil' Skid and Big Dave don't know what we're up against. She does."

The sheriff shot a familiar look at Talbot, forcing him to keep his mouth and take photographs of the body—or what was left of the body. The side of its face was completely ripped off, exposing the skull underneath. The part of his face that still remained was hardly recognizable. The eye was sunken into the socket; what little skin remained was black and purple in color and it appeared as if it was starting to grow into the earth. There was hardly any flesh on the bones from the animals, mostly scavengers, which had picked through it.

With the crook of his elbow wrapped around his nose—which, by the way, wasn't helping at all with the smell—Deputy Twiggs threw out the question that was on everybody's mind: "You think it's Jude Guidry?"

"I dunno," the sheriff muttered.

Doing his best to block out the smell, Sheriff Barbee grabbed a pair of gloves from the investigator's kit and slipped on the gloves.

He nodded at Detective Zargarpour.

"Give me a hand, will ya?"

The detective, who was already wearing a pair of gloves and was surprised to see the sheriff's involvement, helped him turn over the body on its side.

Sheriff Barbee plucked the wallet from the back pocket of the blue jeans and then rested the body in its original position.

"You gotta be shittin' me," the sheriff said in disgust.

"Is it Jude?"

The sheriff nodded.

"It's him," he said. "It's Jude."

"He's the man who's been missing for two weeks?" asked Bexley.

"That's right," the sheriff said. "Him and his wife, Adalynn, are good friends with Cheyenne."

"Who's Cheyenne?" asked Bexley.

"Thought I mentioned," the sheriff said. "She's my wife."

"I see," Bexley said. "Were you two close?"

Sighing, the sheriff removed his hat and ran his hand through his hair, which was thinning.

"Not particularly," he said. "But he was good people. Worked the graveyard shift as a security guard at LabInc. I remember he told me that he switched shifts so that he could see more of Adalynn, who works the third shift as a nurse at Saint James Memorial."

"The things you do when you're in love," Deputy Twiggs said dearly.

However, the comment wasn't at all received well by the sheriff.

Ignoring his mouthy deputy, Sheriff Barbee said to Detective Harlem, "What in the hell was he doing all the way out here?"

"We don't know yet, Sheriff," Detective Harlem replied. "The bayou is past those trees over yonder," he nodded toward the sun glaring off the water past the trees. "Maybe he came out here to collect his thoughts."

"All the way out here?" the sheriff returned, looking around.

"I reckon a man would travel lengths in order to find quietude."

"Not Jude," Sheriff Barbee said. "Wasn't the type. Then again, who knows exactly what goes through a man's head except for the man himself?"

The question left everybody in a contemplative state.

Except for Bexley, who was inspecting the clumps of frizzy black hair below an oak tree that had several long claw marks along the base of its trunk.

"Donovan," Bexley said, waving the sheriff closer.

"Find something?"

"Right here," she said, as she pointed at the claw marks, as well as a clump of tightly curled black hair on the ground. "Sometimes, the werewolf snake will rub against a tree. Think of it as a way of marking its territory."

The sheriff mumbled, "Huh?"

Marking its territory.

He was ready to hear more about what Bexley had to say.

Meanwhile, Floyd and Julien were making ground on their side mission; in fact, they could hear Sheriff Barbee and Bexley talking from a distance.

As Julien inched closer to the "perfect shot" at the crime scene, he tripped—or better yet—slipped on what he thought was a bunch of slick leaves. Turns out it was a pile of shedded skin that Julien had tripped over. Julien gathered himself, placed the camcorder down to the ground, and picked up the skin.

"Is that what I think it is?" asked Floyd in a state of awe.

Julien held up the brownish yellow skin to the sunlight stabbing through the overhead treetops and stretched it outward. He could even extend his arms as far as they could go and still, he had a blanket-worth of skin leftover.

"How exactly big is this fucking thing?" asked Floyd.

"I'd say at least twelve feet long—*at least.*"

"Let's grab Bexley and get a shot of her holding up the skin," Floyd said, just as Sheriff Barbee and Bexley approached from behind.

Julien suddenly tossed the skin behind an overturned tree trunk as soon as he acknowledged their presence.

"Knew I heard someone sneakin' 'round here," the sheriff said. "Thought I told you two to stay put."

"Jewels had to take a leak," Floyd said to the sheriff as he acknowledged Julien, who, in return, pulled his eyes from the skin and went along with Floyd's lie. "There's no way I was going to let him go alone."

"Floyd's right," Julien said hesitantly. "No way in hell I'm pissing out here alone."

"So you hold it for him too?" teased Bexley.

"Funny woman."

"Meet us back at the car," Sheriff Barbee said to Floyd while keeping a close eye on him. "You know the way you came in?"

"Yeah," Floyd said and pointed to the trail. "Over there."

"Good."

The sheriff waited till the two walked off.

Then, headed back the other way.

One of the investigators called out to the sheriff.

"Found some tracks over here, Sheriff," he said, examining the set of tracks on the ground. "They look like gator."

<hr/>

DESPITE the recent—and rather untimely—discovery of which Sheriff Barbee believed to be a local security guard named Jude Guidry based on the personal items found on his person, the production continued to push forward with the shooting schedule; however, Sheriff Barbee couldn't stress enough to Bexley and her crew that, mainly out of respect for Jude Guidry and his wife now widower, Adalynn, they leave out their names while filming the show. In other words, the sheriff was not only saving his own ass from litigation, but also Bexley Hun and every single person associated with *Unleashed*.

With hopes of Bexley utilizing her expertise to assist with tracking down the so-called "unknown thing" responsible for Guidry's death, Sheriff Barbee agreed to let Bexley and her crew film at the Crime lab where the skeletal remains of the John Doe were being held, only if they stayed out of Susanne's hair.

In the time being, the sheriff had the responsibility to perform the one task that he hated about his job.

Since the body was obviously in no condition to be identified by Adalynn at the morgue or any loved one for that matter, he brought a manila folder carrying a couple of photographs of the body that were recently taken at the crime scene. Each one of the photos was intimate: mostly close-up shots of areas on the deceased's body, including two distinguishable birthmarks, one along the right breast of his chest and another four inches below his bellybutton, as well as a faded tattoo of a shotgun on the inner part of his right bicep. The sheriff made sure to cover up the face—what was left of it—as well as any wounds that were too graphic with yellow stickies.

After Sheriff Barbee showed the photos to Adalynn, she confirmed that it was her Jude.

RELYING on forensics, including matching dental work, as well as Adalynn identifying the body based on the photographs that were provided to her, Susanne confirmed that the body belonged to a one Jude Guidry.

As the night pressed on, Bexley, who, after secretly learning about the werewolf snake's skin from Floyd, was left in a difficult position that she preferred not to be in, met up with Sheriff Barbee at the Calssier Parish Sheriff's Office to discuss the details on her findings. She so desperately wanted to tell Sheriff Barbee about the skin that Floyd and Julien found while snooping around the crime scene earlier that day. Floyd's main argument: "It's not withholding evidence, Bexy, if we don't *physically* have the evidence in our possession." Having known Floyd for three years now and realizing his passion to get a "perfect shot," it was clear to Bexley how far—and low—Floyd was willing to go.

The sheriff told one of his deputies, who was playing the role of babysitter, to go home. Then tended to Bexley and a younger man, who were combing through a stack of old cases, which, out of good faith, were given to her by Detective Harlem.

Sheriff Barbee had an answer for Bexley, who had been waiting to hear back from him. After speaking with Bill Kopeck, Adalynn permitted Bexley and her crew to mention her husband's name in the show; in fact, when asked out of respect, Adalynn's response was a seething "Hell yes." After all, it was the Sheriff's Office that brought in an expertise like Bexley to solicit her help.

"At least there's one thing we share in common," he said, taking a seat across from Bexley.

"Oh yeah," she said, taking a sip of cold coffee. "What's that?"

"We're both night owls."

"You got that right," Bexley replied, as she smiled through the comment. "I can't even remember the last time I had a decent night's rest." She turned toward her left and pointed at the younger man sitting next to her. For a moment, Sheriff Barbee thought he was her boyfriend; however, he didn't act as if he was from the same land as Bexley. He struck him as a city boy; wore black-framed glasses for show. He was disturbingly shy, too. Then again, based on the few hours he had spent with Bexley, he knew she didn't come off as the type to chase. "I almost forgot," she said to Donovan. "This is Alfonso Chuke, a close friend of mine who assists me with the show every now and then."

"Call me Alf," he said and shook the sheriff's hand.

"He's a professor over at Christopher Wenport University."

"Christopher Wenport, huh? Isn't that in New York—"

"—Virginia," Alfonso corrected.

"Right," the sheriff trailed off. "Virginia."

"Considering the fact that Alf grew up around here, it's fair to say he's more than qualified to give us a hand."

"Where'd you grow up?" asked the sheriff.

"Just outside Artsville Parish in an itty bitty town called Leblanc," Alf said to the sheriff. "South of Shreveport. If you blink while driving past it, you'd probably miss it."

"I know Leblanc," the sheriff said while he leaned back in the chair. "Yeah. *Small.* See why you left. So," he said, sighing while, at the same time, slapping his hands along the tops of his thighs, "what'd y'all find?"

"Well, after your detectives were kind enough to fetch us these case files, we found a lot actually. Want the good news or the bad news first?"

"No offense, Bexley," the sheriff said tiredly, as he checked his wristwatch, "but it's a quarter past eleven and I have to wake up at the butt crack of dawn to inform our mayor that we have ourselves one helluva alligator out there that's eating our people."

"Not an alligator, contrary to what *your* people suggested," she said and then made sure to emphasize. "That's just the *good news.* The bad news: We are dealing with a creature that's far deadlier than any alligator."

"You mean that *thing* you were talkin' about at Lake Wilshire? The. . . "

The sheriff had a momentary brain fart.

"The steckophorus," Bexley said to the sheriff, who was staring at Bexley as if she was from the planet Saturn. "The werewolf snake," she clarified, as her response was met with more trusting eyes. "Yeah," she said. "That thing."

"How'd you explain the gator tracks leaving Jude's body?" asked the sheriff.

Bexley shook off the question. "Those tracks could've wound up there after Jude was killed. Considering how fresh the tracks were, those two swampers who discovered the body could've scared it away. As you're aware, Donovan, alligators are considered opportunist scavengers. For all we know, it was about to enjoy a late-morning brunch before they showed up."

"Lil' Skid or Big Dave didn't mention anything about a gator."

"And you believed them?" asked Bexley.

The question forced a heavy silence between the two.

"Okay, so," Sheriff Barbee said and breathed deeper, "do you have any concrete evidence to support your claims that we're dealing with this werewolf. . ."

". . . Snake," Bexley finished his thought. "Werewolf snake. I sure do." She showed Sheriff Barbee the two photographs, one of Beaux Cormier and the other, Geraldo Vosper, whose bodies were both mutilated by what was ruled as an "alligator" on the night of June 17th—which, by the way, Bexley pointed out yet again to the sheriff, happened to be on the night of a full moon. "These indentations," Bexley specified, holding up yet another photograph taken at Lake Wilshire, "see them?"

The sheriff nodded.

"Yep."

With her finger, she traced the jagged indentations along the back of a skull college kids found at Lake Wilshire.

She pulled out yet another photograph taken of John Doe's bones.

In particular, a close-up of John Doe's humerus.

"Same indentations along the sides of the humerus," she pointed out, as Susanne had pointed out to him two weeks ago. "These are teeth marks. Literally, the teeth scraping against bone. Now, take a look at these other photos." She referenced the first two photographs, the ones of Beaux Cormier and Geraldo Vosper. "These indentations on our John Doe match the same exact ones found on both the bodies of Cormier and Vosper." She showed the sheriff the same indentations, one along Cormier's scapula, or *shoulder blade*, and another along Vosper's sternum. She said to the sheriff, "See."

With his eyes tracing deep trench-like marks along the bones, Sheriff Barbee made an utterance of what sounded like a "Yeah."

"Having only photos to prove our theories, I would suggest. . . excavating the remains of Cormier and Vosper in order to be a hundred percent certain—"

"—Out of the question," the sheriff said, leaning away from the photos. The blood was rich in his cheeks. "There's no way in hell I'm gonna let y'all dig up those boys' bodies. Their families have already been through enough as it is."

"Fair enough," Bexley said. "I knew you were probably going to say that, so I ended up having some of your fine deputies—who, by the way, are fantastic—to pull up all records from your archives on victims who have been killed by alligators in the past decade. Altogether, there was over a dozen—thirteen to be exact. *However*, it doesn't count all the missing person cases. That's another story. Regardless, based on what I've seen and read of each victim, they were *not* killed by an alligator. Either the person or persons who ruled these deaths as alligator attacks were clearly not in the right state of mind when they examined the bodies or they don't have a single clue as to what they're doing."

"You're talking about Susanne Gloss," Sheriff Barbee said. "She's been with us for a while."

"One of your deputies, Afolabi, I believe, introduced me to her."

"She's good at what she does."

"Maybe," Bexley said, holding up a photo of a past victim found along a riverbank, "but the evidence doesn't lie."

"How can you determine that by just looking at a photo?"

She compared the tooth found in the skull to a tooth of an alligator. Opposed to an alligator, it was much longer, narrower, and looked similar to a bird's beak knife. Then, compared the photos of each victim to the photo of John Doe's skull.

"It's right here, Donovan," Bexley said. "All you have to do is look closely. Plus, like I said earlier, an alligator is an opportunist. Rarely do they ever prey on humans."

"But they've been known do so before?"

"Sure," Bexley said. "They've been known to kill and eat humans. *But* the bite marks on these bodies aren't from an alligator."

Sheriff Barbee inspected the photo closer, briefly, had already seen it over a million times, then leaned back in his chair and folded his arms over his chest.

"You know what some people used to call this town?" asked the sheriff.

Bexley shook her head no.

"The Bermuda Triangle."

Neither Bexley nor Alf understood the nickname.

"You two are aware of the Bermuda Triangle, right?"

"Sure," Alf said. "It's where a lot of ships have been known to mysteriously disappear."

"Well," the sheriff said, "as I'm sure you've already read, Sinclair Leprieur is no stranger to missing folks. Times, I think this town is cursed."

"The facts," Bexley said, as she pulled out a map of Sinclair Leprieur, "don't care about curses, Donovan. All we know for certain is where 'it' likes to hunt." On the map, she already circled with a red Sharpie the areas where each victim was discovered and except for the John Doe, they all concentrated along Fontenot River. "By marking these locations of where each body was found, I was able to get a better idea of where we can track it down."

Bexley pulled out the same red Sharpie and circled a good chunk along Fontenot River.

"Except for one of the town's finest cuckoos, Leonora Weiskopf, who lives near Burgaw Junction, there's nothing out there but mostly wetlands."

"What's her story?" asked Bexley.

"Leonora?"

"Yeah."

"People around town call her Ms. Necro."

"Interesting."

"She certainly interestin' a'ight," the sheriff said, more tensely. "People say she's into black magic, voodoo, that sort of stuff." He drifted off in thought for a moment and then shook his head from the very idea. "Way back when, somewhere between '77 and '78, Leonora Weiskopf was one of the main suspects in a missing case. I'd say she was around your age at the time. Today, you probably wouldn't recognize her. Man was she mean as hell, still is. Swear she had a gaze colder than Medusa. The kind of look that'd cut right through ya." Sheriff Barbee recalled the time after she was arrested. He was a young cop, then, dumb and anything but numb. Since he was the arresting officer who had nabbed her one night when she was drinking and driving, he was sitting at the trial. He remembered—in fact, he couldn't get that image of Leonora sitting with her lawyer out of his head—those beady dark eyes, as still as a doll's eyes, mechanically turning toward his direction and as he put it, *"cutting right through him."* "Everybody knew she was responsible for the Pearl boy's disappearance; however, our DA at the time was inexperienced and for whatever reasons, couldn't find enough evidence against her. So, she walked."

"Well," Bexley said, doing a little cutting herself as her words severed a settling tension, "apart from the Wicked Witch of the East—"

"—Times I wish a house would fall on that woman," the sheriff said over a minor pause.

The comment drew a smile from Bexley.

"She sounds like quite a character."

"Take my advice," the sheriff said, "avoid that woman at all cost."

"Duly noted," Bexley said and took a moment to gather her train of thought. "As I was saying, we may run into an issue with transportation."

"That shouldn't be a problem," he said. "I know some folks who'd be glad to give you a hand."

"Great," she said shortly. "The sooner, the better. How about tomorrow after we interview Mr. Hoper?"

The sheriff was hesitant to give Bexley a crystal clear answer.

"Donovan," Bexley said clearly, "full moon or not, it's going to kill again."

"It don't make any sense, that's all," Sheriff Barbee said as if he was thinking out loud. "How come we haven't seen this thing before?"

"Well, all I can say: you and your men were looking for the wrong species. Werewolf snakes are land animals, not water."

Sheriff Barbee's eyes fell in deep thought.

Bexley studied the sheriff strangely, "You know something, don't you?"

"Two weeks ago, in fact, the night before Jude Guidry was reported missing, one of my deputies was dispatched to Ms. Stower's place to investigate a suspicious call about an animal prowling around Ms. Stower's backyard. Whatever it was, it apparently killed Ms. Stower's pug. She's an old lady, pushin' three digits, senile, her husband, Frank, good man, passed a few years ago after battling cancer. My deputy believed that maybe it was a fox or coyote."

"Did your deputy call animal patrol?" asked Bexley.

"Animal patrol?" The sheriff cringed his face. "You're looking at it. Anyway, according to Ms. Stower's claims, we weren't exactly dealing with a fox or a coyote or even an animal for that matter. She told my deputy that she saw it from her kitchen window. She was—and still is—convinced that it was, get this, a man dressed in a Halloween costume. I figured it was a junkie hopped up on PCP or something. Or, bath salts. Lately, I heard that's been a cheap way to get high."

"A Halloween costume?"

"Right," Sheriff Barbee said quietly. "She told my deputy she saw it with her own two eyes. I figured Ms. Stower was watching one of those shows on TV and she got herself spooked—"

More seriously, Bexley asked, "Why didn't you tell us about this sooner?"

"You don't actually believe what she said was true, do you?"

"I do," she said, "but we're a long way from Halloween."

"Let me guess," he said scornfully, "a werewolf snake?"

Bexley was already nodding her head before the sheriff could finish the rest of his sentence.

∦

THADDEUS "Tad" Hoper had nearly driven himself sick by getting all worked up before Bexley's scheduled visit.

For the past two weeks, both of his parents, Gene and Rakayla, who had reluctantly taken, not welcomed, their twenty-six year old back into their home after he was viciously attacked last year behind Suck The Head, received the brunt of their son's mood swings, including slamming his fists against the table and storming off after taking a bite of a burger Rakayla accidentally overcooked or scrounging around for food in the kitchen during the middle of the night and disrupting any uninterrupted sleep that his parents needed or blasting Slipknot's *Iowa* album in his bedroom to drown out the noise—mostly the vacuum cleaner that sounded like a jet engine—of his parents obtrusive cleaning of the house during random parts of the day or the rage-fueled pacing from one end of the house to the other while seeking the mysteriously "missing" sock to match his outfit that he was going to wear when Bexley Hun arrived and blaming its disappearance on anybody but himself.

Despite Tad being a complete nervous wreck, Gene and Rakayla looked at Ms. Hun's visit as, of all things, a godsend.

On the morning of the shoot, Tad woke up earlier than usual, the usual wake up time being around nine or ten o'clock. He used the restroom three times, went number two all three of the times. His stomach was in knots and anything he put his body came out runny from the other end. He knew that, once he met her, then it'd be okay. The nerves would disappear like a magic trick. All of that pent-up frustration he had been building up for the last two weeks would all melt away.

Both his parents walked on eggshells all morning long and made sure to stay out of his way. Rakayla had even washed and pressed his outfit the night before and had it waiting for Tad on the closet door next to his bedroom that way it'd be the first thing he saw when he exited from his bedroom. Most importantly, they both made sure not to bring up the shoot for it would only add more pressure and most of all, stress to an already stressed out kid.

Once Tad received a phone call from Bill Kopeck saying "they" were close to the house—even from the moment he answered the call to the moment he hung up with Bill, he still couldn't believe that he was going to be on TV!—Tad made sure to thank his parents for putting up with all of his shit. In a way, he could breathe a little easier knowing that his story was going to be told to a larger audience and that people would *finally* listen, including the two people who he cared about the most.

When Bexley Hun, Julien Etheridge, and Bill Kopeck pulled up their SUV in front of the house, Tad was already waiting outside to meet them. He didn't even have to utter a single word about the shoot to his parents that morning. Since Tad was in such a fragile state, they knew ahead of time to stay out of his way, even though the natural parental urge to welcome these folks from Los Angeles to Sinclair Leprieur with hugs and hot breakfast was at the forefront of their minds instead of the wishes of their son. Tad had no other choice than to introduce Bexley, Julien, and Bill to his parents; the sight alone of Bexley made him feel more at ease. They sat down briefly in the living room to discuss the details and format of the show, where cameras were going to be positioned throughout the house—possibly in the kitchen, if that was doable—what certain items in the living room needed to be removed and repositioned for sound and most importantly, lighting, which, according to Rakayla, was extremely poor in the late afternoon since the sun set behind the house. During the planning, Tad was becoming somewhat anxious again.

Acknowledging the soon-to-be explosion from her son, she redirected the attention back to Tad, giving him the floor to talk about any concerns or questions he had for the producer. He had none; in fact, he was ready to tell his story.

After the quick run-through, the folks from Los Angeles thanked Gene and Rakayla for allowing them to use their house and told them that they'd see them again later this afternoon.

Bexley convinced Tad, who insisted on following them in his car, to ride with them to the location of the shoot. The whole time during the ride, Tad tried not to throw up. The nerves were still there, obviously; however, like before, Tad told himself that once the shoot started, the nerves would go away.

When they arrived at Growlers Steakhouse, which was formerly named Suck The Head before the owner sold the place to a couple of New Yorkers, who happened to be stockbrokers in a past life, the rest of the film crew was there and had already started to set up their equipment next to a dumpster behind the restaurant. Except for an indoor/outdoor patio and a fire pit that was added two months ago, the building looked the exact same as it did before. However, for Tad, the memory of that awful night was still screaming inside his head.

The two owners, Giovanni Ricci— or "Gio," which was the name that he preferred to go by—and Logan Dijkstra, both business and life partners, were first to greet Bexley and company.

"Thanks for having us," Bexley said first off and introduced everybody to the owners.

"You must be the Great Tad," Gio said and extended his hand.

Tad quietly shook his hand.

"You're a brave man," Logan said while elbowing Gio on the shoulder. "If Gio had *half* your courage, then he'd finally explain to his ex-wife why he moved to the middle of nowhere to start up his own restaurant."

Gio looked at Logan with mild disgust: "Why you always busting my chops, huh?"

Logan, a bona fide opportunist who couldn't be more excited to have Growlers on TV, waved off Gio's remark.

"He's so sensitive," he hissed, as if Gio was no longer standing in the same vicinity as him.

"Tad," Gio said, trying to ignore Logan, "it's a pleasure to meet you. If you need anything, just holler."

"Thanks," Tad said, as Gio's graciousness killed any nerves he had about being on film. "Appreciate it."

Bexley looked around the inside of the restaurant.

"Nice place you have here," she said, admiring the lodge-like ambience.

"Well, thank you, Ms. Hun," Gio said kindly. "It's funny. We've only been open for a month and Satterwhite is already trying to run us out—"

"—There's no amount he can throw at us that would make us sell this place."

"Funny," Bexley said. "I've heard his name a lot around here."

"Well, get used to it because he ain't going anywhere. I swear the man's like a lion pissing on everything he owns. All people like that care about is money." Gio paused and said from the corner of his mouth, "Don't tell him I said that."

"Of course."

Bexley made sure Jewels wasn't filming the conversation.

He wasn't.

"So can we see it?" asked Logan, as he lips curled beneath his nose.

Tad already knew what Logan meant by "it," even though he remained quiet.

Bexley stepped in and said, "Excuse me. That's uncalled for."

Logan shrugged.

"What? Really?"

"It's no problem," Tad said casually over the sudden awkwardness and didn't waste anytime lifting up the bottom of his shirt.

The pink wrinkly scar diagonally ran across his upper abdomen and chest like a lightning bolt.

"That is *im-pres-sive*," Logan said, his voice stretched out.

The comment was met with a light smack from Gio on Logan's arm.

"Have some courtesy, will ya?" said Gio.

"It's all good," Tad said, lowering his shirt.

Even though Tad said it was "good," he carried a weight in his eyes, one that Bexley only saw a glimpse of when they first shook hands and spoke their names; and it was anything but good.

Now, she saw his eyes for what they were, tampered with, manipulated, and all of the upheaval stemmed directly from underneath that nasty façade along his flesh, a newly installed hub that, when opened, released a magnetic pull with the propensity to switch the polarity of the most innocent of eyes.

Another scar had been formed from the entanglement.

One that nobody could see.

⚡

THE shooting was behind schedule, yet the day roared onward.

Tad shifted the momentum to his two friends, who had died last year.

"That thing should've taken me instead of Beaux or Gerry," Tad said to Bexley. "Beaux was a volunteer firefighter who had aspirations to open up his own chain of food trucks called Firemouth Rescue. Dude would never shut up about it. Gerry was studying at SLU. Only had like a year left till graduation. Bet you didn't know that?"

Bexley said, "I didn't."

"Gerry wanted to become an engineer and fix roads and bridges. Normally, most people set the bar pretty high after graduation. But Gerry, he was set on repairing our infrastructure. As for me, I had nothing. No aspirations. No goals. Till this day," Tad said, thinking about those strange days that followed the attack, "I don't know why it didn't kill me. Sometimes, I think that it *did* kill me and this is the afterlife."

"Well, you're not dead," Bexley said, as if she resumed the undertaking of a role as Tad's shrink. "You wouldn't be here talking to me if you were."

Bexley grabbed the sweaty glass of water from the Mickey Mouse coaster on the kitchen table—before Rakayla left Bexley and the rest of her crew alone with her son, she couldn't emphasize enough for the members of the film crew to use the coasters in order to prevent any water rings on her "brand new" kitchen table, which was made out of oak—and took a sip of water to help loosen her dry throat.

With a nod at Floyd, she asked, "Why don't we take five?"

"When I woke up in the hospital. . . ." Tad said abruptly and seized not only Bexley's attention, but also Floyd's.

Once more, Bexley turned to Floyd, who was rolling his hand and giving her the "continue" sign behind the camera.

". . . Nobody believed me. Nobody *wanted* to believe me. In a way, they had already made up their minds. Everybody thought I was nuts, that I 'made it all up in order to get attention.'" Tad, who had been mostly fidgety throughout the interview, readjusted himself on the chair. "Call it whatever you like: A werewolf snake, Swamp Devil, Shadow Monster, 'Devourer,' as I've heard it being called once. I know what I saw. Whatever it is, it's in pain."

"Pain?" said Bexley, intrigued by the comment. "How do you mean?"

"Ever since the attack," Tad said carefully, "I haven't felt like myself—you know when you feel like you're coming down with a cold? And everything about your body feels, I dunno, not right? That's how I felt or feel. Like I have a virus living inside me, like it's been dormant inside me ever since the attack and every now and then, it'll awake."

"Awake?"

"Sometimes, my body will get really hot," he said. "Other times, I get really cold, so cold that I can see the goosebumps on my skin. Like, for instance, like when you jump in a lake during the springtime after a cold winter and the water is still freezing cold. That sudden shock when your body hits the water. That's how it feels."

"Have you told anybody about these symptoms?" asked Bexley.

Tad shook his head.

"Why not?"

"Mainly because they go away." Tad took a moment to collect his thoughts. Bexley remained quiet, patient. "Nights are the worse, though?"

Bexley asked, "What happens at night?"

"I can't sleep," he said. "I have these terrible night-mares. Yet, they're all the same, only with different peo-ple. I mean they're more like visions."

"Visions?" Bexley said, "In the statement you gave to the police, you never mentioned anything about experiencing 'visions.'"

"That's because I didn't see them until weeks after I was attacked," Tad said, which gave way to more silence.

Again, despite that urge to break after spending hours interviewing Tad, Bexley remained saintly patient.

Tad said over the silence, "They're getting more vivid."

"What is?" asked Bexley.

"The visions," Tad mumbled, then clarified with more energy, "Even when I get all feverish and my body starts to burn up and I start sweating, I can see these visions inside my head. I've learned that taking a couple of z-bars helps—"

"Z-bars?"

"You know, like sleeping pills," Tad said. "If I take them before I go to bed, they mask the visions, nightmares, whatever." He perked up all of a sudden as he had been doing throughout the interview, as if his emotions could go from cold to hot in seconds. Trying to get a grasp on his words, he pointed at Bexley: "It's like that movie, *Nightmare on Elm Street,* where all of those kids try to stay awake in order to survive, only, for me, it feels like the opposite."

"Do you feel as if these 'visions' are trying to tell you something?"

"Two weeks ago," Tad said hesitantly, "I saw that man who went missing in my dreams."

"What man?"

"You know, the guy they were talking about on the news the other day?"

"You're talking about Mr. Guidry?"

"Yeah," he said. "Him."

"In this dream, I was. . . "

The image in his head was so heavy that it caused Tad to catch his breath.

"What were you doing, Tad?"

Tad looked up and met Bexley's eyes.

"I was killing him."

N

NOT even a minute after Bexley wrapped up the interview with Tad in the backyard, Sheriff Barbee shot Bexley a text, saying that he was going to stop by Tad's house to check in, but he wasn't planning to stay for long. Bexley took the downtime to text her new agent, Paulie, who had texted her earlier about whether or not she was interested in doing a TV commercial for one of her sponsors, RuggedDuds™, a brand which specialized in outdoor attire and accessories. Before Bexley could send a reply, the sheriff was already outside Tad's residence. She decided to save the text for later. Paulie could wait.

Considering Sheriff Barbee had his own personal opinions about Tad and his so-called "story," Bexley assumed the sheriff wasn't coming inside. She decided it was not only in Tad's best interest, but also her own best interest to meet Sheriff Barbee halfway.

"How'd it go with Tad?" asked the sheriff, as he stepped outside his car.

"It went well," Bexley answered while approaching the car.

Sheriff Barbee said, "That's good."

The sheriff walked around the car and met Bexley at the passenger side.

The car was idling and inside the AC was blasting, which didn't sit well at all with any of the crewmembers, who had already started to load up their equipment into utility cases and large black crates. It was so cool inside the sheriff's car she could feel the cool air blowing from the driver's side window.

"So, you want to come in and join us?" asked Bexley, pointing at the lit, active house where crewmembers were packing up their equipment into the back of a white truck. "Tad's parents just got back from the casino. His mom, Rakayla, has had a crock-pot going all day. She's been slow cooking a Cajun-style chicken gumbo, which she says is to die for. She's made enough food to literally feed an entire army. You should hang out. The food smells delicious."

"Oh, I'm sure it does," Sheriff Barbee said, as he could feel the acid rising in his chest from the thought of gumbo. "But I'll pass. I'm afraid my stomach ain't like it used to be. Trust me. I'll be up all night if I eat that stuff."

"Your loss," Bexley said, grinning.

"Maybe so."

"Listen, Donovan," Bexley said and paused as she changed to a more serious tone, "there's something that Tad said to me that had me concerned. Did he or his parents ever mention anything to you about visions he was having?"

"Visions, huh?" He frowned while shaking his head. "I can't recall him sayin' anything about that."

"He was very specific."

"And you believe him?"

"I do, actually."

"Could be PTSD."

"Well, whatever it is, he told me some things that I think you should be aware of."

The sheriff crossed his arms over his chest.

"I'm listenin'."

"The night before Jude Guidry went missing, Tad had a vision—or, what he compares to having a dream—that he was killing Jude Guidry. Well, let me take a step back. He said he wasn't exactly killing Jude Guidry. He could see through the eyes of the werewolf snake. If that makes any sense?"

"As a matter of fact, Bexley, it don't make any sense," he said, losing his patience. "The guy's dealin' with something you and I could never understand."

"You're right, *but* if we give him a chance then he can help us understand," Bexley said, more passionately. "Ever since the attack, these so-called visions that Tad's experiencing have been getting stronger. I'm going to throw it out there," she said while expecting a more-than-likely unpleasant reaction from the sheriff, "but *what if* this creature has somehow attached itself to Tad? In other words, like a virus that's using Tad's body as a host?"

The sheriff didn't have a response for Bexley. Yet, he tried—and he couldn't put enough stress on the word *tried*—to remain open-minded, conscientious, and most importantly, willing to hear the rest of what she had to say.

"I know," Bexley said, holding out her hand, "it's hard to digest, but according to several of these unexplainable cases dating all the way back to the early eighteen-hundreds, the steckophorus—or Phoenix Snake—acquired its nickname, 'Werewolf Snake,' from the mythical creature, the werewolf, and its shapeshifting ability. *What if* Tad was somehow infected by the werewolf snake after he was cut? It wouldn't be out of the ordinary," she said, more defensively. "Would it? I mean, it's no different than a person without a tetanus shot getting trismus—or 'lockjaw'—after stepping on a rusty nail."

"Yet, a person, who doesn't get a tetanus shot, doesn't actually turn into the rusty nail after steppin' on a rusty nail," Sheriff Barbee said smartly. "Do they?"

The sheriff was tempted to stop Bexley before she got all revved up, but he decided to bite his tongue.

"All I'm saying, Donovan," Bexley said after taking a breath, "is there's a lot of information out there that we still don't know about the steckophorus. Like for instance, maybe it carries unique properties on its claws and when it cuts its victims, somehow it transmit this, let's say, virus into its victims. Tad has agreed to let me take some samples of his blood. Now, if I can find out what's inside him, then I'll know exactly what we're up against. I know you and your team want to track down and kill the creature responsible for taking the lives of some of your residents and I understand that, but I don't necessarily agree with it and trust me, if word gets out—if it hasn't already—that it wasn't an alligator that was responsible for killing these people, but rather a creature far more dangerous, then you're going to have an entire town gunning for this thing. It's going to be a witch-hunt. I'm talking Salem times ten. Torches and pitchforks. The whole works. Except in today's world, you bet there's going to be people carrying around a little more firepower, if you know what I mean. And I'm sure the last thing you want hanging over your shoulders is a bunch of trigger-happy folks running around town—"

"—You don't have any faith in people. Do you, Bexley?"

"I do," she said, "surprisingly, but in times like these, people have a tendency to show their true colors."

"I know someone who might know what you're up against," the sheriff said, the words coming out almost forcibly.

"That's great," she said. "At this point, we could use all the help we can find. No offense, Donovan, I'd rather have people who are more experienced with dealing with this creature."

The sheriff gave Bexley a heavy look.

"Wouldn't exactly say he's experienced—"

"—So, who is he?"

"He's a local author named Wyatt Whyte."

"Yes," she said thoughtfully. "He once wrote a book on his encounter with a werewolf snake."

"So, you've heard of him?"

"Of course I have."

"Right," the sheriff trailed off. "Who hasn't?"

"Our producer, Makana, tried numerous times to reach out to Mr. Whyte over the phone in hopes to possibly have him on *Unleashed*, but he was unavailable." Bexley turned toward the house and felt incredibly satisfied with today's shoot. "Tad was the next best thing."

The sheriff pictured Zip with a glass of Sazerac in hand, particularly his left, his right gripping a rein, and sipping away his days on one of his many horses and giving a new meaning to the term "unavailable."

"Yeah," Sheriff Barbee said. "He's a hard man to track down. A wild spirit, that one is."

"It's funny you mentioned his name because when my crew and I were doing research on various locations to shoot our next show, one of the show's producers actually recommended to me one of Mr. Whyte's books."

"Let me guess: *The Zigzag Man*."

"So you've read it?" asked Bexley.

The sheriff hesitated and then delivered what sounded like a rickety "no."

According to Sheriff Barbee, he only heard about this book called *The Zigzag Man*.

Which, Bexley knew, was farthest from the truth.

"It was quite an interesting read to say the least," she said, as if she was trying to stimulate a broader reaction from the sheriff.

"Don't be so diplomatic, Bexley," he said.

"I'm surprised you haven't read it. I did, however, find out the publication of one of his books didn't come without its fair share of scrutiny. Apparently, the book *Journeyz* was surrounded by controversy after marketing itself as 'based on a true story' when a lot of the details in it were, according to relatives, 'tweaked.'"

"Let's just say the man has a knack for exaggeration."

"I thought you said you haven't read his book."

"I haven't," he said, more uptight. "But I've known him ever since he was as old as the number of digits on my hands. He's always been the type to tell a convincin' story, fictional or not."

"And after the new evidence that has come to light, you still believe he's not telling the truth about his encounter with the werewolf snake?"

"I believe Wyatt Whyte saw what he wanted to see," the sheriff said, dropping his guard. "It's up to you, though. He may be of assistance. He may not."

Bexley swallowed the sheriff's answer; however, it didn't sit well inside her.

"Let me ask you something, Donovan, if you don't mind."

"No," he said. "Go 'head."

"Do you believe in monsters?" asked Bexley.

Sheriff Barbee didn't put much stock in the question.

"No," he said bluntly. "Monsters only exist in the movies. I believe people create monsters in order to exaggerate a personal issue they're dealin' with. I believe *they* believe it's another way of destroyin' their so-called monster. After all Bexley, you and I both know what eventually happens to the monster at the end."

"What's that?" asked Bexley.

"It gets destroyed."

"So you're saying you believe in destroying a monster before trying to understand the monster? If we learn how it came to be a monster to begin with, even if that means putting *everything* on the line, then based on our data, Donovan, we'll be able to prevent it from becoming a monster."

The answer to Bexley's question was right there on the very tip of the sheriff's tongue and what a warm-blooded answer it was! *What nerve,* Sheriff Barbee thought hotly. *What's there to understand? We can't coexist or walk it around on a leash and grab a cup of coffee with it! If this thing that's killing the people of my town is what you claim it to be, it's already past being a monster. Soon, it's going to be a dead monster!*

As though the timing couldn't have been more perfect for the sheriff, Floyd interrupted from behind, "Hey, Sheriff, sup?"

"Floyd," he said. "How's it goin'?"

"It be goin' all right," Floyd said, more laidback.

The sheriff didn't quite understand the response.

Hollywood, he thought.

"Listen, Sheriff, Jewels wanted to know if you, by any chance, had any extra body cams on you. Not on you per se," he corrected, "what I meant is back at the Sheriff's Office."

"Body cams?" Sheriff Barbee recoiled from the question. "Does it look like we're the type to wear body cams?"

"I thought it was like against the law not to wear a body cam."

"Never heard of that," he said, retaining a more stern composure. "Besides, the Sheriff's Office can't afford 'em. You'd think with all the money pourin' into this town as of lately we'd be armed to the teeth with the latest technology."

"Strange," Floyd said.

He placed his hand underneath his chin, as he delved in deep thought.

"Tell that to Satterwhite," Sheriff Barbee said without thought.

"I swear I've heard that man's name a gazillion times ever since we've been here."

"It's that one guy who we bumped into the other day when we were leaving the set," Floyd said, as if he was provoking a memory. "You know, Blue Eyes?"

"Him?"

"Yeah, deep pockets," the sheriff said over Floyd. "Man's so rich he probably paid for new eyes."

"Right," Bexley said. "The investor who Jewels was talking about."

"That be him."

"He didn't seem too thrilled about our presence," Bexley said and pointed at Floyd. "In fact, I remember him acting like a real jerk towards you. I got this bad vibe from him."

"What can I say?" Floyd shrugged. "I'm a jerk magnet."

"Don't let Satterwhite run you out of town," the sheriff said to Bexley. "His money may look intimidatin'. Believe me, he's harmless."

Floyd started to feel as if his presence was unwanted or untimely. He asked the sheriff what he needed to ask and then he was back to the grind.

Sheriff Barbee kept a close eye on Floyd as he marched his way back toward Tad's house. Even with the uncanny camaraderie the sheriff witnessed among the production crew, he still couldn't trust, as politely as he put it, the unconventional director—as in that most sensitive organ inside his body which he called his gut sending him signals every time he found himself in Floyd's presence. The sheriff knew his type; in fact, the type that, frankly, had a look in each and every gesture he or she made, a sort of camouflaged twinkle. He had seen such a distinct look from those who impetuously broke the machine which was the law throughout his career as an elected officer who was responsible for keeping his townspeople safe.

"About Mr. Whyte—"

"—Right," Sheriff Barbee interrupted Bexley before she could finish, then he observed the changing color of the sky, "looks like it's gonna be gettin' dark here soon. Tell you what. How 'bout I take you to see him first thing in the mornin'? *And,*" the sheriff said before Bexley could give him an answer, "it might be better if it's just you and not your crew. I think Mr. Whyte may get spooked if he sees a film crew with you. Being the opportunistic capitalist that he is, he may use your show for his own self-interest. I wouldn't put anything past him."

"Sure," Bexley said with a closed smile. "It's a date."

⚡

Ms. Necro, who normally bought her groceries at the family-owned store Everyday Pantry right before owner, Wilma Clapton, flipped the OPEN sign to CLOSE at nine o'clock on the dot, knew something wasn't right when she parked her brand spanking new agate black Ford F-250 Super Duty Platinum in the driveway.

When she stopped the ignition and opened the door, the running board below the cab extended forward, allowing her to step down from the truck. Since Ms. Necro was only five feet tall, the power-deployable board happened to be one of the many key selling points for her.

She grabbed both armfuls of groceries from the cab and shut the door behind her. The sight of board retracting after she closed caused her to giggle.

"Never gets old," Ms. Necro said to herself and looked around the front yard, first, then the back yard. Her eyes caught the sight of her old truck parked alongside the house like a neglected member of her family, one with whom she had shared many hardships and losses. For Ms. Necro, the new truck was good and all, like something straight from the future; however, a part of her was left in a state of morose from the sight of her old truck.

She looked past the truck and noticed that the door to the shed was wide open and a light was beaming along the grass on the side of the house like a lit sword.

She placed the two bags of groceries on the front door step and instead of going inside, walked around the side of the house to check out the shed.

From a distance, she could hear Bubby restlessly moving around and making a particular hissing-like noise that he was known to make whenever he felt rather uncomfortable or, dare she'd say, threatened.

When Ms. Necro made it to the doorway of the shed, she witnessed a barefooted man standing in front of Bubby's pit. He was thin and ungainly-looking, possibly under the average weight of a young man of his height. Even when she stepped forward and made her presence known, he didn't budge an inch.

Instead, he remained still above the pit.

"Another stray, huh?" she said to herself, as she inspected a track of muddy footprints along the floor.

She approached the young man. He was wearing gym shorts and a tee shirt. His feet were caked with clumps of dried mud, which indicated that he had been standing there for quite some time. But how long?

What stood out the most were his eyes and they were both rolled over white. Ms. Necro leaned forward and got a closer look at his face. She immediately recognized the young man for she had seen his face all over the news last year.

The Hoper boy, she realized. Went by a name that rhymed with *fad*.

At first, she thought he might've been sleepwalking. But then again, the boy wouldn't have been the first one to show up unannounced at her house. Over the years, there had been many others, just like "Tad," ones compelled by something they had no control over.

Ms. Necro snapped her fingers in front of Tad's face.

He didn't even bat a single eyelash.

Yet, his eyes remained big and white.

"I know just the trick," she said and stepped away. "I'll be right back."

Ms. Necro excused herself and walked to the house where she picked up the bags of groceries and placed them on the kitchen countertop. She went into her bedroom, headed directly to a wooden cabinet along the side of the wall, opened the cabinet, and reached for one of many Mason jars, in particular one containing a special red powder labeled with the Latin word "*Imperium*," which sat between two other Mason jars, one containing a pale blue powder labeled "*Rigescunt Indutae*" and the other containing dried leeches labeled, "*Vim Extermina*." Each label was written with a black bold Sharpie on a strip of scotch tape that appeared decades old, dark yellow, and had lost its adhesiveness and was starting to peel from the top of each jar's lid. Next to the jars were other jars of animal parts, including crow's feet, reptiles, including organs and eyeballs, puffer fish, and other marine life forms, as well as rare plants found deep in swamps, all of which were poorly labeled. On the bottom shelf was an open box of red candles, one of the candles had what looked like part of a black fingernail embedded in the wax.

Confident of its potency, Ms. Necro grabbed a jar of *Imperium*, spun open the stainless steel lid, and pinched herself a thumb-index fingers worth of red powder. She sprinkled flaky powder inside a green leaf-like rolling paper. After she rolled a joint, she headed back outside to the shed where she pulled out a lighter and ran the flame underneath the freshly rolled joint, still moist with saliva.

"A'ight, Zombie Boy," Ms. Necro said, as she walked into the shed. "I got a lil' sumtin' sumtin' that'll put cha'mind at ezz—"

She lit up the joint and took a drag but didn't inhale.

Before she could finish her sentence, she walked into an empty shed.

"Where'd you go?" asked Ms. Necro.

She walked to the pit and glanced down at her Bubby, who was much quieter; in fact, he was sleeping soundlessly.

"Weird?"

She shrugged off the strange encounter and made her way from the shed. She decided to put out the joint on the side of the doorway and save it for later.

N

SHERIFF Barbee picked up Bexley in front of Sneak Peek Inn, a hotel where most of the crew had been staying throughout the duration of the shoot, and drove her to Wyatt's place along Lacombe Island Cutoff which, as the sheriff pointed out to Bexley, was considered "tricky to find, even on that there map." Bexley had absolutely no idea as to why she brought it with her and most importantly, why she had opened it like an umbrella—she had a living, breathing, walking, talking map sitting directly to the left of her.

"Can't *always* rely on GPS," Bexley said.

The morning gaffe had her shrinking in her seat.

After several awkward exchanges, most of the ride involved conversation that had little to nothing to do with the case or any details of the case. Instead, Sheriff Barbee asked Bexley about herself. She was rather short with each one of her responses; however, she answered each and every question Sheriff Barbee threw her way such as the following: *"Where'd you go to college?" "Where's that? In California?" "Are you two, you know, what the kids would call 'a thing?'" "Not your type, huh?" "Then, what?" "Sorry to hear—" "Hey! Isn't that where what's his name—" "So, what exactly got you into the animal biz?"*

As fluent as water, Bexley answered each question.

"First, Cappasaw State University where I obtained my Bachelor of Science degree."

"No. It's in Virginia. In fact, that's where I met Alfonso."

"A *thing*? Not hardly."

Bexley smiled off the question.

"Alf can be—how do I put this politely? A complicated man. But to follow up on your other question: We're just friends."

"Then," Bexley let out a sigh, "after Cappasaw, I took a year off to deal with a death in the family." Bexley cut the sheriff off before he started to sound like an owl, "In a way, it was expected. My grandfather, who was eighty-four years old, smoked for most of his adult life. He was diagnosed with pulmonary emphysema when I was a senior in high school and he had it so bad that he to be put on oxygen. Right before I graduated from Cappasaw, he was hit by influenza. A couple of weeks later, after he started to recover, he came down with pneumonia. He did all he could to fight it off, but his body was too compromised. After his passing, I went back to school and obtained my Master of Science in wildlife at the University of Massachusetts Amherst."

"—That's right. Jeff Corwin."

"I was what most of the *kids* would call a 'weirdo,'" Bexley said. "Strange to say this, but I don't blame them for calling me names. Most of them didn't know what I was going through. Who could? I was only six years old when my parents died in a car crash. I remember I didn't even shed a tear at their funeral. I guess a part of me thought that maybe they would return one day. Then, after a while, I stopped thinking about them. I went to live on the Tescalero Reservation in New Mexico with my grandparents on my mother's side. I only met my other grandparents once before they passed, but I wasn't old enough to remember them. I was told most kids, who've dealt with deaths in the family, take out the frustration on other kids. Me, I just shut off."

"Sounds like you've been through a lot," the sheriff said quietly. "More than most kids."

"Believe it or not, it was being around animals that helped me get through an adolescence that was filled with lots of anger and anxiety. And believe me, New Mexico had its fair share of animals to play with. Even the dangerous kind. Rattlesnakes, hairy scorpions, you name it, I was drawn to them."

"Animals are known to be therapeutic," Sheriff Barbee said and then from the corner of his mouth, "So I've heard."

"No," Bexley said. "I mean, for me, I wouldn't call it therapeutic. I suppose, at that particular time, they kept my attention more so than the ones who walked upright."

"Well, you're a lucky woman," the sheriff said. "I reckon most people would do about anything to have a job that they were happy with."

"I hate to sound like Debbie Downer, but this job has an expiration date," she said bluntly. "I am what most in the industry would call 'expendable.' It's only a matter of time before I'm replaced with someone much *younger* and *prettier*. It's just the way it is."

"Yeah," he said. "I see the way some of the younger women look at you on the set, especially that one. What's her name? Posie, I think."

Bexley grinned.

"That poor girl doesn't know what she wants."

"But," the sheriff said with consideration, "it don't have to be that way." He corrected, "I mean, you being expendable and all."

"Well," Bexley sighed, "it's the biz."

It wasn't until they reached Lacombe Island Cutoff when Sheriff Barbee finally decided to ask Bexley a question about the show.

"I was meaning to ask you," the sheriff started while taking a right turn along a fork in Levee Road. "When you were interviewin' Tad yesterday, did you notice anything unusual about him?"

Bexley said, "I'm afraid I don't know him well enough to know when he's acting unusual. Why do you ask?"

Sheriff Barbee shook off the suspicion.

Bexley had a way of pulling it out of him. Maybe it was her looks. Maybe it was her kindred spirit that was unlike anything Sheriff Barbee had ever seen from another human being.

"It's nuttin, well," he corrected, "this mornin', before I picked you up, one of my deputies got a call from one of the locals who thought she saw him wanderin' around Gruyere Highway in the middle of the night. She specifically said that he wasn't wearin' any shoes."

"And this person was positive it was Tad?" asked Bexley.

"Ms. Keifer," he said, "she's about as honest as they come."

"I'm going to see him later this afternoon to take some blood samples," she said. "I can ask him—"

"—Why you takin' samples of his blood, again?"

"It's for my own curiosity," Bexley said.

Which left Sheriff Barbee at a loss for words.

Silence filled the car; however, the sheriff wasn't at all inclined to kill any of the silence. Surprisingly, he felt a sense of comfort in the silence, especially with Bexley.

On the other side of the car, the silence started to eat at Bexley. With the recent question still lingering on her mind, the one where the sheriff asked her if she noticed anything unusual about Tad—which now that she put more thought into it was a big fat "yes!"—she turned her thoughts to the obvious: that hazy, winding-down part of the night after eating gumbo at Tad's house when she excused herself to use the ladies room and accidentally—or *purposefully*, Bexley didn't know which—coming across a bunch of random sketches of a circular Ouroboros symbol scattered all over Tad's bedroom. Could've been a gang symbol perhaps or even something straight out of one of these visions that Tad was apparently experiencing. The symbol, Bexley recalled, was the same exact symbol that she witnessed spray painted along the murky pane of a shattered window on the side of abandoned high school, which was located not too far from where Jude Guidry's body was discovered. The fact alone that she wasn't going to tell the sheriff about this so-called symbol—at least, not yet—or where she originally saw it made her wonder if her fearless director, the one and only Floyd Bivins, was starting to rub off on her. He was known to bring people to the dark side. Ask Jewels.

Before another subject naturally came to mind, Sheriff Barbee passed a sign on the side of the road that read: "Avery Bayou."

"We're gettin' close," he said, pointing at the sign.

✳

ABOUT a mile from the sign, the sheriff slowed down in front a crooked mailbox next to a dirt road surrounded by thick woods.

"You're right," Bexley said, as she peered down the dirt road that stretched as far as her eye could see. "I never would've found this place."

"Well, you know how these eccentric types can be. They love their privacy."

Sheriff Barbee drove down the dirt road, which, turned out, was probably the longest driveway that Bexley had ever seen.

After another mile of driving down the dirt road, they arrived at a rusty metal gate with a "No Trespassing" Sign.

While keeping the engine running, Sheriff Barbee stepped out of the car and swung open the gate. Then, proceeded down the driveway.

Finally, after reaching the end, they arrived at a run-down plantation along the Avery Bayou.

"Does he know we're coming?" asked Bexley, becoming slightly more skeptical about seeking Wyatt's advice.

The sheriff parked the car underneath a canopy of aged oak trees, which lined the driveway.

"Nope," Sheriff Barbee said, as he shut off the engine. He acknowledged the change in Bexley's demeanor. "Don't you worry 'bout that sign back there. It's just a deterrent."

"Right."

Bexley followed suit and stepped outside with Sheriff Barbee while making sure to keep close to him as he walked toward Wyatt's off-white, two-story Greek Revival home. The house was originally built in 1839 and from the appearance of the exterior, it was clear to Bexley that the owner struggled with the upkeep. The paint along the pillars was chipped and worn with age, practically everything was worn down and ready to collapse. Several boards along the balcony were broken and dangled off the side of the house. The bushes that lined the front of the house were overgrown and unkept as well. Some were dead and bare or plagued by disease. Wandering around the premises were at least a dozen cats, mostly tabbies, which looked like strays. *Perhaps Wyatt's own exterminator*, she thought. *Kitty Terminix.*

Sheriff Barbee walked up the wobbly front steps.

"Watch your step," he said, pointing at a loose board that had the potential to jump up and whack them.

Mindful of the aged, more-than-likely termite-infested wood, she did as the sheriff demanded and watched her step.

The sheriff knocked on the front door, the *thud* of his knocks causing an echo effect throughout the interior of the house.

"Wyatt," he declared, "Sheriff Barbee here."

The sheriff didn't hear a peep inside, only distant thuds of his own doing.

"Wyatt Whyte," he said yet again, this time louder and more agitated. "Calssier Parish Sheriff's Office!"

Again, nothing but the trailing echoes of his own voice.

"He must not be home," Bexley said over the sheriff's shoulder.

"No," he said and pointed at a rust-colored truck parked alongside the house. "He's home. Trust me. He's probably off *playing* somewhere."

"Playing what?" asked Bexley.

The sheriff nodded to the side of the house where they saw more cats wandering around. Among the cats were a few tortoiseshells and calicos.

Another thought came to mind.

After witnessing more cats, Bexley uttered to herself, "Playing with cats?"

"Stay close," Sheriff Barbee said, sighed, and walked around the side of the house, searching the premise for any signs of Wyatt's whereabouts.

Once they reached the back of the house, which opened up to a wide vista of Avery Bayou, Bexley heard—or at least, thought she heard—a noise coming from the woods.

"You hear that?" said Bexley, listening closer.

The sheriff mimicked Bexley: head slightly lowered and tilted to a sixty degree angle, eyes narrowed, ears like a cat, the look of a man who was putting all of his energy into one sense.

"Listen," she said sideways.

Ricocheting through the woods was the sudden *snap* of a tree branch.

Easing closer to the woods, the sheriff unbuttoned his holster, his hand hovering over the handle of his Glock 22.

That *crah-crunch* sound of footsteps coming from behind the thick shrubbery along the edge of the woods forced his hand closer to his firearm. Each footstep was deep, layered, and didn't sound like human footsteps. Most of all, the sounds were getting closer and closer. . .

"Sheriff Barbee," Bexley warned from behind, as she started to take a couple of steps in the opposite direction, "you might want to take a step back."

The footsteps increased, becoming much louder and closer and denser.

The shrubs, tree branches, as well as the overgrowth of vegetation started to move and shake.

Through the narrows cracks of the trees, the sheriff witnessed a massive dark figure approaching and approaching fast!

As soon as Sheriff Barbee withdrew the Glock 22 from his holster, Wyatt and his Rocky Mountain horse leaped from the woods and nearly caused the sheriff to fire his weapon.

The silver dapple—or "chocolate," as Wyatt preferred—colored horse with a wavy, flaxen mane let out a sudden neigh, startling the sheriff.

More amused than shocked from Wyatt's grand entrance, Bexley found herself holding in a laugh. She didn't know the sheriff well enough to know when he was pissed off; however, the bright color along his face was a sure indication that he was about to make quite a scene.

"If it ain't our great Sheriff Barbee Doll," Wyatt said flippantly, as he used a rein to turn the horse. Wyatt's attire was the first thing to catch her eyes, then his game show host-like personality. He was wearing a holey black WCW's N.W.O. T-shirt. The words *New World Order* were inked out and in their place, he handwrote the words, *Niggas With Obligations*. Both of the short sleeves had been cut off, frayed, revealing a couple of tattoos that were so badly faded that they looked like ink blots along his triceps. His black, tightly worn jeans were faded too; in fact, the jeans were so faded they appeared gray, which made the brown cowboy boots pop in color. "What the hell brings you all the way out here on such a fine and dandy day?" He removed the snakeskin cowboy hat from his head. The sun hit the golden cross earring on his left ear, causing a glare. His short hair was dyed the color purple, which he sophisticatedly called "French Violet." As he circled the horse around the two, he turned his sights toward Bexley; his eyes, heavy and lustrous. He said, "See you brought a guest for me."

Sheriff Barbee suddenly bellowed out, "Goddamn it! You nearly gave me a heart attack!"

"Hey, my man," he said, still as cool and laidback as Bexley imagined him to be, "well," his voice got all thick and Cajuny, "maybe you should cut back on all dem pralines. I see ya, Don Juan," he said mockingly. "You must've at least put on a few since we last saw each other. Must be all dem pralines you be eatin'."

"You did that on purpose," Sheriff Barbee said, still heated.

Wyatt smacked his gums.

"I dunno what you be talkin' 'bout," he said. "I didn't hear shit from you."

"I called out your name several times, *Wyatt*."

"Now that I think 'bout it," he said, tilting his head in reflection, "I did hear what sounded like a faint oink followed by a phlegmy snort—that's right," Wyatt said, "a *phlegmy snort* comin' from over yonder. I tell ya it must've been a wild hog or sumtin. Swain be tellin' me all 'bout an infestation the other day."

The sheriff holstered his firearm, planted both hands along his hips, and took several deep breaths.

"Are you through?" asked the sheriff.

"Nah," he said while the horse gaited around the sheriff in an upbeat trot. "I ain't through. I can tell from ya jumpiness you didn't come all the way out here to say hello. Nah. What is it this time, Sheriff? Let me guess: you got yourself a big bull on ya hands—"

"—How about a werewolf snake?" said Bexley, acting as a mediator.

As though his mannerisms were operated by the flip of a light switch, Wyatt turned quiet, opening his mouth while nodding his head.

For the slightest moment, Bexley thought he was actually frightened of the name. His horse, as though instinctually, let out a similar noise to a man who was trying to blow out air with his lips loosely pressed together while giving a shake of a head, as if it was either shaming or admonishing Bexley—or, it was doing a little bit of both. He brushed off the name and did so quickly, as if it was nothing more than dirt on his shoulder.

"A werewolf snake, huh?" he said more comfortably, as he flicked his head at Bexley. "And who may you be, sweetheart?"

The sheriff said to Wyatt before Bexley could respond, "Sweetheart is Bexley Hun. She's currently in town filming a show about your werewolf snakes."

My werewolf snake!

Wyatt was tempted to lash out at the bold sheriff who had a lot of nerve coming down here to his plantation barking orders as if he owned the goddamn place.

Then again, he wasn't so prepared to show his ass in front of such a familiar-looking face that made his insides tinkle.

"Now," Sheriff Barbee said, surprisingly calm, "if you would, please show a lil' respect to the lady and get down from that—"

"—*The* Bexley Hun from the show *Unleashed?*"

"That's right," Bexley said humbly.

Wyatt let out a booming chuckle. "I thought I've seen you somewhere before," he said, more ecstatically. "I didn't even recognize you from up here."

"It's a pleasure to meet you, Mr. Whyte—"

"—Please," he said, "if you would, drop the mister bullspit. Call me Zip."

"Zip, huh? Why do you call yourself Zip?"

"I like to zip around—I'm *zippy*, they say. So, chomp off the *py* and you got Zip."

"Can you help us out, *Zip?*" asked Bexley.

"Well, before we start talkin' *entreprise*," Wyatt said, "how 'bout a drink?"

Sheriff Barbee, who was regretting coming out here, couldn't help but interject, "It's not even noon yet, Wyatt."

Wyatt ignored the sheriff, as he had been trying to ever since his arrival, and asked, "Who's thirsty?"

Sheriff Barbee and Bexley had no other choice than to follow Wyatt toward a covered dock along the Avery Bayou stretching out into the open wetlands, which were partly choked with lilies.

Wyatt's sidekick, Swain "The Hand" Echols, who had what Wyatt called the "Benjamin Button-disease," was taking a nap—better yet, was past out inside an airboat next to the dock. Empty beer cans were scattered along the dock. He had one leg resting on the gunwale with both of his arms folded over his chest as if he was cradling his heart. Wedged between both arms was the brown-spotted peel of a banana.

Bexley followed the snoring and observed a skinny scraggly-haired man—or boy, she couldn't tell which—inside the airboat and gave the sheriff a bump in the arm. "Isn't it bad luck to bring a banana on a boat?" she asked Sheriff Barbee.

"Hey," he said, grinning, "you're catching on quick."

Wyatt rode the horse to the edge of the dock, jumped down, and tied the reins along a post next to the dock. He patted the side of the horse's neck.

Sheriff Barbee placed his thumbs underneath the belt.

Pointing at Wyatt in disgust, he uttered, "A real Creole Cowboy, that one is."

"Yeah, that's right, John Wayne," Wyatt said while running his hand over the horse's mane, "eat ya heart out." He briefly rotated his shoulder and shot a lazy-eyed glare at Sheriff Barbee while speaking from the corner of his mouth, "They don't call me the black John Wayne for nuttin."

"Not only was he one of Louisiana's finest gator wranglers, but he's also one helluva comedian."

"Comedy is only part time," Wyatt said, more ticked off with the sheriff and his unwelcoming presence. He directed his undivided attention back to his horse. "Atta, Bitch," he whispered to the horse. "You a Good Bitch, aren't you?"

"*Bitch?*" Bexley said. "Your horse's name is Bitch?"

"Yeah," he said and walked over to a table where an orange cooler sat. "So?"

"It's just," she said while halfway through the sentence remembered that she was here to ask for Wyatt's help, not to judge him, "it's just an interesting name."

"If you think that's interesting, wait till you meet my other horses—"

"—How many horses do you have?"

Wyatt placed the cowboy hat on the table and stopped to count the number of horses with his fingers.

"Let's see," he said, counting off, "there's Shithead, an Arabian. Then Dumbass, a Mustang, then Muthafucka, Asshole." So far, that was five horses, including Bitch. Then, he used his other hand to count the remaining horses. "Son-of-a-Bitch, a crossbreed of Bitch and Shithead. Last but not least, Big Dick, a black spotted Appaloosa, which I had shipped here straight from Arizona."

"*Big Dick*, huh?"

"Yeah," he said, his voice drawn out with a high pitch. "He got a big dick."

"Very, how do I say," Bexley said, combing through her thought for the right word to use without offending Wyatt. "Colorful," she said, raising her eyebrows at the sheriff, "wouldn't you say?"

"So," he said, "seven horses total. There ya go—"

"—Where do you keep the horses?" asked Bexley, as she looked around Wyatt's many acres of property.

As Wyatt opened the cooler, he nodded toward a general eastern direction of where these horses were being kept.

"I got myself a ranch more inland," he said and pulled out a cool bottle of V8 juice from the ice, as well as a bottle of his own vodka *Snakebite* in which he invested a good bit of the money he earned from book sales. He grabbed three cups from the bar area inside the shed, went back to the table where he placed a stick of celery, as well as a handful of ice cubes inside each cup. "Breakfast of champions," he said, mixed the three drinks, added a couple extra ingredients, including a sprinkle of sea salt and a splash of hot sauce, making his own version of a classic Bloody Mary drink. "Guess you can say," he said while handing Sheriff Barbee and Bexley their Bloody Mary, "I learned my lesson last time I had my horses out here. I had 'em over yonder in that field some years back. Then, after Katrina came and made herself a mess 'round here, flooding nearly this whole area, turning it into an island, I had no other choice than to relocate the horses. Talk 'bout a nightmare." He nodded at the airboat next to the dock. "Good thing I bought the airboat before Katrina hit us; otherwise, I'd be shit outta luck. I never wanna experience that ever again. For sure. That's why I moved 'em much farther inland. So does that answer your question, Ms. Bexley?"

"Just Bexley, please."

Bexley smelled the drink and smiled politely.

She bit her tongue, literally.

Wyatt showed the two a couple of lawn chairs on the edge of the dock.

Bexley immediately sat down. Sheriff Barbee was hesitant but eventually sat down as well.

"You know, *Bexley*," Wyatt said, as he sat down next to Bexley and Sheriff Barbee, "I have to admit. I'm a fan of your show."

Wyatt took a sip of his Blood Mary, savored it.

"You are?"

"Oh yeah," he drawled. "That one where you were chasin' around that glowy frog in those caves—"

"—The neon frog."

"That's the one!"

Sheriff Barbee interrupted, "We came here to talk about the werewolf snake."

"Yes," she said, acknowledging the sheriff's lack of patience, "of course."

One of the strays, a white shorthaired, jumped up in Wyatt's lap.

"I see you're a cat lover."

"Yep," he said. "They protect the horses and keep away the snakes—that is, the lil' ones. Not the ones you be talkin' 'bout."

"Right," Bexley said. "The werewolf snake—or the 'Swamp Devil,' as you referred to it in your book."

"So, you read the book, huh? If you don't mind me askin', which one?"

"All of them," Bexley said bluntly, "well," she back-tracked, "at least the four surrounding your encounter with werewolf snakes."

"Ain't that sumtin! The lady has done her research. That's what I like about people, that hustle. Being pre-pared yet remaining open to question the establishment, which, time and time again, has created way more doubt than reason. There are things out there that people ha-ven't seen or chose not to see. Bexley here is a seer." The comment was, more or less, an indirect insult at Sheriff Barbee. "See, Sheriff, when I was on the road doin' my book tour for 'The Series,' I met all walks of life and you know what the one thing all of 'em had in common?"

Sheriff Barbee was no longer hiding his discontent for Wyatt. He was wearing it on his sleeve—or in this case, all over his face.

"What's that?" the sheriff said, restraining his anger.

"Appreciation."

Reprising her roles as mediator, Bexley said, "I appreci-ate you, Zip. And I'm sure Sheriff Barbee here, in his own subtle way, appreciates you for what you've done."

"Thank you, Bexley," Wyatt said graciously and toasted his Blood Mary.

"However," she continued, "as I'm sure you're aware, there has been a recent death in Sinclair Leprieur—"

"—Jude Guidry, know him?" asked the sheriff.

"Can't say I do."

"Bexley believes he was killed by a werewolf snake."

"And what you think, Sheriff?" asked Wyatt.

"Call it whatever makes you more comfortable but I think there's something out there and we'd," the sheriff pointed at Bexley, "*appreciate* it if you'd give us some insight as to what exactly we may be dealin' with here, since you claim to have firsthand knowledge of these werewolf snakes."

Even uttering that name, "werewolf snake," was like using an overused word that was so 2019.

"So Sheriff Barbee is asking for Wyatt Whyte's assistance in what would be considered a police matter?"

The sheriff forced out a *yeah*.

"Sorry," Wyatt said over a tense silence. "Can't do it."

"What do you mean you can't do it?" said the sheriff.

"Sorry," he said and sipped from his Bloody Mary. "I'm retired."

"Retired my ass," the sheriff retorted. "What was this whole thing you said a couple of years ago about bein' in your prime and comparin' yourself to Denzel Washington and how he was around your age when he made that movie *Training Day* and how he was still at his prime; in fact, has been at his prime for past—and I'm paraphrasin' here—for the last twenty-sumtin years?"

"You remembered all of that, huh?" He shrugged his shoulders. "I was shitfaced, Barbee Doll."

The sheriff waved off Wyatt.

"Let's go, Bexley," he said. "We don't have time for this clown's games."

Bexley didn't budge from the chair.

"In your book," Bexley said thoughtfully, "*Journeyz*, you wrote about how nervous yet excited you were to come back home to Louisiana after having spent most of what you called a good part of your 'rebellious twenties' on the road living your life as a drifter, bouncing from one town to another; however, you never mentioned why you decided to come back home, especially with everything you went through as a child. I guess, my question for you, Zip—"

"—None of it was true," he said, more seriously. "The rumors, that is. All of those claims you read 'bout were fabricated by a jealous cousin who only had one goal in mind."

"Which was?" asked Bexley.

"Money," he said, as he couldn't even speak her name. "*She* wanted to squeeze every penny from me cuz, for some reason, since I was your blood, she had every right to that money as I did. She wasn't fam. She was a leech, plain and simple."

"Considering this place was surrounded by so much pain, why did you come back home, Zip?" asked Bexley.

As Wyatt hung his head, he took a small sip of his Bloody Mary and thought extra carefully about Bexley's question.

"I didn't want to, at first," he said, looking up at Bexley. "You're right, with everything that happened, what's the point? One night," he said more clearly, as he leaned forward and rested his elbows along his thighs, "when I was on the road passing through a small town between Nashville and Memphis called Brockett, I decided to grab a drink at the local bar, which was so local it was named *The Bar*. It was dead inside, almost desolate, only two or three people either killing time or waiting to kill sumtin; like straight out of an old Western. I ordered a PBR with a shot of Beam. Two PBR's turned into three, then four, then you get the idea. On my seventh PBR, this woman sits down right next to me. Tall, dyed blonde hair, blue eyes, long legs. Trouble, if you know what I mean?"

"Is there a point to the story, Wyatt?" asked the sheriff.

"Let him finish, Donovan," said Bexley.

"You see, I've run into my share of people, unusual people who most normal people would tend to avoid. But this woman there was just sumtin about her. She saw things most people couldn't see. For instance, that night, she saw a man who had lost his way. A man who needed sum correctin'. So, later that night, after a couple of more PBR's, she invites me back to her place—"

"—Where's this going, Wyatt?" asked the sheriff.

Bexley immediately threw out her hand, as if she was silencing the sheriff.

"Turns out the woman was into psychology, said that one day she wanted to be a shrink. She was takin' classes at a college in Memphis. So, she wants me to be her lil' guinea pig for the night. So while I'm under the influence, I say 'Why not?' What the hell, right? As the kids say nowadays, 'Yolo!'" Wyatt reached in his pocket and pulled out a gold antique watch attached to a chain. "She pulls out this here watch, tells me to relax, and starts swingin' it back and forth in front of my face. Next thing I know I'm driftin' through this dream but it ain't no dream. I'm re-livin' my childhood."

"Sounds like she put you under a state of hypnosis," Bexley said.

"Yeah, sure," Wyatt said, "maybe, at one point in the night, I might've mentioned sumtin 'bout my childhood, 'bout havin' this *wall* inside me and somehow, I couldn't penetrate it. When I came to," Wyatt said, his brow furrowing, "it was like that wall was completely gone and I could see everything on the other side. Memories that had altered over the years." Wyatt paused for show, accessed the memory of that one time when he was just seven years old wandering through the woods in the middle of night underneath a full moon. Before his seven-year-old eyes, he witnessed a man without an arm, *not* a "wild hog" missing a leg, running, *not* limping, at him, then being eaten by a werewolf snake, *not* an "alligator," as the police later reported. He could hear that man's screams, *not* squeals cutting through night darkness. "For so many years," Wyatt said, "police, *doctors*, my mama, even my Gramma Eunice, who was as tough as a two dollar steak and often warned me of the Swamp Devil, practically raised me, they had convinced me that what I witnessed in those woods that night when I was seven years old, was nuttin more than what we'd call one big ass bull havin' himself some pork chop—'Good ole nature at work,' as Mama said. It was with their convincin', as well as me lockin' away the trauma of that awful memory and over time, learnin' how to convince *myself* that what they were tellin' me was the Lord's truth, that left me with this impenetrable wall inside me, you see, a wall created by both myself and those around me. However, over the years, I've learned a lot 'bout time. You see the funny thing 'bout time. *Time don't give a rat's ass 'bout you. But with nuff time, anybody*, I reckon, *can turn an anthill into an empire*."

Wyatt finished the rest of his Bloody Mary as Sheriff Barbee looked around Wyatt's property, his so-called "empire."

Bexley asked, "Did the police ever give you any reason as to why it would've been a wild hog and not this man who you wrote about in your book?"

"Yeah," Wyatt said shortly. "Two weeks later, they found a dead hog not too far from the house. They even showed me it, so I could see it with my own eyes. And that was that. Case closed." While running his tongue over his lower gums, Wyatt shook his head and drifted into a state of reflection. "Till this day, I sometimes ask myself why it didn't kill me that night. It could've," he snapped his fingers, "*just like that*. Then, I get to thinkin' that maybe it had already eaten and wasn't in the mood for dark meat. Then, it hits me. You know why it didn't kill me?"

Sheriff Barbee finally spoke and did so with authority.

"Why's that?" he asked, his voice gravelly.

"It chose me."

Once more, the sheriff waved off Wyatt and his story.

"So," Wyatt said, ignoring the sheriff, "to answer your question, Bexley, as to why I came back to Sinclair Leprieur: I came back here cuz the werewolf snake wasn't through with me. And I wasn't through with it."

"Wasn't through with you?" said Sheriff Barbee.

The cat jumped off Wyatt's lap as he stood from the chair and said to both of them, "I'll show ya."

Both the sheriff and Bexley remained seated and hesitant.

Wyatt, who didn't even bother to wipe away the white cat hairs along his lap, stopped and turned to the two. Both Bexley and the sheriff acted as if they were hard of hearing.

"Follow me," he said and waved them to his house.

⚡

WYATT walked into the house where, no surprise, it felt warmer than outside.

"Watch ya step, you hear?" he said, immediately pointing out the overturned lamp on the squeaky hardwood floor.

"What the hell happened here?" asked the sheriff.

"Damn cats got into it," he said. "They do that from time to time. You know how cats can be. Besides I wasn't expectin' the Great Sheriff of Calssier Parish to grace me with his presence today."

As Wyatt walked them farther into the somewhat untidy house which, for the exception of two leather recliners in front of 60-inch television in the great room, was rather sparse of furniture, he pointed at the posters of his life's work hanging on the hallway wall leading toward his office: the Z series, including the first volume, *Zigzag Man,* the second, *Lost Yearz,* the third, and most controversial, *Journeyz,* then finally, the fourth and final volume, *Catalyzt.*

"These here are some of the few alternate covers of second and third editions of The Series," Wyatt said, stopping for a moment to admire them as if each one was his own La Gioconda—or "Mona Lisa," as most people knew it—hanging in the Louvre. "Had these babies framed a couple of months back."

What really caught Sheriff Barbee's eyes was the stark silhouette of a werewolf snake along moonlit trail on the cover of *Catalyzt.*

"Let me guess," the sheriff said, as he pointed at the one poster, "a werewolf snake?"

"Had the cover drawn from memory," Wyatt said. "Found me this great artist who was from, of all places, Belgium. Lars Peeters. Thought I was eccentric. Dude was outta his mind."

"Right," the sheriff said, rather sneeringly.

"Lotta readers I met while I was on tour were particularly drawn to *Catalyzt,*" Wyatt said. "Mainly cuz it was my most personal."

"—Right," the sheriff interrupted Wyatt, "so, what was it that you needed to show us?"

Bexley had at least a million questions to ask Wyatt about the Z series and the werewolf snake he had spent most of his adult life searching for, as well as his own personal encounters with the elusive creature; however, it was obvious to her how pushy the sheriff had gotten ever since they arrived at Whyte Plantation; yet, despite all of the soiled looks he received from Sheriff Barbee, Wyatt stayed cool. But, Bexley wondered, *for how long?*

Wyatt kept the tour moving toward his office, which was located at the end of the wide hallway.

They entered a massive room with high ceilings, which was Wyatt's office.

As with the other rooms throughout the Greek Revival house, they was very little furniture. The only pieces of furniture were a desk at the end of the room, as well as a table with picture frames along the side of the room.

Two of the four walls were lined with cardboard boxes of hardbacks and paperbacks and every single edition from the *Z* series, as well as merch, including *Z* lettered T-shirts and coffee mugs with Z-shaped lightning bolts.

Sitting on the center of the desk was a computer that looked as if it was one of the first computers ever invented. It was a rather boxy Word Processor, its sole purpose to churn out one story after another. On the end of the desk was a typewriter for moments, as Wyatt put it so nicely, he "felt like tappin' into the days of yore." Bexley could imagine Wyatt sitting in this massive room, shirtless, in his Z-patterned boxers, clobbering away at those keys, the meditative *clicking* of each stroke reverberating throughout the entire house as if he was prodding at ghosts.

While lagging behind, Bexley was drawn to the table with picture frames of what looked like family members.

She picked up a photograph of Wyatt's mother, Anastasia and his father who shared the same name as Wyatt, his father being The Second.

"That there was my father," he said, nodding at the picture frame in Bexley's hands from across the room. "He was killed in Vietnam. Me, I was just a lil' shit stain at the time. He was part of the last remaining troops before Ole Tricky Dick decided to pull the plug."

"Sorry to hear," Bexley said solemnly.

"Nah," he said, waving his hand. "It's a'ight. Didn't know him. After I had the old house torn down and donated the land, as well as quite a *substantial*," he shot a glance at the sheriff, "amount of earnings from my books to the state, I decided to build the park. The least I could do was name it after him." He kneeled down and opened up the bottom drawer of the desk. He pulled out a small black box and carefully placed it next to a stack of old manuscripts on top of the desk. He opened the lid, pulled out an object, which was covered in bubblewrap, then began to slowly unveil his prize.

More intrigued by his grand unveil, Bexley drew her attention away from the family photographs and inched closer to the desk where Sheriff Barbee was waiting in anticipation.

Wyatt peeled back the final sheet of bubblewrap.

"Is that what I think it is?" asked Sheriff Barbee.

"Yep," Wyatt said, as he revealed the fully intact skull of a werewolf snake.

"Where'd you find it?" asked Bexley.

"Burgaw Junction," he said. "I found it in an overgrowth on the edge of the woods along Fontenot River." He specifically pointed out the hole in the back of the werewolf snake's skull. "See the hole." Both the sheriff and Bexley nodded. "Capped straight to the back of the skull. Execution-style."

"Have any theories?"

"I got plenty," he said, chortling. "Based on the cut marks along the sides of the skull, I'd say it was a scrapper back in the day. Eventually, it got old, maybe even got hurt, you know, *Old Yeller*. We all know what happened to *Old Yeller* in the end."

Bexley looked closer and examined the circular-shaped hole, as well as several marks—or "indentations"—along the sides of the skull.

"The skull is old," Bexley identified. "Based on the deterioration of the bone I'd say this one was over a hundred years old."

"And is that old for one of these things?" asked the sheriff.

"I'm afraid we don't have enough information on this species to answer your question with confidence. See these marks here," Bexley pointed out to the sheriff, who, after a thorough study, nodded his head, "look familiar, don't they?"

Immediately, the sheriff was on the same page as Bexley.

"You sayin' there's more of these werewolf snakes out here?" asked the sheriff.

"Why'd you get it was just one—"

"—From the looks of the skull, it was in a fight."

"How do you explain the gunshot to its head?"

"I dunno yet."

Next to stand out were the teeth. One tooth was missing.

Perplexed more so about the missing tooth, she turned to Wyatt. "How come you didn't mention this in your book?"

Wyatt thought carefully about the question and then answered with outstanding confidence, "If I wrote about it in my book—no offense, Bexley—I'd have a thousand people like you knockin' on my door with blank checks. Askin' me to name my price. Catch-22, right?" The remark didn't draw any reply, yet it gave Wyatt a moment to further explain himself. "For as long as I can remember," he said, more so in a similar reflective state, "I've been tryin' to make people believe my story. So what better way than to make 'em believe is by providin' 'em with hard evidence to back up my so-called monster story? I'm still not quite ready to share this with the world, but I can make any exception for you. Well," he said, letting out a heavy sigh, "here you go."

More studious, the sheriff said, "Are you aware of the human remains which were found at your daddy's park?"

"Do I look like someone who keeps up with current affairs, Sheriff?"

"A group of college kids found skeletal remains in Lake Wilshire," the sheriff said. "When I had my investigators examine the remains, they found a tooth similar to this werewolf snake lodged in the back of its skull. By you withholding this information, Wyatt, you could've saved us a lot of time."

"Donovan," Bexley intervened, "the man just said he didn't know about the remains. Besides, we still don't know if it's the same tooth. Do you mind if we take the skull back with us, so we can examine it with our own equipment?"

Immediately, the thought of the human remains Sheriff Barbee spoke of possibly sharing a connection to his past left him in an almost paralyzed state.

"I dunno," Wyatt said doubtfully, and then shook his head in disgust. "Shit. Yeah. *Whatever.* But only if you bring it right back to me."

"This is now considered evi—"

"—Of course," Bexley said over the sheriff. "We'll bring it back. Actually, I have a better idea," she said more directly. "How would you feel about being on camera? Believe it or not, one of the show's producers tried to get in touch with you. I mean you don't even have to be on camera, if you don't want to. You can just tag along with us," she said over the waves of pauses from Wyatt. "We need someone who has firsthand experience with these things."

Finally, after careful deliberation, Wyatt shook his head, this time more worried than disgusted.

"Nah," he said. "That'd be a hard pass, Bexley. Sorry. I thought I told you. I'm retired—"

"—Come on, Zip," Bexley said, more convincingly. "This is your chance to prove to all those who doubted your story."

With a more serious demeanor, Wyatt said, "Let me ask you sumtin, Bexley: What you gettin' outta all this? Is it for the science, to study these creatures? Or, is sumtin else drivin' you? Tell me, Bexley: What makes you any different than any of those kids who've read one too many Wyatt Whyte books, who venture out into these lands with their cell phones, tryin' to snap 'em a shot of the mysterious Swamp Devil in order to post it on the Internet and become the next viral sensation?"

"I have sponsors," Bexley said teasingly.

"Forget it," Wyatt said, more turned off by Bexley's presence. "The skull is not for sale."

As Wyatt placed the skull back into his drawer, Bexley blurted out, "It's *not* my show, never has been!"

Wyatt stopped what he was doing and listened.

"The show was originally intended to educate people," Bexley said sentimentally, "to show them another side of life, a side that wasn't so different from their own even as far down as the microscopic level. It was meant to provoke the most basic idea that each and every organism on this planet does, in fact, have a singular purpose. I thought, by making people more conscious of every life form—big or small—all around them, I'd be able to make this cruel world a little less cruel. A place where every living thing could thrive in harmony. *But* education, Zip, it wasn't paying the bills. Studios saw what people really wanted, straight down to their core, and they exploited it. Now, I'm just their puppet that they fly around the world. Which, believe it or not, isn't even the sad part of my story. When I returned home from filming a show in Thailand, I was involved in a car accident no more than two miles from my home in Los Angeles."

"One of my deputies told me about what happened," the sheriff said tenderly. "They said you were in some bad shape."

"I suffered a collapsed lung, a severed spleen, several broken ribs, as well as internal bleeding. Up until that point, I've traveled around the entire world, gone on adventures, explored the most dangerous parts of the world, and yet, when I come home, I nearly die by someone who was texting while driving. So I was forced to ask myself: Who's more dangerous? Them, the creatures I've spent my entire life studying, or us? I'm leaning toward us. But a part of me *still* clings onto the idea that we can do much better."

Once more, Wyatt found himself diving back into thought.

He placed the skull back on the desk and said mindfully, "I lost its trail back at the abandoned paper mill, which ain't too far from Burgaw Junction."

"You talkin' 'bout the Jean Bordeaux Paper Mill?"

"What other paper mill is there?" asked Wyatt, then turned to Bexley. "Take my advice, Bexley: Stop while you're ahead. It's not worth it."

"I don't get it, Zip," Bexley said. "Why the change?"

"You want the straight up answer? Or, do you want the diluted one?"

"Straight up, Zip," she said, starting to lose her restraint. "Anything you can tell us will be a great help."

Wyatt nodded at Sheriff Barbee.

"Sheriff knows."

"I know *what*?"

"Necro."

Bexley turned to the sheriff.

"The crazy lady?"

"Leonora Weiskopf is completely harmless."

"She's anything but harmless."

"Did she say something to you?"

"It's more like what she didn't say." He directed his attention toward Bexley and made sure to look her in the eyes when he spoke his next words. "Whatever you do, just stay away from that woman. She dangerous."

Throughout the silent car ride home, Wyatt's argument while defending his novel *Catalyzt* stayed with her: "*If we humans could use science to create and manufacture a weapon that could literally wipe out the entire human race, then why in the hell couldn't nature create a weapon to defend herself?*"

"*Defend itself?*" Bexley returned.

Which prompted Wyatt to respond, "From us."

Bexley turned to the sheriff, who hadn't spoken a word to her ever since she entered the car, and said, "I can give you my copy to hold onto while I'm in town. I don't mind at all."

Sheriff Barbee shook his head, "No. That's a'ight."

He turned quiet again, this time wrestling with what Bexley had just said.

Finally, he redirected his attention from the road to Bexley, who was scrolling through her contacts on her phone.

He couldn't hold it in any longer. He had to speak his mind.

"You know that was mistake exchangin' your info like that," he said to Bexley. "I sure hope you know what you're doing."

Bexley shrugged.

"He seems harmless," she said innocently. "Maybe a little bit full of himself. Besides, I've dealt with far worse men. Trust me."

"Yeah. I know how you Hollywood types can be."

The sheriff acknowledged the road sign "BURGAW JUNCTION," which was the next street coming up.

Bexley followed the sheriff's eyes.

"It's on the way home," she said, as if she was making a suggestion.

The word was on his mind.

Bexley extracted it from the sheriff with her "pretty-please" eyes.

"*Witchcraft*," Sheriff Barbee said. "You actually believe that man?"

"Donovan, aren't you the least curious?" Bexley asked but was immediately forced to reconcile with the truth.

"You know what I think?" he said, wearing his heat. "I think he made all of this shit up to sell a book, to create himself a legend like all of those assholes did with the Loc Ness."

"I tell you what," Bexley said after calming herself. "Let's just check out the place. And if we don't find any-thing, including any *concrete* evidence to support Wyatt's claims, then I will forget even coming here."

"Is that so?"

"We'll shake hands," Bexley said, even more heated than the sheriff, "go our separate ways. And the great legend of the 'mysterious Swamp Devil' will continue live on. Deal?"

They approached the road to Burgaw Junction.

Again, Bexley looked at Sheriff Barbee with those begging eyes.

"Deal," he said and at the last second, took a sharp right onto Dumont Road.

◢

AFTER about fifteen more minutes of driving, they arrived at the abandoned Jean Bordeaux Paper Mill, which hadn't been in operation since the Great Depression. The sides of the brick structure were covered with an overgrowth of vines. Even the weeds around the building were as tall as the sheriff, who needed a weed whacker in order to walk to the paper mill. Fortunately, Bexley located a dirt trail a couple of feet wide.

"This is a mistake," the sheriff said to himself, as the thought of going anywhere near the abandoned structure made him hesitant about following Bexley.

"Be on the lookout for snakes," she said, as she grabbed a flashlight from the sheriff and led the way, "in particular, Agkistrodon piscivorus. You may know it as the *pit viper*— or 'cottonmouth'—for the white ling of its mouth. Their bite packs a punch all right."

"Yeah," Sheriff Barbee said skeptically while looking around, "and the nearest hospital happens to be at least twenty-five miles away, Bexley."

"I wouldn't worry too much about it," Bexley said, as her voice trailed off in the field of tall weeds. "About twenty-five percent of pit viper bites are considered 'dry,' meaning they don't contain venom." She stopped and saw that Sheriff Barbee was no longer following her. "Don?"

With no other choice in the matter, the sheriff figuratively put on his big boy britches and followed Bexley toward the paper mill.

"Just watch your step," she said motherly.

"Got it," he said and changed the subject to one that didn't involve snakes or deadly snakebites. "So what exactly we lookin' for?"

"Well, Wyatt said his search ended around here so, more than likely, it was either doing two things: One, either it was nesting—after all," she said, as she approached the dilapidated building, "dank, dark, undisturbed structures such as this one would make ideal places to build a nest—or two, it was feeding."

"Nesting," the sheriff repeated, then said in disbelief, "Great."

Once he noticed that Bexley stopped talking, in fact, she had stopped walking as well, Sheriff Barbee removed his eyes from the ground and glanced up.

In a trance-like state, Bexley was standing in front of a symbol of a serpent eating its own tail spray painted like graffiti along the side of the building.

The Ouroboros.

"Something wrong?" asked the sheriff.

Again, Bexley was almost transfixed by the symbol of Ouroboros.

"Bexley?" the sheriff said, closer. "Ms. Hun—"

"—Ouroboros," she said, finally pointing at the symbol.

"I'm not following."

"It's an ancient symbol that represents the cycle of life."

"Okay. And. . . "

"I've seen this before," she said. "Last night, before the crew and I left Tad's house, I saw images like this in Tad's bedroom. He had dozens of them sketched on paper like something you'd most likely see coming from the artwork of a small child. From the many passes of scribbles, I could tell it was drawn rather quickly, like he was trying to get it out of his head. Or something, I don't know."

Bexley caught herself thinking about that "other" thing, as in the other place where she saw the symbol.

As far as she knew, it was a gang or some kind of cult symbol.

Or, maybe even a bunch of bored adolescents playing sort of a "find me" type of game on social media. Find it, snap it, hashtag it. Move onto the next location. Let the *cycle* continue.

Whatever the case may be, she decided to keep it to herself.

At least, for the time being.

Think of it as a temporary lapse in memory.

"It could've been anything," Sheriff Barbee said, taking a second look at the symbol on the wall.

Bexley pushed a few times on the cracked door before she released it from its jammed position. All three of the hinges were so badly corroded that it prevented the door from opening all the way. She ended up shouldering her way through the narrow entrance. Sheriff Barbee sucked in his gut, cautiously entered as well. He turned on a flashlight, hand shaking. Bexley followed suit, only without the shaking, and gave a left-to-right scan with her flashlight. Then aimed the light on the dark silhouette of a man, who turned out to be an oddly yet humanly shaped pile of bricks that had been constructed like Frosty the Snowman. You didn't want to know what was used for a pecker. Bexley shook her head—*Damn kids.*

With their beams of light cutting through the dusty insides, they crept farther into the paper mill. From a distance, part of the roof was collapsed, which left a hole wide enough for the afternoon sun to blast through that opening like a waterfall of sunlight; however, it was still way too dark to venture without any portable handheld lights. Rusty scaffolds and towering balconies surrounded the center of the mill in a perfect square, arena-like. Directly below crooked walkways were smothered cigarette butts as well as an artwork of at least a thousand of unrecognizable shoeprints, both adolescent and adult; however, the freshest ones appeared to be from adolescents.

"Must be a hangout for the homeless," Bexley suggested.

She kneeled down and placed the beam of light over one particular cigarette that had a faded shade of red lipstick on the filter. She found herself backtracking the comment. She didn't know any homeless people who wore lipstick.

"All the way out there?" the sheriff said doubtfully. "They tend to stick close to the cities."

"Whatever went on here," she said, coming across a beer bottle, "it looks like a party."

Even the smell had a particular metallic ulcer-like aroma hidden under an old distillery odor.

Bexley kept moving farther into the mill. She arrived at another space, possibly a storage room, where she found old, rusty machinery that, like the exterior of the building, was covered with overgrowth. A couple of rats—or mice, Bexley couldn't tell which—scurried from the stacks of bare rollers as soon as they were struck by a heavenly beam of light. She rejoined the sheriff in the main open area and arrived at two massive chains that were wrapped around two support beams.

The sheriff shined the flashlight on the support beams and noticed the slight bend on each beam, as if the beams were about to buckle.

Bexley was more interested in the dark spots and puddles along the ground.

The sheriff moved the flashlight toward Bexley's and together with both light beams, brought out more of those dark continent-like shapes on the ground.

"This here looks like old blood," he said.

"A dog fight perhaps," Bexley made another suggestion.

"Perhaps," he said. "Wouldn't be the first."

"Hence the chains."

The sheriff couldn't help but draw his attention back to the beams, then those chains. He reached into his pocket, pulled out a handkerchief, and lifted up part of the chain.

"These are some awf'lly big chains for a dog."

He found himself backtracking.

I'd say it was a scrapper back in the day. Eventually, it got old, maybe even got hurt, you know, Old Yeller. We all know what happened to Old Yeller in the end.

Bexley inspected the end of the chain and found more of that clotted blood.

"Well," the sheriff said, his voice trembling, "we won't exactly know for sure until I can bring in a team of forensics and have them comb the entire area. For all I know, we're standin' smack dab in the middle of a crime scene."

"Looks like our friend, Zip, was telling the truth," Bexley said, as she moved the flashlight to the winding three-foot wide track along the dusty ground.

She knew of only one animal that left such a track.

※

WHILE forensics had set up shop inside the mill, Sheriff Barbee instructed Bexley to catch a ride home with Deputy Twiggs and specifically told her that he'd contact her later, regardless if he found anything or not.

※

IT was a quarter after three o'clock in the afternoon when the deputy dropped off Bexley at Sneak Peek Inn. Bexley thanked Deputy Twiggs and rested inside her hotel room, changed her nicotine patch while she had the time, and spent the better half of the afternoon debating whether or not she should inform Floyd about the meeting with the elusive author of the Z series, as well as the discovery inside the abandoned paper mill. Knowing Floyd and his knack of capturing the perfect "money" shot—and there were plenty of them inside the paper mill!—Bexley was most definitely convinced that he'd want to shoot at the paper mill as soon as the scene was cleared. What better way to build anticipation leading up to the inevitable encounter with the werewolf snake than by filming at such an unsafe location where its presence lingered far beyond the tracks it left behind! The fearless tracker herself, Bexley Hun, one step closer to picking up the beast's trail! Floyd would say in such vim and vigor, "It's all about creating tension so real it's palpable. The audience is *always* less frightened by what they see and more frightened by what they don't see."

With the pressure of the day mounting, Bexley decided to take a hot shower in hopes, by the end, she'd make up her mind.

By the time she stepped out of shower, dried herself, and stood in front of the mirror, she was more indecisive.

She stared, even ran her fingers over the jagged scar along the side of her rib cage.

Her phone rang, sending a shiver of panic through her body.

Please be Donovan, she thought to herself.

Longing to hear the sheriff's voice, she hurried to her phone, which was resting on the nightstand. She checked the number on the screen.

Again, she couldn't have been more hesitant about answering a call.

⚡

ON the way home from Jean Bordeaux Paper Mill, Donovan stopped at the local bookstore called Da Book Nook right before they were about to close shop for the night. He grabbed himself the last copy of Wyatt Whyte's paperback, *Catalyzt*.

⚡

"SOMETHING smells good," Donovan said, rolling his window farther down as he drove past Growlers.

The parking lot was fairly crowded. Patrons were coming and going from the restaurant, ready to feed or already fed.

He thought about how much he could use a stiff drink right now, a nightcap to wash away the day; however, with the fresh case sitting heavily on his mind, the thought came and went.

⚡

AFTER Donovan parked the car inside the garage, it just dawned on him that he was supposed to pick up food for Cheyenne. He scratched his red, tired eyes, as if, by doing so, he'd rid away the day. Then, placed the brown paper bag with the book inside the glove compartment. The only books she ever saw him reading were ones with pictures in them, and the only question he wanted to answer right now was "With ice or without ice?"

As soon as he stepped foot inside the house, he heard the roaring sounds of a vacuum cleaner running throughout the house. Which, he knew, was a bad sign on how the rest of the night was going to pan out. She always cleaned when she was in a bitchy mood and did so, loudly and violently, as if she was taking out her frustration on naughty bacteria and rebellious dust mites. *Why is it that long days are always met with the bitchy wife?* Of course, he'd never verbalize such a question aloud. Otherwise, Pounding Stare would tear him a new hole.

Cheyenne turned off the vacuum once she saw her husband through the bedroom doorway.

She was dressed, too, Donovan also noticed.

Another bad sign—or good, he didn't know which.

"You're home," she said, out of breath. "I didn't hear you come in—"

"—Cleaning, huh," he said, cutting her off. "This late?"

Cheyenne looked down at the vacuum cleaner, as if, for a moment, she was completely unaware that she was recently using it.

"I was trying to keep busy until you got back."

"You didn't get it, did you?" asked the sheriff.

"No," she said, her tone higher. "In fact, I did."

Donovan dropped the car keys in the small clay dish on the nightstand.

"Congrats," he said, more relieved and kissed his wife.

"It came down to me and, of all people, Lahela making the final call."

"Tom's wife?"

Cheyenne nodded her head.

"So, she gave you the loan?"

Once more, Cheyenne nodded, this time with a broad smile on her face.

"Starting next Monday I'll be meeting with the architect and we'll start going through designs. It's really happening, Don. I can't believe it. I'm going to open up my own store. *And,*" Cheyenne said, more excited, "get this: I had a cool idea where every Thursday night I'll offer free pottery lessons for adults. I'm thinking of calling it 'Pottery and Play.' I'll only charge for the wine, of course."

"If you're gonna be servin' up alcohol, you gonna need a license."

"Don't be such a Party Pooper, Don," she said. "I will. Besides, the concept is to hang out with friends, make pottery while enjoying a glass of wine."

"How's someone gonna drink wine when your hands are gonna be all messy from wet clay?"

"I'll serve the wine out of plastic cups," Cheyenne said. "Or, even better, I'll give them a straw that way their hands will be free to get as dirty as they want."

"Well, let's not get ahead of ourselves."

Donovan leaned down and kissed his wife once more. Halfway through the kiss, she recoiled and said, "You forgot to pick up food, didn't you?"

"Long day," he said, bracing for impact.

"Well since I didn't have time to cook," she said, "let's go out and celebrate." She looked down at her outfit. "I'm already dressed. How about Enzo's? Come on, Don. You can use a break from work."

"A'ight," he said, "but you mind if we go somewhere else other than Enzo's? Lately, my stomach's been actin' like it has a bone to pick with ole Enzo."

"Have any other suggestions?"

"I could use a burger."

Only one place came to mind.

GROWLERS was still crowded when Donovan and Cheyenne arrived; in fact, it appeared to Donovan as if it had gotten even more crowded than the time he drove past the restaurant about an hour ago.

While waiting to be seated, several of the patrons shot glances at Donovan, not the sheriff.

"You're off the clock, Don," Cheyenne said in his ear. "Don't mind them."

"It's hard not to," he replied.

Finally, the hostess showed them to the booth, which Donovan had asked for instead of a table.

The hostess handed them their menus and told them that their waiter, Julio, would be with them shortly. On the front of the menu was the food while on the back, the booze. Donovan immediately flipped to the back.

Before she left, she apologized once more for the wait.

"Not a problem," Cheyenne said, as her husband contemplated whether or not he should start out with a shot or a beer.

Cheyenne immediately noticed his interest in alcohol.

"Eat first," she said and reached over the table to flip over his menu. "Drink later."

"Excuse me, lady."

"Well," she said, leaning over the table, "I was thinking maybe we continue our celebration later this evening."

"Is that so?"

Cheyenne's face was warm. She slowly bobbed her head up and down, up and down, while wearing the face of a woman who was twenty years younger, a face that Donovan missed dearly.

"On that note," he said and skimmed through the menu, "I'll skip the burger and go for a salad."

Cheyenne couldn't help but let out a thunderous "Ha!"

As though he couldn't arrive at a more perfect time, the waiter, Julio, arrived to take their drink orders.

"I'll take a Coke," he said. Then, emphasized, "Diet."

"And for you, ma'am?"

"Do you have sweet tea?"

"Of course," he said. "Best in town."

"One sweet tea with a slice of lemon."

"Absolutely."

The waiter memorized the drink orders and then poured them both a glass of ice water.

As the waiter was filling Donovan's glass, he noticed a tattoo of a Japanese symbol on his wrist. It wasn't the content of the tattoo that caught his eye. It was the position of the tattoo.

Right then and there, Donovan realized where he saw the symbol.

Last year, he thought, *one of the witnesses, big guy, worked nights here.*

"Is something wrong, Don?" asked Cheyenne.

"I can't believe it," he said, his eyes widened. "I have to run."

"What? Donnie, you're serious?"

"I'm so sorry, Annie," he said while acknowledging the sudden change in her demeanor and how, in an instant, she had gone straight from his beautiful, lovely Annie Pie who was the mother of his daughter, to the fierce, plucky warrior who was Pounding Stare. "I'll make it up to you. Promise." Donovan waved down the waiter, Julio, who hadn't ventured off too far from their table. "Can I get a to-go order?"

Cheyenne had no words.

"Donovan?" she uttered, trying to make sense of her husband's behavior.

◢

CHEYENNE was livid and had every right to be; however, her husband's explanation regarding his epiphany on the ride home, including the circular snake symbol—*aurora borealis* or whatever Bexley had called it—as well as the two places where he had seen the symbol, one of them being on the wrist of a former employee who worked at Suck The Head before it was bought out, renovated, and renamed Growlers, helped snuff out that flame which was igniting her anger until he mentioned "her" name, the person whom he had made this so-called "other" discovery with, the person whom he had been spending *way* too much time with, which was met with those inevitable five words, spoken in all caps: *ARE YOU HAVING AN AFFAIR?*

She repeated the words for him, adding a couple of extra words each time.

"Are you having an affair *with this woman?*" asked Cheyenne.

Donovan was through arguing with Pounding Stare; in fact, he couldn't drop her off at the house quick enough.

N

DETECTIVE Zargarpour managed to track down the address for Austin Hirsch, also known as "Hunchback." Accompanied by Detective Harlem and Deputy Afolabi, they escorted Austin to interrogation where only a few minutes later, Sheriff Barbee, who was dressed in plain clothes, entered the room.

Austin Jericho Hirsch, who preferred to go by his new nickname "Bear," told the sheriff everything that he knew about the symbol. He didn't exactly spill his beans, but he came damn near close. He even had that Ouroboros tattoo removed by laser. Saved up six paychecks to pay for the removal. After working part time at several jobs, one including Suck The Head as a bouncer, another as an orderly at Saint James Memorial, and lastly, a job similar to the one at Suck The Head, however, with more of a tightlipped responsibility, he created his own landscaping service called Serenity. Having served three years in the United States Army and doing a tour which resulted in a nearly crippling lower back injury branding him the name "Hunchback" when he returned home from Afghanistan, Bear only hired retired vets, like himself; however, Bear rarely spoke about his medical discharge from the Army.

Sheriff Barbee was more interested in the job that required a "tightlipped responsibility."

When pressed by the sheriff, who, after arguing with Cheyenne and missing a golden opportunity for makeup sex—which, as of lately, was the only kind of sex he was getting, hence why the celebration sex was bound to be one for the ages—wasn't in any mood for bullshit, Bear couldn't name the person who had hired him for the job. The only details he could give the sheriff were how it went down: First, he'd receive a text of the location from a "Blocked" number, meaning if he ever got caught and had to hand over his phone to the police, it'd be one helluva hard time for police to track down the number; then, when he arrived, he was greeted by the muscle, usually a different guy each time, however, Bear never got a name and conversation was kept to a minimum; after he was shown around the perimeter, detailed over each exit, which doors were to remain locked, which ones were for emergencies, and whatnot, and then, finally given the lowdown, as in how many people were going to show up that night, as well as a list of names, which, after the "show," which was what they called it, was to be destroyed, as in burned, he took his post by the main entrance and kept a lookout. He didn't know anything about the "show," what it was, who was in it. All he could hear were the animalistic sounds of chaos: *screams, screeches, cries, chants*—both rally and kill chants—*grunts, groans, ewws* and *ahs*, as well as primitive roars of carnage seeping through the walls. In his own words, he could only describe the experience as "disturbing."

"Disturbin' how?" asked the sheriff, as he leaned in closer.

"Disturbing," he said, thinking wisely, "as in some nights I had to bring a pair of ear buds to block out the noise."

The sheriff digested the comment—or at least tried to. Only a couple of seconds of trying to comprehend what Bear was saying, the comment wasn't at all sitting well inside him.

"I want a name," Sheriff Barbee said fiercely. "Any name."

Bear embraced a deep breath, as if he waiting for this exact moment where he'd be coerced to saying something that he'd later regret. Like in all of the crime shows on TV where the weak-looking nark ratted out the more sought-after perp.

He thought about his mama and one day earning enough money to buy her a house of her own. He was tired of talking about it. This was going to be the kick in the rear that he so desperately needed.

"*Rome*," he said clearly. "They call themselves Rome."

"They?"

"It's like a club."

"You mean a gang?"

"No," he said, more expressively. "You know, like a club-*club*. You got fat cats with boatloads of cheddar, gamblers who owe enough money to loan sharks to buy two houses, even your everyday fools who show up with their life's savings. *It's Wall Street without the Wall Street.*"

Bear looked away for a moment and then looked at the camera in the corner of the room.

Sheriff Barbee was quick to acknowledge his interest in the camera. Right then and there, he realized Bear was about squeal a one-hit wonder.

"Camera is off, Austin," he said to Bear.

Bear moved his eyes toward the sheriff's.

"I've even seen your kind, Barbee," he said with a loss of color in his face.

TWO DAYS LATER

AFTER wasting an entire day combing for more evidence at Jean Bordeaux Paper Mill, Donovan woke up on the farthest side of the bed to the phone call of Deputy Twiggs informing him about the death of Austin "Bear" Hirsch.

When asked about the "how" of Bear's death, the deputy had a hard time explaining the details. It was one of those "you have to see it to believe it" types of situations.

N

THE sheriff pulled up to the Hirsch residence where a HAZMAT team was securing the inside of the house. Austin's neighbor was the one who first called about the disturbance, said she heard Austin's truck running inside the garage right before she went to bed, which was about eleven-thirty, then heard it again when she woke up the next morning about six o'clock. She said she was a light sleeper and she swore that she heard the truck running throughout the night. Based on the initial findings, there were two bodies inside the house: one, Austin's mother, Sheryl Hirsch, the other, Austin himself. Both were found lying in their beds, dead. The batteries inside the carbon monoxide detectors in every single room had been removed from the devices. The two ends of water hoses had been duct taped around the exhaust pipe of Austin's truck. The two hoses snaked inside the ranch-style house, one of the hoses going underneath the doorway to Austin's bedroom while the other one going inside Sheryl's bedroom in similar fashion. Even the narrow openings along the doorways of each bedroom had been clogged with bath towels and then sealed with duct tape; *however*, the only difference between the two bedrooms was that Austin's bedroom was sealed from the inside of the room, *not* the outside. Later, once the house was safe to enter, Sheriff Barbee also pointed out that the window to Austin's bedroom happened to be unlocked.

Considering that Austin didn't exactly live in a safe neighborhood, he knew it couldn't have been a coincidence.

N

BACK at the Calssier Parish Sheriff's Office, Sheriff Barbee spent most of the afternoon inside his office, skimming through a stack of old case files that Bexley had ruled, based off her educational background as well as the evidence provided, both relative and irrelative, death by a werewolf snake, not an alligator, as the initial report stated. One name had stood out throughout each report.

N

SHERIFF Barbee managed to catch Susanne as she was leaving the morgue.

Susanne, who, once casually strolling to her car in the parking lot, acted as if she was in a hurry as soon as the sheriff made his presence known, told the sheriff that she had somewhere to be.

"Can we talk, Susanne?" the sheriff asked Susanne, who went straight for the keys in her purse.

"Sorry," she said. "I'm late to an arrangement."

"Let me guess," he said with a hint of sarcasm in his voice, "Landon's takin' you out to that new fancy restaurant, The Roux, over on East Pointe."

"I wish," Susanne said, as she stopped, faced the sheriff, then motioned to her car. "Do you mind?"

"How 'bout you join me in a cup of coffee?" asked the sheriff, more persistently. "I just have a couple of questions to ask you."

"Regarding?"

"Well," the sheriff said, looking around the parking lot. "I'd rather not say at this moment."

"I'm sorry," Susanne said. "If you would excuse, I have to be somewhere."

She walked past the sheriff.

Only a couple of steps in her pace, the sheriff said from behind, "I know what you've done, Susanne. All I want to know is how much they're paying you."

Susanne stopped in her tracks and slowly rotated around. Her face was pale white. She looked at the sheriff as if he had cracked about her late father.

"Excuse me?"

"What did they promise you?" asked the sheriff.

"Who's they?"

"I dunno," he said. "You tell me."

She swallowed the next words down her throat and glanced around the parking lot in what the sheriff perceived as paranoia.

"What do you want?" she asked.

"Just a couple of answers."

"You know where the old Guillory casino used to be?"

"Sure," the sheriff said. "I know where it's at."

Susanne said, "Meet me there."

N

INSTEAD of grabbing a cup of coffee, which Sheriff Barbee really wasn't going to do, Susanne led the sheriff to the outskirts of Sinclair Leprieur in a smaller town called Mafadaux. There, standing next to an overgrown field where a dilapidated house, King Guillory Casino, which used to be one of the most popular casinos west of the Mississippi, Susanne told Sheriff Barbee about the false reports, why she did it, how she did it, and *who* was the person pulling her strings.

"Satterwhite," Sheriff Barbee repeated.

"Why do you always have to get involved, Donovan? Can't you just turn the other cheek, let nature sort this thing out?"

"Where's the next fight gonna be?" the sheriff asked Susanne, who was hesitant about answering.

Her lack of answer had only accentuated the severity of her situation.

"Susanne? Come on now—"

"—I dunno," she blurted out, her eyes gushing tears. "I think I heard something about a gas station."

"When?"

"Tomorrow night."

"Be more specific."

"They usually have them at areas that are abandoned."

The sheriff only knew of two abandoned gas stations in the area, one of them happened to be more than a gas station and in the past, was known to draw criminal activity.

"Benoit's?"

Susanne struggled to nod her head.

"I think so," she said. "That name rings a bell—"

"—Listen, Susanne," the sheriff instructed, " you and Landon need to lay low for the next couple of days. Y'all have anywhere you can stay? Somewhere outside of town? How 'bout any relatives?"

"Landon has a brother who lives in St. Louis."

"Good," he said. "Go there as soon as you can."

"Donovan," Susanne cried. "I'm sorry. I didn't—"

"—Susanne, you don't have time for this," he said. "You hear?"

Sniffling up the loose phlegm from her nose, Susanne nodded.

She did as the sheriff asked and started making her plan to leave town.

WHILE shooting at Rue Wabash High School, Bexley received a phone call from Sheriff Barbee while she was in the middle of a shoot inside a ruined gymnasium, which was a similar condition to that of the paper mill: cigarette butts; holes in the walls, as well as ceiling; debris and trash scattered everywhere; crime scene-like *blood* decorated the walls, the backboards, the hardwood floors, surface-level as well as between the cracks, even specks of blood on the ceiling; two similar industrial sized chains, this time each one wrapped around each opposing basketball goal posts; even those cracks in the warped hardwood floor, which weren't caked with blood, started to sprout weeds, as if the natural outside world was consuming the inside of the manmade structure. It was as though the carnage from the paper mill had been copied and pasted into the gymnasium.

Floyd slammed his arms against his sides and cried out Bexley's name, as she excused herself.

The director wasn't the only one left reeling with vexation. Other crewmembers, who were on edge and itching to wrap up the shot, occupied their headspace with work by tending to whatever equipment he or she possessed. Grippers made sure their rigs were tight, double—even triple—checking their setup. The guys in the lightning department rechecked lights, making sure there weren't any unnecessary shadows in the shot. Sound guys tested their mikes, even though the mikes were good. The script supervisor, who often pulled Houdini's during a shoot, was talking shop with one of the wardrobe ladies.

Bexley stepped outside the gym into a narrow, moldy hallway where the echoes of her voice were less transparent.

"Donovan," she whispered into the phone, "I thought I told you to text me."

"Right," the sheriff said, the sound of Bexley's voice making the tone he was originally going to use less rigid. "You know I'm old fashioned. Anyway, the reason I'm callin' is to inform you that some important information has recently come to light."

Bexley asked, "What information?"

"It's probably best that I not say over the phone," he said.

"Donovan," she said, more straightforwardly, "whatever it is you have to say, then say it. I don't have time for this—"

"—There's this old gas station off Cherry Grove Road called Fill'R Up, was once owned by a fellow named Marceau Benoit. Benoit died some years back—can't remember when—but his son took over his business. Not too long after the son took over, the place ended up going to pot. Word has it that there's supposed to be an event there tomorrow night."

She mentally highlighted the name of the street, *Cherry Grove Road*, and that name, *Marceau Benoit*, repeated them both several times in her head as if she was cataloguing them into her thought bank.

"What kind of an event?"

"The kind we saw back at Jean Bordeaux Paper Mill."

"Where did you get this information?"

"Doesn't matter," he said. "Where y'at? I can meet you somewhere."

"I'm afraid that's not possible," she said. "I'm actually on set right now."

"Where?"

Bexley paused.

"We're filming a quick scene next to Fontenot River," she said. "Nothing too big."

"Well, that's not too far from where I'm at," he said. "I can pick you up—"

"—No," Bexley interrupted. "How about I meet you somewhere after I finish up here."

"Okay. I guess I can do that," sheriff trailed off as he tried to think of a place where he could meet Bexley without drawing too much attention. Only one place came to mind, and it was the closest place from his house. "I'll tell you what: there's a taco truck called El Delicioso, which sets up shop next to the Gator Hole around six o'clock. How 'bout you meet me there at around, let's say, seven?"

"How about eight o'clock?"

"I can do eight," he said.

"Sounds good."

"Well, see ya at eight."

Bexley hung up with the sheriff and walked back into the gymnasium where a thinly-reserved Floyd was walking straight toward her.

He stopped in front of her, held out his right hand, palm side up, and said sassily, "Hand it over."

"Hand what over?"

"Your phone," he said, clapping his fingers against his palm.

"I'm not handing over my phone, Floyd," Bexley said with resentment. "And you don't have to talk to me like I'm four years old."

"We're on a tight schedule here, Bexley, and frankly, you're being rude."

"Rude? You're one to talk."

Bexley stormed off, shouldering her way past Floyd.

He rotated around, shifted his weight to one side of his body, and folded both arms across his chest.

"Excuse me," Floyd said, his tone drawn out, hostile.

Bexley applied the brakes to her firm stride and marched back to Floyd.

She asked, "How much longer can we continue to lie about what we're doing here? Huh, Floyd?"

Floyd perversely looked over Bexley as if, in some diabolical way, he got off on watching mad women.

"Let me guess," he said, his queer eyes lowered under a finely sharp ridge of a brow, "that was your new boyfriend on the phone."

"Fuck you, Floyd," Bexley said bitterly. "I'm done lying to him. Got it?"

Floyd held up his hands in surrender.

"Sure," he said. "I got it. Now, are we gonna finish this scene or what?"

SUSANNE was packing her luggage, including a suitcase, a cosmetic bag crammed with makeup and feminine hygiene, as well as a Ziploc freezer bag filled with generic OTC medications, when she heard a strange noise coming from outside.

At first, she suspected it was Landon, who had come home earlier from work. She didn't think anything of it until she heard the noise a second time.

She stopped packing and left the bedroom.

"Landon, Honey," she said, poking her head from the bedroom.

She heard no response.

As she went back into the bedroom and prepared to pack, she heard the noise yet again, but this time much louder and more distinguishable. Immediately, she recognized the sound for she had heard it thousands of times over those scorching summers when Landon, who was very particular about the upkeep of his lawn and at times, made her question who Landon loved more, his wife or his zoysia grass, turned on the water sprinklers. That choppy, rapid-fire *hiss–hiss–hiss* sound of the impulse sprinkler head spraying water over the lawn had become one of the many melodies of her seasonal music.

Susanne went downstairs, first noticing the empty driveway, in particular, the Australia-shaped oil spot where Landon usually parked his car, then hearing what she concluded was, in fact, the sprinkler running in the backyard.

With caution, Susanne switched on the floodlight and walked toward the outdoor faucet, which happened to be located behind a couple of holly bushes along the side of the house. She straightened and thinned out her body, shuffled sideways between the two bushes, leaned down, and turned off the faucet while casting a tall shadow along the house.

As she pulled herself away from the faucet, the floodlight revealed a yellow lighter lying in the mulch. She picked it up and while making her way from the bushes, closely inspected the lighter.

Psst!

Susanne turned to the noise behind her.

Before she could recoil from the sight of Ms. Necro, who was wearing a raggedy navy blue bandana the same way an outlaw would sport it over the lower half of the face, a pair of swim goggles worn enough to make her dark eyes bulge, and holding out a lime green latex dishwashing gloved hand in front of the straw that had been inserted inside a centimeter-long slit over the bandana, a pale blue cloud of strange powder was blown directly in Susanne's face.

Susanne initial reaction was to wave the cloud of powder from her face. The pale blue powder had gotten into both of her eyes, which caused them to burn, as well as her nose and mouth, which caused her throat to tickle.

Rubbing her burning eyes, Susanne started to hawk, first softly, like someone trying to extract phlegm or a piece of food lodged in the back of the throat; then the more she hawked, the more she violently coughed.

Underneath the pale blue powder that wore like makeup, Susanne was turning red in the face. She dropped the lighter from her hand and staggered back and forth. She dropped to one knee, then two, looking up at Ms. Necro, who was towering above her. Once the air was cleared, she removed the bandana with the straw from her face and watched Susanne, whose vision doubled, then tripled.

With her eyelids fluttering like bird wings, she heavily fell to her side; however, she was still conscious. Yet, she remained still, her entire body paralyzed.

Ms. Necro removed the contaminated glove from her hand and picked up the yellow lighter off the ground and handed it to the burly, bearded man named Mutt, who emerged from the dark shadows outside the floodlight. He was dressed in a black and red tracksuit and from his dumb facial expression, looked as if he had a hard time registering why Ms. Necro was handing him a yellow lighter.

"You moron," Ms. Necro seethed, slamming the lighter in his catcher's mitt of a hand. "Bad enough you nearly killed the sheriff's wife, *Mutton*. Next time be a lil' more careful. I'm not gonna tell you again. Got it?"

She patted Mutt on the side of the face, as if he was an obedient pet.

Eventually, after taking a moment to register the words, in cartoon-style Mutt bobbed his head three times, the third time he forgot what he was agreeing to.

Ms. Necro animatedly instructed Mutt to pick up Susanne, whom she referred to as "the woman," and bring her upstairs. Mutt followed commands and grabbed Susanne underneath her arms and picked her up as if she was a dumbbell.

Once inside, Ms. Necro looked around and said amusedly, "Sweet crib."

Mutt carried Susanne up the stairs to the bedroom where Ms. Necro instructed him to place her body in the bathtub inside the master bathroom.

Susanne's eyes remained open while Mutt roughly handled her body.

"Gently, you dumb ape," Ms. Necro seethed.

Once more, Mutt bobbed his head like the good pet he was and while combing the side of Susanne's mane, placed her body into the tub.

"Good boy," Ms. Necro said, as she started to remove Susanne's clothes. She stopped while removing Susanne's bra, admired her D-cup sized breast as well as her slim, toned figure, and said casually to a gawking Susanne, who was able to move both her eyes toward Ms. Necro, "Such a shame to let a beautiful body go to waste. Most women would kill to have a body like yours." Once more, Ms. Necro eyed Susanne's rack, held her eyes on it, then flashed her a wicked little smile. "Well," she said, moving her eyes up to Susanne's, "the worms are gonna love ya."

Ms. Necro made a weasel-like noise by clapping her tongue against the backside of her teeth.

DALIVIA PLAUT

"You gonna stand there or you gonna help me?" Ms. Necro asked Mutt, who, after registering the words, finally assisted her with the rest of Susanne's clothes.

Once Susanne was undressed, Ms. Necro turned on the water and let it run to the very top.

While that was happening, Ms. Necro, with her smooth, fingerprint-less fingertips smooth and papery from the many years of cooking, pulled out a bottle of Aleve from her pocket, unscrewed the cap, and dropped a couple down the sink.

Then, she carefully placed the open bottle along the side of the vanity.

She turned to Mutt and winked at him.

"For the *aesthetic*," she said.

Mutt clearly didn't understand the word or its usage.

The bathwater was now up to Susanne's chin and was only a couple of minutes away from reaching her nose.

Ms. Necro took the last remaining minutes to make sure the scene was staged according to plan. She placed Susanne's clothes on top of one of those remote controlled beds like she had seen on TV, which, like the interior decor, impressed her. She started to unpack the luggage that Susanne had already packed when all of a sudden her eyes shot back to the bathroom where Mutt was kneeling beside the bathroom.

"Hey," Ms. Necro shouted out, as she stormed to the bathroom.

Mutt's right arm was submerged in the bathwater. Ms. Necro shouted out his name. He rotated around, as he was slow to remove his hand.

"What da hell you think you're going?" asked Ms. Necro.

Mutt had no response for her.

Ms. Necro slapped him across his meaty face.

"Don't touch her again," she demanded sharply. "Got it?"

With his head lowered and his eyes drooping like a sad dog, Mutt bobbed his head as if the simple command was quite an arduous task.

With Susanne's body, including her head, fully submerged, Ms. Necro went back into the bedroom to finish
the job.

She saw the beam of a headlight cross the bedroom wall.

Then, moments later, she heard the sound of a car door
closing.

She walked back into the bathroom where Mutt was
staring at Susanne as her wide eyes stared back underneath
the rippling water.

"Meet me outside," Ms. Necro said to Mutt. "I can
handle the husband."

Mutt looked at Ms. Necro with that same dumb expression.

"Yeah," she said, as if she was reading his expression or
lack thereof. "I'm sure. Now, go on."

Ms. Necro pulled out a joint that had been smoked
down to a roach from her pocket, inserted it into the corner
of her mouth, and quickly snapped her fingers a couple of
times at Mutt before he exited the bathroom.

"Lighter," she said, snapping away. "Gimme. Now."

$$\textit{N}$$

EARLIER that day, Donovan told Cheyenne over the telephone that he'd try best he could to make it home in time
for dinner as soon as he finished up at the Sheriff's Office,
but he ended up arriving at least two hours past after the
time he originally said, which was around a ballpark of five-
thirty. Donovan figured he'd check on his wife, run to the
nearest Chicken Shack to pick up her favorite three piece
meal if she wasn't able to go to the grocery store, make sure
she was fed and taken care of, then he'd use an excuse that
he left something behind at the office, which he hadn't
used since the time they went through a rough patch in
their marriage six years ago when they hardly spoke a word
to one another and spent most of their time in separate
rooms as if avoidance had become a popular trend that was
destined to end with violence. He was certain the excuse,

as much as he hated using it, would give him enough time to meet up with Bexley.

When he closed the front door behind him, Cheyenne was waiting for him by the kitchen doorway.

"It's freezin' in here," Donovan said, shivering from the coolness of the living room.

The temperature inside the house was at least fifty-nine degrees Fahrenheit. He could hear the AC unit running at full blast outside. All he could think about was the cost of having to replace the fifteen-year old unit, especially with it being on its last leg and all. He ignored Cheyenne in the corner of his eye, immediately went straight to the thermostat, and noticed the temperature had been set to fifty-three. He wasn't aware the temperature could go that low—frankly, the lowest he had ever seen it was at sixty-eight, but during those cold years, that sickness in his wife's body liked it cold, preferred it actually, as if it was more cozy in cold, dark places; regardless, the sight of the temperature sent a flash of anger throughout his body. Using his thumb as support underneath his straightened index finger, which was like a tiny mallet pounding away on the up arrow, he jacked up the temperature back to its normal setting of seventy-four degrees. *What'd hell is that woman thinking, running up the goddamn bill like that?* As Donovan stormed toward his wife, who was standing in that same position he last saw her when he first entered the house, a grim thought caused him to slow down his pace. The possibility alone of that "it was back" melted any hostility he had surging through his body.

"Anne, Honey," he said, approaching her, "have you been messin' with the thermostat?"

With her arms held down by her side, Cheyenne snapped from her trance as if it was one of those little black bugs pestering her face and turned to Donovan.

"So sorry about that," she said, "I meant to put it on seventy-three. Must've been a glitch or something."

"You're not cold?"

"No," she said casually yet confusedly, as if she wasn't so sure which to feel, calmness or confusion. "Not really?"

251

Donovan touched his wife's forearm, then placed the backside of his hand on her forehead.

"You don't seem cold."

"Why should I be?" asked Cheyenne.

He teased, "Guess you're just a cold-blooded gal, huh?"

The comment barely provoked any emotion from Cheyenne.

"You sure you're okay?"

She bobbed her head, obediently.

"Why shouldn't I be?" she asked.

"Nuttin," he said, not thinking too much about her strange behavior. "Sorry I'm late. I got caught up at work. Have you eaten yet? I can pick you up something, if you want."

"I'm fine," she said robotically. "I ate a bowl of cereal for dinner."

"You're not hungry?"

"Nope."

"Well," he said, as he walked toward the cabinet to grab himself a glass from the shelf, "I think I might just make myself a sandwich." A new excuse sprung up in his mind, and it'd certainly be better than using that old one. *Why not say you're going to pick up food? Fast food,* he thought, *something I could eat in the car.*

As he opened up the cabinet door, he noticed a small blotch of what looked like a spill of paprika along the tile countertop. He ran his fingertip over the reddish powdery substance. Then rubbed the substance between his index finger and thumb. He closely inspected his red fingertips. He held it up to his nose and took a sniff. He suddenly recoiled from the fishy, pungent stench.

⚡

PARKED somewhere along an empty cul-de-sac, Ms. Necro sat on the tailgate with her hand resting along the truck bed floor and keeping her upright while her other hand was holding a squeezable pouch of Musselman's applesauce. She squeezed a mouthful of applesauce into her mouth, smacked her gums together in exaggeration, and said coolly to the night darkness, *"What is it, Honey?"*

N

CHEYENNE repeated the question to her husband.

"Oh," he said, trailing off. "Nuttin. A lil' case of déjà vu. That's all."

As soon as he grabbed the cup from the shelf and rotated around, Cheyenne was holding a glass of milk in front of her.

"Save yourself the trouble. . ."

He was somewhat baffled from the sight of Cheyenne and her speediness to pour him a glass of milk before he could even reach for a glass.

"You read my mind," he said.

"Please," Cheyenne said, as if she was returning the tease. *"You're predicable."*

She handed him the glass of milk, which was slightly lukewarm.

"Thank ya, ma'am," he said and sipped from the glass.

He received a strange aftertaste in the back of his throat.

"You sure the milk is still fresh?" he asked, smelling it first but not reacting much to the smell, then placing aside the glass on the countertop. He opened the fridge, grabbed the milk carton from the side of the door, and checked the date. It had two days left before expiration. He smelled the inside of the carton, but it had no funky smell to it.

"Does it taste funny?" asked Cheyenne.

"A little," he said, drifting off.

"How about a glass of tea?"

You know I don't drink tea woman, Donovan thought, but said instead, "You know caffeine keeps me up a night."

Everything about Sheriff Donovan Barbee faded, his thoughts, feeling, even his own identity. Somewhere among that downward spiral, he didn't even know where he was or how he had wound up inside this strange kitchen. He redirected his attention toward his wife,

Cheyenne, and for the briefest moment, didn't recognize the woman standing next to him. He shook his head, snapping from what Cheyenne referred to in the past during her chemo as "brain farts."

"Then, *how about a beer?*"

"Nah," he said, waving off Cheyenne. "It's been a long day."

"*You're tired?*"

"Yes," he said in that same robotic tone. "I'm tired."

Donovan walked into the dark living room, sat down in that comfy recliner of his, grabbed the TV remote wedged between the seat cushions, and flipped it on *Shark Tank*.

✗

AS Bexley paced laps around a picnic bench next to the Gator Hole where, not too far away, a handful of late-nite stoners and foodies were ordering tacos at El Delicioso, she checked the time on her watch.

The time read, "8:13."

Bexley waited a couple of extra minutes before she finally decided to give the sheriff a call.

✗

SPACED out in a coma-like state with his eyes glazed over and glowing from the flicker of the TV screen, Donovan reached for the cell phone on a side table next to the recliner and answered the call without even glancing at the phone.

"Hello," he said in a monotone voice.

✗

BEXLEY'S brow furrowed from the sound of his gruffly voice, which sounded like the voice of a man who was in the middle of catching z's.

"Where are you?" asked Bexley.

"Home," he said over the other end.

Bexley was even more confused by the sheriff and started questioning if she dialed the wrong number.

"Am I calling at a bad time?" she asked, waiting in anticipation.

✕

GIVEN more life by the question, Donovan pulled the wooden handle along the side of the recliner, which sprung his once relaxed body forward.

"Who is this?" he asked.

"It's me," the caller said over the phone. "Bexley," she said. "*Bexley* Hun."

"I don't know any Bexley Hun," he said.

"I'm sorry," Bexley said. "Is this Sheriff Barbee?"

He thought carefully about the question, more so the word or title.

Sheriff?

Then, answered with a drawn out voice as if he was reiterating Bexley's own question, "Yes." He gained more confidence in his response. "This is the Sheriff of Calssier Parish. Who is this?"

✕

"IS this some sort of joke, Donovan?" Bexley asked, as she stopped pacing.

Everything about her stopped, except for her mind, which was racing.

✕

MEANWHILE, Ms. Necro was having the time of her life as she sat relaxingly on the bedding of the truck.

She grabbed the invisible phone from the empty space to the right of her, held her right hand in the comical shape of a phone, pinkie finger and thumb extended to their extremes while her remaining three digits were tucked into her palm; and then she placed her phone-hand to her face and made a stupid, cross-eyed expression on her face.

"*Who is this?*" said Ms. Necro, with her voice cute and child-like.

✎

ANOTHER voice came on the phone.

Bexley was at a loss of words.

Logically, the only person whom she could think about was Donovan's wife; and somehow, during the time spent together, Missus Donovan had gotten the impression that her husband was not running around doing police work; instead, he was out involving himself in nefarious activities with a lady on TV.

✎

CHEYENNE towered over her husband and asked once more, this time with energy, "*May I ask who's calling?*"

"This is Bexley Hun," she said finally. "Who is this?"

"*I'm the sheriff's wife, Cheyenne Barbee.*"

✎

"IT'S nice to meet you, Cheyenne," Bexley said, more re-lieved by the fact that she called the right number, not the wrong. "I've been helping out your husband on the new case."

Yet again, Bexley started pacing around the picnic ta-ble.

"*Right,*" Cheyenne said, more casually, "The *Bexley Hun. Yes. I've heard a lot about you. As a matter of fact, my husband won't shut up about you.*"

"Is that so? Well," Bexley said and for a moment, stopped pacing to think of something nice to say to her, "your a lucky woman to have such a good man."

She resumed pacing.

However, the phone on the other end went silent, dead.

Which had Bexley wondering if Cheyenne heard the compliment.

"In case you weren't aware," Bexley announced over a phone noise, "I have a show on the streaming service S-H-H."

"*Oh!*" Cheyenne said. "*You mean, Shh!*"

The only follow up she could come up with was a trendy expression that avid Shh! viewers jokingly used to rebuke questioners. Unlike its competitors known to live and die by the "dump it all at once" motto, Shh! released each one of their episodes from the premiere shows, or "shush shows," every Friday. That whole Whatever N' Chill was more like Shut the Fuck Up N' Have Some Fucking Patience You Entitled Little Shit!

"Did you just *shush* me?" asked Bexley.

"*No,*" Cheyenne said. "*I mean the name, Shh!*"

"I know," Bexley said, playing off the harmless comment. "It's a silly comeback that the kids use nowadays. Anyway, do you mind putting Donovan back on the phone? I just need to ask him about the details surrounding tomorrow night."

N

CHEYENNE'S face slackened until she no longer wore any expression.

"*Tomorrow night?*" Cheyenne repeated, wearing the expressionless mask of what looked like another entity that had taken over her body.

"Yes," Bexley said. "He mentioned something about some event going down at an abandoned gas station."

"*An event going down, huh?*" Cheyenne said, as if she had turned into a parrot. "*I don't understand.*"

"Is your husband available?" Bexley said with more frustration.

"*If you would, please forgive Donovan,*" she said, as she eased from the living room while her husband's mind was lost watching some overeducated twenty-something pitching a new—and affordable—device involving paperless bathroom tissue to the sharks. *"He's a little tipsy,"* she said and poked her head into the living room, *"as in he had one too many for supper. I'm afraid he's in no condition to be discussing important matters."*

"I see," Bexley said, disappointed. "Well, can you at least give him the message that I called? Again, it's really important that I talk to him."

"I sure can, Bexley," Cheyenne said, grabbed a picture frame from the lamp table, and looked over a photograph of her and Donovan, which was taken on a private beach off the Florida coast. *"Say,"* she said as she set the photograph back down on the table, *"I was meaning to ask you: How's the show going so far?"*

"It's good," Bexley said, her voice jumped and sounded slightly higher.

"It must be kind of cool, having a film crew follow you around. I wish that Donovan and I filmed each other more often. I mean, not like that, but you know, film each doing stuff, like traveling and whatnot. Mainly to leave behind for our daughter and her future kids—that is, if she can find a decent man to settle down with. I swear, her last two boyfriends she had were something else."

"How old is your daughter?" asked Bexley.

Cheyenne tilted her head to the side and paused as if she wasn't thinking but, more or less, frozen in that same coma-like state. She rapidly blinked her eyes as if her mind was being rebooted, then suddenly snapped out of whatever trance she had fallen into.

"Nineteen," she said over the pause.

"Well," Bexley said, "she's young. She has plenty of time before she settles down."

"There's never enough time," Cheyenne said, strangely morose in nature.

"Anyway, it was nice talking to you, Cheyenne," Bexley said, more louder as if it was her cue to end the conversation. "But I have to run. How about we get together before I leave town? I would like to meet you—that is, in person."

"Really?"

Cheyenne's eyes started to water.

"Sure," she said. "We can grab lunch."

"Well, then, I would be delighted."

"Sounds good, then. And please tell Donovan I called."

"I'll pass along the message."

Cheyenne hung up the phone. She walked into the hallway bathroom, broke the cell phone in two, and flushed it down the toilet.

✗

MS. Necro wiped the tear from the corner of her eye, sniffled up the phlegm from her nose, and shouted out at Mutt, who was sitting in the passenger seat, "There's been a slight change in plans!"

Mutt ignored Ms. Necro for he was too busy playing the game *Splatoon 2* on his new Nintendo Switch.

"Mutt!" Ms. Necro shouted out.

✗

BEXLEY was still having a difficult time making sense of the previous conversation with the sheriff's wife by the time she reached the hotel. *As for Donovan,* she wondered, *what was he on?* She found it strange for such a respectable sheriff to put his interests first before the town's safety. She sat on the edge of the bed and pulled out the phone from her pocket. She scrolled through her contact list until she came across Wyatt's phone number at the bottom under the letter Z (for Zip) and contemplated calling him. *What was I going to say to him?* She decided after more thought not to call him.

✗

BEFORE the sun was out the next morning, Floyd and Makana were both waiting alongside Cherry Grove Road until Bexley arrived with the PA, Posie, who ended up dropping off Bexley, who, in return, told her that she'd give her a shout when she needed her again.

Makana, who was driving a rental, last year's model of a Mustang, was shining the high beams on what was left of Fill'R Up.

The location was, as Sheriff Barbee mentioned, an old, rundown gas station, "abandoned," clearly from the desolate appearance. Weeds choked tarnished gas pumps that were definitely old school: no touch screens, keypads, or slots to insert a plastic card.

Next to the gas pumps was a ramshackle convenient store called BENOIT'S. The letters *B*, *E*, *I*, and *S* were missing from the original sign, removed, leaving only a scabby outline of the letters, however, deliberately spelling the word *NOT*. Inside, some shelves had been gutted of food and merchandise while others overturned. The repulsive trend flowed like a disease toward the refrigerators, which were gutted and completely stripped. Several of the front windows were partially shattered in spider web-like patterns by projectiles, more than likely, rocks and bricks, which covered the ground like an untouched crime scene. Regardless of the devastation, when Bexley set her eyes to the next filming site, an eerie feeling came over her.

Floyd said while Bexley was giving a hard study to the area, "You sure this is it?"

Bexley, who remained studious, nodded.

"That's what the sheriff said."

"You know we could've rode together."

"I had to stop by the Sheriff's Office."

"To see your boyfriend?"

Bexley moved her laser-sharp focus to Floyd.

Acknowledging the look, Floyd threw up his hands.

"Friendly," he said, drawing more awkwardness than needed. "So," he said over the bird chirps, "how da good sheriff doin'?"

"I dunno," she said flatly. "He wasn't there. He was probably hungover."

Bexley walked past Makana and flicked her head in a nod.

"Hey, Makana," she said to Makana, who responded in same taste.

Floyd said over more slippery thought, "Hungover? What? Okay." All of a sudden, he turned excited. "I want details, Bex."

"Floyd, please," Makana said, rolling her eyes at the well-caffeinated director, "it's too early."

"A'ight," he said. "Straight to business."

They went straight to business, as Floyd said, only speaking in regards of the show, where to place the camera, mapping out the lighting by tracking down the direction of the sun, which was peeking slightly over the horizon and casting a red wash of light over the eastern sky. The three of them spent a good hour surveying the area, as well as the space in and around Benoit's—or "Not."

N

WHILE Bexley and Floyd were planning for the shoot, Posie drove past the long driveway, which lead into the woods.

Thinking more about what the old creepy woman had promised her last night, she decided to put the gear in reverse. She reversed the car and parked in front of the driveway. Then, put the gear back in drive, then reverse, and then drive again. She did this a couple of times before she finally drove down the driveway. At the end of the driveway was Ms. Necro's house.

Inside the dusty house, Ms. Necro was raging on her new 65-inch smart TV with 4K Ultra HD that she recently bought with the money Satterwhite had given her.

"Work goddamn it," Ms. Necro seethed, as she was struggling to change the input on the smart TV.

In a heap of rage, she chucked the owner's manual across the living room, its pages flailing like a fleeing duck. Next, she banged on the universal remote with her hand. As though, like all manmade things, a good smack would do the trick, she constantly tapped at the "HOME" button, but the TV still wasn't working.

"Fucking technology!" Ms. Necro shouted out. "Haven't even had my cup of coffee yet and this piece of shit is already pissing me off! Smart TV... My ass! More like dumbass TV!"

She slammed the remote on the floor, causing it to shatter in pieces.

"What do you know?" Ms. Necro said, that rage cooling as she looked down at the backside of the remote. More amused, she kneeled down.

The batteries were missing.

With her cat-like hearing, Ms. Necro heard a car pulling up the driveway outside.

She hurried to the window and saw the approaching car. She went back into living room. The first item she went to was the picture frame of the six-year-old boy, Kareem Pearl, who went missing over forty-two years ago.

In the photo, Kareem and Ms. Necro, who was wearing the same black duster that she always wore, only it was much nicer and cleaner, were making silly faces for the camera. Behind them was a carnival, which included a Ferris wheel and a line of booths where various games were being played. In one of Kareem's arms was a stuffed animal of a pink pig. The other arm was wrapped in a navy blue cast.

After much deliberation, Ms. Necro placed the picture frame flat side down on the mantle.

She stepped outside on the front porch and waited for the visitor to arrive, as if, in a supernatural way, she knew exactly who was driving the car without even seeing the person behind the steering wheel.

※

THE sun was high enough in the clear blue sky to draw out light from the shadows. Among those shadows was a small building that Bexley had overlooked earlier that morning.

Intrigued, Bexley pointed out the boathouse across the street along the side of Fontenot River. She checked it out, Floyd and Makana tagged along.

As soon as Bexley entered the boathouse, the idea manifested in her head and it was as though Floyd's unorthodox
work ethic of being reactive opposed to proactive, of pos-
sessing a thinking-on-your-feet mentality, started to rub off
on her.

While examining the fishing nets hanging on the walls
and ceilings, Bexley said to Makana, "We need to find the
owner of this place."

"Shouldn't be a problem."

"What are you thinking, Bex?" asked Floyd.

"*Sea cucumbers*," she said abruptly.

"Ooo-kaaay," Floyd said, brow furrowed. "What about
'em?"

"I'm thinking this is where we trap it." Bexley showed
him the two barn-like doors and the down slope of the hill
leading toward the boathouse. "We can lure it straight
down the hill and trap it in these nets. There's a local
author," she turned to Makana, "I'm sure you've heard of
him."

"You're talking about Wyatt Whyte."

"Yes," Bexley said. "He wrote in his book that the dial-
lyl disulfide, one of the principal components of garlic, is
known to burn the skin of a werewolf snake, which would
inevitably weaken it."

Floyd was already given her a look from across the boathouse.

"Hear me out," she said before Floyd could protest, "if
we can rub garlic over these nets, then it'll only increase
our odds at catching this thing."

"If what you say is right, Bexley," Makana said, "then
we're going to need a shit-ton of garlic."

Floyd didn't make the ineluctable wisecrack about, of all
creatures, vampires; however, Bexley could sense him itching to capitalize on the opportunity.

She held up her hand and said before Floyd could utter
a word, "Save your breath, all right."

Floyd shrugged.

"I didn't say anything."

"But you were."

263

She backtracked and went over the final scene, or scenes, with Floyd by suggesting using a handy cam while the rest of the crew hung outside, perhaps "along the edge of the woods for a wide shot," then have another camera inside the boathouse, perhaps "put Jewels right there in the corner," waiting to capture the final shot of Bexley luring the werewolf snake into the trap.

Floyd asked, "What the hell are you going to do after you capture it? These nets," he said, grabbing one of them which was made out of thread, "aren't going to hold it for long. And garlic, won't that make it even more agitated?"

"Maybe," she said, "but if I can get close enough to it, I can hit it with ketamine-xylazine or a general anesthesia."

"You want to kill this thing or put it to sleep?"

Makana suggested, "How about a tranq dart?"

"That's a possibility," Bexley said. "But its hide might be too thick for a dart. If we trap it in these nets, I can use a jab stick on it."

"It's risky, Bexley, but. . . "

"*But* it'll work," she said. "You know it will. So, what do you think?"

"Well, it *will* work but only by using a smaller crew," Floyd said. "Six people tops. Plus, we need to cut down on the budget—"

"—Don't worry about the budget, Floyd," Makana said. "I'll worry about the budget. I have to get back to LA for a meeting tomorrow morning, so there you go. You'll have one less person to worry about."

Floyd said, "Also, I'd really like to have Whyte in these scenes. Perhaps we can film an interview with him later in the timeline."

"Well," Makana said skeptically, "we can try again."

"Well, let's do. I think having his expertise on werewolf snakes would make for a good opening for the show. So, can you reach out to him?"

"I can try—"

"No," Bexley said over Makana. "I'll call him."

FLOYD was having second doubts and was ready to call off the shoot after waiting over an hour for Wyatt to show. Everything was already set up, including microphones, cameras, as well as lightning; each and every crewmember were hanging back, making sure to stay out of sight, and were exactly where they needed to be. The boathouse along Fontenot River, which had been given a green light for production and cleared by the owner, Sid "Sarge" Farley, smelled like the inside of a pizzeria.

"Give him another ten minutes," Bexley said, as she waited next to Floyd on a small dock behind the boathouse. "He said he'd be here."

"We don't have ten minutes, Bexley," Floyd said sourly. "Call him again."

Once more, Bexley tried Wyatt but received only his voicemail: "*Yo, you've reached the Z Man. Drop a line at the tone.*"

She didn't bother leaving a message.

"So?"

"I dunno," Bexley said unsurely. "Maybe something came up."

Floyd said to Bill, who had his arm crossed over his chest while the other one supported his head, "Did I not tell you this guy was unreliable."

"Yeah," Bill said sharply. "You did."

Bexley turned to the rest of the crew who was having a small powwow and found Posie, who was hanging just outside the clique like an odd woman out. Posie immediately looked away as soon as Bexley glanced in her general direction. She moved her eyes back toward the crew, spotted the biggest guy in the crew, a gripper who happened to be one of those guys who competed in those hot dog eating competitions every Fourth of July. He was stocky, American built, and could certainly throw down, if it came to it.

"I'm going to borrow Ocelot for a sec," Bexley said. "Wyatt lives not too far from here—"

"—What? No. I need him here. I can send one of the assistants to fetch him down."

"I wasn't asking, Floyd," she said and then asked for Posie's car keys. She thanked Posie, told her she'd bring her car back, then said to Floyd while walking toward Ocelot, who was eating a power bar underneath the portable tent, "Make sure you keep your phone handy. I'll call you when I have him."

Floyd removed his floppy hat, ran his hand through his hair while shaking his head in disgust, and said to Bill, "Told you we should've went to Loveland."

N

AT nightfall, Bexley and Ocelot pulled up to the front gate of Wyatt's plantation. Bexley told Ocelot to wait inside the car while she opened the gate; then once the gate was open, she cruised down that narrow stretch of shaded driveway. Only a couple of lights were on inside the house, two dimly lit ones on the first floor, one of them was flickering like a bug zapper, another one, a bright one, at the far end of the second floor.

"Looks like someone's home," Ocelot said, leaning closer to the windshield for a closer look.

"Something's not right," Bexley said, as she parked the car.

She tried calling Wyatt once more, but he didn't pick up.

She even left a text message saying that she was outside his house.

Once more, she received no response.

She decided to give Donovan a call yet again. So far, Bexley had called him five times and each time, he didn't pick up; however, this time, she didn't even get a tone. The call went straight to voicemail. Which meant that either he turned off his phone or something was wrong with his phone. Or, thirdly, which Bexley worst suspected, he was blocking her calls.

"Fuck it," she seethed. "Let's go."

Bexley stepped out of the car and gently closed the door behind her.

Ocelot mimicked Bexley by carefully easing the passenger door against the frame of the car and then giving it a light push.

"Stay close," she said, more quietly.

Bexley walked up to the front door and pushed on the doorbell. She listened closely for the doorbell, but she heard nothing in return, only the distant sounds of 2Pac rapping "Hail Mary." She knocked a couple of times on the door.

"Wyatt!" Bexley shouted out. "It's Bexley Hun!"

She even tried to open the door, but it was locked.

She knocked again, this time louder, like a cop.

"Zip!"

Bexley pressed her ear to the front door.

"Hail Mary!"

She stepped back and looked for another way in. She motioned toward the side of the house.

"Come on," she whispered, waving Ocelot to follow.

They walked around the side of the house.

Bexley stood on her tippy toes and peeked through one of the windows along the side of the house and witnessed the destruction inside the house highlighted by the flickering beam of an overturned lamp. Which Bexley highly expected that it wasn't from cats. There were various sized holes in the walls. Part of the living room ceiling was caved in. All kinds of debris, mainly from the foundation, was scattered all over the hardwood floor: remnants of a chair, which had been torn to shreds, cotton balls of what little furniture he owned, chunks of drywall, all messily thrown everywhere.

Surprisingly enough, when Ocelot and Bexley tiptoed their way through the back door, which had been ripped off its hinges with the remaining pieces of door strewed across the back lawn, the stereo was perhaps the only item still intact.

In the corner of her eye, Bexley couldn't help but notice the upper part of the destroyed doorway. She immediately

267

recognized a circular pattern, as well as the tiny holes from a buckshot round. She found blood spatter along the floor, as well as a streak of blood smeared down the marred doorway panel.

She nodded toward the direction of the stereo, which was bumping 2Pac.

"Do you mind?" she asked Ocelot, who eased into a debris-laced living room, stepped over the leg of a table, and turned off the music.

"Looks like a hurricane swept through here," Ocelot said over loud silence.

He slowly moved his eyes upward to the ceiling above where he found more blood splatter, as well as tiny holes from buckshot peppering the drywall.

Among that silence, they heard a loud *thud* from what sounded like a piece of debris falling to the floor.

Bexley tried Wyatt's phone, again.

As she waiting for a response, again, the anthems of 2Pac chimed throughout the house, however, this time through the muffled sounds of a ring tone.

She followed the ring tone and unearthed Wyatt's phone from a pile of broken drywall.

Ocelot drew his attention back to the blood on the doorway.

"Whose blood do you think that belongs—"

Before Ocelot could finish his sentence, Bexley shushed him after hearing the sound of someone moaning.

"You hear that?" asked Bexley.

This time, Ocelot heard the moans. Together, they tracked down the moans toward the hallway, which led toward Wyatt's office. The ceiling in the hallway, like the living room, was partially caved in; the opening of the doorway in front of the office was blocked with debris, making it completely impassable. Below the dark triangular opening of the blockage, Bexley witnessed two feet sticking out.

"Zip!" she shouted out and rushed over.

She heard a faint voice speak her name from underneath the destruction.

"Yes, Zip," Bexley said clearly. "We're here. . ."

Ocelot helped Bexley remove the debris, starting with the smaller, easier-to-move pieces and then working to the heavier pieces. It was like playing the game, *Jenga*. They were both mindful not to remove a piece that would cause the rest of the ceiling to collapse on top of Wyatt. Eventually, they removed enough debris to slide Wyatt from the dusty hole. He was wearing a deep gash along the side of his abdomen, wasn't bleeding out exactly, but was bleeding badly enough that the wound would require plenty of stitches. He had several cuts and bruises along his forehead. Overall, he was, as he said, "Good. Banged up. But still kickin'."

"You don't look so good, Zip," Bexley said. "You need medical assistance."

"Hell nah," he said. "I ain't going to no doctor—"

"—Zip, look at yourself," Bexley said motherly. "We need to take you to the hospital; otherwise, your wound is going to get infected."

"I appreciate the concern and all," he said, nursing the wound by pressing his hand against the long gash, "but I told you, 'I'm good.'"

Bexley ordered Ocelot to grab a first aid kit.

"In the bathroom," Wyatt said to Ocelot, "you'll find ya some gauzes in the bottom drawer."

"Where's the bathroom?"

Wyatt nodded toward the general direction of the bathroom.

Bexley helped Wyatt sit against the wall, which made the pain worse. Wyatt eased on his side, relieving the pressure against the wound.

"Back where you came from," he said, grimacing. "To the right of the living room."

While Ocelot fetched some gauze for Wyatt, Bexley lifted up Wyatt's Macho Man "Oh! Yeah!" T-shirt, which was no longer white, and took a quick peek at the wound.

"This doesn't look good," she said and pulled his soaking wet Tee back down.

"Believe me now, Bex?"

The comment left Bexley in a state of confusion.

"How'd this happen?" she asked.

"That crazy fuck'n bitch, fuck'n Ms. Necro," he said bluntly. "She knew she couldn't use her lil' spells on me, so she decided to send in the *big guns* to do her dirty work."

"Who?"

"Oh," Wyatt said animatedly. "Not who. *What*. You know exactly what."

She turned away and noticed the long and dark tire track-like marks along the white walls, as well as small crater-like footprints in the hardwood floors.

"Least now," Wyatt said with another grimace as he re-adjusted himself, "I've got more material to write about. Huh?"

"Did you kill it?" asked Bexley.

"Does it look like I killed it?" Wyatt returned, more frustrated with the lady.

"I saw the gunshots in the wall."

"I think I might've clipped it when it was leaving," he said, "maybe. I went to grab more ammunition from my office. Then, next thing I know the damn ceiling came crashin' down on my ass before I had myself a chance to chase it outside. One thing's for sure, tho. Ms. Necro ain't gonna be messin' with me no mo. I put a buckshot straight to that ugly mug of hers when I was playin' possum on her witchy ass. Bitch thought I was dead."

"Where is she?" asked Bexley, looking around.

Wyatt eyes widened.

"You mean you didn't see her on your way in?"

Bexley shook her head.

"No," she said.

"There's no way she would've survived that blast. Here," he said, repositioning himself toward the pile of debris next to him. "Grab the shotgun. It should be underneath all this shit."

Bexley used the flashlight on her phone and aimed the light into the dark recess where Wyatt was once lying.

"I think I see it," she said, shining the light on the butt of a shotgun.

She got down on her all fours and crawled into the narrow hole.

"Be careful," Wyatt said from behind.

Bexley managed to pull out the shotgun from the hole; however, the box of ammunition was too far back to reach without getting stuck or worse, having the rest of the ceiling caving in on both her and Wyatt.

Ocelot arrived with an armful of medical supplies, including a first aid kit.

"Have you gotten a hold of the sheriff?" asked Bexley, as she began to work on Wyatt's wound.

"Me?" Wyatt said and smacked his gums. "Hell nah. He ain't gonna help us. I'm afraid we're on our own, Ms. Bexley."

"Maybe you're right," Bexley said, applying gauze to the wound in order to stop the bleeding. "I've been trying to reach him on his cell all day, but I'm getting no answer. Honestly," she said, shaking her head in disappointment, "I don't know what his deal is." As soon as she removed the gauze, she realized the severity of the wound. "Wyatt," she said, showcasing a stern composure, "we need to take you to the hospital ASAP."

"No," he said over Bexley. "You specifically told me you had a plan to catch this thing and that you could only do it with my assistance. So, *Bexley*, I'm gonna help you cuz you ain't gonna get in that place without my help."

Bexley had no other choice than to go along with Wyatt. After all, she knew it was his choice to make, not hers. She looked over the medical supplies presented before her. She found a roll of athletic wrap.

It would have to do.

For now.

N

MS. Necro managed to drive back to her place in one piece.

She stumbled her way to the cabinet of her special potions and remedies. She grabbed a jar of dark green jam from the shelf and carried it to the bathroom. She forced herself to look at the gunshot, even though the sight of it was disturbing to look at. With her right eye closed—the other one being missing—she opened her eye. The left side of her face had been blown off, exposing skull underneath. Her shaky hands reached for the jar. She even had to hold her hand while unscrewing the lid of the jar for the shaking was nearly crippling. She used a tongue depressor— "spatula" or "popsicle stick"—dipped it in the thick jam until the end of the wooden stick was covered and then smeared it along the open wound on her face.

The feel alone of the jam touching her face caused Ms. Necro to scream out in bloody horror.

N

ONCE Wyatt was all bandaged up with a silver, sparkly windbreaker jacket worn over his shoulders like a cap, he, Bexley, and Ocelot exited from the house.

On their way out, they heard a disturbance coming from the hallway closet. Since Wyatt couldn't reach the rest of the ammunition box for it was buried underneath the rumble, he only had two rounds left in the chamber. Bexley insisted on handling the shotgun for Wyatt—clearly, the recoil only would reopen the wound that she had just dressed—however, after he turned to her with a hard glare worn tightly on his face, she knew the only way she'd ever touch Wyatt's shottie again was by prying it from his cold, dead hands.

With Bexley and Ocelot following close behind Wyatt, they approached the closet.

"Is it her?" asked Bexley.

"Maybe," Wyatt said, as he tenderly nursed the butt of the shotgun against his shoulder.

He nodded at Ocelot, cuing him to open the closet door while he took aim.

On a silent count of three, Ocelot swung open the door.

Wyatt eased his finger on the trigger.

Cowering in the corner of the closet was Swain.

"Don't shoot!" he shouted out, as he threw out his arms.

Wyatt pressed the trigger but didn't pull the trigger.

Finally, he removed his finger from the trigger and lowered the shotgun.

"Swain?" Wyatt said, perching the shotgun against the wall. "I thought your ass was dead."

Wyatt and Bexley gave Swain a hand by pulling him from the closet.

"Not dead," he said unsteadily. "But damn near close. I... I hid as soon as I saw that dinosaur-looking monster sneakin' into da house. I... I just didn't know what else to do."

Wyatt wrapped his good arm around Swain and held him close.

"It's a'ight," he said and kissed Swain on the side of the forehead. "I'm glad you're alive, boy. For a sec, you had me runnin' through lines in my head as to what I was gonna say to ya daddy." He rubbed the top of Swain's head the same way a proud father would playfully rub the head of his son. "Come on," he said to Swain, first, then the other two. "Let's get outta here."

Together, they exited the house.

Once they made it to the car, Ocelot agreed to drive while Swain rode shotgun. Bexley rode with Wyatt in the backseat in order to watch his injuries.

"Are you sure you want to do this?" Bexley asked one last time before entering the car.

"Please, for the love of all things holy, don't ask me that again. My ass ain't dead yet," Wyatt said, as he was beginning to lose his patience with Bexley.

"Good," Bexley replied. "And let's keep it that way. Shall we?"

Once everybody was in the car, Ocelot drove off.

*

ABOUT five minutes into the drive, Bexley told Ocelot, who was driving just below the speed limit, to speed it up.

"We're not joy riding here," she said bossily.

Ocelot accelerated ten miles per hour over the speed limit, which was 45, and kept the speed between 55 and 60.

While eyeing over Bexley in an admirable sort of way, Wyatt said to Bexley, "You're a rare breed. You know that, Bexley?" She gave him an almost identical look that he had given her while asking to hold his shottie, one that suggested that he better further explain himself by what he meant by "rare breed," otherwise he was going to get an earful from her. "It's just," he said, as if he was backpedaling his remarks, "I never met a woman like you before."

"And what woman is that, Zip?" asked Bexley.

"A woman who knows exactly what she wants."

Bexley shook her head.

"Honestly, I just want this to be over with already."

"Right," Wyatt said, turning his eyes to the blur of white lines running alongside the road. "Over the phone, you asked me about Benoit's place, if I knew it. I apologize. I wasn't exactly being forthright with you."

All of a sudden, Bexley repositioned herself until she was facing Wyatt. Her eyes were fully open as she studied Wyatt.

"I'm listening," she said professionally.

"There's a place underneath Benoit's, which was originally made to serve as a hideout for slaves. Then, over time, it turned into a bunker. Then, eventually, it became something else."

"Like what?"

"Back in the day," he said, glancing over at Bexley in the dark car, "it was used as a hangout during Prohibition. Folks used the place to drink and blow off steam. Some years back right before I did a lil' soul searchin', I got myself into a lot of trouble—you read about it the book, I'm sure. I was on pace to be dead by the age of twenty-five. I never wrote about the 'Spot,' tho. That's what we used to call it. *The Spot*, as in few people knew about it. And I felt if I wrote about The Spot, then I'd be breakin' an oath."

"So, what did you do in 'The Spot'?" asked Bexley.

"Stuff that, even till this day, I'm still ashamed of. But I was young—people like to twist that around, like bein' young is a poor excuse for wild behavior. But that kind of talk comes from people who hadn't lived. I admit it I was dumb back then. Partyin' all the time. Doin' all kinds of stupid shit. Who didn't? Right?"

More thoughtfully, Bexley said to Wyatt, "Sheriff Barbee, he said something about Benoit's son taking over the place."

"I heard he did," he said. "I was long gone by that time. When I came back some years later, the place had shut down."

"But not anymore, right?"

"If what you told me over the phone is true, then, yeah, I guess so," he said. "But times have changed."

"Changed?"

"Same party, different players," he said, then, once more, backpedaled. "I've only heard the rumors 'bout them, an organization usin' secret codes to flock from one place to another, Illuminati-type shit."

"Did you ever get involved in this organization?" asked Bexley.

"Me?" Wyatt frowned. "Nah. I don't mess with that. Besides, I've been too busy with my books to fool around with fuck'n cults."

"Well, if this *cult* is involved in what I think they are, then think about it, Zip: This *cult* would make for one heck of a book. Don't you think?"

Wyatt grimaced slightly, as he readjusted himself in the seat. He checked the wrap, making sure it was still on there good but not too loose or tight or too anything for that matter.

"Back at your house, you said something earlier about Ms. Necro using spells on you. Who is she, really?"

"Right," Wyatt said, more laidback. "That. Yeah. She's a witch. For real."

"A witch? Right." She turned her eyes to the passing trees outside the window and then glanced back at Wyatt. "Let me guess. You're a dragon slayer."

"Not any more I ain't," Wyatt teased. Then, thought more about Ms. Necro and her evil ways, *that goddamn Witch-For-Hire using her black magic to cause all kinds of trouble*. "I knew for sure that she was one screwed up individual, but I never thought, in my wildest dreams, she'd go so far as to kill a nigga."

"Well," Bexley said, "the way I look at it, Zip, you're not dead yet."

Wyatt couldn't agree more.

N

THEY made it back to the site of the filming location across the street from Fill'R Up, as Floyd was minutes away from canceling the shoot.

Wyatt pulled Bexley aside before she joined the rest of the crew.

"Do me a favor," he said, nursing his side as he stepped out of the car, "don't tell your people about what happened back at my place, you hear?"

"What? That you might've murdered some woman named Ms. Necro, who, by the way, happened to be a Witch-For-Hire?" she said, more at ease after spending a twenty-minute car ride with Wyatt and his good pal, Swain, who, turned out, happened to be highly skilled in handling the yo-yo, his most famous trick being "Walk-Da-Dog."

"Yeah," Wyatt said. *"That."*

Bexley ran her two fingers across her mouth as if she was zipping her mouth closed.

"They won't hear a word about it," she said and paused, "but maybe—that is, if you make it out of this thing alive—you'll write about it."

"Yeah," he said, giving Bexley a common bro-handshake. "Maybe."

Bexley eased away from Wyatt and in the quietude of the night, she heard the throbbing heartbeat-like pulse of what sounded like a techno song.

"You hear that?" Bexley said over the quietness.

Taking a closer listen, he tilted the side of his head and picked out the sound with his good ear.

"Yeah," he said. "Sounds like music. Must be from your people—"

"—No. They no better," she said and nodded toward Fill'R Up. "It's coming from across the street."

Much more subdued and stealthy in nature, Bexley, Wyatt, Swain, and Ocelot joined Floyd and the rest of the crew.

Floyd was first to acknowledge Wyatt's banged-up condition.

"What the hell happened?" he asked, trying to keep his voice down.

Floyd's almost hushed tone was a sure indicator that there had been a development in the situation. Bexley glanced across the street where she witnessed two cars, parked to the left of Fill'R Up.

"I thought you told the crew to park next to the Red Zone."

"They're not with us."

"Then, who are they—"

Bexley tracked down movement coming from behind Benoit's: two heavyset men dressed like the night, one of them was bald while the other one had a bushy beard, and they were both smoking cigarettes in front of another car, the tarnished frame of a 1977 Pontiac Firebird missing wheels. Earlier, Bexley and Floyd came across the old shell of a car when they were surveying the land; however, neither of them thought much to take a peek inside.

"I don't know," Floyd said. "They just pulled up about ten minutes ago."

"They must be guarding the entrance," Wyatt said over the two.

"Entrance?"

"Floyd," Bexley said, introducing Wyatt to the anxious director, "this here is Wyatt Whyte—or 'Zip,' as he prefers."

Floyd shook Wyatt's hand.

"Nice to meet you," he said. "So, is everything all right?"

"Wyatt here ran into some trouble back at his place," Bexley said for Wyatt.

"Werewolf snake got a hold of me," he said over Bexley. "But I'll live."

"Wait! You were attacked?"

"Yeah," he said, waving it off as if it was no big deal, as if he normally got attacked by werewolf snakes, as if he and werewolf snakes often quarreled. "But it's no sweat. I'm ready." He looked around the small site next to the river. "So, what? Do I need to go to makeup?" He combed the side of his hair. "I could use a cleanup. Gotta be lookin' tight for the cameras."

"I'm afraid, Zip, this isn't that kind of production," Bexley said while touching Wyatt on the shoulder.

"Bexley," Floyd said to Bexley and pulled her aside away from Wyatt. "Can I talk to you for a minute?"

She walked over to a vexed Floyd, who said quietly to her, "Should I be worried, Bex?"

"We've come way too far to turn back now, Floyd. You want your shot. I'll get you your shot."

"At what cost, Bexley?" Floyd pointed at the local celebrity, Wyatt, who was currently in the middle of checking out the PA's *tight* body. "Was he really just attacked by a werewolf snake?"

Bexley nodded.

"Yeah," she said shortly. "He's fine."

"Fine? The man looks like he needs to see a doctor."

"Well," she said, "you can have Frank take a look at him, if it makes you feel more comfortable."

"I sent Frank home."

"Whatever, *Floyd*," Bexley said, more sharply, "we're doing this—"

At least a dozen cars and SUVs, the expensive kind, high end, luxury, as well as two vans, pulled up around the side of Fill'R Up.

Bexley, as well as the rest of the film crew redirected their attention toward the beams of bright headlights cutting across thick gray clouds of gravel dust and remained eerily quiet and subtle with their movements, "soft feet," as if they were in the middle of recording.

Both men and women—but more men—who were all dressed as if they were hitting a club, stepped out of each vehicle. There had to be at least two to three dozen people inside the two vans.

When Bexley thought the last person had stepped out of the van, another one stepped out, then another, as if there was a never-ending assembly line of clubbers inside each van.

One of the heavyset men walked up to the gathering, escorting them in a single-file line to the gutted Firebird.

"Maybe there's something we missed," Bexley whispered to Floyd.

"I told y'all," Wyatt pointed out, "see that old car in the back?"

"Yeah," Bexley.

"That's where they enter."

"Through the car? But how?"

"Just watch," Wyatt said. "You'll see."

Bexley and Floyd watched carefully.

The other man, the bald-headed one, popped open the hood of the Firebird.

The muffled-sounding techno music became clearer as a burst of light shot up from below, revealing a staircase underneath the car.

The bald-headed man helped each person onto the bumper of the Firebird and down into the area of the car where an engine normally rested.

"I can't believe it," Bexley uttered in disbelief. "It was right underneath our noses this entire time."

"There's another way in," Wyatt said, drawing a wave of silence. He looked at everybody who was staring at him with wide please-tell-me-more eyes. "You didn't just ask me to be here cuz of my looks. Now, did y'all—"

With a cup of coffee in her hand, Posie walked up to Bexley and offered her the coffee.

She didn't even have to ask. She already had it the way Bexley wanted, with a little bit of cream, no sugar.

"Thanks, Posie," Bexley said, as she grabbed the cup of coffee from Posie's hand. "You read my mind."

She sipped from the coffee and slightly tilted her head to the side with both of her eyes narrowed with great concentration. She moved around her tongue along the top of her palate and picked up a sharp, nutty aftertaste. She took yet another sip of the warm coffee and finally, acquired the taste.

"Is something wrong?" asked Posie while studying Bexley.

"No," Bexley said, sipping from the coffee. "Not at all."

"—What another way?" Floyd asked to the side of Bexley.

Wyatt threw his head in nod toward the woods next to Fontenot River.

"In there," he said emotionlessly.

�

WYATT showed Bexley, as well as the rest of the crew this *other* way inside the underground hangout, which was once known as "The Spot." Of course, it wasn't an actual door or an easily accessible entranceway for that matter. However, it'd require Bexley to hunch; nonetheless, it was just wide enough for her to fit without having to crawl.

"There?" Bexley said, pointing at the sewer drain next to Fontenot River.

"Yep," Wyatt said, clutching his side. "There."

�

FIRST, Jewels started by attaching the body camera to Bexley's breast pocket and making sure it was secure. Once the body cam was properly secured in its place, he moved to Bexley's ear where he inserted an earpiece into her ear.

"Say something," Jewels said to her.

"Something," Bexley repeated, waiting to hear a voice in her ear.

Wyatt, who was hanging back with Floyd and other crewmembers in front of the monitors underneath a tent stationed at the bottom of a hill next to the woods, said over the microphone, "Can you hear me, Bexley?"

"Yeah," Bexley said, touching her ear. "I can hear you, Wyatt."

"How about visuals?" Jewels asked through a walkie-talkie.

"Roger," Floyd said over the walkie-talkie. The feed from her body cam was somewhat fuzzy on the monitors. "Can you readjust the camera a little?"

Bexley did as Floyd directed and gave the camera a slight adjustment.

"Good," Floyd said, as the monitor became clearer. "Right there."

Once Bexley was all geared up, she shined the flashlight into the dark pipe.

"Be careful," Jewels said before he rejoined the rest of the crew.

"Break a leg, Bex," Floyd said through Bexley's earpiece.

"Thanks," she said and didn't waste anytime entering the sewer.

Meanwhile, back at the monitors, Wyatt was struck by a sudden dizzy spell. He closed his eyes for a moment while pinching the bridge of his nose. When he opened his eyes, he was no longer staring at the monitors in front of him. Yet, he was looking at himself, as well as other crewmembers through the narrow gaps of trees. His vision felt as if it was pulsing. He snapped from the vision—or whatever you wanted to call it—and found himself glancing toward the woods.

"Wyatt?" he heard a voice next to him. "Zip, you a'ight?"

Wyatt turned to Floyd, who was sitting next to him in the director's chair.

"You got anything to drink around here?" asked Wyatt.

Floyd waved down the PA, Posie, and had her fetch Wyatt a bottle of water.

Back in the sewers, Bexley arrived at an intersection.

"Which way, Wyatt?" she asked, while Wyatt was taking a sip of water.

"Right," he said into a handheld microphone. "Take a right, Bexley."

Bexley took at right down another pipe.

"Then where?" Bexley asked. "I'd like to know where I'm going before I get there."

"If my memory serves me right," Wyatt said, "then you're gonna continue on that path for about two minutes or so until you reach another intersection. There, you gonna wanna take a left."

"Got it," Bexley repeated, as talking helped keep her calm. "Two more minutes. Then, take a left."

"How you holding up, Bexley?" asked Floyd.

Bexley sighed.

"Good so far."

In a left-to-right scan, she moved the flashlight across the large concrete pipe. A small creature darted past the light beam, causing Bexley to cry out.

"What is it?" asked Floyd.

Bexley tracked down the creature with the flashlight.

"Rat," she said, more relieved as she shined the light on the rat.

"Let's keep it moving, Bexley," Floyd directed.

N

WHILE Tad was standing in front of the bathroom mirror brushing his teeth before heading straight to bed—well, it wasn't exactly straight-straight to bed. First, bed usually started with a game of *Call of Duty*, then maybe an episode or two or even three of *American Chopper*, then whatever book was on the nightstand, either a Manga or Stephen King novel, and then, finally, lights out. But before all that, he was precise with his teeth, first brushing for a good two minutes, then came flossing, then, lastly, gargling mouthwash.

By the time he was finished with his dental hygiene, a feeling suddenly came over him, familiar in its bite and the way it caused his vision to double. He tried to flicker away the spell; however, that warm, fuzzy feeling overwhelmed him.

As Tad braced himself along the edge of the vanity, he flexed the muscles in his neck.

"Not again," he groaned with his teeth barred.

His eyes rolled over white and the last image he witnessed before he blacked out was one of a film crew standing—and sitting—in front of a group of monitors.

N

AFTER two minutes of walking down the pipe, she arrived at yet another intersection where, as directed, she took a left.

As she proceeded forward, she didn't even have to ask for directions. Wyatt already beat her to the punch, "Now," he said carefully over the microphone, "up ahead, you should see a ladder on the side of the wall."

Bexley shined the flashlight ahead but didn't see any ladder.

"Am I missing something here?" she asked.

Wyatt leaned forward and pointed out the ladder on the monitor.

"There," he said with a grimace while mentally trying to put himself in Bexley's point-of-view. "Eleven o'clock."

"I don't see it," Bexley said, searching her eleven o'clock.

"Right in front of you, Bex," Floyd said.

Bexley narrowed her eyes and peered closer.

"I see it," she said. "Yeah."

"After you climb that ladder," Wyatt said, "head on straight. You should see it not too far ahead."

"Watch your step, Bexley," Floyd directed, as Bexley reached for a holding on the rickety ladder.

She didn't even get as far as touching the ladder before she was hit by a dizzy spell, this one, unlike Wyatt, without the visions. She figured it was a combination of the humidity inside the sewers, which was causing her to sweat, on top of drinking coffee, which was known to dehydrate the body. *What was I even thinking?* She fought through the spell by focusing her eyes on the ladder.

"Bexley?" Floyd said while waiting for Bexley to climb the ladder. "Is everything all right? Talk to me. . . "

"Yeah," she said shortly. "Just give me a sec, will you?"

As the dizzy spell lessened and that throbbing world before her eyes steadied, Bexley forgot where she was or what she was doing.

"Time is not on our side, Bexley," Floyd said, his voice more strained.

Time was the trigger word.

Two minutes, Bexley remembered.

Bexley inspected the ladder by tracing it with the beam of the flashlight, told Floyd that she needed a moment, and then she started to climb. Each step Bexley made was rather loud from the side of the flashlight banging against the ladder.

Halfway up, she started to hear more of that same techno music.

"You hear that?"

"Yeah," Floyd and Wyatt said simultaneously. Then, Wyatt followed on his own: "That means you're probably gettin' closer."

While Bexley continued to climb the ladder, Floyd turned to Wyatt.

"So how you know about this place?" asked Floyd.

"When I was younger," he said shortly, "they used to have these wild parties here. Cops couldn't touch The Spot. Basically, it was a place where you could do whateva the hell you wanted—"

"—I'm here," Bexley said, as she reached the top of the ladder.

On the monitors flashing lights appeared at the end of a dark tunnel. Wyatt listened closer to the sound of cheering over the sound of techno music.

"What is that?" asked Floyd, as he, too, listened closer.

Bexley turned off the flashlight and inched closer to the strobe lights.

As the music turned down slightly, she heard a booming voice coming from what sounded like speakers.

"Now introducing first to the ring," the voice shouted out over the rapid pulse of a techno beat, *"with an undefeated record of thirteen and zero, the fearless, the ferocious Dracule!"*

The music was turned up yet again over the roars of an audience resonating throughout the sewers, which caused Bexley to slow down her walk to a prowl.

"Bexley," Floyd said quietly in Bexley's ear.

"Yeah, Floyd."

"It's not too late to turn back."

Disgusted, Bexley couldn't believe Floyd's comment.

Talk about a confidence boost, she thought. *Thanks a lot, Floyd!*

"Now you tell me this?"

"Whatever you do, you cannot get spotted."

"Got it," Bexley said, as she was stopped in her tracks by the guttural sounds of a werewolf snake shriek coming from The Spot.

The audience cheered in harmony: *"Dracule! Dracule! Dracule!"*

Then, the same gravelly voice of the MC as the music once more lowered in volume: *"Coming next to the ring, the Ragin' Cajun bred right here in the state of Louisiana, a home town favorite, the savage showstopper with a finishing move called 'Slicin' and Dicin',' let's shout 'Geaux!'"*—as though conditioned to follow commands, the audience shouted out the word *"Geaux"—for the incredible, the delectable Geaux Get 'Em!"*

This time, the audience roared even louder, resulting in the sewers to shake.

Finally, Bexley arrived at the end of the pipe and waited at the edge of The Spot, which was roughly the size of that high school gymnasium where they last filmed. Before Bexley an intimate yet decent-sized crowd, as rowdy as hell and thirsty for blood and carnage, was circled around a rectangular-shaped hole in the ground, which looked as if it had been drained of sewage.

The first noises she pointed out were the dull sounding *clinks* and *clanks* of heavy chains dragging along the concrete. Then, the piercing shrieks underneath a flatline of hisses followed by growls, which were so deep and throaty that each one caused the foundation to tremble. Then, shouts of encouragement from humans to the two combative werewolf snakes, *"Rip her fuckin' head off Dracule!"* Or, *"Show 'em who's boss, Geaux Get 'Em!"* Then, on top of all that arena-like chaos, she heard the high-pitched sounds of a wind instrument known as, in India, a *pungi*. However, she didn't just hear one of them. She heard multiple ones. It wasn't until she crept behind the crowd that she realized the flute-like sounds of a pungi were coming from several of these Rodeo clown-esque entertainers dressed in gaudy outfits covered in bright neon lights. She overheard one of the audience members refer to the performers as a "charma"—or charmer.

While circling and racing from one side of the ring to the other, one charmer was holding a cattle prod and dancing around while occasionally zapping a werewolf snake to prevent it from turning its fangs on any of the audience members. Another one was blowing into that pungi, as if, in a way, the hypnotic sounds kept the werewolf snake in order, if not tamed. She couldn't exactly get a good look at the two werewolf snakes for they were circling one another. Every now and then, she'd catch a glimpse of one of them through the gaps of bodies: a dark and scaly human-like hand with claws the size of sabers; the black bushy mane covering its elongated neck; its many layers of fangs dripping wet with drool whenever it let out a shriek at its opponent; or, even for the briefest moment, its sharp red reptilian eyes cutting right through the crowd.

"Are you seeing what I'm seeing?" Bexley asked, as she remained in a state of shock.

Bexley's voice broke up, preventing the others on the other end from hearing.

She stayed close to the shadows behind the audience, making sure not to get spotted.

By shifting her body slightly, Bexley was able to get a better look at the two men—or "coaches"—on either side of the ring: one of them was a short, chubby, lightly bearded fellow who was wearing a lime green jumpsuit and Wayfarers; the other one was much taller and thinner with saggy shoulders, a pale narrow face, sunken cheeks, dressed in a black trench coat and wearing a cowboy hat.

The MC, a hefty, wide shouldered man with red greased back hair and sideburns the size of pork chops, wearing an altered coat with the striped tiger print of a cape on his back, pointed his glittery top hat at the fat man whom he referred to as "*Dr. Fist.*"

"*Are you ready?*" asked the MC.

Dr. Fist lived up to his name and pumped his fist.

Then, the MC pointed at the other man, "*Billy the Vamp, are you ready?*"

Billy the Vamp coldly nodded.

Then, finally, the MC shouted out, "*Let the fight begin!*"

The two coaches released the chains attached to the collars around each werewolf snake's neck.

The charmers stayed on high alert as each one circled around the edge of the ring, preventing the werewolf snakes from turning their fangs toward the crowd.

One of the charmers happened to get too close to the werewolf snake—the one who went by the name, Dracule, Bexley noticed as he identified it based on a distinguishable red strip running down its slumped over back. Smacked directly in the upper abdomen by Dracule's scaly tail, the charmer was sent flying over the crowd.

The charmer instantly getting knocked unconscious after violently slamming against the wall prompted a sonorous wave of "Ohs!" throughout the awestruck crowd.

Two charmers stepped forward and zapped Dracule with cattle prods, which kept the werewolf snake away from the crowd.

While the fight between Dracule and Geaux Get 'Em was raging on, Bexley couldn't help but notice another entranceway, one that Wyatt had completely forgotten about; however, surrounding two massive doors were at least six men who were holding shotguns and assault rifles. The doors, Bexley only assumed, were more than likely used for the werewolf snakes. *What other way would they enter?*

"Sorry, Bexley," Wyatt said, as Bexley aimed the camera on the two doors next to the crowd. "It's been so long. . . "

"Don't worry about it," she said, counting more guards, now eight, then nine. "I wouldn't have been able to get through there anyway."

"The doors were always locked when we used to hang out there."

"It's okay, Wyatt," she said.

"Bexley," Floyd said next, "we've seen enough. Now, if you would, get your ass out of there before you get spotted."

She didn't budge an inch. Instead, she was drawn to the ululating werewolf. She moved the camera back to the fight.

From the angle where Bexley was standing, Dracule wrapped his tail around Geaux Get 'Em's body and applied a nasty bite to her neck.

The crowd was chanting, "*Geaux! Geaux! Geaux!*"

Among the chants arose the *whistles* and *whooshes* of a tail whipping through the air. Bexley drew her eyes upward to the sight of Geaux Get 'Em's longer and much thinner tail waving and thrashing above. Half of the tail suddenly straightened in a steep ninety-degree, aiming downward like a sword.

Before Bexley could make sense as to how a tail was capable of straightening out in such a way, Geaux Get 'Em counterattacked with three swift jabs directly at Dracule's face, in particular, its eyes.

The third and final strike to the eyes resulted in Dracule releasing Geaux Get 'Em from its death grip.

Again, the crowd, which was favoring the hometown fighter, roared over the deep bellow of Dracule.

Drenched with blood, the very tip of Geaux Get 'Em's tail appeared as if it had skewered one of Dracule's eye-balls.

Bexley spotted a familiar face standing at the front of the crowd chatting it up with two fat cats.

"Is that the same guy we ran into earlier?" Bexley asked while moving closer for a clearer shot.

"Who?"

"What's his name?" she said, thinking out loud. "Sat-terwhite?"

Wyatt said, "You must be talkin' 'bout Kenneth Satter-white."

"That's him," she said under another roar of the crowd.

Mutt, who was previously partnering with Ms. Necro on a job, shouldered his way through the crowd and walked up to Satterwhite. He leaned in close to Satterwhite and whispered something in his ear. One could only assume he was giving Satterwhite the recent news about Ms. Necro. Nonetheless, whatever he said resulted in Satterwhite smacking Mutt upside the head.

Bexley read Satterwhite's lips: "You *fuckin'* imbecile!"

Then, after wearing a scowl on his face, he nodded to-ward the first entranceway: "Get the *fuck* outta here!"

If there was one word that could easily be lip-read, it was the word *fuck*.

Satterwhite, who was visibly frustrated with Mutt, turned his attention back to the fight while Mutt walked away with his head down.

As Wyatt continued to watch the shapes of bodies but no actually clear shot of a werewolf snake displayed on the monitors, he was hit by yet another one of those strange dizzy spells, this one more debilitating. His skin turned hot, feverish. Sweat beads formed along his forehead. He rubbed away the grayness from both his eyes and when he reopened them, he fell witness to not himself but that same force creeping up behind Bexley. Both eyelids flickered. His eyes partly rolled over white as he lost himself in the monitors. However, instead of seeing what Bexley was seeing, he was seeing from the eyes of what something else was seeing.

He snapped from glitch-like trance and refocused on the monitors.

"Bexley," he said, out of breath, "get outta there. Hurry. . ."

"What?"

"I said, 'Get outta there.' Now!"

Unaware of Wyatt's vision, Floyd turned to Wyatt: "So you seeing something that we're not? What is it?"

Then, he leaned in closer to the monitors and focused.

"Bexley," Wyatt said, "it's behind you."

"What's behind me?" asked Bexley, as she rotated her shoulder.

The sudden jerk of her body caused the body cam to slip from her shirt and fall to the ground.

Her eyes fell onto the two slit pupils of Bubby's crimson red eyes. Standing roughly seven feet tall on its two arms—and twice that height when erected upward on its tail—Bubby stalked right by Bexley.

"Bexley?" Floyd said into Bexley's earpiece, "what happened? Talk to me!"

On the monitor the only part Wyatt could make out was part of the werewolf snake's tail slithering past the camera.

"Bexley?"

Remaining dead still and watching with great trepidation, Bexley waited for Bubby to creep past before she responded to Floyd: "Did you just see that?"

"See what?" asked Floyd.

Bexley felt for the camera but came up empty. She looked down, realized the camera was no longer clipped to her shirt; then she searched the ground.

By the time she picked up the camera and clipped it on her shirt, Bubby had already slithered from view.

"There," she said, picking it up back up on the other side of the crowd. "See it?"

"See what, Bexley?" said Floyd, as he gave an innocent pat to the side of the fuzzy-screened monitor. The silhouette of a crowd flickered on the screen, causing him to give the monitor a good smack. However, Floyd's attempts were only worsening the picture.

Dracule body slammed Geaux Get 'Em, causing another uproar; however, yet another cry from the crowd amplified, and it wasn't coming from the fight.

Bexley witnessed what appeared to be the top half of a torso being flung upward in the air followed by the scattering of a crowd.

As half of the crowd parted ways, Bexley tried to adjust the camera as Bubby tossed aside the other half of a body and set his eyes on Satterwhite, who was redirecting the closest charmers away from the fight and instructing them to "control" Bubby. The charmers had little-to-no effect on the werewolf snake.

Satterwhite grabbed anybody he could find and pushed him/her at Bubby; however, Bubby wasn't at all interested. It was as though he was targeting Satterwhite.

Before Satterwhite could make a run for it, Bubby pounced on his back and began to tear Satterwhite to shreds. This had given Bexley enough time to escape without getting spotted.

As Bexley ran back the way she came in, the images on the monitors became clearer.

"Please tell me you got that," Bexley said, her breath labored from running.

"Got what?"

"You're kidding me," she said, as she climbed down the ladder.

"Doesn't matter," Floyd said with urgency. "Just get out of there. . . "

Floyd searched for Posie, who was no longer standing behind them; in fact, she was nowhere to be found. He found the closest person he could find, which was Ocelot.

"OC," Floyd demanded, "go to the drain and meet Bex when she comes out. Hurry back here once you got her."

Ocelot did as he was told and took off running toward the river.

N

AFTER Tad managed to crawl from the bathroom to his bedroom, he stopped short of his bed and fell onto the floor where his sweaty body curled in a fetal position.

With his eyes rolled over white, Tad blindly reached for a stack of blank copy paper, as well as a pen on his desk and started to sketch the phantasmagorical images streaming before his eyes.

N

AS Bexley neared the exit of the pipe, she slowed down her pace from the blankness, which plagued her thoughts. Her face went long, eyes glassy. Bexley didn't know what she was running from, only that something was, in fact, chasing her.

It wasn't until Bexley shined a light on Ocelot who was standing on the slick concrete surface at the edge of the pipe that she realized the urgency of the situation. Even that name when he repeated himself for Bexley, "Ocelot," as well as that round face, not only looked, but also sounded strange. Somewhere lost in the blackness of her thoughts, Bexley thought of one thought, which had many other thoughts lined up behind it: *Donovan*, Bexley thought, and that strangeness in his voice when she called him on the phone. She had most certainly been around her share of drunks during her brief existence and whatever the sheriff was on, it certainly wasn't the sauce. Perhaps it was a chemical in the air. *Or. . .* Bexley traced the rill of dirty water flowing down the slanted runoff into Fontenot River.

As she approached Ocelot, who was waving her closer, she immediately recognized the change in his face. The fear gripped Ocelot like a vise, tightening all mobility. He stood trembling. The color in his face, extinct.

With his eyes wide and attached to a dark silhouette creeping behind Bexley, he said carefully, "*Do not move. . .*"

Bexley slowly lowered the flashlight from the gripper's face.

�

IN the garage, while kneeled on a Kazak hand-knotted wool rug laid over the hard slab of concrete, Ms. Necro, with the left side of her face covered in a hardened, gummy substance, meticulously moved a red coarse candle over a professionally looking black and white private investigator-style photograph of Ocelot, which was taken across the street from Lake Wilshire; in fact, the photo was taken on the first day of the *Unleashed* shoot at Wyatt Whyte Park. With the flame still burning along the aged wick, she dripped hot red wax down the photo in a zigzag pattern. Next, she grabbed hold of the ancient weapon, which was lying by her side. On top of the smooth wooden handle was a curved blade, like a bird's beak knife; however, the blade wasn't metal. It was the claw of a werewolf snake. Part of it was chipped. Even the color of it was brown and faded, like old bone.

Gently, Ms. Necro inserted the sharp tip of the claw into the photograph and drew the letter "X" over the face of Ocelot.

✶

AS soon as Ocelot was marked, Bubby leaped over Bexley and pounced on top of Ocelot and began to tear him to shreds.

Bexley threw the flashlight at Bubby, striking him in the side of the face. It had absolutely no effect on the werewolf snake.

Crying out, Ocelot shouted, "*Run, Bexley! Run...*"

His screams were cut short as Bubby ripped out Ocelot's jugular.

✶

INSIDE the circle of candles, Ms. Necro placed the marked photograph of Ocelot next to another PI-style photo of Kenneth Satterwhite, which like Ocelot's photo, was covered in red wax and x'd out. She proceeded to pull up other photos from a stack of photos lying next to her.

⚡

BEXLEY ran into the woods, and Bubby chased after her.

"I'm not going to make it to the trap in time," she said out of breath.

Her voice was choppy, her throat parched and scratchy.

"What happened to Ocelot?" asked Floyd.

"Goddamn it! Just do what I said, Floyd!" she said more loudly this time, as she glanced over her shoulder and saw a massive dark figure appearing behind the trees.

While Bexley was being chased by Bubby, Floyd got back on the radio and told Jewels that there had been a change of plans.

"I need you back at camera one right now," Floyd said with urgency.

"But what about the boathouse?"

"Camera one," Floyd demanded. "Right now!"

Jewels left his position in front of the lure inside the boathouse and joined the other cameraman, Marco, who was stationed at the edge of the woods.

"It's coming for us," Wyatt said expressionlessly, as he turned to Floyd. "*All* of us."

"You still have that shotgun on you?" asked Floyd.

⚡

IN order of Bubby's targets, Ms. Necro lined up each photograph of the film crew, which were taken either on the first day of the shoot or at the hotel where the film crew was staying.

First, Ms. Necro started with the cameraman, Julien Etheridge, and placed his photo in front of her.

ONCE Bexley sprinted from the woods, Brice was there to hand her a rifle, which was already loaded with a dart syringe of ketamine-xylazine.

"Get back," Bexley said to Brice, as she moved into position on a grass field.

As Bubby stormed through the woods, knocking over smaller trees and trampling shrubbery, Hans, who was in charge of lighting, slowly brightened the lights, which were strategically placed at the edge of the woods. Ashley, who was holding a boom mic, aimed the microphone toward Bubby's direction. Jewels, as well as Marco had both of their cameras in place. Jewels was handling his camera on a shoulder rig while Marco was operating the jib of a camera crane next to the trees. Each one of the cameramen had their cameras aimed at a shadowy figure that was quickly approaching.

Brice said to Bexley, "Make sure to aim for the shoulder, in particular the bicep or triceps. If you have a clean shot at the hindquarter, then take it."

Bexley nodded, but she didn't even know what she was nodding at for Brice's words went straight over her head.

Bexley stood motionless in front of the bright lights while Marco panned the camera toward her direction.

In those few moments of anticipation—a calm before the storm, if you will—Bexley staggered and nearly lost her balance from yet another dizzy spell. As her thoughts started to turn black, only one remained the most vivid inside her head: the plan. *Was this how it was always going to be?* For days, they had planned the show, location and whatnot, storyline being Bexley uncovering the truth about the werewolf snake and hopefully—with fingers crossed—Bexley finally confronting the werewolf snake by the end of the show. As the blackness started to take hold, all she could think about was the end and how people were going to react to it.

The weight of the rifle felt heavier in her hands.

And clearly, the rifle started to lower slightly.

Bexley removed the buzzing voice from her ear.

Before the blackness overwhelmed her, Bexley imagined what would happen if the world found out about Bubby after it opened her up on film. She imagined each viewer sitting in the darkness of the living room and the glow of a TV screen or phone screen or eTablet screen or whatever electronic device they were using flickering on each one of their faces. Then she envisioned each one of them wanting blood, grabbing whatever weapon they could find within their reach and coming after the steckophorus, *not* to study it but to track it down, destroy it, and afterwards, hang it on the wall like a trophy. She knew you'd have people coming out of the woodwork to hunt down this creature and its entire species. *"It's much easier to kill sumtin you don't understand,"* Wyatt said after giving her a tour of his house, *"than it is to take the time and effort to understand what it is you tryin' to kill."*

From the tent, producer Bill Kopeck yelled out to the massive creature and attempted to distract it by waving his arms.

Bexley slowly turned to Bill, then Wyatt, who was sitting in front of a group of monitors. Bexley furrowed her brow as if, at that particular moment in time, she was completely unaware of who these people were, what she was doing here, or how she even got here.

Brice grabbed Bexley's attention by calling out to her, telling her to take the shot, but, as before, his words went straight over her head. The rifle in her arms lowered to the ground. Every inch of Bexley noticeably sagged.

⋏

Ms. Necro dripped the hot wax over each photograph of each crewmember, starting with the two cameramen Julien Etheridge and Marco Estella, who had been a cameraman for the show *Unleashed* for the last two seasons, then next, the assistant director from New York City, Brice Shuffly; then, after the AD, it was Hans Uhlig, who was in charge of the lighting department; Hans was born and raised in

Hollywood; started off as an extra—"background actor," as he called it—for tons of shows and movies before making it on a production team; had been in the film industry for over twenty-three years, had three Academy Award nominations under his belt; after Hans, it was Ashley Dabbs, then wealthy producer Bill Kopeck, then, finally, Floyd Bivins. She set aside three other photographs: the production assistant, Posie Rodgers, Wyatt Whyte—which happened to be a black and white photo that was torn out of the dust jacket of the hardback *Catalyzt*—then, last but not least, Bexley Hun.

⚡

WHILE Ms. Necro began to cross out each one of the crewmembers, Bubby picked off each one as soon as the tip of the ancient claw was pressed against the paper.

With her mind emptied, her face slack, her jaw dropped, and her open mouth shaped like a gaping hole, Bexley watched the massive creature tear through Jewels, first slicing right through the camera and shoulder rig, with his claws.

Trying to shield himself, Jewels dropped the camera and fell to the ground. It wasn't enough, though. Bubby cut right through his flesh, then his bones, then his vital organs.

Behind Fill'R Up, Mutt exited from the hidden door underneath the Firebird and inched closer to the commotion coming across the street.

Then after Bubby dismembered Jewels, she watched the creature tear through Marco, who was steadying the camera on the crane. However, the camera continued to run and film a slack-faced Bexley as she stood and watched in utter horror.

After Jewels and Marco, it was Brice and then Hans, then Ashley: each and every one of them killed, off-camera.

In a left-right combination, Bubby swiped at Ashley once horizontally across the gut, which caused his insides to spill to the ground in a bloody lump, then another time across the neck, which was turned into a PEZ dispenser.

Finally, after all of the waving and hollering, Bubby moved his sights to producer Bill Kopeck, who was standing next to Floyd by the monitors. Bill made an attempt to run away, but Bubby was on him before he could make a run for it.

As soon as Floyd, who previously ignored the massacre for the only footage he received on the monitors were the dark shadows of a creature zooming past the camera lens, came to his senses and recognized the dire situation, he removed the headphones from his head and stumbled from the director's chair.

"Shoot it," he said to Wyatt, who was holding onto the shotgun.

Wyatt turned to Floyd and stared at him with veiny white eyes.

N

Ms. Necro crossed out Floyd's wax-covered photograph with that ancient werewolf snake claw and in return, Bubby tore right through him. She came across the last remaining photos: Posie, who wasn't anywhere near the shoot, in fact, Posie, while crying and at the same time, laughing hysterically from the deceitful act she had recently committed, was in her car driving back home to Los Angeles; Wyatt, who was hanging out at the monitors with Swain attached to his side like a third limb; lastly, Bexley, who was stuck in that mindless state of disrepair. Ms. Necro pushed aside Posie's photograph, then Bexley's, and focused on Wyatt's. Of all the photos, his was the one she had her eye on the most. She carefully poured that red wax over Wyatt's author pic, as if she was solidifying his fate. The crooked smile seemed less crooked along Ms. Necro's mutilated face as her head barely tilted to the side while closely inspecting the photo in her hand.

With the wax-covered photo held in one hand, Ms. Necro picked up the claw from the floor and as she was about to stab the photo, she did something that she failed to do with the other photos: she hesitated.

N

MUTT cautiously approached the light across the street while Swain braced himself against Wyatt's leg and told him that he loved him.

All of the monitors were filled with white snow, except for one of the monitors, which showed a pale-faced Bexley, who was sitting on her knees and gawking at the camera.

As the white snow flickered over his face, Wyatt, whose eyes were still rolled over white, stared back at himself through the eyes of Bubby.

His skin was hot, burning.

Before Bubby was about to attack Wyatt, Bubby was distracted by the sound of Rome loudly exiting through the hood of the Firebird.

Skittish from the sudden commotion, Bubby removed his sights from Wyatt and stormed back home.

N

SEVEN miles away from Cherry Grove Road, Ms. Necro set aside Wyatt's photograph on the concrete floor of the garage. Except for Bexley's and Posie's photograph, which, unlike those other nine photographs carved with a giant X, had been unmarked, Wyatt's happened to be the only photograph covered in *only* wax.

And, for the most part, Ms. Necro planned to keep it that away.

If only for the time being.

But the funny thing about time.

Time don't give a rat's ass 'bout you. Ms. Necro couldn't agree more. *But with nuff time, anybody can turn an anthill into an empire.*

BY the time Calssier Paris Sheriff's Office was called to the crime scene whatever was left of Rome had already scattered before their arrival. Only after a couple of hours of combing the scene, it was dawn. Bexley, Wyatt, Swain, and Mutt were the only four witnesses left on the scene. Back at the Sheriff's Office, each one of the witnesses was called in and questioned thoroughly by the sheriff.

After Sheriff Barbee finished with Mutt, whose statement was about as accurate as a third grader explaining Einstein's special theory of relativity, he brought in Wyatt, then Swain, who explained the werewolf snake to the sheriff, who had absolutely no recognition or understanding of the creature, only that it came from campfire stories, rumors, myths, legends. Since most of the investigators working the case had pointed to an alligator—or alligators—as the main suspect or suspects, the sheriff dismissed Wyatt and Swain and brought in Bexley and showed her the recovered footage of the attack. Except for the footage of the "gathering" at The Spot—because, considering most of what was collected from the body cam was taken from behind the audience, there weren't any clear-cut images of two werewolf snakes fighting, only the dark shapes of what could've very well been alligators—most of the footage collected from Spoiled Monkey Production was useless. The only detail happened to be taken outside The Spot, where part of a shadowy figure darted within inches of the camera's reach. It could've literally been anything; in fact, as soon as the idea of an alligator being responsible for the killings was brought to the forefront, the figure, especially the tail, was similar enough to an alligator to let the imagination fill in those blanks. The other piece of footage, significant or not, was Bexley Hun's horrified reaction, which was captured right on camera.

When Bexley talked to the sheriff, it was as though the two didn't know each other and were meeting for the first time.

Considering Bexley's fragile state, Sheriff Barbee asked Bexley if she wanted anything to drink. He mentioned "*coffee*," but strangely, Bexley refused the very second he mentioned the word.

"My men," the sheriff said from across his desk, "believe a gator was responsible for these murders."

"Maybe," Bexley said unsurely. "Yeah. It's a possibility I guess. Like I said before, it was too dark."

Sheriff Barbee looked over Bexley and asked her, "Is there anything else you would like to tell me?"

As tears formed in Bexley's eyes, she looked up at the sheriff and said with a shaking voice, "I can't remember."

FROM NEW ORLEANS TO LOS ANGELES, CALIFORNIA
THREE DAYS LATER

BEXLEY took a red-eye flight back home.

Throughout the entire flight, while sitting in a window seat, she desperately tried to remember the time spent in Sinclair Leprieur. Everything was a blur; in fact, Bexley couldn't even recall how she wound up in Louisiana in the first place or the people who had been tragically killed by what the sheriff and his investigators believed to be an alligator.

When Bexley arrived at LAX, it was daytime. She hailed a taxi. The driver, a kind man who knew exactly when to be quiet, placed her bags in the trunk. She was driven to her beachside house in Malibu. The house, Bexley remembered—at least, partly. She remembered buying the house from a real estate agent named Rochelle. Her neighbor, Riley, whom Bexley remembered, who had been collecting all of her mail for the past several weeks during her time spent in Louisiana, brought by the mail later that afternoon.

In the kitchen, Bexley sorted through the mail on the granite countertop.

Two pieces of mail grabbed her attention the most: firstly, an envelope which was sent from a company called LabInc with a Louisiana address, and secondly, the latest issue of *BOLD &*. She saw herself on the cover. She was wearing this colorful peafowl-like dress. The title of the cover story read, "*Wild By Nature.*"

She placed the magazine aside and pulled up the other piece of mail. She cut open the envelope with a bird's beak knife and pulled up the blood test results.

One of the tests was from the samples that she took from a young man named Thaddeus Hoper while the other one was collected from the gymnasium inside the abandoned Rue Wabash High School. The blood results were a match!

She set aside the blood test results and moved her eyes toward the front cover of *BOLD &*. She opened up the magazine, went straight to the index, found her name "Bexley Hun," as well as the article "Wild By Nature," then flipped to the interview. She remembered bits and pieces of the photo shoot, as well as the interview in New York. Like before, it was all blurry. Each memory, each thought, whenever she tried to remember an event from her past, it was as though she was staring at a steamy mirror. She could see the shapes, silhouettes. She could hear sounds, voices, but not words. She ran her finger along the page and came across one particular excerpt from the article. In the interview, Bexley was asked: "*What has been your greatest discovery while filming the show Unleashed?*"

Bexley answered, "*Believe it or not, that is the most common question I'm asked whenever I bump into a fan of the show while I'm out in public. I tell them, 'The one inside myself.' Whether it be trekking the Western Ghats or scrambling around on the island of Mineo, each and every time I find myself in uncharted territory I learn something about myself. And that alone is my greatest discovery. I know how cliché it may sound, but it couldn't be any closer to the truth.*"

The magazine slipped from Bexley's grip and fell to the kitchen floor.

She drifted deeper in thought and imagined herself standing on the street corner of Cherry Grove and River Road and staring up at the green road sign.

Cherry Grove Road.

"Marceau Benoit," she whispered to herself, as she snapped from her trance and moved her eyes to the steaming mug of coffee on the countertop.

FROM MANHATTAN TO LAKE OPEAKA, FLORIDA
SIX MONTHS LATER

INSIDE Freidman hotel's swanky French restaurant called Le Palourde, Wyatt and his agent, Payman Foster, who found a home for his new book *Afterthoughtz* at the big house publishing company, Mersey and Sons, were having a celebratory lunch when halfway through enjoying hors d'oeuvres Payman popped the question that had been on his mind for the past six months: "So tell me, Zip," Payman said after swallowing the bite of escargot, "is it true?" Wyatt didn't immediately answer, as he took yet another sip of his domestic beer from the cool, tall glass. "Let me be as clear as possible: Do I need to push the book as fiction or nonfiction?"

"You and I both know I ain't in the fictional business, Pay."

Payman asked, "Why not go back there?"

"If you mean 'there,' as in Sinclair Leprieur, the answer is a no-brainer, Pay," he said, thinking not about himself but his horses he set free in the wild. "There ain't no chance in hell I'll ever go back there."

"Why not—if I may ask," Payman said, leaning back in his chair. "You were born and raised in Sinclair Leprieur. Some of us," he pointed around at the other patrons inside the restaurant, "don't get the privilege to call a place where we currently live as home. It's either home away from home or a transitional place."

"Bottom line," Wyatt said over Payman, "if I return, I'm a dead man."

"Ms. Necro, right?" Payman said, then joked, "You wouldn't be the first man to leave the nest because of a woman. Aren't they all the same?"

"No," Wyatt said, thinking. "This one here's much different," he said, more seriously. "She pure evil."

After lunch, Wyatt parted ways with his agent and spent the rest of the afternoon walking through Times Square, which was decked out for the holidays.

As he was about to hail a cab back to the airport, he noticed a billboard promoting a new show featuring Posie Roxx—or who Wyatt knew as Posie Rodgers, the intern lady who drove around crewmembers or fetched them coffee. He could never forget such a pretty face.

The new TV show was similar to Bexley's, an explorer type show; however, instead of tracking down rare and unique species or debunking legendary tales of monsters or fairytales, her show focused more on lost treasures.

Wyatt sighed and shook his head and said to himself, "New name, new face, same shit."

He got inside the taxi and rode away.

By late afternoon, he was already on a flight back home to Florida. He made it back home in time for dinner. He was currently living in a two-story house on a lake that was only a couple of miles from the beach.

After Wyatt put some leftover lasagna in the oven, he grabbed himself a beer from the fridge and went outside where he sat down in a lounge chair on the back porch. Before Wyatt could even take a sip of beer, he heard the *snap* of a branch coming from the woods surrounding the lake. He moseyed from the back porch and checked out the noise.

As Wyatt reached the backyard, every muscle in his body suddenly tightened. His eyes rolled over white, his body started to burn up. He found himself standing outside his own body.

The bottle of beer slipped from his fingertips and fell to the ground, most of the beer spilling onto the lawn.

Wyatt froze and lost all mobility in his body.

In his mind, he could see the force creeping up behind him until it was looming over his own shoulder. However, Wyatt never turned around nor did he ever bat an eyelash. Yet, he remained still with those white eyes staring vacantly at the tranquil water before him. He turned feverish, face slackened. The fear gripped him. The horror had left him in a paralyzed state. The only part of his body that he could move was that mind of his, and he was trying to catch each thought but each one was filling with another. Among a whirlpool of thoughts only one stood out the most, that being the idea he was no longer a man nor an author, a friend, or a lover. He no longer bore any name. Yet, he, the necessity, was no different than the very food that he ingested in order to maintain the burden of survival.

The very last time Wyatt experienced that same upending feeling which made everything he had achieved prior seem so extraneous was six months ago when he found himself face-to-face with the mysterious creature. Very few had ever experienced such a feeling throughout their lifetime. And for those fortunate enough to have survived—whether they were chosen or they happened to find themselves in the right place at the right time—they'd tell you there was nothing quite like it.

TAKING in gulps of fragrant hotel room air, Sandor let out a grunt as he finished making his fourth and—based on what little he had left to show for the woman—*final* transaction. His shoulders, as well as the upper half of his body, including his head and neck, which were arched upward in the posture of a wolf howling to the moon, deflated. Every muscle in his body, which had been wrought for hours, slackened and swelled.

With sweat dripping down his face, he rolled off Vera's body and plopped to the side of the bed.

Eventually, he caught his breath and turned to Vera, whose cheeks were both clouded with red. The sheets beneath her were soaked with mostly his sweat.

Vera excused herself for a moment while she traipsed to the bathroom where she grabbed a hand towel from the basket of toiletries, held it under the faucet, and soaked it with warm water. She wrung the towel and wiped herself clean, starting with her chest first but doing so briskly as if she was brushing off dust. She spent more time rinsing her private area, giving it a more thorough cleansing.

Afterwards, she tossed the soiled towel into a pile of dirty clothes next to the shower.

With less stumbles and staggers, she strutted back to the bed and as she was about to slip into her black lingerie, which included a sheer lace cup bra with adjustable spaghetti straps, satin bow accents, a hook back closure, as well as a high waist garter belt with metal clips, matching panties with cut-out panels and thong cut back, and thigh high stockings, each and every highly detailed piece of garment draped along the backside of a chair, Sandor patted on *her* side of the bed—he had already claimed his side. The gesture alone caused Vera to pause.

He said bluntly, "That can wait."

"Again?" Vera said, startled by the old man's energy. "You know it's going to cost you extra."

"Whatever," he said, once more patting that wrinkled indentation on the bed.

Vera set aside the panties and eased into bed next to Sandor and began to kiss him on the nape of his neck. However, he didn't show any affection toward Vera; in fact, he placed his phone back on the nightstand and carefully pushed her away before she could kiss him again.

Turned off by Sandor's withdrawal, Vera leaned away and asked naively, "Is there something wrong?"

"Let's just hang out for a while," he said, more seriously, as if he was starting the beginning process of a less showy, less *spunky* transaction. "Can we do that?"

"But isn't that what we're doing?" asked Vera.

Sandor didn't answer. Yet, he let out a deeper sigh, one knotted with anger, which made him appear more agitated by the woman's response.

For Vera, it wouldn't be the first time a client wanted to "extend" time with the so-called product. Vera had been with many other clients, more than could be accounted for (in other words, ones destined to be what she called "regulars," who were what Vera deemed as more talkers than doers and would say about anything considering their circumstances. Those who were the antithesis of your everyday "Wham bam, thank you, ma'am"-ers. She wasn't a shrink by any means nor was she one to hand out advice; however, she'd listen; and sometimes, despite the heat of the night, listening was all of what the job entailed. Because, for Vera, at the end of the day, that was all it was, nothing personal, just a job, bang, bang.

"Yeah," she said shortly. "Okay. Sure. You just want to *hang out*. I can do that."

They rested in silence, Sandor lying flat on his back and Vera, after pushing a pillow against the headboard, lying in an upright position.

Vera pointed at a faded scar running down Sandor's hairy forearm.

"What's the story here?" she asked and gave a tap on the scar as if it was her own subtle way of pounding on emotional floodgates.

Sandor traced the tip of her finger; and for a moment, he needed the woman to further clarify her question.

"This, huh?" He noticed the scar and then, *finally*, the story behind it. "I got it when I was younger."

Despite Sandor's silence, Vera patiently waited to hear the story.

"I was, maybe, I don't know, in my early twenties. Twenty-two maybe," he said, as the AC shut off and gave way to more authentic silence. "A bunch of us used to get together in one of my friend's garages every Saturday night and we'd have these boxing matches. Nothing too serious. You know, just a bunch of guys with high testosterone blowing off steam. We had gloves and everything—even had a couple of girls from the sorority act as the ring girls. They'd hold up signs between each round. To us, it was like Pay-Per-View."

"How many rounds did you guys have?" asked Vera.

"No more than three," Sandor said, intertwining his fingers over the patch of hair along his chest. "Most of us couldn't get past the first round. At least one of us would get knocked out by the end of the night." He held up his arm and once more, looked over the scar, then poked at it.

"I got it when I was boxing this one kid named Derrick De Long. We used to call him Rhino, though, because he was born with this defect where his forehead protruded outward like the horn of rhinoceros. So, yeah, Rhino was what we called him. Story goes that during delivery Derrick was, let's say, stubborn and didn't want to come out of his mother's womb, so his father used a plunger to pull him out, resulting in his head looking the way it did. I guess it's because the baby's head is soft—or whatever. Derrick and I weren't at all close. We were once, but ever since I hooked up with his ex girlfriend back when I was a freshman in high school, there had been bad blood between the two of us. In a way, it was *always* there, that resentment. I grew up in East Side, a wealthy part of town. He grew up in Regal Park, which was where most of the crime took place in the city. So, I think, fundamentally, the only reason we were friends was because, one day, we knew we would be enemies. That night, we were beating the dog shit out of one another. I won the first round, but barely. The second round belonged to Derrick. I had him exactly where I wanted him though, if he hadn't thrown a cheap blow. He was a dirty fighter, did anything to win a match. As we were going into the third round, it's anybody's fight. But I know in order to beat him I have to get dirty as well. So, as we tangled up toward the end of the round, Derrick's got me in this headlock while, at the same time, he's throwing these cheap blows to my body. He leaves me with no other choice. So, I pull a Tyson on him."

"A Tyson?"

"You know Mike Tyson," he said, glancing over at Vera, "the famous boxer, probably one of the greatest of his time?" Vera was left expressionless, as if she was waiting for Sandor to give her another description that would piece together a face to the name. "You don't have a clue who I'm talking about, do you?"

"Yeah," she said shortly. "Sure. Mike Tyson. The boxer. I've heard others talk about him."

"Then, I'm sure you're aware of the Holyfield vs. Tyson match."

"*The Bite Fight*," she said, recalling one of her clients in Las Vegas from way back when mentioning that particular fight, as well as the infamous "bite" heard around the world, and doing so with so much hostility. "Yeah," Vera said, using a shorter tone with Sandor. "I have."

Sandor was somewhat taken aback from Vera's knowledge of the fight, considering she must've been no more than six years old at the time of the Bite Fight.

"So, anyway," he said, starting the thought by trailing off, "I pull a Tyson on Derrick. To say Derrick got what he deserved would be an understatement, but if I would've known, you know. . ." he paused, thinking more about what he really wanted to say to Vera, how the bite was going to haunt him later in life and *bite him* right *in the ass*, ". . . certain ramifications, I probably would've never bit Derrick in the first place. But thinking back now, someone really needed to put him in his place. If it wasn't me, eventually, it would've been someone else." Sandor's eyes darkened, as if the thought itself spread directly to both his eyes. "Derrick recoils, touches the side of his head, and pulls away a handful of bright red blood. Then, his face changed, and he was now wearing the face of a man who wanted to kill me. He removes his gloves, charges at me, throws me against the wall, and starts kicking me while I'm down before the others pull him off. Once the chaos dies down, I look at my arm and it's covered with blood. My blood, *not* Derrick's. I follow the blood trail to the floor, then the wall where I find a nail sticking out of the wall. When Derrick threw me against the wall, my arm ran across that nail. The cut wasn't nearly as bad as Derrick's ear. I mean, the poor guy was missing a piece of his ear. Eventually, he had it reattached. He didn't press charges even though he threatened me that he would. As for my cut," he said, raising his arm to glance at the scar as if each time he took a glance at it another new detail came forward, "well, you get the idea."

"Did you get any stitches?" asked Vera.

With his lips hung loosely in a frown, Sandor shook his head.

"No stitches," he said. "A buddy of mine had some superglue. Which made it even worse. The cut got infected. When it finally scabbed over, I remember for weeks I'd pick at it and try to make it worse."

Vera asked, "Why would you do such of thing?"

"At the time, I thought that the longer and uglier the scar you had the tougher you were." Sandor blew out a sigh from his mouth that sounded like a cross between a snort and a sigh. "Talk about the insecurity."

"Who isn't, right? Especially at that age."

Like she would know, he thought. *She's only seven years older than I was at the time* of the scar story.

Sandor rolled his head toward Vera and looked at her as if he wanted her to further explain her response.

"Isn't it natural for a person to feel insecure when he or she is surrounded by other people?"

"Only when you're young," Sandor said coldly, as he rolled his head forward. "Besides, you don't need a scar to prove to others that you're tough. It's all in the past, though. If anything, the only burden leftover from my rebellious days is the appearance of the scar and having to find ways to cover it up."

"You mean, like at work?"

"Yeah," he said hesitantly. "Sure."

As though Sandor had purposefully—or mistakenly—opened the door for yet another topic for conversation, Vera asked, "What do you do for a living?"

"Enough about me," Sandor said, putting aside Vera's question. "How about you? What's your story?"

In a way, Sandor's unwillingness to answer the question or even divulge any information about his work wasn't at all a surprise to Vera; in fact, she didn't expect anything less from a man who was worth so much money.

"I'm afraid my story isn't nearly as interesting as yours," Vera said bashfully.

"Yeah," Sandor said darkly, "but everybody has a story."

"I don't."

"Of course, you do."

"My story may put you to sleep, *really*."

"Start with where you came from," he suggested. "Where were you born?"

"I was born in a small town in Russia called Sviyborsk. I only lived there up until I reached the age of nine. I don't remember much, only that the winters were quite brutal."

"Do you have any siblings?" asked Sandor.

"No," Vera said. "Just me."

"How about your parents? What did they do for a living?"

"My mother cleaned houses for most of her life. We moved around a lot, especially when I was younger. She'd basically find whatever she could find. She ended up finding a sales job when we settled down in London."

"How about your father?" Sandor asked, turning to Vera.

"Daddy lives in the States, like you."

"I take it Mommy and *Daddy* are separated."

"Yes," she said. "They are."

"And let me guess, your Daddy doesn't approve of your profession."

"Actually," she said bluntly, "he does. Believe it or not, ever since I was little, he encouraged me to be whoever I wanted. He felt as if it wasn't his responsibility to get involved in the way I lived my life. No question I definitely take up after him, opposed to my mother."

Sandor asked, "How so?"

"We're both hardheaded."

While she was talking about her father, Sandor carefully watched her, in particular, the expression on her face—or lack thereof. Vera spoke about "Daddy" with a dark stillness, as if, whenever there was any mention of him or the subject of him, whatever followed was delivered with poise and grandeur.

"How's your relationship with him?" asked Sandor, as if he was being more polite.

"Good," Vera said, her voice rose a little from her answer. "Twice a year, I pay him a visit and check on how he's doing."

"And what does 'Daddy' do for a living?"

"He owns a couple of restaurants, one in New York City, the other one in Los Angeles."

Sandor drifted off for a moment. Food—or even the notion of food—had an uncanny way of putting him at ease.

"You know," he said, more loosely, "I've never had Russian food before."

"I don't think Daddy has either, at least not till he moved to the States," Vera said, more laidback as well. "The restaurant in Manhattan is Mongolian. The one in LA specializes in a fusion of North African-Mexican cuisine."

"You'd think one would start a restaurant based on their heritage."

Vera didn't have any response for Sandor. Instead, she turned to him and at the same time, raised both her eyebrows and widened her eyes as if the expression itself was her way of holding back any words.

Losing confidence, Sandor said over the silence, "But what do I know?"

"Well," Vera said, more smoothly, "he looks at the restaurant business as any other business in the service industry: What's the key to success?"

"Supply and demand, of course."

"Let's just say Russian cuisine never quite found its footing in American culture. Can you see the average American eating *borscht*?"

"What's that?"

"It's a sour soup served chilled."

"Who doesn't like cold soup?"

"You?"

"You underestimate us, *Vera*," Sandor said. "We'll eat anything, literally."

"But you've never eaten Russian."

"Well, except for tonight," Sandor teased.

He laughed from the joke; however, Vera barely brought herself to laugh and when she did laugh, it appeared as if it was forced.

Sandor's laugh soon turned to him clearing his throat, which led to a cough.

"You okay over there?"

"Just got something in the back of my throat." He rubbed his neck region as he continued to cough. Eventually, Sandor decided to roll out of bed. He grabbed a pair of silk boxers lying on the floor next to the bed, told Vera that he'd be right back, and walked to the bathroom.

After putting on his boxer shorts, Sandor leaned down into the sink and took a sip of cool water from the faucet, helping ease off the coughing spell a little. He touched his cheeks with both the front and backside of his hand. Then, he felt the top of his forehead. He was incredibly warm to the touch, which didn't cause any need for alarm, considering he had been drinking a wicked combination of alcohol throughout the night, starting off with a couple of glasses of Cabernet Sauvignon, then switching over to shots of hard whiskey chased with brown ale. Sandor didn't think much of his temperature, considering the recent "release," as he was known to call it; however, he felt slightly warmer than he normally did after his nocturnal activities. He splashed his face several times with cold water, which helped cool the warmness in his cheeks; in fact, the feel of cold water was surprisingly soothing to the touch.

As he pulled himself from the sink, he caught an object moving from side to side in the corner of his eye. He glanced into the mirror and witnessed the lower half of a naked man's body swaying back and forth, back and forth like a pendulum, behind the bathroom doorway. Both feet were at least three feet from touching the floor and each one was much darker than the color of the rest of his slender, spotty body; each foot bloated and swollen with blood.

From the ghastly, macabre nature of the man's gentle pendulum-like sway—Sandor thought maybe a draft in the room was causing the body to move like that, even after death—he looked as if he had been dead for quite a while, maybe days, maybe weeks.

In that throbbing silence, he heard the twisty, wringing sound of leather tightening.

Sandor forced himself back to the sink where he splashed his face with cold water. Even shook away the hallucination—because, he knew, it was *only* an image spawned from the darkest recesses of his mind—then he glanced more wearingly into the mirror. The body was gone. The sound of leather replaced with the rushing *shhh* of water.

As the coughing mellowed, he could feel a headache coming on, only a slight pecking of blood along the sides of his forehead yet it had the potential to worsen and completely wreck the rest of his evening. He grabbed two pills from the bottle of Aleve inside a small travel bag along the back of the vanity and washed the pills down with another sip of water. He followed with a sample of peppermint mouthwash inside that complimentary basket of *hotel* brand toiletries. He gargled for about ten seconds, then spat out the mouthwash into the sink.

Once more, Sandor cautiously glanced into the mirror, *not at himself*, but at the doorway.

Holding onto a silver-colored comforter held between her arms while, at the same time, shielding her breasts, Vera was sitting upright against the headboard.

"Should I leave?" she asked as soon as Sandor stepped out of the bathroom.

"Do you want to leave?" asked Sandor, who was approaching the side of the bed.

Vera gave him a child-like shrug.

"It's your money," she said.

"Yes," he returned flatly. "You're right. It is."

He picked up the phone, dialed the front desk, and ordered a bottle of Chardonnay. Before hanging up with the front desk agent—or "receptionist," as Sandor referred to them back in the States—he turned to Vera, who was still hugging the end of the comforter, and asked, "Would you like something to eat?"

Vera declined, said she was fine; however, Sandor insisted she'd eat. "Whatever you like. Let me treat you."

"I'm not hungry," Vera said defensively.

Which came off as, more or less, an insult to Sandor—a *bullshit answer from a bullshitter*, he thought. *She could have* literally *anything she desired* and even if the kitchen staff couldn't make what she wanted, he could have them fetch whatever it is that she wanted: a filet mignon or any cut of meat for that matter, even a stack of pancakes from iHop, which he'd have flown in from across the pond on his own private jet; yet, after spending hours in bed with Sandor, she wasn't at all comfortable enough to share a meal with him.

"Suit yourself," Sandor said to Vera, then ordered a hamburger, cooked "medium-rare," and hung up with the receptionist.

As Sandor sat on the edge of the bed, he checked his business phone. He received two messages on his phone since the last time he checked his phone. He glossed over the messages, then switched his phone from the silent setting to vibrate, then placed the phone back on the nightstand.

Vera asked, "Business?"

Sandor immediately straightened up from the comment. Way more serious in nature, he glanced over his shoulder at Vera with a slanted, narrow eye and said to her, "Yeah. None of your business."

Vera shot her eyes to the time on the large clock hanging on the wall next to the TV set.

"Do you have somewhere you need to be?" asked Sandor, as if he had eyes in the back of his head.

Vera wasn't quick enough to respond.

"I'm starting to think you have become more attracted to that clock than the client whose about to make you a rich woman."

Sandor propped up a pillow against the headboard and sat back in bed.

"It's nothing personal," Vera said quietly. "Bad habit, I guess."

Sandor said thoughtfully, "*The two most powerful warriors are patience and time.*"

"Profound."

"You should know," Sandor said. "It's Tolstoy."

"I still have Daddy's copy of *War and Peace*," Vera said, as if she was trying to win back Sandor's trust. "Still haven't read it, though."

"You know your writers, huh?"

"Tolstoy was before my time," Vera said, then threw it back at Sandor. "I'm more of a '*Time is Money*' type of lady."

"Of course," Sandor said. "The First American." With a grin on his face, he glanced over at Vera. "I get it. It's all about the Benjamins."

Sandor slid farther down in the bed and rested more comfortably on his back while Vera attempted to make herself content with the extended time with Sandor by uncoiling her somewhat tight grip around the comforter. Sandor made it easier for Vera as he carefully pulled down the bed cover, drawing her close to his body. She cuddled up to Sandor's side and with her fingers, played with a dark patch of hair along the center of his chest. Vera made certain to keep her hand on his chest and not once did she venture anywhere near areas that might draw arousal, like a nipple, which was known to be an erogenous zone for some men, the loin, or any other sensitive area around his abdomen. After three hours spent with Sandor, she was plenty sore and knew she'd be twice as achy in the morning. The thought of going yet another round with Sandor bored her—and just the notion of him having his way with her, especially after his last mediocre showing, she knew Sandor wouldn't finish until sunrise. Her vigilance was even more fortified, each maneuver of her hand strategic yet retaining its soft sensuality.

While on the subject of time, Sandor found himself falling back into a memory. He said more casually to Vera, "When I was your age all I cared about was money—still do, still nice spending it on beautiful things." Smirking, he glanced over at Vera. The word *thing*, with its usage solely held in the same context as a product, overshadowed the compliment and if the prize wasn't as great as the profession, it might've bothered Vera to the point where it only added more cynicism to her perspective of each one of her clients, in particular, men; and without further explana-

tion, she'd put an end to whatever he thought he was buying and give him a refund. She forced herself to acknowledge Sandor, even though it appeared as if one half of the
smile was being pulled by a string. "But it isn't as important to me as it was when I was younger," he said in reflection. "When I was younger, it was my *Holy Grail*. It was
everything. Anything else, relationships, my marriage, it
simply fell to the wayside."

As though the pale outline of a wedding band wrapped
around his ring finger didn't give away the answer, Vera
asked anyway, "Are you still married?"

"No," he said despairingly. "After the third, I gave up.
What's the point?"

Vera didn't answer; and in a way, Sandor wasn't expecting one.

"When I was younger, I thought, without money, a man
was nothing. He was no different than those dirty, sun-
burned-faced people who use to tap on the passenger side
window and ask my father if he could spare some change. I
remember he'd yell at them the same way he yelled at me
whenever I was doing something I wasn't supposed to be
doing, tell them to get a job. All I could think about
throughout the entire school day was the rage inside my
father. It was so visceral that I felt as if it came from a
place that was all but foreign to me. So, whenever I saw
one of those people on the side of the road, begging drivers
for money, all I could think about was my father and that
rage of his. Sure, money may be able to buy a temporary
solution to a problem. But it can't fix the damage a man
leaves behind in his wake. The ripple effect doesn't waver
for anybody—it doesn't care who you are or what you've
done—and those affected the most are left with only a tarnished image of the man whose selfish actions were based
solely on the curse which he had been given: feeling. *Sadie*,
my third wife," Sandor said, a glimmer of reconciliation
rising in his face, as well as his voice, which carried a spiri-
tual calmness, "she was the only person in my life who saw
me for who I was and who I could've been. She saw the
resentment I had for my father, who, when finally con-

fronted, had given me the excuse that he had given me everything." He sighed and scrubbed away the rage that his
father had passed down to him by turning all of his
thoughts toward his third wife. "*Sadie,*" he said more
clearly, "she grew up in a home with absolutely nothing; in
fact, her father, a welder, who, unlike my father, used to
make his living with his hands, was once homeless and living on the streets. When he was younger, he traveled
around the world, spent years in India, learning from a
guru, then lived in Alaska where he was a deck hand on a
fishing vessel. He told me stories about being stuck out at
sea, surviving off whatever he had at his disposal. He had a
story. In that story, he raised a girl who would later grow
up to be my wife, a girl who was surrounded by the uncon-
ditional love that every child deserved. So, when I think
back, about my father, *that rage*, I wonder if there was
something *more* to the rage. For a man who was all about
the rules—about order—I often wonder whether or not it
was those very principles he lived and died by that inter-
nally eroded and eventually, over patience and time, became the foundations of his rage."

"Without order," Vera said wisely, "there is chaos. Life
is founded on chaos, both deliberately and accidentally. If
it wasn't for chaos, then life would cease to exist."

Sandor nodded his head in subtle agreement. More or
less, he was somewhat surprised to hear those words coming from a young woman who was mature beyond her years.

"Honestly, though," Sandor said abruptly, that glimmer
back in his face as he nestled his head against the sunken
pillow, "I didn't know what in the hell Sadie saw in me.
She didn't marry me for my money, if that's what you're
wondering."

Having spent more time around people and listening to
their deepest, darkest secrets, Vera only partially believed
him and his comment about his ex wife, who, clearly, still
weighed heavily on his heart.

"If anything," he said, "she showed me the man I had
become. And that man scared the living shit out of me. I
commend her, though, for trying to clean me up and get

me sober. She had recently gotten over a damaged relationship before I met her. Maybe she needed something to
fix during that time of her life. Maybe she looked at me as
her own personal project. Either way, she recognized who
I was and saw who I could've been. *Sadie,*" he said, clearing his throat, "she was exceptionally good like that. She
could see beyond things that any normal person couldn't
see. You could say she had an eye for it. Fully aware, no
distractions, in tuned with her surroundings, a constant
observer. Which I believe had way more downfalls than
perks." He readjusted himself by sitting up more in bed,
causing Vera to follow suit. Once Sandor was all situated,
Vera rested back down against his side and placed her
hand on a bare spot along his left upper pectoral muscle.
"There was this one time," he said and coughed a little and
then reached down for a deeper breath, "we hired a contractor to build us a swimming pool in our backyard. It
was all my choice, not Sadie's; in fact, from the very get go,
Sadie didn't like the idea. I went ahead and paid the contractor the money he needed to do the job. After the designs were finished, he said it'd take about two months to
complete. Which, I thought, was pretty short for the size
of pool I wanted. Sadie told me, the moment after she met
him, that he was nothing but trouble. It was almost as if
she knew what he was up to before he even started the job.
He digs the hole in the ground, makes it look like he and
his men are working. Then, a couple of weeks in the job,
he or his workers don't show up one day. The next day
passes, still they're a no-show. I try to contact him, but the
phone number is no longer in service. I try to track him
down, but it's like I'm tracking a ghost. One neighbor says
he knows the guy, pulled the same shit on him a couple of
years back. Then, I hear other stories about the contractor.
Each story is the same: starts a job, takes the money, then
runs. But Sadie knew the contractor's intentions all along.
She saw right through him, like she did with me."

"Did you ever get your swimming pool?" asked Vera.

"No," Sandor said seriously. "And yes," he said, now
comically. "Couple of weeks later, we got a terrible storm.

Rain flooded the hole. Made an entire mess in the back-yard. We had the hole pumped. Then, eventually, we filled the hole back up. No pool."

"Sorry to hear," Vera said but the comment didn't come off the least sincere.

"Nah," he said, waving it off. "It was for the best—"

Sandor paused from the sound of a *knock-knock* on the door.

"Expecting someone?" asked Vera.

"Must be room service," Sandor said.

As soon as Sandor said "room service," a voice behind the door said, "Room service."

"Told you," he said, rolled out of bed, and answered the door.

Sure enough, a room service attendant was standing at the door. Once inside the hotel room, he pushed in a cart carrying a tray with a closed metal lid, as well as a bucket of ice with a chilled bottle of Chardonnay, and rolled it to the front of the room.

"Good evening, Mr. Horvath, I have one hamburger and one bottle of Chardonnay."

The attendant asked if Sandor would like for him to open the bottle; however, Sandor declined, told him to leave the bottle opener, and then slipped him a hundred dollar bill into his breast pocket. The attendant thanked Sandor, left the cart, and then left the room. Sandor placed the "DO NOT DISTURB" sign on the handle of the door and closed the door behind him. He walked back into the room, first lifting up the lid over the warm plate. He turned to Vera, asked if she'd like part of his burger, which was surprisingly gentlemanly of him. She gave him the same answer she had given him the first time. He con-structed the hamburger, removed the slice of onion, then took a bite. He pinched a piece of meat away with his fin-gers and further inspected the hamburger, which was cooked just the way Sandor had wanted—*Gotta love those goddamn Brits!* And you thought good ole America was the only place where you could find a good burger. He chased the burger with a couple of "chips," or French fries. He

DALIVIA PLAUT

had also heard people call them by the name "crisps" during his visit. They weren't as good as the fries he had back home; but they did the job, which was not only to slay that rumbling, pissed-off dragon throwing fits inside his belly, but also help mellow the headache.

He swallowed roughly.

"Damn," Sandor said, clearing his throat, "if I was on death row and about to get executed," he held up the hamburger in his hand as if it was a trophy, "I have 'em call up whoever made this burger before I get the big needle."

"How dark of you," Vera said dryly.

"Just saying," Sandor said, as he took another bite of his hamburger. He said from the corner of his mouth, "Best burger I've ever eaten. You don't know what you're missing out."

Vera listed, "Bad cholesterol, heart disease—"

"—Right," he said callously. "You're one of those people."

While chewing the rest of his food, he inserted the bottle opener by twisting the corkscrew into the cork of the bottle *La Prairie*. He pulled on the lever, releasing the cork with a tiny *popping* sound. He poured two glasses of Chardonnay, one for himself and another for Vera.

Before bringing the glass to Vera, he took a small sip of wine to wash down the remaining food bits inside his mouth. One sip led to a chug. And by the time he lowered the glass, the wine was gone. He coughed, not a full cough but, more or less, another clearing of his throat.

As he was about to pour himself another glass of wine, he glanced into a mirror on the wall and in the reflection, saw Reagan lying where Vera should've been lying. She wasn't at all what he remembered of her. Her body was emaciated, her eyes and cheeks sunken in the sockets of her skull, which was visible underneath a thin layer of skin worn like an oversized body suit. She was reaching out to Sandor, as though for help, to end her suffering, to rescue her from hell itself.

As before, Sandor shook away the image from his head and witnessed Vera, *not* Reagan, waiting for him to join her in bed.

He refocused on Vera, her beautiful, healthy, toned body, and poured himself a glass of wine.

Somewhat satisfied by having a little bit of food inside him, Sandor carried the two glasses over to the bed. When he reached the bed, he realized the bottle opener was still partially gripped in his hand. He placed the bottle opener next to the phone on the nightstand and with his unrestricted hand, handed Vera the glass of wine. Vera, who was sitting juvenile-like on her crossed legs, held up her glass in a toast; and together, they basked in celebration.

"To good health," Sandor said.

Beneath Vera's smile, another smile was forming: a longer, wider, more sinister smile that barely formed along the dimples of her cheeks.

A darker smile under a smile.

"*To good health*," she repeated, as they clinked the sides of their glasses together.

Sandor ignored the strangeness of Vera's look, that sinister smile, and refocused on those calming hazel eyes underneath a curl of golden blonde hair.

Together, they sipped wine.

As Sandor lowered the glass from his lips, he glanced down at the sheets and found a black speck on the corner of the pillow. He picked up the insect by pinching his finger together. Once he realized what was squirming between his fingertips, he smothered it with a massage-like motion and then flicked away its crumbly remains onto the floor below.

"What is it?" asked Vera.

"Bug," Sandor said, glancing at Vera through the corner of his eye.

Sandor reached across his body and placed the glass on the nightstand. The move caused him to cough; however, he made sure to cough away from Vera. He checked his phone for any messages. He had "1" new one from a woman named Tatiana. The message read: "What are you doing?" Which, Sandor knew, was a covert text for "I need money."

More conflicted, he decided to close the phone and tend to the other woman, Vera, who, for some reason—maybe it was the alcohol—carried a glow about her, had these angelic vibes about her, as if she was luring him back into bed and ripe and ready to go another round; however, as much as he wanted to jump her bones, he was growing more tired by the minute. His eyelids were getting heavier, too. He just wanted to lie down.

So, he did.

And Vera made more room by placing the glass of wine on the nightstand on her side of the bed and lying back down as well. He pinched the upper bridge of his nose and rubbed the backside of his eyelids.

"Headache," said Vera.

"Yeah," Sandor said. "A little."

She patted on her stomach.

"Lay down," she demanded.

Sandor slid farther down the bed until his feet were hanging over the edge of the bed and rested the backside of his head against Vera's stomach. In return, she massaged the sides of his temples.

"How does that feel?"

"A lot better," Sandor said.

"It's a little trick Daddy used to do whenever I was feeling under the weather. He'd rub my head, and afterwards any pain that I had simply went away."

"Well, whatever you're doing, it seems be to working."

For a moment during that relentless circular motion of Vera's fingers caressing the sides of his temples, the ends of her fingertips suddenly changed texture. Sandor didn't think anything of it; he thought it was the repetitiveness of rubbing, like, for instance, when you loosened your fingers and lazily shook a pencil back and forth between your fingertips and after a while, the pencil felt as if it was no longer made of wood but rather made of soft rubber. The more he thought about it, the more the panic rose inside him. Her touch started to feel liquidy, as if she was digging further and further into his skin, beneath the epidermis, and swirling around his precious blood.

He cracked open his left eye and witnessed a lengthy leg of not a woman but a black, veiny, thorny leg of a sleek and shiny skinless creature that had the similar shape of a woman's leg. He snapped open both his eyes, lifted his head from her grip, and rotated around to Vera, who was concealing a smile on her face and holding back laughter.

"What?" said Vera in an innocent tone, as she waited for Sandor to respond.

Sandor was left speechless, as though, even if he found the right words to say to her, he didn't know where to begin.

"It's okay," Vera said to a more concerned Sandor. "Lay back down."

"I swear I thought. . . "

What the hell's going on with me?

"Why don't you try to get some rest?" she asked over his trailing thought.

"Yeah," he said, slightly slurring. "Maybe that's a good idea. You mind?"

She shrugged.

"It's your money."

Sandor sighed and rested the back of his head against Vera's stomach. Vera hushed him and stroked what little thinning hair he had left on the top of his head, as he took a moment to glance at her bare leg, which was sticking out of the comforter, then, after feeling the softness of Vera's touch, returning both of his weary eyes to the crown molding along the ceiling above.

"So," Sandor said relaxingly, "what was it like growing up in Sviyborsk?"

"It was cold," Vera said, relaxed as well as she carefully rubbed the sides of his head. "I know, right? Russia? Cold? I don't care who you are. Spending the winter in subzero temperatures isn't easy to get used to."

"No wonder you Russians drink vodka like it's water."

Vera smiled from the comment.

"Yes," she said. "We've been known to drink like fish."

"Well, who can blame you?"

"It's fair to say, for some, it helped get them through the day. I mean, there was absolutely nothing to do in Sviyborsk. For me, I remember being on my own a lot. I didn't have a lot of friends. I was alone but not lonely. I had this Teddy bear that I named Vasilii after a popular Russian fairy tale called *Vasilii the Unlucky*. I took that bear everywhere with me, on my journeys through the countryside. Having spent most of my life living in the city, there's still a part of me that longs for those days where I had nature at my disposal."

"Have you ever thought about going back?" Sandor asked.

"Yes," she said. "Sometimes. I suppose one day I'll go back to see what became of it and if it's the same as I last remembered. To me, I consider Russia like an old friend. One day, when I'm least expecting, I'll somehow find myself there again, in that coldness, in some shape or form, skating along the frozen lakes with the abyss below me. A casual misadventure perhaps."

Or bump in, Sandor thought.

He snorted from the very idea.

Then, shook his head with mild disgust.

The headache eased away as though it receded into his heavy bones.

"A few years back I ran into Derrick De Long—*Rhino*."

"Your friend from college?"

"Yeah," he said, trailing off. "That one. . . he'd changed so much I couldn't even recognize him. He had longer hair. That edge he once had—that look, that fierceness— not entirely gone, more like hidden, domesticated. He looked. . . " he searched his mind for the right word, ". . . *content*. He told me that whatever happened between us in the past was all 'water under the bridge.' He sounded genuine, even though there was still a part of me that thought it might've been a front. So, Derrick and I grab a drink at this local spot not too far away from where I was living at the time. We have a few drinks and play catch up," a faint smile grew on the side of his face, "even joked about all of those boxing matches we had. Derrick did most of the talking. He told me about his business, sort of Mom and Pop-type of vitamin shop. He was successful in his own way. He has a child, too, not a child, actually more like a teenager. Said he got married right after college; in fact, his wife was six-months pregnant when they got married. She gave birth to a baby boy. What was his name?" Sandor paused, thinking of the boy's name. "It was a strange name, I remember—Thrace. The boy's name was Thrace."

With the circular motion of her fingers slowing down over Sandor's temples, Vera narrowed her eyes into sharp slits from the sound of the name.

"He was high school age, I remember. Derrick was proud of him. He played football, had potential to play college. After we catch up, we say goodbye and as we're about to go our separate ways, Derrick invites me to a party. His birthday is next week, and he's invited some old friends from college. I should've told him 'no' and kept on walking. I don't know whether or not it was pity—or something else—but I accept his invitation. Next week, I show up at his party after spending days leading up to it contemplating whether or not I should go. Only a couple of guys show up. Those who said they were going to attend ended up canceling at the last minute due to business and family matters. Derrick is already tipsy when I arrive. I knew I should've left the second I walked into his house. Derrick introduces me to his wife, Reagan. Immediately, there's attraction, this connection, *not* just on my end. Till this day, I don't know what it was she saw in him. I end up talking to Reagan as the party starts to die down. We had been shooting looks at one another across the patio throughout the night. She doesn't love him. She doesn't say it, but I can hear it in her voice whenever she mentions his name. I leave; however, the next day, I call up Derrick. We hang out for a while. We end up rekindling a friendship. In the following weeks, we start to hang out more on a regular basis: fishing trips, basketball games, even a trip to Las Vegas. Derrick started to suspect what was going on when I invited Reagan to Vegas with us. I kept hanging around, but really I just wanted to see her. Derrick knew it, but he couldn't do anything about it. The only reason why they were still together was because of Thrace. In a way, she was stuck with a man whom she didn't love anymore. And I expose the cracks in their relationship. When Derrick was away at a small business conference in San Francisco, I get a call from Reagan. It was the first of many times she'd call me over whenever Derrick wasn't around. Toward the end, we started to take more risks: hotel rooms, the park, parking lots. Do I feel wrong about what I did? Looking back," Sandor thought, then said without any hesitation, "no. I don't. But what I didn't realize was that I was the one who was coming out on bottom."

Keenly invested in the rest of what he had to say, Vera asked Sandor, "What happened?"

"I later found out Reagan was sick," Sandor said, his red eyes filling up with tears. "Bone cancer. Doctors told Reagan numerous times that she only had six months to live. She defied them each time. But I could see—toward the end—that she was getting worse. She refused treatment for the cancer. I ended up writing a check for her treatment. She never deposited it. That's when I realized I was expendable. Some fantasy-fuck. A middle finger to Derrick. Which had me thinking back: Was the time we spent together real? Or, was it one-sided? After she died, I then started to question my own intentions. Was I getting back at Derrick for what he did to me years ago? Had the hatred—that rage—gone dormant and somehow manifested itself the day I bumped into Derrick after years of shoveling him away in my thoughts? Not too long after Reagan died, the son, Thrace, found his father's body when he came back home from his Spring Break. Investigators ruled his death a suicide. A few days later, after Derrick was found dead inside the master bedroom, Thrace was found unresponsive by one of his friends. The friend called the paramedics. But Thrace was already dead. An 'overdose of VP-23' was the official ruling of Thrace's death. A couple of his friends blamed it on a bad batch of *red rocks*. But everybody knew what really happened."

"That's terrible," Vera said, unable to find anything reassuring to Sandor.

"Well, that's not even the worst part," Sandor said more quietly, as he started to drift off. "I have to live knowing that I was responsible for destroying an entire family. My whole life I was the one who was always in control. With Reagan, I had no control. It just. . . " Sandor closed his eyes, ". . . it just happened."

Vera held Sandor in both of her arms while the tears ran down the corners of his eyes. Some of the tears pooled along the inner part of the eye socket and then funneled down the side of his nose.

While stroking Sandor's greasy hair across his forehead, she shushed him to sleep.

The sound of shush trailing like a snake's *hiss*.

Hissing Sandor into a deep black sleep.

Once the *hissing* faded into a heavy silence, a panic rose inside Sandor, gripping him tightly, demanding attention. Under his sun washed eyelids, he charged from the darkness and suddenly bolted upright in bed. His eyes were wide open, as he looked around the hotel room, which was empty. Vera was no longer lying next to him; in fact, the impression she once left on her side of the bed was gone. The sheets were unruffled and strangely pulled tight, organized. And, both lamps on the nightstand were on as well.

Before Sandor could make sense of the last moments leading up to him falling asleep, the bed springs below him twisted and popped!

He sat on his knees, pulled back to the comforter, and closely inspected the bed, which he swore was moving. He leaned closer to the sounds of moaning—a deep, painful kind—coming from underneath the bed.

The moaning sound started to intensify.

As his ear inched closer to the bed, a hand shot up through the mattress and caused Sandor to jerk his head

away.   The hand, which was veiled by the white bed
sheets, reached for Sandor; however, he backed away before
the hand could grab hold of him.

He attempted to jump out of bed, but yet another hand
shot up from the mattress and prevented him from leaving.

One of the hands grabbed him by the ankle.   Another
hand grabbed him by the forearm.   Another, his wrist.

Once Sandor freed his arm, yet another hand shot up
from the mattress.   The hands, which were slightly re-
stricted by the bed sheets, managed to pierce through the
thin fabric with jagged, gnarly nails.

Sandor fought off each dark, spotty hand; however, by
the time he used up all of his energy, there were too many
hands—at least two dozen of them—grabbing at him, fon-
dling him, scratching him, and pulling him into the gummy
mattress.

The moans, the groans, and screams of torment, became
louder and louder as his body began to sink into the mattress with its center caving inward.

In one last desperate attempt, Sandor reached up to the
ceiling, hoping to grab something, anything, even it was
only air. . .

Reaching deep for a breath, Sandor's eyes snapped open,
only to witness a dark figure with glossy reflective eyes staring down at him in the pitch-black.

The strange figure leaned down, the shadows along its
face peeled back and revealed. . .

". . . Vera," Sandor said feverishly, as he witnessed the
lower half of her pale face in the soft beam of moonlight.

The bed sheets below him were drenched with a pool of
sweat underneath his body.

She combed back his soaking wet hair from his sweaty
forehead, which was incredibly warm to touch.

"It's just a dream," Vera said tenderly, kissed him on the
center of his forehead, and walked away.

Sssleep now, Sssandor, a staticky, hissy-like voice said in
the night darkness.

A yellowish beam of warm light speared through the
room from where Vera had cracked open the door, the nar-

row doorway leaving behind a sword shape of light along the patterned carpet.

Sandor wrestled open his eyelids, only to witness Vera's dark, slender figure standing in the lit doorway. She looked over her shoulder at Sandor and then, as quietly as a whisper, closed the door behind her.

In the pitch-blackness of the room, Sandor heard those familiar sounds of anguish rising from the below like an approaching storm.

Ready to shroud him in misery and eventually pull him under to a place that never slept.

꒐

IN the lit hallway outside the hotel room, Vera strutted toward the elevator. Once she pushed on the down arrow, the doors immediately opened. She stepped inside the elevator, pushed the "L" button, and during her descent, pulled out Sandor's belongings from her purse. Vera made sure everything was accounted for before she exited the hotel: *Sandor's smartphone* (since she secretly watched him punch in the password into his phone throughout most of the night, Vera didn't have to worry about entering the wrong password—after all, 1-1-1-1 wasn't a hard one to remember); the business card with the name, Vera Fedorov, a "companion" for an escort agency called *Loyal Companion*, which, earlier that night, she had handed to Sandor while he was slumped over the bar and enjoying a pint of brown ale at a local pub not too far away from the hotel; Sandor's passport, as well as his wallet, which contained a driver's license, a couple of platinum credit cards, and at least three hundred pounds, consisting of banknotes of £50's and £20's; however, Vera was more interested in Sandor's *keycard*, which granted him access into the main headquarters of Neuvak Corporation.

After she double-checked each one of Sandor's belongings, she arrived at the lobby floor.

She passed the main check-in desk. The doorman held open the door for her as she exited the hotel. She stopped a couple of feet outside the hotel, kneeled down, and closely inspected a lone *Centaurea cyanus*—or "cornflower," as it was commonly known as—which had absolutely no earthly business being there. The native flower was protruding from the crack in the sidewalk. She plucked the bright blue flower from its droopy steam, carefully held it in the center of her palm, then crushed it in her hand and sprinkled the crumpled florets on the sidewalk as she walked away. The doorman, who was standing not too far away, couldn't help but stare at the young woman in a state of bafflement.

Driven by the night, Vera bravely strutted down a grungy alleyway alongside the hotel. She cut through the shadowy London streets until she arrived at a desolate rundown factory building tagged with various landscapes of graffiti and high-fantasy combined with horrific art. She stopped in front of one particular cartoon-like drawing and found herself admiring the piece, yet, at the same time, loathing it: a stereotypical image of a Grim Reaper, albeit with a vulgar spin, spray-painted on the side of the wall. The title above the piece read in a bubbly font: "*Death or Glory.*" Slightly crouching downward with his black cloak animatedly flapping in the gusty wind, the Dark Angel himself was spinning around his bony cock with a cartoon bubble above his mouth reading, "Helicopter!" In one skeletal hand, the Dark Angel was holding his large scythe while, in the other hand, he was holding up the sign of the horns.

"*Psst.*" Vera said amusedly from the side of her mouth, "Humans."

She continued walking through the trashy, rat-infested, disease-infested area. The insides of the building were rather gutted and hollow and appeared to be used mostly as a skate park and a hangout for troubled teens during the day and a shelter for the homeless at night.

Attracting the eyeballs of three homeless men huddled around a small campfire-like flame inside a rusty oil drum, Vera, who was dressed in a skintight dress and wearing a pair of black stilettos, strutted straight toward to the three homeless men, who were left gawking at the approaching woman, as well as her expensive yet seductive attire. Each step she made sounded like the *clip-clap, clip-clap* of a horse echoing throughout the grand space.

Vera removed the contacts from her eyes and flicked them on the ground.

"You lost, Love," one of the raggedy-dressed homeless men said to Vera.

"Fuck off," Vera said coldly, as she stepped into the glow of firelight.

Her eyes were all black, demonic.

As soon as the three homeless men noticed those eyes—the tone of her voice was deeper, throatier, and rather disturbing as well—the two homeless men hurried away. One of them stayed behind and was left staring at Vera.

"Give me your coat," she said.

The homeless man didn't bother to question Vera's intentions.

He removed the raggedy hooded black coat from his shoulders, placed it on the ground, and then ran off.

Once all three homeless men faded into the night darkness, Vera stood over the fire and began to toss in Sandor's belongings. She threw each artifact into the fire, Sandor's phone, the business card, as well as Sandor's wallet, including everything inside the wallet, except for one particular item: the keycard. She placed the keycard in the pocket of the coat, which was lying on the ground. Then, Vera proceeded to remove her skirt by unzipping the back of it. She kicked the skirt up to her hand, threw the skirt inside the fire, then, next, her top, and then, each piece of lingerie that she was wearing, including her bra and panties.

Stripped naked, Vera removed the final article of her clothing: her skin.

With the tip of her extending needle-like stinger of her index finger, she cut a slit down her face, starting with the top of her forehead and slicing down her nose and mouth, over her chin, and finally, stopping at her trachea.

With both of her hands, she peeled off her face. Then, once the skin was removed from her head, she slid the skin

336

off one shoulder, then the other. Once the skin was removed from her upper torso, she removed the rest of the skin from her body like a sock made of Velcro, revealing nothing but a gummy, thorny blackness underneath. The manikin-like body had neither male or female genitals, nor any breasts for that matter; in fact, it carried no sexual orientation at all.

Finally, the creature tossed the skin suit of Vera Fedorov into the flames, kneeled down, and slipped its arms into the coat first, then, second, placed the frayed hood over its head, then, finally, watched all of the evidence burn, blacken, and melt in the fire.

꒦

THE next morning, one of the staff members of the hotel, who was concerned after Sandor didn't answer the second wake-up call, checked on Sandor; however, the guest wasn't answering the door, either. The attendant opened the door and made sure to announce his presence when entering. He only took several steps into the room before he realized something was terribly wrong. The tray, as well as food on the cart, had been knocked over on the floor. He discovered a body, more than likely, Sandor's body, lying facedown on the bathroom floor. A small puddle of blood was formed into a dark red puddle beside the side of his mouth. The frantic attendant kneeled down next to Sandor and felt for a pulse but couldn't find any.

ONE WEEK LATER

"TWO of our board members have mysteriously died in the past couple of days— one of them now missing—how the hell do you think I feel, Anya?"

Grant's secretary, Anya, stopped walking and stood still with the pointy tip of the stiletto inches away from the narrow, isosceles-shaped streak of sunlight shining a distant mountaintop through the three story-tall window pane covering one side of the massive hallway wall and running across the floor like a starting line. She readjusted a stack of folders from one side of her body to the other and waited for Grant to acknowledge her.

"Mr. Mallory," said Anya, but didn't grab her boss's attention until she spoke his name once more, this time with a tremble underneath her voice, "Are you saying they're *not* coincidental?"

Anya left Grant with no other choice than to stop and acknowledge his secretary's concern.

"It's too soon to tell," he said. "We won't have test results back until tomorrow—"

"—Tomorrow can't wait," Anya said, trying to keep her voice down as other employees walked past them in the hallway. "What does your gut say?"

"My gut says wait until the test results come back before we make any rash decisions." He walked back to Anya, touched her on the shoulder, and said, "Just be mindful of who you interact with. Right now, the only person you can trust is yourself." Another employee walked past them, even eyed them as he walked by. "We'll get through this. Trust me."

"Should I reschedule your lunch with Mr. Silva?" asked Anya.

"Just tell him I'm going to be running a little bit late," he said. "Right now, I could really use a cup of coffee."

"Certainly," Anya said without missing a beat. "Where do you want it—"

"—No," he said abruptly. "I can manage."

"You don't trust me?"

"Of course, I trust you, Anya."

"But I would strongly advise against—"

"—I'll see you back at the office."

Grant started to walk away; however, Anya had so many other questions and concerns to voice after listening in on the board's latest meeting where one of the board members, Salazar, without any proof, boldly suggested that Sandor Horvath and Tomas Zajac were both targeted.

"*But Mr. Mallory . . .*"

Ignoring Anya, Grant kept on walking. He swiped his keycard on the elevator and rode it to the ground floor where a couple of security guards were waiting at a desk. Etched along the marble flooring the golden emblem read: "NEUVAK CORPORATION: PHARMACEUTICALS AND MORE." He walked along the company's trademark emblem as he exited Neuvak Headquarters.

Glancing several times over his shoulder while crossing the street, he made it to a small café called eXpresso. The café sign on the front of the building consisted of a larger, redder, glowing "X" in the word *expresso*, opposed to the other letters, which appeared to fade in the background.

As soon as Grant walked into eXpresso, the barista, a young woman named Lillian, knew exactly what Grant wanted without him even having to say it.

"One regular sized black coffee," she said, as she punched in his order along the touch-screen.

Before Lillian completed his order, Grant eyed a dark chocolate croissant sitting at the front of the pastry case, as if, strangely, of all the times he had bought coffee at eXpresso and skipped on the alluring sweets next to the cash register, the croissant had a spotlight highlighting it. Grant couldn't resist.

"I'll tell you what, Lilly," he said, as Lillian paused midway through tapping her finger against the screen, "add one dark chocolate croissant."

"Feeling adventurous today. Huh, Mr. Mallory?"

"Yes," he said smoothly. "You can say that."

"Will that be all?"

Grant glanced around the café. His eyes found a brunette with greenish-blue eyes dressed in a black cape-like overcoat sitting at the far end of the café.

He couldn't help but notice how long she had been sitting there. Did she follow him inside the café? Or, had she been sitting there this whole time?

After a sudden pause, he turned back around to Lillian, who was smirking by Mr. Mallory's interest in the lone sylphlike woman.

"Yes," he hesitated. Then, smiled back. "For now."

Lillian's smirk rose higher on one side of her face, as her eyes flickered toward the vicinity of the other woman.

Grant held up his smartphone to the scanner and finished the transaction.

As Lillian prepared Grant's order, first by grabbing the dark chocolate croissant from the case with a prong and neatly placing inside a to-go bag, then pouring the coffee from a pot into a cup, Grant waited by the pick-up counter.

During his wait, he shot glances at the greenish-blue eyed woman with long dark hair.

In return, the woman shared a glance or two with him. A rogue strip of hair fell forward over one side of her face, causing her to comb it back over her ear.

First, it was the hair, the primp.

Then came the eyes, both of them looking up from her phone to fully acknowledge Grant.

The eyes were more seductive, pulsing.

"Mr. Mallory. . . " Lillian said from the side. She was standing on the other side of the counter with Grant's order in her hands.

Grant turned to the sound of Lilly's voice.

"Yes, Lilly," he said and grabbed the black coffee and dark chocolate croissant. "Thank you."

Grant found himself at a table next to the window not too far away from the interested woman, sat down, and placed everything on the table, first his phone and then the coffee and the croissant. He first tended to his phone. Before he could scroll through his most recent emails, he saw a dark figure standing over him. He turned his eyes upward and saw that same woman standing at the table.

"Hi," Grant said, surprised by the speediness of her pursuit. He figured that he'd sip from his coffee, check the messages on his phone—or at least act like he was checking messages on his phone—then pull himself away from the device to play a little eye-tag foreplay by occasionally shooting glances at the woman until he finally warmed-up to the inevitable conversation.

"May I join you?" asked the woman.

He loosened the red tie around his neck, pointed at the empty chair, and said, "Please."

She placed her coffee on the table and sat down across from Grant.

As the natural light brought out more details of her face, he couldn't help but stare at her features. He knew her face, had seen it before. It didn't take him long to remember where he had seen her and then the app where he had *swiped* her. As soon as she spoke her name, "Tatiana Lebedev," Grant realized it was the same woman from his phone. Which, to say the least, was shocking, considering he thought most of those photos were stolen and their real identity happened to be some fat guy dressed in his underwear sitting in front of a computer.

"Grant," he said, maintaining his coolness, "Grant Mallory."

"Pleasure to meet you, Grant Mallory."

He looked around the half-full café, only to find Lilly turning away the moment his eyes crossed hers.

"So," he said plainly, shifting his focus toward Tatiana and nobody else but Tatiana, "you come here a lot?"

"First time," she said villainously.

"Best coffee in the valley," Grant said and took a bird-like sip from hot black coffee.

"Well, I didn't come over her to talk about the coffee."

Grant could feel the blood moving around his body.

"Is that so?"

Tatiana nodded her head.

"You live around here?" asked Grant.

"I have a place up near Rock Creek."

"Nice place," Grant said. "Quiet. Me and a buddy of mine used to take hiking trips up there. One time, we nearly got mauled by a mountain lion, who was looking at us as if we were its next entrée. If we hadn't run into a couple of other hikers, who were more experienced, then you probably wouldn't be talking to me right now."

"How did you defeat it, the mountain lion?" asked Tatiana.

"We didn't," Grant said. "We were told to scream and make loud noises and show dominance. Eventually, it ran away."

"So, why'd you stop?"

"Stop what?"

Tatiana asked more clearly, "Why'd you stop going on hiking trips with your friend? Was it because of the mountain lion?"

Grant blocked out the memory as soon as it came to him.

"He passed away," he said politely.

"Sorry to hear," she said.

"It's okay," Grant said. The last angle he wanted right now was a sad angle, even worse play the sympathy card. But then again, at this point, he had no angle, no card. She was, more or less, the aggressor. Which meant he already had her in his pocket—or, the other way around. He straightened his shoulders, reaffirming his superiority.

Tatiana pointed at Grant's phone and said, "May I?"

Without thinking, Grant unlocked his phone, then handed it to Tatiana, whose hand deliberately and flirtatiously grazed the side of Grant's hand during the exchange. She entered her information into Grant's contacts and then slid the phone back to Grant.

"I have to run," she said. "But if you want to hang out later—perhaps tonight if you're not too busy—or, we can just talk. It's up to you. Either way, you have my number. Don't be afraid to call it."

He scrolled to her name under the letter "T" in his contact list, clicked on it, and found her phone number.

"I won't," he said and checked out Tatiana's backside as she exited from the café.

He couldn't help but shake his head in amusement.

Too easy.

𝔇

LATER that same night, Grant kissed his wife, Nadia, goodbye, as well as his three children, two who were still young enough to embrace bear hugs from their father, and one, technically not a child, who had reached an age where an electronic device and the alternate world inside it received way more attention; and the only form of affection Grant had to look forward to was an involuntary nod of the head coming from a person, who, each semester, was slowly turning into a stranger.

With his travel bag packed for the supposed business trip, Grant felt nothing but relief as soon as he pulled out of the driveway.

Once Grant reached the hotel, which wasn't too far away from the airport, he checked in. He made sure not to draw any unwanted attention by checking in under a different name. On the way to his room, he received a text from Tatiana, saying that she'd be at the hotel in "ten minutes." Which left Grant some time to get comfortable inside the room, mainly making sure that he was presentable and looking and smelling his finest by brushing and flossing his teeth, gargling mouthwash, trimming any unwanted nose and ear hair, as well as doing some last minute manscaping.

As soon as he finished in the bathroom, he stepped back into the room where he received a text message on his phone. The text read: "I'm outside."

Shortly after reading Tatiana's text, he heard a *knock* on the door. As Grant arrived at the door, his heart started to race. Through the tiny peephole, he witnessed the dark figure standing behind the door, waiting for Grant to open the door. He followed a tip his yoga instructor had given him and breathed in deeply through his nose and exhaled through his mouth. He was already past the point of no return. Yet, Grant no longer carried any rational thought inside his head nor, at this time, did he ever welcome such reason. Instead, his actions were solely driven by a primordial force. She was there, waiting for him. And he was there, standing with only a door separating himself from her.

Grant reached for the door handle, and as he was about to open the door, his hand started to tremble.

343

www.ingramcontent.com/pod-product-compliance
Lightning Source LLC
Chambersburg PA
CBHW030249270626
47156CB00021B/299